THE
ICELANDERS

—for Ann Smith, in memoriam

THE
ICELANDERS

SJ

ISBN: 978-1-943661-58-9

Sij Books
booksbysij@gmail.com

Printed in the USA

GWAR, ETHIOPIA, 1987

On June 8, 1783, the craters of Mount Laki in southern Iceland erupted, spewing an estimated 3.4 cubic miles of basalt lava and emitting vast clouds of sulfur dioxide and hydrofluoric acid. The five-month eruption killed half the livestock and twenty-five percent of the people, ten thousand no less, during a time of suffering known as the Móðuharðindin or Mist Hardships.

Dr. Gudmunder Thorsonn often listened wide-eyed as a child growing up near Reykjavik to stories of the fire, gas, poisoning, crop failure, and famine. His grandfather Jon, a Lutheran pastor, had instilled in him a respect for the power of God's earth and a responsibility to watch over those in need. First, Thorsonn studied theology at the University of Iceland, but being taken with the words of the Apostle James to care for the body before the soul, he took up general medicine, becoming a doctor in 1981.

To the sound of roosters crowing, Dr. Thorsonn awoke inside his white tent. The ground beneath his back was rocky. The small net hanging above his head held his black glasses, a cigarette lighter, and a pack of crackers. He wondered how well the American, Reece, had slept. Having killed five bottles of Awash white wine the night before, he guessed that the two nurses, Eydis and Svana, should have slept well.

Outside in the foggy morning chill, the guard Gebremariam, hired to keep watch over the compound, walked a muddy path holding an ancient teakettle, steam sniffing from its spout. Feet clad in tire sandals, with strong ankles and muscled calves, he navigated the rocky trail with ease. He approached the doctor's tent, walked around it, and then scraped his dirty nails across the slick cloth.

"Hallo!" said Gebremariam.

Dr. Thorsonn unzipped his bag halfway, sat up, and unzipped the fly. He looked up at Gebremariam, who gazed down at him with a bountiful smile.

"Chai," said Gebremariam, holding forth the pot. "Moqa," and he whistled, suggesting that the tea was very hot, but good to warm the body. He admired the doctor's puff of red hair that reminded him of a rusted plow point.

"Amenseganalo," said the doctor. He reached for his steel cup and held it to receive the spiced tea.

Gebremariam visited the other tents, calling out his morning greeting.

Inside the largest tent, a dark green affair acquired from the Polish Army via the Baptist Mission in Addis Ababa, Eydis stiff-armed Svana. "Vakna! Wake! It is time for tea, sleepy bones." Svana loomed large, with a shock of short black hair, over the slender and blonde Eydis. Svana liked clear nail polish and Eydis liked pink.

"Ugh!" said Eydis. She rolled over, trying to remember the dream she was having, something with water, a boat.

"Tenesteling!" said Svana. She stood, stooped, grabbed her lower back, and untied the inside flap. The cups, where were they? She looked around. There, each sitting inside a hiking boot.

"Hallo," said Gebremariam. The cloud of fog seemed to descend to his shoulders, misting his face and head, wrapped in a dirty shamma. He laughed and poured the tea. He pointed to Eydis and made a snoring noise.

"Eydis, wake up!"

In his tent, Reece listened. High above the clouds, a MiG-21 jet screamed across the rugged Highlands. From the administrative compound a hundred feet away, the sound of a crackling two-way radio blared in bursts, the new Transitional Government in action. The whole thing operated on a truck battery. Why they ran the sound so loud, Reece couldn't understand. He listened as Gebremariam walked up to his small pup tent, bought at a Kmart back in Alabama. Gebremariam scratched on the fabric as if gently waking the King of France.

"Abet?" said Reece. He had only been in the country for two weeks, but it seemed that the Amharic spoken by the people was strangely familiar. He found himself using words and phrases just minutes after he had heard them. The Icelanders were impressed, although Doctor Thorsonn's knowledge of Ethiopian history seemed to be bottomless. Reece unzipped and, still wearing his dirty hiking boots, crawled out of the tent, shivering, careful not to knock over the tent pole. He coughed and held out his green plastic cup. "Amenseganalo," he said.

"Minem aydelem," said Gebremariam, and then with a thick accent, "No problem."

The pop and putter of the grain mill mingled with the calls of roosters all around Gwar, and the team readied to split up to accomplish their respective duties. Dr. Thorsonn was administering vaccines at the government clinic. Eydis and Svana were weighing and measuring the children in the area. Reece, doing research for his master's thesis in public health, spent the days interviewing the local people, inquiring about their health with his interpreter Afewerki.

Four folding chairs sat around a fire pit made of fist-sized rocks.

"So, where do you go today, Mr. Reece?" asked Dr. Thorsonn. He stood and adjusted his outback-style hat.

Reece ran his hand through his hair, wildly crimped from sleep. "I'll just follow Afewerki. We go in different directions each day." The morning fog was lifting, the grass damp with dew. Otherwise, all was dry, and the hot sun would soon take charge.

"So, perhaps there is randomization?"

"That's my idea. We have no system, just head out and meet people. We try to get as many men as women, but the men are usually out in the fields or hanging out in the tejj bars."

"Look at these two clowns." Dr. Thorsonn pointed.

Eydis stood at the nearly empty rain barrel beside the crude cook house filled with smoke, trying her best to dip a cupful to wash her face. Svana, a strong woman with high cheekbones, held Eydis's belt so that Eydis wouldn't fall into the barrel. Both were laughing.

Reece watched them from across the empty yard, a space that the Baptists had once used as a compound to house their workers in Gwar. Down the steep hill was another dusty, sloping field where used to stand a warehouse for grain, a clinic, and a helicopter pad, and beyond that, worn mounds of the dead from cholera outbreaks gone by.

The bright orange sun with its permanent black spot peered through the breaking fog. Once the fog lifted, the temperature would climb rapidly. Afewerki, in blue jeans and a plaid shirt two sizes too big, walked through the broken gate. He greeted Gebremariam and said hello to the young woman making kita in the cook house.

"Hallo!" said Afewerki. He greeted the doctor and shook his large hand, laughing nervously.

"Come and eat with us, my friend," said Dr. Thorsonn. He rubbed his thin red beard.

"No, I cannot. It is a time of fasting."

"Not even a cup of tea?" asked Reece.

"Yes, tea without the sugar is good."

"Ah, the tea is very sweet. You can blame Gebremariam," said Dr. Thorsonn. He rocked back in his chair.

Svana headed to the outhouse, and Eydis came near the small fire. She looked small beside Svana and had a ready smile. "Good morning to all!" She cupped her green plastic mug and took a sip of the sweet, hot tea spiced with cloves.

As Afewerki moved to shake her hand, Reece stood and gave Eydis a hug. Afewerki cleared his throat and stepped back, not sure of how to proceed. The night prior, Eydis had been drinking wine with Svana and made Afewerki dance with her. Then Svana had squeezed him tight and spun him around in a circle until they both fell dangerously close to the fire. The whole night Afewerki had been barely able to sleep, thinking of Eydis, her blonde hair, and somewhat puffy but pink cheeks.

"Goh-than dai-yin," said Reece, using his Icelandic to say good morning.

Eydis pushed him away playfully. "You think you are from Iceland, no?"

Dr. Thorsonn laughed. He liked Eydis's vitality, as he

called it.

Afewerki walked back to the cook house to see if there was plain tea, a lump in his throat.

TWO

After eating his kita, a round of flatbread rubbed with oil and dried red pepper, Reece brushed his teeth, spitting into the grass. This made Afewerki gag, and he looked away.

"Where to, my friend?" asked Reece. He wore a wrap of local white cloth over his short-sleeve shirt. The others had already left.

"We shall go toward the river. A few are living there. They will complain if we do not go. There is a school-teacher who lives there. She is my friend."

"Do you have a girlfriend?" asked Reece.

"Oh no, I cannot to support a wife. I am still young."

"What? We're both thirty-two. We're getting old."

A woman begging met them at the gate. Afewerki whistled.

"What does she need?" asked Reece.

"She needs a husband but is asking for food."

The woman's rags were stiff with dust and limp with dew. A greasy covering lay over her shaved head. She put her hand to her mouth.

"Well, dang, let's get her some dabo or kita. Is the cook still here?"

"No, she has left. She will be angry if you take some breads."

"Well, who cares? This woman needs food." Reece trotted to the cook house, still smoky, and lifted the lid from a straw basket. He took two kitas without the oil and pepper and brought them to the woman.

She bowed her head and lifted her hands. "Xavier meskin."

"Minem aydelem," said Reece.

"Shall we go?" asked Afewerki, hands in pockets.

"Sure thing. Are you annoyed?"

Afewerki put his hands behind his head. "I am noid? What does it mean?"

Reece laughed. "No, not a noid, annoyed. Are you angry at me?"

"My goodness, no." He had learned that phrase from Dr. Guthrie.

"Okay, just checking."

The fog seemed to have been sucked away by God's vacuum cleaner, and a bright morning sun illuminated the path between compounds. The spot on the sun was barely visible in the glare.

A thin man walking their way stopped and took Reece's hand. He spoke in a quiet voice.

Afewerki explained. "He is asking when will again come the grain." He looked impatient and was eager to get the interviews underway.

"That was ten years ago, right?"

"God will provide," Afewerki told the man.

The man bowed his head and withdrew.

They meandered through Gwar and began the long downhill walk, holding back to keep from breaking into a run. Rocks clogged the path. Afewerki greeted all those they met along the way. They reached the former site of the Baptist Mission's feeding compound. All that was left was the helicopter pad and the cement floors of the warehouse and clinic. The buildings' poles and tin roofs had long been stripped.

"Supposedly, someone, a mission worker, was shot and killed by the town administrator," said Reece. "Is that true?"

"He did not die. He is flying to Addis and then to home. This is the story."

"Jeez, that sounds harsh. Wonder what happened to him?"

"Only God knows," said Afewerki.

"I suppose."

They walked away from the main village of Gwar and descended to a ridge where stood a gathering of ten tukuls, each with its own walled compound. "Ferenj!" came the call from a young boy with a toy whip. Within half a minute, a group of ten children had gathered. Reece smiled and was at once holding hands on both sides. He marveled at the little bunches of hair on the boys' heads and the serious braids on the girls. Afewerki did not look pleased. The children were filthy, and as far as he was concerned, they were just little diarrhea machines.

A young woman emerged from a compound and, smiling, asked if they would like some coffee. Afewerki realized it would be an hour-long process and answered for Reece. "Yellum." But he asked her if she would like to participate in an interview.

The woman, who had intricate line tattoos on her forehead, laughed and said no problem.

"Our first interview," said Reece. He hoped to do at least ten before calling it a day. He needed two hundred to make his quota for a significant sample size. The questionnaire consisted of forty questions and a visual assessment that did not involve any invasive procedures. Following the routine agreement to consent to the interview with explanations of its purpose, the process began.

"How is your family?" Reece used this as an ice breaker.

The woman spoke for a minute, and Afewerki summarized her words. "Her family is suffering due to a lack of money."

Reece was in the middle of his public health master's degree at Yale University and knew the rules of seeking information. If you discovered someone with high blood pressure, you couldn't just record the data and move on. You had to have a treatment option ready. But did that include not having enough money? He wrote down the response and asked the next question.

"What is your family's biggest health problem?" He shifted his buttock on the low stone he perched on. He tried to get at eye level, a fig tree partially shading him. All around, children scurried, eyes bright with flies. A group of women had begun to form within earshot. That was not good. They could be influenced by their neighbors' responses if they were interviewed.

"Her family's biggest health problem is lack of food," said Afewerki.

"Make sure she knows that Eydis and Svana are weighing children. Their data could result in a feeding program if warranted." Reece felt a bit like a snake oil salesman, but it was true, right? Dr. Thorsonn had said so.

"Yes, they have been there, but one of her childs has been afraid and would not be weighed."

"That sucks," said Reece.

The woman smiled and looked to Afewerki for an explanation.

"God will provide," he told her.

Reece wiped sweat from his eyebrows. They had not brought water, and he was thirsty. "What is her biggest personal health problem?"

The woman knotted her long dress hem and said that she suffered from severe pain in her joints. Did they have any medicine?

Reece grimaced again and wished that he had a portable pharmacy. He wrote down the response and continued questioning and writing. Nearly forty-five minutes had passed by question thirty-nine. Still, the group of women stood close by, some with fingers in their mouths. The temperature had crept to eighty in the shade.

"How is your health different from one year ago?"

Afewerki translated: "It is the same every year, but only gets worse." He picked up a small stone and threw it over his shoulder.

As part of the protocol, following the interview, Reece took a black-and-white photo of the interviewee with his Ricoh 35mm and promised that a print would be delivered. It was the first photo ever taken of her, and Reece felt a great burden to get the photos back as promised.

Another hour passed, and Reece had to excuse himself to the bush to urinate. Another hour passed, and at the end of an interview, a man appeared, the first of the day. He wore a ragged hat and carried a doolah, a short stick with lead wrapped around the end. Right away, Afewerki stood from his squatting position.

"What's the problem?" asked Reece.

"Mendeno?" asked Afewerki. The man staggered into

the middle of the lane. He pointed his finger at Reece and spoke in an angry tone.

Afewerki spoke to the man. The man's eyes were red from katikala. "He is drunk. He says that you have come to steal the tabot."

The man, wearing green patched shorts and an old shirt made from a grain bag, walked closer to Reece. Afewerki moved between them.

"That's crazy," said Reece. Dr. Thorsonn had told him about the tabot. Every Orthodox church had its version of the tabot, the tablets carved by God on Mt. Sinai and given to Moses.

"He believes these things," said Afewerki. He knew the man. He had worked with the Baptists back in 1980, unloading hundred-pound grain bags from the helicopter and stacking them twenty high in the warehouse.

Reece stood and spoke to Afewerki, saying that he respected the man's fears but that he was only there to help, to do the survey. Did he want to do the survey and have his photo taken? This seemed to calm the man, and he took off his hat and sat on the stone opposite Reece.

"How is your family?" asked Reece, feeling like an automaton.

Ten interviews and eight hours later, Reece and Afewerki trudged uphill to the Icelandic camp. They were both parched and starving. Plumes of white smoke from the cook house made them both smile. In his backpack, Reece had the numbered hardcopy interviews, two black pens, and a roll of toilet paper. Dr. Thorsonn, who preferred to be called Gudmunder, and Eydis and Svana were standing around the tents, waiting for dinner, which would be served on a tarp on the ground.

"Hallo!" Eydis ran up and hugged Reece and then gave Afewerki a side hug. Svana said hello and asked how the day had gone.

"I don't know, pretty good," said Reece. He had felt Eydis's breasts with that hug. They'd been working together for two weeks, and he didn't know if she was single. Svana wore a ring on her middle finger, but Eydis had none.

"How was the vaccine clinic?" Reece said to Gudmunder.

"Very fine." He held a green plastic cup filled with katikala. A hard day's labor deserved alcohol in his world, and the local vodka was dirt cheap and tasty, much better than the weak beer, which tasted like smoke and gesho leaves. "Have a drink?" He picked up an IV bottle from Iceland filled with the clear liquor.

"Hell yeah," said Reece.

Afewerki did not drink katikala, finding it much too strong. He could drink the sweet honey mead, tejj, and beer, but that was it.

Gudmunder told Reece to get his cup, and he did.

"What's for dinner?" asked Svana. She tousled her black hair. She was "beefy" by her own admonition, but curvy nonetheless. Most men were shorter than she was, but she was used to that.

"Gebremariam!" Afewerki called to the guard, asking him what was for dinner. With a broad grin, he announced that ox tail was on the menu. The wot would be accompanied by a thick layer of spongy enjera made from sorghum. The ox tails were cut from living beasts, the hairy end of the tail becoming fly swatters.

Gudmunder, already known in Gwar as the red rooster for his bright orange hair, moaned with approval and toasted Reece from his camp chair. Reece looked above the broken fence wall at the clear blue evening sky. Already, the brightest of stars could be seen. Nightfall was a kind of miracle of lights.

Reece sipped his drink, making a sour face. The clear liquor was warm and strong. He sat in the grass, leaning back on one arm, and looked up at Eydis, who was drinking a warm St. George beer. He admired the outlines beneath her white scrub top. He looked over at Svana. She was a handful, a party animal.

"Eydis? Any interesting stories to tell?" Reece could smell the spicy wot in the smoke from the cook house. His stomach grumbled. Often the cook, Abebe, cooked topless, a kind of phantom stripper, stirring and stoking.

Eydis looked at Svana and laughed. "This day we have been weighing the children, no? And measuring their height, no? One woman is coming to us." She paused and looked to Svana, who was shaking her head. "This woman is saying that she is pregnant by seven years. She wants us to deliver the child because it is eating her body."

Gudmunder frowned. He thought of a particular Icelandic saga where a similar situation was reported. "She is crazy," he said.

Afewerki nodded his head in agreement. He knew exactly who the woman was. She claimed to have been raped by a man from the heavens. He would return when she gave birth.

"Wow," said Reece. "That's a new one."

"And you?" asked Eydis. She picked up the bottle of katikala and poured herself a good half cup.

Reece glanced at Afewerki, who dug his toe in the grass. "Well, today I had a guy who was hanging around the interviews. He was wearing the shorts and shamma and a dirty hat. He had his doolah. He was about thirty, with really muscular legs. I just assumed he wanted to be interviewed, and so we invited him over. He sat on the stone and crossed his legs. He seemed to be very bright." Reece began to laugh. "I asked him how his family was doing..." Reece looked to Afewerki for sympathy but received none. "He, he, he started to talk..."

"What is this funny business?" asked Svana. She was interested.

Reece collected himself, taking a deep breath. "So, he responds. He has a serious speech impediment. He can't pronounce his r's."

"So what happens next?" asked Eydis. Her blonde hair and rosy cheeks complemented the blue sky.

Reece sipped his katikala and frowned. "I wasn't expecting the speech impediment. I was tired. My legs were falling asleep. My butt hurt. What could I do? I just started to laugh. I had to hold my breath. I jumped up and turned my back. I just started coughing, trying to pretend that I was sick or something. Holy cow, I was mortified. I walked away from him about thirty feet while I composed myself."

Afewerki nodded, affirming each step of Reece's reactions.

Gudmunder chuckled, and Eydis and Svana laughed.

"I was so embarrassed," said Reece.

The evening attracted bats circling in the rapidly cooling air. Emerging from the cook house, Abebe brought out the first platter of sorghum enjera. She wore a long, patched dress that had never been washed. She had four children, one of whom was an epileptic. Because of this child, she never left a fire burning, fearful that he would fall into it.

Each person breathed "Amenseganalo."

Abebe returned with an ancient pot filled with spicy ox tail meat and a handful of the spicy berbere powder.

Reece's mouth watered, and his forehead broke out in a sweat. He imagined the result: squatting in the outhouse with his anus on fire. But it tasted so good.

"Let's wash our hands," said Gudmunder.

THREE

The next morning, Dr. Thorsonn arrived at the government clinic. He didn't need an interpreter to do his job, just a long line of those who needed vaccinating against measles, mumps, and rubella. The clinic, funded and staffed by the Ethiopian government, also offered very basic healthcare at very cheap prices. The clinic's "doctor" was Berhanu Nega, known simply as Berhanu. Of all the people in Gwar, Berhanu had the most prominent afro. He was plump, revered, and known to offer Western medicine while appreciating the role of demons and ghosts in sickness.

"Hallo!" Gudmunder greeted Berhanu's assistant, a young, attractive woman with the unlikely name of Lilly. Her ass in Gudmunder's eye was picture perfect. As long as he could work with Lilly, he would vaccinate every man, woman, and child in Ethiopia.

"Tenesteling," said Lilly. She spoke no English. She opened the propane-powered fridge and glanced at the remaining forty-five doses of MMR vaccine. Who knew when the next delivery would occur? She flashed an ultra-white smile at Dr. Thorsonn.

Berhanu emerged from behind a curtain and smiled at Gudmunder. They shook hands as usual, and Berhanu looked outside at the long line of patients, perhaps forty, a light day.

Dr. Thorsonn had to take each patient's word on whether they had been vaccinated for MMR. No one had a vaccination record. He figured that a double vaccination couldn't hurt anything. If there was one thing that the villagers loved, it was the murphy or injection. The needle meant cure. Pills were inferior and often sold.

Lilly directed traffic, dividing the line between those who needed the vaccine and those who needed to see Berhanu. A young woman entered, her head covered with a white cotton cloth. She spoke in whispers. Her husband insisted on raping her, and what could be done?

"How old is he?" asked Lilly.

"He is a shimogele, an old man."

Lilly wanted to give her a sharp knife to cut the shimogele's throat, but the best she could do was to prescribe a sedative to help ease the distress and pain. "Do you need medication?"

"Yes, please."

Lilly surveyed the medications in stock and prescribed thirty milligrams of phenobarbital daily for one month. At least she would be able to forget.

The next patient, a woman with ten children, complained of dizzy spells. Dr. Thorsonn watched Lilly draw up the long dress with one hand and inject 10 ccs of sterile saline into the woman's emaciated buttock. It would give her hope. Even he realized that.

He surveyed his third vaccination patient, a young man dressed in military garb. He carried an old rifle and had a hand grenade pinned to his uniform shirt. He looked worried.

"Mendeno?" asked Dr. Thorsonn

The man replied at length that he feared death and needed an injection.

Gudmunder nodded, patted the man on the shoulder,

and sent a dose of saline into his right deltoid muscle, followed by the vaccine.

The day revealed itself with hot sun and no clouds, unusual for seven thousand feet in early spring. The Baptist helicopter that visited Gwar on occasion, to bring supplies and mail to the Icelandic team and Reece, relied on such days as ideal.

Reece lay inside his unzipped sleeping bag, discriminating the various small rocks beneath him. He decided to name them, lying still, and he did. The largest he named Darnell. Only thoughts of hot tea caused him to rise and put on his pants. He usually slept in the shirt he wore the day before. He thought about his ex-fiancée, Kristin, back in the United States. She seemed to be a dream, a thin gauze.

Outside the tent, wearing his unlaced hiking boots, he stood and looked around. The compound was fenced in on three sides. He spied the outhouse, the shintabet, which he needed.

A sound of ripping nylon. Eydis unzipped her tent and poked her head from within. Reece preferred blondes, and Eydis was sexy in her scrubs.

"Hallo," said Eydis.

"Tenesteling," said Reece.

Eydis crawled on all fours out of the tent. She sat back and put her feet into her tennis shoes. "You are up early? No?"

"Yeah, early."

In walked Afewerki. He had been up for an hour or more.

"Good morning, brother," said Reece.

"Praise to God," said Afewerki.

"Hello, big blue world!" said Eydis. She stood and stretched.

"Go to hell," said Svana from within the tent. Her back hurt. She cursed God.

Reece extended his hand to Afewerki. The two shook and exchanged knowing looks.

Inside the cook house, Abebe sampled the berbere wot, an ongoing work of culinary art that stretched from day to day. She took ten eggs and beat them in the steel skillet, adding the wot and a scoop of butter. The breakfast would be greasy as usual, but tasty beyond reason.

Reece and Afewerki set off for the small village of Aferbiny. Whereas the women of Gwar had to walk thirty minutes downhill to obtain water in their clay water pots, the women of Aferbiny had an hour's walk. The land around Aferbiny was no different from that of Gwar, rocky, black, and dry except during the two rainy seasons: one short, one long.

"Why don't you have a girlfriend?" asked Reece. "I mean, really?"

"My goodness," said Afewerki. He led Reece eastward toward an enclave of essentially divorced women. Their men had left to find work and never returned, children or not.

The first woman they interviewed was very young, sixteen, with high, shiny cheekbones and large breasts swinging beneath her dress. She reminded Reece of a pirate. Her husband had left over a year ago to work with a friend at a restaurant in Gondar that specialized in fish from Lake Tana. He sent a little money once every three months, just enough to keep her and their two daughters from starving to death.

She invited them into her hut and motioned for them to sit on the homemade bed. A large battered pot hung from a peg on the wall. A fire of hot coals sent a spiral of smoke up the tukul's center to eke through the pointed straw roof. The littlest child with wide eyes sat near the fire, holding a stick. The other, a pretty girl of five with tightly braided hair, stood in the doorway with a huge grin.

Before they could begin, the woman, who was named Zubeda, offered to cook their lunch. She would make a spicy lentil wot. Afewerki explained to Reece.

"Tell her we can come another day. Is that okay?"

Afewerki relayed the information, and Zubeda agreed, all smiles.

Reece removed a survey from his backpack and asked Afewerki to explain the study and obtain her consent. He sat on the edge of a crude bed. Reece waited until he was through and launched into the interview. "How is your family?"

"We are poor, but praise to God for life," said Zubeda. She then went on to explain that her husband had given her gonorrhea and that he had refused to go to the clinic for an injection. She had gone, but they would not treat her unless her husband accompanied her. "Is that fair?" she said.

Reece didn't quite know what to say. "What is your family's biggest health problem?"

"We are poor and have little to eat."

"What is your biggest personal health problem?"

"My husband has given me a terrible disease."

Reece leaned forward. The bed, which was laced with leather to support the crude mattress, sagged in the middle. His feet barely touched the floor. He wondered if asking these questions would ever benefit anyone. He would take the woman's photo, so there was that. He felt defeated. He looked to Afewerki for some sort of support. Afewerki had stood and was stooping beneath the roof next to the wall. He seemed to be a million miles away. Reece thought of his grandmother frying okra back in Alabama. The age spots on her hands had merged, making the backs of her hands brown. She had warned him not to go to Africa. It was too dangerous.

Gudmunder walked from one end of the compound to the other. He needed the exercise after standing in the clinic all day. He had given the last of the MMR vaccines and then stayed to help Berhanu with patients. He held a green cup of katikala, but yearned to have ice in his drink and sat in a folding chair.

Reece followed Afewerki into the compound, greeting Gebremariam. They had met the creepy village administrator, the Snake, on the walk back. He had cocked his finger, pointed it at Reece, and said the Amharic equivalent of "Bang!"

"Hallo!" said Gudmunder. He raised his glass. Eydis and Svana had stopped at a tejj bet to drink mead on their way back to the compound. It was causing quite the scandal, as typically only men were allowed inside. Gudmunder was not pleased.

Afewerki said hello.

Reece took a roundabout path to Gudmunder, pausing to peek into the cooking hut. Hot smoke seeped through the straw roof. He wondered how Abebe could breathe. The goat meat sizzling made his mouth water. Her face emerged from the cloud, and she smiled at him. Reece could barely make out the green tattoos along her lower jaw.

Reece came near the fire pit, now cold. Gudmunder held out a wine bottle filled with clear liquor. "Good for your digestion, no?"

Afewerki settled into a squat, hungry and tired. Reece took a chair across from Gudmunder. Reece estimated Gudmunder's age at forty.

"How was the vaccine clinic?" asked Reece.

"Was good, but we have no more vaccines. We must wait for the helicopter to bring more." He sipped and smacked his lips.

The shift to evening was perceptible to Reece, as if someone was dialing down the light ever so slowly and adjusting the contrast. Early stars he could see above a group of bats diving and dashing for bugs. The moon had not yet risen.

"Afewerki, why so quiet?" asked Reece.

"Hmm," said Afewerki. He switched from squatting to sitting in the grass cross-legged, chewing on a green stick. He was thinking of Eydis. She made his breath catch, although he imagined her teeth weren't as white as they should be. If she were to tattoo her gums blue, like the local women, they would shine.

"He is thinking," said Gudmunder, and held forth his

cup in cheers.

"Long day," said Reece. He thought about the rocky ground beneath his tent. He thought about breaking up with his fiancée, Kristin, just one week before he came over. He had decided while eating a fish sandwich at McDonald's. He needed to be free to experience all that the world had to throw at him. And now he had to find out if Eydis was single or not. Svana was cute, but he imagined that she could lift and toss him like a fruitcake. She needed a swarthy man, and Reece was not that.

"Eydis and Svana must return soon. It is not good that they are drinking with the men," said Afewerki. He was horrified.

"I think they can handle themselves," said Reece. "Especially Svana." Reece mimicked a bodybuilder's pose.

"They work very hard and so must play very hard," said Gudmunder. "But they must respect local traditions. I know the mother of Eydis, and she would be very worried." He sipped from his cup.

"They will be rap-ed," said Afewerki. He knew it to be true. The Snake, the village administrator, was liable to drop in and begin flashing his gun, bragging of the men he had killed, the women he had raped. He had raped the blind woman who lived near the airfield. Everyone knew that.

"I'll have some of that," said Reece. He walked to his tent, kicked off his hiking boots, which were too small, slipped on his flip-flops, and grabbed his green plastic cup. A thin veil of nausea swept through his body, and then a chill.

Gebremariam, holding his ancient rifle, a Czech make,

came and asked if they would like to eat or wait on the nurses. He smiled his infectious smile and adjusted his hat, a gathering of cloth scraps sewn into a circle.

"Let us eat," said Afewerki. He wanted to return to his house. He wanted to go to the tejj house and check on Eydis.

"We can wait," said Reece.

"No, let us eat," said Gudmunder. "They will come soon enough and eat, or not." In the glowing of evening, his red hair softened. His head looked very square.

Afewerki explained to Gebremariam, and he went to the cook house to help Abebe serve dinner.

FOUR

Eydis and Svana sat opposite one another alongside a narrow table made from pallets. The pallets had been used to drop wheat from cargo planes during the famine in 1985. Even though equipped with parachutes, the loaded food pallets often exploded upon hitting the ground, scattering grain and wood. The hard stools were locally made. A small radio suspended from a yellow wire played music from a shortwave station in Addis Ababa. Two men played checkers in the corner.

Yellow plastic lined the inside walls of the square building. The roof was corrugated tin, and there were no windows, with just a low open doorway. Inside, ten men conversed in low, shy tones, drinking the dull orange tejj from the ubiquitous green cups, relics of the famine.

"You see?" said Svana. She'd had three cups of the mead as opposed to Eydis's one. "Tejj and teff. These are the lifebloods. No? F and J. In between is GHI. Ghee, which is clarified butter. No, Eydis? How is your English?" She drank half of her fourth cup. The man next to her, a farmer who rented land from his brother, tried to avoid touching her shoulder with his, but the tiny room was packed.

Eydis noted the recessed tooth of Svana. It was very sharp and out of place. Otherwise, she was beautiful. "Dinner will be soon," she said.

A young man with a masinqo, a one-stringed instrument, scraped out a tune with his bow, competing with the radio. Laughter and loud talk filled the room. The hostess, a pregnant woman, went from cup to cup with her large blue bottle filled with tejj.

Eydis waved off the hostess and watched as Svana put her arm around the man to her right. He was handsome, with a kind of goatee, perhaps in his twenties. She couldn't tell. "Svana?" she whispered.

Svana didn't hear her and kissed the man on the cheek and then withdrew her arm. The din of the room shallowed as everyone digested Svana's actions. The man she had kissed was married, a Muslim cleric who liked tejj.

"Svana!" said Eydis a bit louder. She shook her head, no. As she did, her cup was refilled before she could put her hand over it.

Abebe brought out the enjera on a large steel platter that she placed on the tarp near the fire pit. Gebremariam brought out the wot, goman, a green like collards made with niter-kibbeh, butter simmered with spices. The pot steamed in the cooling evening air, and the smell caused Reece's scalp to sweat.

Gudmunder missed the seafood of Iceland, but he loved Ethiopian cuisine. "Let me tell a story," he said, wrapping some goman in enjera.

"I will go to the tejj bet to see Eydis and Svana," said Afewerki.

Reece was thinking the same thing.

"No, no, they are fine. They will be okay," said Gudmunder. "They will miss this meal."

Afewerki had stood and remained standing.

"Let's eat," said Reece. His stomach was feeling queer.

Afewerki put his hands in his pockets. He seemed confused. He tried to sit and lost his balance, almost falling into the fire pit. "Shite!"

"Ha!" said Gudmunder. "Eat. I will tell a story."

Afewerki squatted. Reece wondered how he could squat like that. He fell over backward when he tried to squat.

"Do you know the story of Moses and the freeing of the Israelites?" asked Gudmunder. He did not wait for a response. "In this story, Moses leads the Israelites out from the power of the Egyptian king Ramses II. To do so, he battles with the royal court's magicians. They throw down a staff, which becomes a snake. Moses throws down his staff, which becomes a snake, and eats the staff of the magicians. He warns the Pharaoh that many plagues will visit Egypt if he does not free the Israelites."

"Frogs, the river turning to blood?" asked Reece. He'd been raised Southern Baptist, but had given up his religious heritage when both of his parents had been killed by a madman with a gun in a Luby's restaurant in Texas.

"Darkness, and death of the firstborn," said Afewerki. As an Orthodox Christian, he was very familiar with the Old Testament.

"There were ten plagues visited upon the Egyptians, sent by God to convince Pharaoh of his power. You know this, it seems?" He poured warm water from an Icelandic IV bottle into his cup.

Afewerki and Reece ate their first bites of goman and enjera.

"Delicious," said Reece. He loved collard greens, and these were especially good, although spicier and more bitter than he was used to.

"About two thousand BC, a volcano on the island of

Thera, in the Mediterranean, north of Egypt, erupted. It has been judged to be one of the most powerful volcanic events in ancient history. This occurred at the same time as Moses petitioned for the release of the Israelites from Ramses II. Many of the plagues can be explained by this eruption. There is a book which explains these things," said Gudmunder.

"Really?" asked Reece.

"The water into blood would be red volcanic ash in the rivers. The darkness is explanatory as the eruption would obliterate the sky."

"What about the frogs?" asked Reece.

"This is explained in the book, but I am not remembering," said Gudmunder.

"Interesting," said Reece.

"I fear they will be rap-ed," said Afewerki. He stood and took another bite of goman wrapped in enjera. He felt like he was looking through the wrong end of a telescope, even though he'd never seen one.

In the tejj bet, time slowed and became like amber. No one there would forget the night. It was magical. On her sixth cup of tejj, a full liter, like drinking a bottle of rice wine, Svana stood and began dancing to the rhythm of the masinqo. The radio spluttered with static. The pregnant woman pouring the tejj prayed that nothing bad would happen.

Eydis, now on her third cup, began to feel a warm glow. She thought about her father committing suicide back in Iceland. He had rented a hotel room, eaten an entire lemon meringue pie, and then shot himself in the roof of the mouth with a rivet gun. He was forty-seven, an embarrassing death, like drowning in an inch of water. She sipped her tejj.

The men hunched over the narrow table, all with eyes on Svana. She wore a loose blue scrub top with tight blue jeans. She was circling her hips. An older man named Mulu stood. He rounded the skinny table and took the hand of Svana. She twirled him. She pulled him close, felt his erection, and then pushed him away. Only the radio static played.

"Svana, please..." said Eydis.

Dusk meant sleep. Afewerki had left, returning to his house inside his parents' compound. Hopefully, his two younger brothers had managed to herd the goats into the pen. If one were lost, it would mean a late-night search. Hyenas made short work of a goat. He could only think of Eydis and Svana.

Both Gudmunder and Reece lay in their tents, waiting for Eydis and Svana to return. A rock poked Reece's left kidney. Reece looked at the ceiling of his orange tent. The fabric was tight. It was pitch black except for the rising moon. Surely Eydis would be back soon. Kristin seemed like a distant memory. Her parents had not liked him. Kristin was gorgeous but had not understood his need to leave the United States and travel halfway across the globe to Africa. Eydis could understand him. For the first time in over two years, he prayed to God. A line from a Rolling Stones song intervened. Was the katikala making his legs itch? He scratched hard and drew blood. He could smell it, red and full of iron.

Afewerki's prized white hen, a gift from a German sustainability group, roosted overhead on a pole, sleeping.

He was full from dinner and looked down at his dusty tennis shoes, a gift from Reece. They were too big, but that was okay. He thought about the local women and how sassy they were, even the young ones. No wonder so many women were divorced. Eydis, by comparison, was polite and liked to laugh. Before Reece came, he had imagined marrying her. She seemed now less interested. And why would she and Svana stay so long at the tejj bet? He could not imagine Eydis drunk, but had seen Svana drunk on two occasions.

Afewerki sat on his bed and began to untie his shoes. No, he could not sleep. He had to go and check on Eydis and Svana. He stood. The night was beginning to chill, and he put on his Exxon ballcap.

Nearing midnight, Gudmunder checked his watch. He had not heard the nurses return. He could hear Reece snoring in his tent. Still dressed, he sat up and put on his hiking boots. The air was cold. He slipped on a red sweater and unzipped the tent. The bright moon washed the compound in a magic glow. He could see Gebremariam with his rifle, watching him near the break in the fence.

"Abet?" asked Gebremariam.

"No worries," said Gudmunder. "Chicorilla." He stepped through the fence gate and turned left to follow the path to the tejj bet. He had been once and cared little for the sweet mead. In the distance, within minutes, he could see the red light of a kerosene lantern emanating through a plastic flap over the door. A faint sound of music and laughing. He tripped on a rock, "Djöfulsins helvíti!" He approached the door and hesitated. Should he knock or just enter? He hoped to God that Eydis and Svana were inside. He had no way of explaining his visit without Afewerki to interpret.

He pulled the plastic to the side, and the screech of the masinqo and the laughter ceased. All eyes were on him. The lantern's brightness blinded him. He surveyed the two packed benches. The smell of honey, sweat, and alcohol filled the room.

"Hallo!" said Afewerki.

Gudmunder's eyes began to adjust. To his surprise, he saw Afewerki with Eydis sitting on his lap. She sat facing forward with a cup in her hand, wearing the Exxon ballcap, staring into space. He did not see Svana. "Shit."

Several men, all drunk, started to stand and give him a seat. He waved them off and pointed at Eydis.

"Eydis." He walked closer. "Eydis. Come with me." He nodded at Afewerki, who seemed to be the only sober one in the room. "She must come with me. She must rest."

Eydis looked up and smiled. "You devil! Oh, where is Svana?"

Afewerki was in full bliss. His hands were in Eydis's lap. "No, she is fine. I will to you bring her very soon."

"Afewerki, please. Svana, where is she?"

"She has left? She has not returned?" Afewerki had not even noticed her leaving with Mulu, the farmer with the wide-legged shorts, who was muscular with a shaved head.

"No, she is missing. Eydis, please, come with me." Gudmunder pulled her chin sideways so she would look at him.

Seeing him, Eydis closed her eyes and moved her head from side to side. She realized that she was drunk and sitting on Afewerki's lap. She could feel his boner pressing into her. This was not good, and she tried to stand and wavered. Gudmunder gripped her elbow, steadying her.

Afewerki felt a course of anger rush through his fogged brain. "Eydis?"

Eydis leaned into Gudmunder and let him lead her beyond the plastic flap and into the night. The cool air felt distant. The night was black for a moment before her bleary eyes adjusted. Gudmunder knew it was fruitless to hunt for Svana, and he walked Eydis back to the compound, where she collapsed into her tent without a sound.

Eydis awoke early to the sound of cocks crowing around Gwar. Her eyes hurt, and she remembered the long night of drinking. Svana, she was not in the tent. Eydis was fully dressed and could smell her dirty hair. She would need to bathe and shampoo. Where the hell was Svana? She squatted and then stood in the tent opening. The morning seemed raw and cruel, like an ocean beach in winter. She was thirsty and had to use the bathroom badly.

"Hallo!"

Eydis, bent slightly because of the fullness in her bladder, turned and saw Afewerki emerge from the cook house. "Oh, hello." She turned and trotted to the far end of the compound and the shintabet. She opened the crooked door and stepped inside, breathing fumes of feces and urine. Eydis squatted with head in hands and tried to figure out when Svana had left. Had she left alone or with someone?

Gudmunder was up, having heard someone emerge from the nurses' tent. He put on his glasses and pressed back his red hair. He first looked into the tent. No one. Eydis must have gone to the outhouse. It was then that he noticed Afewerki. "Good morning," he said.

"Good morning," said Afewerki. He had not slept the entire night, thinking of Eydis.

"Tell me, Afewerki, do you know where Svana may be?"

"Yes. She has left with Mulu, the farmer. It is nearby. Do you wish me to take you there?"

Eydis strolled back to the tents. She knew they were talking about Svana.

Gudmunder felt like a father to Svana and Eydis. "If she does not return by breakfast, yes, we will go."

"Hey!" Reece was up and calling from inside the orange tent.

"My brother, join us," said Afewerki. He stood with his hands in his pockets. Eydis had stopped short of him by ten feet. He wondered if he should hug her.

Gebremariam emerged from the cookhouse, surprised that everyone was up so early. He called Afewerki and asked if he should prepare the tea.

Svana awoke with her head on fire. She lay on her back in the middle of a sagging bed made of skinny poles. She was wearing a top but had no pants or underwear. No one was in bed with her. She looked at the steep tepee roof. The room was cold and smelled of smoke. On the wall made of poles daubed with mud hung an enjera basket. Pages from a magazine were pinned here and there. She moved her toes to make sure she was not paralyzed. She had no memory of the night before other than the sweet taste in her mouth. What had happened? She realized she was naked from the waist down. She sat up quickly and nearly passed out. She stood, bent over, and grabbed her knees to keep from falling. Her jeans and underwear were on the dry mud floor. She dressed, sitting on the bed, moaning. She could tell that she'd had sex, but with whom? Had she been raped, or was it consensual? Visions of her father loomed in her mind.

Outside, roosters crowed. The hut was inside a small compound. An old dog skulked, growling. Svana looked at the steeply pitched roof, wondering if she could climb it. There was a door made of scraps in the fence. She made it there without falling and pushed. The dog barked, teeth bared. She pulled, and the door opened. She stepped onto a wide path with a huge pothole, mud in its bottom.

She turned left. Nothing seemed familiar. She turned right and headed downhill. No, the compound was near the highest point in town, and she reversed course. She met an old woman piled high with firewood. The old woman paid her no mind, stooped with her load. She smelled fire and milk as the wrinkled woman passed. Svana walked, stepping over stones, and reached the village square of a sudden. Chickens scuttled to and fro, clucking.

FIVE

Gudmunder, tea in hand, watched Svana trip through the fence opening. Angry, he stood. Reece, Eydis, and Afewerki sat in chairs eating breakfast, eggs with hot pepper and bits of enjera.

"What the hell, Svana?" asked Gudmunder.

"Stop," said Svana. Her black hair stood on end. She angled toward an empty chair and fell toward it. She fumbled to the ground in a heap.

Reece, Afewerki, and Eydis jumped up. Eydis pushed them away, and she helped Svana to a folding chair. "You will eat," she said.

Svana contemplated that. She smelled of vomit. "Okay." She put her head into her hands.

Afewerki said, "Tsk, tsk, tsk."

Reece didn't know what to do. He looked to Gudmunder, who now looked more concerned than angry. Gudmunder had Afewerki bring Svana breakfast and an IV bottle full of filtered water.

Svana sipped the water. She ate a bite of the eggs and gagged.

"Kita. She needs kita," said Reece.

Afewerki went to the cook house and asked Abebe to prepare a plain flatbread for Svana. Abebe frowned. She needed to get back to her four children and make breakfast for them as well.

With Eydis and Svana taking a day off from weighing children and Reece and Afewerki out doing the survey,

Gudmunder walked the steep paths of Gwar. He walked toward the peak of the village where sat the Orthodox Church, dedicated to St. George. Inside, he knew, was the Holy of Holies, the maqdas, where was kept a replica of the Ten Commandments given to Moses from God on Mt. Sinai during the Exodus and wandering of the Israelites. It was long rumored that the original tabot was inside the Ark, housed in a chapel in Axum, farther north. Gudmunder also knew that the Ark sometimes was moved to prevent its capture. An island on Lake Tana was rumored to harbor the Ark at one time to protect it against those who would steal it. Where was it now? He thought about his research into the matter, specifically the Icelandic saga of Gaukur, the Lost Saga.

Gudmunder approached the Church of St. Gabriel, a large round hut of poles and mud topped with a straw roof and a wooden cupola. A crude metal box secured by a padlock accepted donations to the church. The church was not occupied full-time by a priest, which caused Gudmunder to doubt that the church could harbor the real Ark of the Covenant.

He traversed the rocky ground and walked a circle around the building. He paused at the wooden door and pushed it, but it did not move. He sensed a power emanating from the church. He wanted to see the maqdas, but knew that he would never be allowed to do so. Only the priest could enter the Holy of Holies. A stray dog appeared and turned tail as soon as it saw Gudmunder.

He walked higher and visited the site of a former Baptist Mission shelter that had housed widows and orphans. Nothing remained. In the distance to the north, he could see a river valley. Crocodiles lived there. To the southwest was a flat-topped amba, more than ten thousand feet high.

He returned to the offering box, slid in a one-birr bill, and made his way back to a main path, heading downhill.

By dinner, Svana and Eydis had somewhat recovered. Svana sat in a chair, elbows on knees, looking into a fire that Reece had built. He had bought an entire load of firewood from an old woman for seven birr, a week's wages. Eydis stood with her hands toward the flames. She considered making fire a kind of magic.

"How did the survey go this day?" asked Gudmunder.

"Not so good," said Reece.

"What do you mean?" asked Gudmunder.

Reece thought about how aloof Afewerki seemed to be that day. "We interviewed an old woman, the oldest woman in Gwar, it turns out. She only had one tooth. Well, we interview her and then she insists that we interview her entire family, who have been gathered around us, listening to her responses."

"So you are worried about the integrity of their responses, no?"

"Yeah, I guess. But what could we do?"

Eydis spoke up. "You could eliminate their responses from your survey?"

"That would be a whole day wasted," said Reece. He thought about how he had two months left to complete his survey *and* do research in Addis Ababa.

"A difficult decision," said Gudmunder.

Gebremariam announced that dinner was ready. He walked from person to person with a bar of white soap and a pitcher full of water.

Svana let the water trickle over her right hand as she soaped it and then rinsed. Her period was due in a day or two. She'd had sex at the height of her fertility cycle. Would she bear a café au lait child like the Polish soldiers had left in Gwar?

The next day, Reece and Afewerki walked downhill. Three gunshots. "What the hell?" asked Reece.

Afewerki motioned for him to stop. The shots had come from near his parents' compound, which was next to the village's prison compound. They waited for a moment, not hearing further shots, and continued. They walked to another small village nearby, thirty minutes or so, just a few huts, known as Diray. There was a flat stone low to the ground, in the shade, on which Reece sat. Right away, he was uncomfortable.

The first interviewee was a mother of three children. She reeked of smoke and stood six feet tall. Butter oiled her short hair.

Reece asked the initial questions, and the woman replied in a sad voice. She interjected that she had lost four children, the last one to a snake bite. He wondered if the snake was a black mamba. She didn't know, only that God had chosen to punish her for not sending her oldest son to study for the priesthood.

"How is your hearing?" asked Reece.

Afewerki said that the woman reported she had good hearing.

"Do you have any pain?" asked Reece.

The woman appeared to be puzzled. She said that, of

course, she had pain. "My husband has died. I have lost four children. God keeps me alive to care for the others, but that is the only reason."

Reece nodded to Afewerki, waiting for the translation. He fidgeted on the low stone. His butt hurt. His back ached. He scribbled the responses onto the response form and completed the interview with a photo.

The next person walked forward. He wore a pristine, tailored suit made from the polypropylene grain bags dropped years before during the great famine. He sported a mustache, and he appeared calm and confident.

The interview progressed. "What do you use for cooking fuel?"

The man looked perplexed. "The wood," he said.

Reece thought about the electric stove in his apartment back in the States. All he had to do was turn a knob. Here, one had to walk at least forty-five minutes, gather wood, walk back uphill, and then build a fire to cook. He thought about the Winn-Dixie filled with fresh vegetables and cans of soup.

"Have you ever been injured as a result of military activity in this area?"

Afewerki yawned. Within a few hours, he would be eating dinner with Eydis. How would Svana act? Had she had sex with Mulu? Life was so much more interesting since the Icelandic team and Reece had arrived.

Eydis and Svana had wandered down the road that led to a village called Sokol. All of the residents were known to have the evil eye, known as buda. They were the primary metal workers and weavers in the area. As a result of their outcast status and poverty, health was miserably poor. Unknown to the Icelandic team and Reece, residents of the town were banned from seeking help from the foreigners. They attended the Saturday and Tuesday markets in Gwar, but they dared not make eye contact with anyone, which made them seem humble and afraid.

Svana, with the portable weight scale in a backpack, led the way. The road was wide and rocky, hurting her ankles. "We are going down, down," she said.

"And up and up on our return," said Eydis. The sun breathed heat through a thin layer of high-altitude cloud.

They passed gigantic fig trees. The road wound about with high banks of rocky dirt. There was no smell to the air, just a heaviness as if the altitude added weight to their existence. After half an hour, a tukul appeared in the distance and then more. A smell of smoke. Two children, bottomless boys with stiff shirts of burlap, spotted them and ran uphill to greet them.

"Ferenj!"

Svana smiled. One boy took her hand, and the other took the hand of Eydis, leading them to their village. A recent survey indicated that food assistance was not needed in the area. The survey, though, had only kept to the main roads, ignoring small enclaves such as the one they were approaching.

Upon reaching the first walled compound, they found a level bit of ground and set up the scale beneath a tree. A cloth sling held the child. They measured height with a simple tape measure. Soon, the first women emerged. From experience with other aid organizations, the women recognized the scale, and they knew what to do.

Their first patient was a malnourished child of seven years. His eyes seemed twice the size they should be. Eydis frowned at Svana. This was a case of very severe malnutrition, but they had no way of asking questions. The child was nearly four feet tall but only weighed thirty-five pounds, a skeleton. Svana filled in the data on the yellow card. A constant bead of sweat played in her eyebrows despite the arid conditions. She promised herself that she would never again drink to excess.

Gudmunder spent the day at the camp, sitting in the shade of a thorn tree, reading from his book of Icelandic sagas, the *Íslendingasögur.* He loved the intricate details, the disputes over land, the bloody acts of retribution. Snorri Sturluson was his favorite narrator. The best story, though, was that of the Lost Saga, that of Gaukur Trandilsson, an Icelandic adventurer who became one of the first Icelanders to convert to Christianity around 1,000 BC. Alone, he had set out on a quest to acquire the Ark of the Covenant for his people, first traveling to Jerusalem and from there to Egypt and then to Ethiopia. Due to his large stature and stiff yellow hair, the Ethiopians had received him as a lost son of God and provided him with food, shelter, and even a wife.

Inside the cook house, Abebe poured enjera batter onto a hot round steel pan. The thick gray liquid bubbled, forming a thin porous layer of the spongy enjera. Standing in smoke, she wiped sweat from her forehead and pulled her ancient dress down from her shoulders to her waist. Sweat streamed between her large breasts. After three minutes, she lifted the hot round and laid it in the enjera basket. She would make enough to last for three days or more. She peeked through the haze into the compound yard where sat the doctor. She hoped he would come and watch and perhaps see how beautiful she was. It was difficult being a divorcee with four children, and it was rumored that the doctor was single. He slept alone in his tent.

Gudmunder paused in his reading. Coming into the compound were Afewerki and Reece. Overhead, the hot sun indicated noon. They had left a small line of people waiting to be interviewed, promising to return within the hour. Afewerki peered into the cook house and asked what was for lunch. Abebe, half-naked, had no effect on him. He grinned and had Reece take a look. Reece peered into the smoke. He smelled onions and oil. Abebe, stirring a pot, gave him a working smile.

"Uh, tenesteling," said Reece. He ducked out, and Afewerki slapped him on the back. Reece imagined that it must get pretty hot in the cook house.

"Reece and Afewerki, have these chairs for your tired feet." Gudmunder placed his book on his lap. He noticed that Afewerki, although a bit short, had nicely toned forearms.

"Are you reading the sagas?" asked Reece.

"Yes, always. It is a hobby. It is the only book I have brought." He scooted his chair a bit for more shade.

"What is the story?" asked Afewerki. He imagined Iceland as a vast sheet of ice with only snow and volcanoes. It seemed a harsh place. He wondered if Eydis and Svana would come for lunch.

"It is the story of a man named Gaukur. He was from Iceland, an adventure seeker, like me, no less." He laughed. "There are many sagas, but one was lost for many years. It has now been found in a monastery near Kirkjubæjarklaustur. A place for nuns." He unfolded three sheets of paper from within the large book. "The lost saga is here. It is a photocopy. Afewerki, you will be interested. Do you know the Ark of the Covenant?"

"Yes. We say that it is in Axum at the Church of Our Lady Mary of Zion, in a chapel there. It has been brought to us by Menelik from the Holy Land."

Reece perked up at the mention of the Ark. He'd read a book on the subject. "Do you think that the Ark is hidden, though, and not where they say it is? Why would you tell everyone where it is?"

"Abet?" Afewerki tried to remember what they were talking about. He inspired through his mouth.

"Gaukur found the Ark in Ethiopia. The priest recognized him as a son of God. He was allowed to enter the maqdas and see the Ark. Because he did not die, the priest knew that he was truly a son of God."

Afewerki was listening once again. "If this is true, perhaps he came to steal the Ark. But it is unbelievable that he has seen the Ark. Only the blessed priest can do such a thing."

"Yes, that was his plan. But when he saw the Ark, he had a vision from God, instructing him to return to Iceland, to have his story written, and then to live as a woman begging for food."

Afewerki watched Abebe coming with the enjera platter. Gebremariam was behind her with a pot of shurowot, spicy lentil stew.

"And here is our food," said Gudmunder.

"Some of the people have been murmuring," said Afewerki. He looked at Reece and then Gudmunder.

"Of what?" asked Gudmunder.

"They say you will try to steal the tabot from the church."

"Really? I have visited the church, but that is all."

"Ah, but you said that you must see the maqdas, the holy place. The people are listening," said Afewerki.

Reece ladled wot for Afewerki and then for Gudmunder. He served himself last. It smelled delicious. "Why would he want to steal from the church? That's crazy."

"Dr. Thorsonn is a good man. He will not do such a thing. But the people is talking."

Gudmunder took a wad of enjera and beans and chewed. "This is good to know, Afewerki. I will have to be more careful. I do not want the people to distrust me."

"Ah, they are watching you," said Afewerki. He laughed and began to eat.

SIX

Svana and Eydis wound up staying the day in Sokol and eating with a very poor family. The enjera was made from sorghum. The spicy wot was runny. After eating, they resumed their busy work, having weighed all of the children. Both had basic medical supplies in their backpacks, including peroxide and antibiotic ointment. Sounds of metal being pounded reverberated through the dusty lanes.

A mother presented her daughter. The girl of twelve turned and buried her head in the folds of her mother's dusty dress. The mother explained at length in Amharic that the girl refused to have sex with her new husband. She had hit him and bitten him. There was an infection, and she wanted to have his wound treated.

Svana and Eydis listened, trying to glean a clue as to what was wrong.

"I will try," said Eydis. She bent down and turned the girl's face toward hers. A look of sheer terror was there, but why? "Ishi, ishi," she repeated, meaning okay. "Mendeno? What is wrong?"

The girl's eyes grew bright and flickered at the sound of the ferenj speaking her language.

Eydis noticed rough, bumpy patches on her arms and diagnosed scabies. But she did not have medicine for that. She touched the girl's warm, dry face and pulled down a lower lid, checking for anemia. The flesh was pale. She was malnourished for sure. Hopefully, the data they were collecting would result in food aid to the area, but for now, she could only give money. But if she gave money to one, then she would have to give money to them all.

"Svana, what to do?"

The girl's mother reached out and touched Eydis's blonde hair.

Svana shook her head. She was feeling hungry. "I feel it is something bad. We must return with Afewerki."

"Naga. Tomorrow. We will come again. Ishi?" asked Eydis.

The girl blushed and nodded.

"What's next? This is killing me," said Svana. Around them had gathered a crowd of twenty-four. The villagers were not used to having visitors, let alone foreigners with pale skin.

A man, speaking in a loud voice, stepped forward. His eyelashes had begun to turn inward, and he was slowly going blind. He went to his knees and begged them to help. He was a metalworker, and if he went blind, how would he feed his family? His wife was dead. He had five children and no livestock.

Relieved that she could do something, Svana pulled a tube of tetracycline eye ointment from her backpack. They had plenty at the compound. His was a nasty case of trachoma. Hopefully, the damage was reversible. She put on a latex glove and slipped a bead of ointment beneath his eyelids. Yellow debris spilled down his face, dislodged from his eyes. Svana shuddered.

The man held the tube of ointment. He knew the medicine. It had helped him before. He knew to use it three times a day. "Xavier meskin," he said, praising God.

"You must wash your face very well, and hands, every day," said Eydis. She mimed washing her hands and face.

"Samona. Soap."

The man shook his head in agreement and heartily shook her hand, leaving sweat on her arm.

Svana gazed around at the group. It seemed they had all taken one step forward. She could smell the collective body odor, a smell of hot steel. She felt a bit dizzy and looked up at the bright blue sky. Circling were two buzzards. She suddenly wanted to be far away. She wanted to lose herself in a haze of techno, dancing, vodka, and maybe some amphetamines, at one of her favorite clubs in Reykjavik.

"Svana? You are okay?" asked Eydis.

A woman ushered her small boy forward. He was five and wore a rag of shirt that barely reached his navel. The woman was pointing to his uncircumcised penis.

Svana looked at Eydis and stifled a laugh. The woman wanted them to circumcise her boy. And it was the case each day that the weighing of children turned into a spontaneous and frustrating clinic for them. If they could prove there was a need for food relief in Gwar, then perhaps the Baptists would help them build another clinic.

By five o'clock, everyone except Afewerki was back in the compound. He was at home shaving and taking a bath from a plastic pan. He had bought some menthol powder and planned to rub it liberally in his fine chest hair.

Abebe had spent the afternoon washing clothes and was behind with dinner. Her children would have no dinner, and she was angry, rushing about. To save time, it looked to be more shurowot fortified with niter-kibbeh.

Reece emerged from his tent. He was tired, having

walked several kilometers that day. He passed the Icelanders, all speaking Icelandic. Eydis smacked him on his butt as he walked by on his way to the water barrel. He turned, came up behind her, grabbed her shoulders, and began to massage her neck. She sank into her chair and made suggestive moans, much to the delight of the others.

"Oh, Reece has the magic hands," said Gudmunder.

"Hey, I am jealous," said Svana.

"Okay, you're next," said Reece. Eydis's skin was soft and warm, sunburned above her collar.

Gebremariam and Abebe emerged from the cook house just as Afewerki entered the compound. Afewerki felt a little woozy. He could hear Eydis laughing. He walked past the cook house toward the tents and chairs. Reece was grunting and rubbing Eydis's shoulders. She was moaning, "Oh, baby!" He stopped. What should he do?

"Afewerki! Come and join the party," said Svana. "You come and rub my neck like Reece."

Paralyzed for a moment, he shuffled forward. He made eye contact with Reece, who sensed something was wrong.

"You okay?" asked Reece. He noticed that Afewerki had changed clothes.

Gudmunder surveyed the unfolding drama and deduced that Afewerki might have a crush on Eydis. Gudmunder had been married twice before, briefly decided that he was bisexual, and now was satisfied to live a single life. He liked everyone.

"Ha, is long day," said Afewerki. He could not make himself look at Eydis, as if she were made of fine glass. He withdrew and put his hands in his pockets.

Abebe and Gebremariam set up the meal on the tarp.

Only Gudmunder said thank you, and Abebe left in a hurry to see about her family.

Reece finished his massage with a flourish, and Eydis sighed her approval. Dusk had begun to settle, the bats circling and diving.

"Let's eat!" she said.

There was a sound of loud voices in the lane. They all turned toward the gap in the fence, and there he was, the Snake, drunk off his rocker and waving his pistol.

"Shit," said Reece.

The Snake had interfered in their work, demanding payment for certain "necessary" document stamps. The Snake's favorite act was to use his purple stamp as a symbol of his limited power in a faraway village. In fact, he was being punished, sent to the hinterlands for his general incompetence and alcoholism.

The Snake, his real name being Assnake, staggered into the compound. He holstered his pistol, a Russian Makarov, and motioned for his two "bodyguards" to follow. Each held an AK-47, sixties models, but in perfect working order.

Reece chewed his food slowly and swallowed. He looked to Gudmunder, the elder statesman of the group, for a clue. He stood and went to greet the Snake.

"Afewerki?" asked Gudmunder.

"Yes?"

"Will you translate?"

"Yes."

The Snake unleashed a string of profanities, which Afewerki left alone. He winced as the Snake kept reaching for his pistol, but missing with his right hand.

"He is angry," said Afewerki.

The Snake continued to ramble, weaving back and forth, his gold teeth flashing in the fading light.

"The nurses have visited Sokol, where there is the buda, the evil eye. They cannot go there. The buda will come to Gwar. The people will become hyenas and eat the dead. He believes this thing."

Svana stood and pointed her finger at the Snake. "You are the devil. Don't tell me what I can do. Everyone is equal in God's eyes."

The Snake demanded to know what Svana had said. He called her a whore and said that she had clots of blood in her pussy hole. His minions laughed at that one.

Afewerki, glancing at Eydis, told the Snake that she would obey his orders.

"Would you like to have some dinner?" asked Gudmunder. He thought that was the best way to get rid of this nuisance.

Afewerki translated.

"I would rather eat my shit than eat your sorry food," said the Snake. Suddenly, he seemed deflated, as if a great chemical rush had shut down his body. He staggered and was braced by his bodyguards. He looked as if he would defecate in his pants and turned to leave.

"Good riddance!" said Svana, her shock of black hair trembling with anger.

"Svana, no," said Eydis. She realized she had been holding a bite of enjera the entire time and placed it into her mouth.

"What an asshole," said Reece.

"Yes," said Gudmunder, "but we must try to make a

friend of him. He is too dangerous to ignore. He will hurt someone."

The next day at breakfast, Gudmunder had an idea. "Let us all take a little break, no? I say we take a jeep to Alem Ketema for a short vacation, perhaps just two nights. There is the Beselfui Hotel, no? A pleasant room with a bed. They have electricity from seven until ten p.m. We can drink some in the bar. I will pay for this trip, no problem. What do you say?"

"We need to return to Sokol, the place that the Snake has forbidden," said Svana.

"Afewerki, we need to have you there to translate. There are so many sad cases," said Eydis.

"It is forbidden for me to go there. At night, they eat the dead. They become hyenas. It is unclean and very dangerous."

"Really?" asked Reece.

"Yes, it is true. Everyone knows it."

Gudmunder cleared his throat. "I say this. The deserving people of Sokol can wait for three days. We will figure out a way to translate for you without Afewerki having to go. What do you say?"

Eydis was thinking of sharing a hotel room with Reece. "Sounds good to me. She reached over and squeezed Reece's thigh."

The others agreed as well, and they decided to leave as soon as the next jeep arrived. One should be coming in the afternoon, but one never really knew.

At noon, just as Abebe was about to bring out the meal,

news reached them that a jeep had arrived and would be leaving soon. Everyone sprang into action, grabbing their bags and rushing down to the site of the old Baptist clinic. Gebremariam had bought a leg of goat for Abebe to make tibs, and now there was no one to eat it except for them. They sat on low stools outside the cook house and began their intimate feast.

The jeep, an old red Toyota, already held three persons, each paying twenty birr to ride to Alem Ketema, about a half month's farmer's wage for a forty-kilometer trip. Their bags were piled on top and secured with a ragged rope. Reece and Afewerki sat in the back cargo area, cramped by a bag of teff. Gudmunder sat crammed with three passengers in the back seat. Eydis sat in Svana's lap in the front seat. A late arrival, a young man seeking a wife, crawled to the roof and settled in among the luggage. The driver cranked the jeep and began the slow crawl from Gwar to AK. He was disappointed because he knew he could fit one more person in the back with Afewerki and Reece, a loss of twenty birr.

Reece looked out the back window, seeing where they had been through a cloud of dust. Every rock and rut sent a jolt through his skinny frame. He imagined his grandparents, Dora and Horace, back home in Alabama, snapping green beans and cutting okra. Afewerki's knees hit his knees. His stomach felt a bit queasy.

In the back seat, Gudmunder sat pressed to the window behind the driver. He had to lean forward because his shoulders were so wide. All of the windows were rolled up, as wind was bad for one's health, and the aromas of nine bodies began to mingle.

The jeep descended, twisting and turning, finally beginning a descent to the Wenchit River that involved a never-ending series of switchbacks. The engine roared, and the transmission groaned. Reece's stomach began to bubble, and he burped rotten eggs. *Oh God.*

The Wenchit River was mostly large pools of standing water connected by trickles, being the dry season. They crossed the trussed bridge and began the hilly drive to the next river, the Jara.

Reece felt truly sick. He wondered if he would throw up or if he would shit himself first. He closed his eyes and concentrated on the lake where his grandparents lived. He liked to jog around the lake, a distance of about five miles. The lake was in a valley, Emerald Valley, and the humidity would reach staggering levels, perhaps two-hundred percent, he sometimes imagined. Sweat would stream from his head and body down to soak his shirt and shorts. He imagined it was like a natural form of dialysis, and it felt so good.

Nearing the Jara, Svana had to switch with Eydis as her legs were going to sleep. Svana leaned against the door, facing the driver. He had a scraggly beard and bloodshot eyes. She imagined that he never left the jeep, just driving back and forth, which was more or less true. There was something about the Ethiopian men that she liked. They were thin and muscular, with strong voices. She let her mind wander.

Reece tapped Afewerki on the knee.

"Abet?"

"You have to tell the driver to stop. I have to go to the bathroom."

"You are needing to urinate?"

"No, the other. I have to defecate, right now. I'm sick."

Now that Afewerki looked at Reece, he was very pale. He called over the back seat and yelled at the driver to stop for the ferenj.

The jeep came to a slow halt on a flat stretch of land. To both sides were scraggly trees the height of a donkey's ear and towering above them bedena and soapberry trees. The ground seemed like cocoa powder mixed with rocks.

Reece crawled over the back row, turning upside down in the process. Eydis opened the door, and she and Svana with Reece piled out of the jeep in a tumble.

"Oh God," said Reece. He wanted to run into the distance, away from the jeep, but he was forced to walk. He clenched his buttocks as if he were Superman. Without looking back, he tore loose his belt, unzipped his jeans, pulled them down, and stood stooped over. First, unexpectedly, he projectile vomited, and then came the hot diarrhea. It was over within twenty seconds. He had no toilet paper and searched the ground for leaves, anything. All he could find were two smooth stones.

Too sick to be embarrassed, he returned to the jeep. The driver had opened the back hatch, and he crawled in, worried that he stunk of diarrhea. He felt so much better, though, and thanked God beneath his breath.

SEVEN

The jeep pulled into the town square of AK, actually a circle, around three in the afternoon. Old men sat on a low wall that lined the inner circle. Reece belched rotten eggs.

Gudmunder coordinated the removal of luggage and enlisted the help of two energetic boys to carry their bags to the hotel. As a group, they walked down the wide, dusty lane. Reece felt weak and feared he would ruin their little vacation. He had hoped to hit it off with Eydis, but was now doubting if he would be able to leave his room, except to visit the shintabet. He would need to buy toilet paper and keep his eyes open for a dry goods stall.

As they walked through town, cries of "Ferenj!" greeted them. The hotel was about half a kilometer away, and they made good time with their child porters, laughing the entire distance. Reece had stayed at the Beselfui before and knew that they served good food. He looked forward to having a shot of Johnny Walker Black or Red, whichever they happened to have. *Maybe I will be okay.*

"Hold up," said Reece. He had spotted a small store, just a closet of rickety wood. He bought a roll of toilet paper and three boxes of vanilla crème cookies made in Saudi Arabia, one for himself and two for the porters.

The entourage continued, reaching the Beselfui five minutes later. The proprietor, an unusually fat woman with reddish hair, greeted them at the gate. She talked for nearly ten minutes, during which Afewerki interpreted for just one minute. "She is happy that you have come."

All of the rooms had a single bed made of planks with

a thin mattress. That was it, no chairs or tables. Reece had hoped there would be a room shortage so that perhaps he could share a room with Eydis, but the hotel was mostly vacant. In reality, he was relieved, worried that his diarrhea would return.

The owner of the hotel announced that she would be hosting a special dinner for her guests from Gwar. She sent her nephew to buy a goat.

Reece relaxed on the bed. It was lumpy but more comfortable than his sleeping bag in Gwar. He kicked off his hiking boots and could smell his feet. For the first time, he worried that Eydis might not be attracted to him, especially since he'd had to stop the jeep. What could be done?

The others relaxed as well, letting time pass without care. Only Afewerki was out of his room, sitting in the courtyard at a small wooden table. The weather was warm, but he was in the shade and drinking a cup of hot, strong coffee filled with heaping teaspoons of sugar. He felt fantastic. He felt light. He wished that the others would emerge from the rooms and join him.

Eydis, used to sharing the tent with Svana, admired her private room. The wall was a bright pastel green. It felt cheery. Flies buzzed in and out of the open door. Her feet were hot, and she took off her shoes, resting her toes on the cool concrete floor. She heard a slight commotion outside.

The owner's nephew had bought a black and white goat. He had told the owner that it was for the ferenjis at the hotel, and the man insisted that he come and slaughter the goat himself. To prepare, he had downed a very healthy portion of katikala, which he had been drinking since noon.

Svana and Gudmunder came to the open courtyard in front of the bar/restaurant. A row of rooms flanked either side. The shintabet was behind the cook house. They saw Afewerki and pulled up chairs. An ancient checkerboard with beer caps for playing pieces sat on the table. The owner of the hotel came out, greeted them, and then hurried to buy salt and have firewood delivered.

Coming now to the front of the courtyard was the nephew and the man with the goat. In one hand, he held the goat by a rope around its neck. In the other was a large, sharp knife. He staggered into the dirt courtyard and pulled the protesting goat behind him. The nephew looked worried. Afewerki seemed amused.

"What is this?" asked Gudmunder.

"This man has come to kill the goat for your dinner," said Afewerki.

"Dear God," said Svana. She wasn't interested. "Where, here?"

"No, he will not do it here," said Afewerki.

Praising God, the man reached beneath the goat's neck and slit it. Blood shot from the gash. The man cried out in pain. He had sliced open his palm as well. He let loose the goat. Gudmunder stood. Svana ran inside the bar. Afewerki was stunned. What was happening?

The goat, bleating its last breaths, escaped the drunken man's grasp and leaped toward the rooms. Eydis's door was barely open. The goat entered, spraying blood. Eydis screamed. The goat chased her around the room, begging for mercy. Eydis jumped on the bed. The goat jumped on the bed. Afewerki was inside. He grabbed the rope and dragged the dying goat from the room, where it looked as if a massacre had occurred. Eydis ran from the room into the bright sunshine, blood on her hands and shoes. The man and his nephew dragged the goat through the bar to the kitchen, leaving a trail of blood.

Reece emerged from his room and tried to make sense of the scene.

"Dear God," said Svana.

"I did not think he would do it," said Afewerki. "He is drinking."

"Thank you, Afewerki," said Eydis. She would have hugged him, but he had blood on his shirt.

"Chicorilla. No problem." He felt warm inside. Dinner would be delicious with the meat of the goat. He would drink a Coke, a rare treat. He laughed.

When the proprietor returned with salt and discovered what had happened, all hell broke loose. The drunk man had run back to his shack. The nephew received the brunt of her fury. She made him scrub the bar floor and Eydis's room. She gave Eydis another room and apologized profusely, her ample bosom shaking with her words.

The group sat in the shaded courtyard, chatting and drinking warm St. George beer. Gudmunder tapped out a cigarette from his pack of Nyala's. Very few people smoked in the villages because of the cost. Eydis took a cigarette and lit it off of Gudmunder's. Afewerki frowned.

"I'll take one too," said Reece. He was a social smoker.

"Why everyone is smoking?" asked Afewerki. He waved the smoke away from his face.

"May I?" asked Svana. She took one as well, laughing

at Afewerki.

The barmaid, Lebna, came outside. She was tiny and had a protruding tooth. She wore a bright red scarf. She took Reece's empty bottle. Did he want another? "Certo!" She looked into Reece's eyes. She took his hand and held it for a moment. Everyone stared, and Gudmunder chuckled.

"I think she likes you," he said.

"Hmm," said Reece. "She has that smell of smoke and milk." He wondered what would happen if he had a child with a local woman. What would the child look like? Would it be a boy, a girl?

"She is a very bad woman," said Afewerki. He made a sour face.

"Bad?" asked Eydis. She exhaled smoke and tapped her ash to the ground.

"She is prostitute."

"That doesn't make her bad. Does it?" Eydis had a thing for social justice.

"She is dirty," said Afewerki.

"We are all dirty, no?" asked Svana.

"I am not dirty," said Afewerki.

Gudmunder dropped his butt into the beer bottle.

"No, you must not," said Afewerki. "These bottles will be used again."

"Oh, are you sure?" asked Gudmunder.

Afewerki nodded. He looked cornered and uncomfortable. There was silence for nearly a minute. It was nearing six o'clock, dinnertime.

Lebna broke the tension, bearing a large platter of salted fried potato slices.

"My God," said Reece. "My favorite food." He examined the bottle of Merti Hot Ketchup.

"They are fried," said Eydis. "Yuck."

Everyone except Eydis savored the hot potatoes. Reece focused on using only his right hand. The others were doing the same. The potatoes were from heaven. The ketchup was spicy but not too spicy. From inside the bar, music played. The evening was beginning.

Afewerki asked when dinner would be served. Lebna said perhaps an hour, looking at her broken watch. She desperately wanted one that worked.

"Shall we walk?" asked Afewerki.

"Of course. Good to stretch the legs," said Gudmunder. Everyone followed.

They walked into the lane with immediate cries of "Ferenj!" coming from doorways. The wide path was rocky and light brown with large ruts. Afewerki led them in the direction of the old Baptist Mission. AK had been the base for the helicopter, the hub for the feeding stations, including Gwar. The air was getting chilly, and a wind blew.

Suddenly, Reece felt nauseous. He thought he would shit himself. "Fuck," he said. He looked around. There were large boulders. Without a word, he ran to a rock outcropping and yanked down his pants. He grabbed a heavy rock and tried to lean backward. Liquid diarrhea shot onto the ground. It was over. He had no toilet paper. *Fuck.* He hoped the others had just continued. He pulled up his underwear and pants. He felt disgusting.

The others were still there.

"Are you okay?" asked Gudmunder.

Reece took a deep breath. "I have to go back to the

room."

"Oh, you're ill?" asked Eydis.

He didn't want her to touch him. "Yeah, need to go back to the room." He turned and walked with his hands in his back pockets, praying that he would not be sick again.

Lebna was disappointed to see that the ferenj Reece was not at dinner. She brought a platter of teff enjera stacked high with tibs from the goat, spicy, tender morsels of meat. This was Afewerki's favorite meal, and he moaned with pleasure. He wanted to give the gursha, a wad of enjera and meat, to Eydis, but he was afraid. She sat next to him, and her knee touched his. Instead, he gave one to Gudmunder, who took it. "Amenseganalo," said Gudmunder.

Back in his room, Reece felt some better. There was a chamber pot, and he had used it. The entire room smelled. He was optimistic, thinking that maybe he was okay. There was nothing left in his gut. To pass the time, he read from *2002: A Space Odyssey.* After a couple of hours, he decided to try his luck and see if the others were still eating dinner. Maybe the Johnny Walker would sterilize his bowels. They had the Red.

First, he carried the chamber pot to empty in the shint-abet. The smell there knocked him back. He felt nauseous and held his breath. He entered and poured the contents down the gaping hole. How would he rinse the pot? He wanted to wash his hands, but there was no soap or water. He had some alcohol wipes in his room.

With clean underwear and dirty hands, he walked into the bar lit by a single bulb. The bass of the music vibrated the room. They were there, having eaten and now relaxing, just drinking Johnny Walker Red, except for Afewer-ki, who was drinking a beer.

Eydis jumped up and hugged Reece. She led him by the hand back to the small table. The bar was full, and there were no more chairs. The town administrator was there drinking beer. He had introduced himself to Gudmunder and thanked him for his work.

"Are you better?" asked Eydis. "You sit here." She pushed Reece into her chair and then sat in his lap. Reece felt dirty and unworthy to have her so close. He was look-ing at her back until she turned and put her arm around him. Now he was looking directly at her breasts.

Gudmunder downed his whiskey. He was having a good time. There was something magical about the shad-ows created by the single bulb. Svana was checking out a tall, muscular man in shorts and a farmer's shirt of coarse material. This could be her night, having a single room. How could she navigate her way to him without seeming so obvious?

Afewerki clenched his jaw. He sipped his beer and wished to be back in Gwar with his family. Beer made him feel foolish. He would much rather drink tea, but what could he do? Gudmunder was buying.

A few minutes before ten p.m., the single bulb went dead and the tape player stopped. The generator had been shut off. Lebna hurried to light candles, fumbling with the matches in the dark. Everyone kept their places until the golden candlelight filled the room with velvet shad-ows. The noise had reduced to a hush, but was picking up again. Lebna turned on a battery-operated radio, tuning to a tinny station playing Amharic music. It was the famous

Barra Damte accompanied by an accordion. Eydis was off of Reece's lap, and she pulled Svana up to dance in the center of the room.

"Uh oh," said Reece. "It has begun."

Gudmunder nodded, wondering if it was better that he not see the nurses getting wild. He had notions of visiting the local Orthodox Church, which was just down the road on a small rise. He would leave a donation. Maybe the priest would be there. He ordered one more shot of Red and announced his plan to take a walk. Nicely buzzed, he stepped into the moonlit night.

"Gudmunder has left," said Svana. She smoothed back her black spiky hair and twirled a lock of Eydis's blonde hair.

"He's going to look for hyenas," said Eydis. She let Svana twirl her. All eyes in the bar were on them. The muscular man Svana had noticed earlier was nodding his head, moving to the music. The town administrator stood to leave. He had an appointment with a prostitute at the other hotel, a regular thing. Three other men left with him, making more room to dance.

Lebna zeroed in on Reece. She poured him another Red without asking and gave him her biggest smile, then sat in his lap.

Afewerki couldn't believe it. "Goodness to God," he said.

"What is she saying?" asked Reece. He was surprised to find Lebna in his lap and wasn't sure what to do. Was she grinding on him?

"She says that the night is very early. She wishes to come to your room."

"Oh Lord," said Reece. He was hoping to hook up with Eydis. It looked as if he would have a good chance.

"She is whore," said Afewerki.

"Yikes, that's pretty harsh. She's cute. Tell her I said she is cute, but that I have to rest tonight."

Afewerki, watching Eydis and Svana, rolled his eyes. He spoke to Lebna in a low tone. In response, Lebna put her arm around Reece's neck and tried to kiss him. She shot out of his lap and ran to the bar. The hotel owner had come in. Lebna made her way to the tables, taking drink orders from regular customers who were not pleased at being left unserved.

The muscular man, who was from Addis and visiting his wife in AK, worked his way to Svana and Eydis. Together they swayed to the music.

"I need beer," said Eydis. She went to the bar and waited. The chubby bar owner was behind the counter, keeping an eye on Lebna. Eydis took her beer and headed back to the table with Reece and Afewerki. "Come, let's dance with Svana and her new boyfriend."

Reece and Afewerki shook their heads no, but Eydis insisted. "Come now, little men!"

Reece gave in, rising to the occasion. Afewerki remained frozen to his chair, trusting his instincts.

The muscular man's name was Simon. He smelled of body odor, which Svana found scintillating. She rubbed his bicep and traced a scar there. The music's tempo increased, and Simon began to dance in earnest, impressing her with his footwork. She tried to accompany him, but was a bit drunk. Instead, she maintained her slow undulations, reaching out to touch Simon's body.

Reece danced with Eydis as she drank her beer. She moved in close to him and turned her back, bending over. Reece felt naked standing there with Eydis grooving on him. He grabbed her hips and brought her back upright.

"Are you shy?" asked Eydis.

"Yes," said Reece.

"Put your arms around me. I will not bite you."

He draped his arms around her neck, and they slow danced, bumping into Svana and Simon.

Afewerki sat alone, looking up occasionally from his empty bottle. He could see the lust on the men's faces as they watched Eydis and Svana dancing. Most of them had slept with Lebna, so she was of little interest. The bar owner, satisfied that all was under control, left with Lebna hustling about the room.

There was a scream, and a woman with a two-foot length of heavy sugarcane burst into the room. Simon's wife. She hit him on the head and back. He went to his knees. She attacked Svana, swinging the sugarcane, which flew out of her hands. A table tipped over. She scratched Svana's face, kicking her legs. Reece forced himself between the two as Eydis stood back wide-eyed. The men shouted, encouraging the enraged wife. She turned and began pummeling Simon, who turned and ran outside. Eydis grabbed Reece from behind and buried her head against his body. What the hell was going on? Someone had her by the shoulders. She let go of Reece and faced Lebna. Lebna pushed her and then turned on Reece. She shook her finger at him and turned back toward Eydis. Svana intervened, her face bleeding, and shouted at Lebna to get away. The size of Svana frightened Lebna, and she retreated behind the bar to catch her breath.

Afewerki stood, shaking his head. He could not bring himself to laugh as did the other men in the bar. He had seen enough and walked out to go to his room.

EIGHT

After their "vacation," the team regrouped and assumed their regular roles. Reece and Afewerki set out to do more interviews. They wound up near the derelict airfield at a long, low building with four rooms on each side. Young divorced women with children exclusively inhabited the building. Their first interview was with a tall, chesty woman who wore a black stocking on her head. Reece imagined she was strong enough to beat him at arm wrestling.

Halfway through the interview, the woman indicated she was very worried. Afewerki asked her what the problem was. She replied that she had sores. She lifted her dress and exposed her groin. There, she had draining wounds running beside her pubic hair. Miliary tuberculosis. Reece had Afewerki write down the diagnosis and suggested treatment with INH and Rifampin to be had at the government clinic. He gave the woman ten birr to cover the cost of the medicine. He hoped it was enough.

The next woman to be interviewed was led to Reece. He sat on a bench just beneath the roof overhang. Afewerki said for her to sit on the bench, but she insisted on squatting and holding her hands above her eyes. Both eyes were a cloudy blue, filled with cataracts. The woman told her story.

"She is pregnant by six months. Her husband has left her. Her brother is giving her some food," said Afewerki.

A light rain began to fall. After a few minutes, Afewerki interrupted her and explained the survey. She gave her consent and then cried. A younger woman came to her and said something. She looked up and smiled with wet eyes.

"What is your biggest health problem?" Afewerki began the interview.

"I am blind?" said the woman. She laughed and wiped tears from her useless eyes. Did they not notice?

"She is blind," said Afewerki to Reece.

"I figured," said Reece.

A group of small children had gathered, standing in the light rain with fingers in mouths. The small boys wore no pants. "Ferenj," said a soft-spoken little girl. On her back was her little sister, a five-year-old caring for a two-year-old. The rain poked holes in the dusty ground.

"The helicopter is coming," said Afewerki.

Reece listened, but did not hear it. And then he did, a faint thrum in the air, getting louder.

"Shall we go there?" asked Afewerki.

The blind woman mumbled to herself.

"No, let's finish this interview first, and then we can go." The helicopter sounded like hands clapping in the distance.

They completed the interview with the blind woman, and she began weeping. Reece helped her to the bench and took her photo.

"What a hell," said Afewerki. He wiped his hands on his pants.

They walked back toward the village square and veered down to the old helipad. The red, white, and blue Swiss Helimission helicopter was there with boxes of supplies and an ice chest with vaccines stacked nearby. Gudmunder stood with hands on hips, talking to the pilot Andreas. He called for Afewerki to have the supplies carried to the tent compound. Several men wearing old tire sandals were standing about, and Afewerki conscripted two but got four, all of whom insisted on helping.

"We need to trade out the ice chests. Can you have the empty one brought here?" asked Gudmunder.

Afewerki nodded and went to fetch it himself.

"Hello, Andreas," said Reece. Andreas had brought him to Gwar just two weeks ago. The Baptist Mission was furnishing the supplies.

"Hello, how does it go?" Andreas was short and stocky with a ready smile. He wore a jumpsuit and looked like a pilot with his sunglasses.

"Good. We're into the survey now, Afewerki and me."

"You are the nosy one," said Gudmunder. "Asking so many questions." He laughed and patted Reece on the shoulder.

"Where is Svana?" asked Andreas. He liked muscular women.

"I think they are in Tababit this day," said Gudmunder, "Perhaps forty-five minutes away. They may come. Or maybe not."

Andreas went to the helicopter, an AS-350 BA Ecureuil, and reached behind his seat to fetch the mail pouch. He withdrew the letters and handed them to Gudmunder.

"Here you are, Reece." Gudmunder handed him two letters, both from his grandmother.

"I need to water the horse," said Andreas. He walked off into the bush, behind a section of old fence, and turned his back.

"Do you have any letters?" asked Reece.

"Yes, from the hospital in Reykjavik, and from a friend, Bjarni Vigolsson. He is a doctor working in Sudan with refugees there." He wanted to add that Bjarni was gay, but that didn't seem relevant.

Andreas returned. "Any letters to go?"

"I have three letters. Can you wait? I'll run get them," said Reece.

"Okay, if you hurry. I need the ice chest as well."

"Roger," said Reece. He took off, sprinting uphill, and was winded before he reached the top. He ran through the fence opening, nearly colliding with Gebremariam. He ran to his tent and retrieved the letters. He saw the empty ice chest and looked around for Afewerki. Where was he? He grabbed the ice chest and started back.

Afewerki came out of the shintabet. He saw Reece with the ice chest. "Hallo! Wait. I will carry."

"No problem!" Reece kept going. He didn't want to make Andreas wait. When he arrived at the bottom of the steep hill, Andreas and Gudmunder were talking. Andreas looked worried.

"What's the problem?" asked Reece.

Andreas said, "I stopped in Alem Ketema to deliver some medicine for the clinic there. They were telling me that someone has stolen the tabot from the church."

"The what?" asked Reece.

Gudmunder spoke. "The tabot, the replica of the Ten Commandments that was in the original Ark of the Covenant. Is the priest there blaming me? Dear God, what a mess."

"Yes, it sounds preposterous. It happened while you were there, apparently. Perhaps this is some kind of extortion?" As a bush pilot, Andreas had seen it all.

"I did go by there and leave money for the church," said Gudmunder. "It was dark. I felt an energy. It's hard to explain. But I would never steal such a thing. That would be crazy."

Andreas took Reece's letters and put them in the pouch. "I must go. Better to fly in daylight than dark." He placed the empty ice chest in the helicopter. He had just enough fuel to get back to Addis.

That night at dinner, with warm beer, the discussion surrounded their ill-fated trip to Alem Ketema. Svana had long scratch marks on her face, which had festered, but she rated the overall experience as "exciting." Gudmunder laughed. Afewerki just shook his head.

"It was around 1360 BC that the Israelites left Egypt under the guidance of Moses," said Gudmunder. "As they wandered, God gave them the Commandments, and then directed them to build an Ark to carry the stone tablets, upon which God had written on Mt. Sinai. The Ark was plated in gold and had two seraphim on top. It was between these two seraphim that God would appear and communicate with the high priest Aaron, Moses' brother. The Ark had mysterious qualities and could strike a person dead with a kind of fire." Sweat trickled down Gudmunder's face. He seemed transfixed.

Reece helped himself to more of the spicy fish wot heavy with onions. Using his right hand, he made a neat package of fish within the enjera he had torn from the folded spongy bread. There was the warm St. George beer, but he drank water from the repurposed Icelandic IV bottles, as did Afewerki.

Afewerki said, "The people are murmuring." He knew this was a terrible thing that had happened, especially if anyone thought that Dr. Thorsonn had stolen it. Had he not tried to open the door of the church in Gwar? Yes, he had been seen doing so.

Eydis spoke up. "You say that the original Ark is in Ethiopia, with the Ten Commandments. How do you know this?" She had thought the whole thing ridiculous, but Gudmunder did seem to know quite a bit about the subject.

"Yes, this is true," said Afewerki. "The Ark is with us in Axum. Each church keeps its own tabot."

"A replica," said Reece.

"Yes," said Afewerki. "The real is in Axum."

Svana drank from her IV bottle. There was an ant on the rim, and she blew it off. She'd had enough talk of the Ark. "Dr. Thorsonn? Will you go with us to Sokol tomorrow? There are many patients there who could use your help."

Gudmunder leaned forward, peeling the label from his beer bottle. "Of course. But you see, the Ark was taken from Jerusalem by Menelik the First. He was the son of King Solomon and the Queen of Sheba, who was Ethiopian. Some say that the Babylonians destroyed the Ark in 597 BC in Jerusalem, or others destroyed it at later dates."

"No," said Afewerki. "The Ark is with us. It is true."

"Yes, I believe you," said Gudmunder. "But many do not."

"They are liars," said Afewerki.

"So what do we do?" asked Reece. "Will they try and

arrest you?"

"No," said Afewerki. "The people will murmur. The priest will report the theft to the Abuna, Tekle Haymanot. The Abuna will decide what to do. This is very bad."

Gudmunder felt off. "I pray that this will work itself out." He'd lost his appetite. The food was so spicy. He pondered that for a moment. He knew that in cultures with a high prevalence of intestinal parasites, such as tapeworm, people often ate extremely spicy food. This irritated the worms, causing them to detach and be expelled with bowel movements.

"Well, we will just have to stand together. I wonder if the Snake will try and do anything," said Reece.

Gebremariam came to gather the platter with a layer of soaked enjera on it. He would eat that and the rest of the wot that Abebe left in the cook house. Nothing would go to waste. "Tagabjalo?" he said, meaning, "Are you satisfied?"

Everyone groaned their satisfaction.

As promised, Dr. Thorsonn accompanied Eydis and Svana to the evil-eye enclave of Sokol. The vaccines were safely stored in the government clinic's propane refrigerator and could wait. Berhanu would take care of them.

The weather was bright and airy, hot and dry. Cracks in the earth indicated a need for rain. Gudmunder wore a loose scrub top and hiking boots with a pair of tan hiking pants and his outback hat. He had a medium build but felt that he was gaining weight. That morning's breakfast of eggs with hot pepper had stuffed him. He took a deep breath. Medicine and supplies filled his backpack.

"These people are outcasts," he said. "They cannot even visit the church. They have become pagan."

"They are very poor," said Svana. She wore a light blue dress that came below her knees, her favorite dress.

They continued walking downhill and to the east, stepping over the fist-sized rocks. Eydis wondered how old the rocks were. She pondered the scene at the bar in Alem Ketema and thought she could perhaps write a story about that night. She'd had every intention of sleeping with Reece, but the violence of the evening had caused her to reconsider. The barmaid, Lebna, had attacked her and Svana! She thought about her cousin Sven, who designed furniture. Maybe that was the best direction to take, something safe. He'd recently been on vacation and then traveled to the United States for a conference.

Approaching the cluster of huts without compound fencing, two children ran and screamed that the ferenji were coming. Gudmunder smiled. He only wanted to help as best he could.

Ahead of them, as they walked the dusty road, a man in rags walked with his head down. Svana was in front and reached the man first. Svana called out "Tenesteling!" and the man did not respond. She walked up behind him and touched his elbow. He nearly jumped out of his skin. Upon hearing his voice, Svana realized he was deaf. She wanted to laugh. The others caught up, and she explained. Briefly, there was an uncomfortable silence.

"Xavier meskin!" said Gudmunder. He raised his hands as an offering to heaven.

The man smiled and let them pass, happy to follow in the wake of these three ferenji. What an interesting day he was having.

Within a few minutes, prefaced by the children they had met on the road, they reached Sokol. There was a general air of excitement. Right away, a thin man wearing a farmer's hat approached and insisted they follow him to his hut. They followed and were treated to a large pot of fermenting talla, the local beer. They tried to squat like their hosts, but had to sit on the ground.

A scream. A dog yelping. The man jumped up and ran. Eydis, Svana, and Gudmunder sat perplexed and uncomfortable. The talla was very smoky and served in huge glasses made from gourds. Eydis frowned.

"Dear God," said Gudmunder. "What will happen next?"

The man, with a shaved head and bug eyes, returned with a little girl in his arms. He placed her in front of Gudmunder and pointed to her leg.

Gudmunder examined the puncture wounds. The dog had bitten her. He placed his talla on the ground, and it fell over.

"Svana, do you have the peroxide?" he said.

Svana produced the hydrogen peroxide. She opened a sterile 4x4.

The little girl was petrified. The man held her. Svana poured peroxide over the wounds, which bubbled with fury. The girl cried and kicked her leg.

Gudmunder poured some peroxide on the four-by-four pad and used it to wipe the puncture wounds. Eydis stood ready with triple-antibiotic ointment. He applied a thick coating to the bite marks. The little girl seemed to be in a trance. The man placed her on the ground, and she looked at her leg as if it were a dream.

"She must keep it clean," said Eydis.

A woman ran up to the girl and embraced her. She spoke in hushed tones.

"Give to her the ointment," said Gudmunder.

Eydis replaced the cap and handed the tube to the girl's mother. She took it and that was that.

"My God, what is next?" asked Gudmunder. He swatted at flies trying to drink from the corners of his eyes.

They were all glad to escape their talla through the dog bite incident and walked to a central place among the huts lorded over by a large jacaranda tree.

"Let us begin," said Gudmunder.

As if they understood, the people present made a line.

The first man had worms clotting his rectum, and Svana had to walk away.

On their way to do interviews, Afewerki led the way up and over the hill where the church stood. The sun strained in the high altitude. They passed near a plowed field, and two boys were carrying what looked to be a rocket. It was green, about four feet long, and looked deadly. Afewerki called out to them to put it down and to run. They ignored him and continued toward them.

"What the hell?" asked Reece. He began to walk forward to stay clear.

"It is a BM rocket, fired from the trucks very quickly. The Russians have brought these things. Very dangerous," said Afewerki. "Sometimes the farmers are finding." He waited for the boys and yelled at them to put it down. "You will kill yourselves," he said. They stopped and grinned at him. He knew them and, with an angry voice, said he would see that their fathers beat them for doing such a stupid thing.

A mild fear overcame the boys. Afewerki instructed them to put the rocket on a high place so that everyone could see it. Perhaps the Snake would have sense enough to come out and detonate the rocket with a hand grenade.

"Now go! Go!"

Reece was impressed with Afewerki's sternness.

"Let us continue," said Afewerki.

Within ten minutes, they approached a scattering of huts. No one seemed to be around. One tukul stood alone, without a protective fence around it. Afewerki knew the woman who lived there. He called her name. There was no smoke threading through the straw roof. The poles making up the round hut's wall were not daubed with mud. Reece imagined that the cold night wind must pass through with ease, and it did. The dark doorway stood open. A collection of black tenacious flies clung to the door frame. Someone called out from within, a sound like a little girl.

"She is saying to enter," said Afewerki.

Reece stooped, his eyes adjusting to the dim light. There was no bed, just a pallet on the dirt floor. The fire was out. Sitting on the pallet was a thin woman. Reece could tell that her left leg was withered and useless. She smiled and looked down, ashamed.

"Does she live alone?" asked Reece. He squatted and sat with his back against the rough wall.

"Yes, her husband has left her by many months. She is alone."

"Jesus." Reece looked around the hut. There seemed to be nothing but the pallet, except for a covered clay pot. "Explain to her the survey."

Afewerki gained her consent and said, "How are you doing?" He squatted.

The woman went on at length and began to weep. Afewerki appeared unmoved and scratched his head. "She is being rap-ed by the village administrator. He comes at night, and what can she do?"

"The Snake?"

"Yes, a-bab, the Snake."

"What about the people who live around her?" asked Reece.

"They are afraid and very poor. What can they do?"

"Huh."

"Her husband has left for Gojjam by six months. She is alone and begs for her food."

Reece forgot about the interview. "What happened to her leg?"

"She is saying that it is the work of Satan. She is born this way."

Reece felt in his pocket. He had three birr and gave them to her. She bowed her head and whispered thanks. That was enough to buy food for two or three days. He looked at her face. She was quite pretty, but in a sad way. What if he married her and brought her to the States?

"Ah, the others will complain if they know you are giving money," said Afewerki.

"I would give more. Maybe we can buy her some food and bring it here."

"If you wish."

The woman asked when the grain would come again. She assumed they were surveying in preparation to bring food.

"Tell her we do not know, but maybe," said Reece.

Afewerki told her that no grain was coming.

The woman then asked why she should do the interview.

This irritated Afewerki. Reece watched the exchange, trying to guess at the words.

"It is for science," said Afewerki. He didn't quite know how to respond.

The woman did not understand what he meant.

"You must answer the questions," said Afewerki. He couldn't believe that she was being stubborn. Of all the people!

"My name is Misha, and you must leave my house."

"Is she angry?" asked Reece. He was surprised.

"We must leave." Afewerki stood, stooped, and walked outside, mumbling.

Reece held the questionnaire and his Bic pen. He looked at the woman, and she at him. She smiled and shook her head. "Bucka," she said. "Enough." Reece smiled and stood, his back aching.

Outside in the hot sun, Reece and Afewerki sized up one another. "Where to next, my brother?" asked Reece. He thought about Eydis, about how it would be good to see her at the end of a long day. Perhaps they would go to a bar?

"Oh, just here." He pointed to a hut just a hundred feet away. There was a fence of living green plants and poles that surrounded it. There was a small sign written in Amharic.

They walked through the gate and entered the dark teahouse. A coal fire glowed in the far corner. An ancient teakettle sat on a stone just into the fire. A circular bench went around the perimeter of the tukul. Two men were sitting there. The squatting patroness stood, and she murmured a greeting.

"Shall we?" asked Afewerki.

"Order some tea, sure."

Afewerki ordered for them. The thin woman in a long, dull red dress poured out two cups of tea into white ceramic cups from China.

"How much?" asked Reece. He had no more money with him.

"One birr, that is all," said Afewerki.

The tea, flavored with cloves, contained a deadly amount of sugar.

Reece sat and sipped his hot tea. He nodded to the two men across the room. They sat with legs crossed, feet shod with tire sandals. Both were farmers. He didn't want to waste time and asked Afewerki who they should interview first.

Afewerki knew the men would not be interested in participating, as they were not drinking alcohol, and suggested he start with the patroness. He knew she had an interesting story. Gudmunder had treated her. He obtained her consent and began.

"How is your family?"

The woman, who had stood, gathered her long dress and sat along the wall. She held a steel rod that she used to poke the fire. "My parents have died. My sister has died. My brothers are plowing and planting yellow peas."

Reece wrote Afewerki's translation as quickly as he could.

"What is your family's biggest health problem?" asked Afewerki.

"I am living alone."

"What is your biggest health problem?"

The woman paused and rubbed her belly. "I have been pregnant for many years. The baby will not come out."

Afewerki nodded and relayed the information to Reece. Reece remembered hearing the story from Eydis, or maybe it was Svana. Was this the same woman? It must be.

"Huh."

"The placenta has been born seven years ago, but the baby will not come out. It may be a girl or maybe a boy."

"Does she know who the father is?" asked Reece.

Afewerki interpreted.

"The father has come from the sky. He has rap-ed me. I did not see his face. He took me into a chamber and laid me on a table. It was very hard and cold. What am I to do?"

Reece digested the information. He watched the woman pour more tea for the two men. They did not seem fazed by the story. "Has the father ever returned?"

"Only in dreams," said the woman. She put both hands on her flat stomach, which did not seem pregnant.

Reece sipped his tea. He needed to pee and told Afewerki to move on with the questions.

Dinner that night was kikel, a mutton wot served with enjera. Gudmunder, Eydis, and Svana had had a long day in Sokol, treating everything from tapeworms to delivering the placenta of a woman who had given birth the day before. Everyone agreed it had been a long but productive day. Gudmunder told the story about the man with tapeworms hanging out of his rectum, and Reece shared the story of the boys hauling a rocket.

Gudmunder had been drinking katikala before dinner and was feeling especially joyful. He insisted on feeding everyone at the table the gursha, bite-sized morsels of enjera and wot.

"Afewerki, when you come to Iceland, I will feed you shark meat," said Gudmunder.

"What is the shark?" asked Afewerki. His experience of fish was limited to catfish and a fish similar to tilapia.

"The shark can eat you. It has many teeth."

"Oh my goodness," said Afewerki. He laughed. "Like the crocodile?"

"Yes, like the crocodile."

"Did you know crocodiles can cry?" asked Reece.

Everyone went silent.

"Crocodile tears?"

No one knew what he was talking about.

"I think we have reached what you call an impasse, no?" asked Gudmunder.

"Probably," said Reece. Humor seemed the hardest thing to share across language barriers.

Gebremariam came to the group. The fire Reece had lit had fizzled, leaving only smoke. He was about to rekindle the flame when Gebremariam pointed to the gate. A man stood there in the fading light, holding his hat in his hands.

Afewerki spoke. "The man there says his wife is giving birth. There is a problem."

Svana and Eydis were standing with greasy right hands. "What is the problem?" asked Gudmunder.

"The baby will not come out."

There was silence for ten seconds.

"Let us go then," said Gudmunder. He took one more bite of enjera soaked in the juices of the wot.

As if connected at the waist, everyone stood and followed Afewerki, who followed the short man in farmer's shorts. The light was still strong but fading in stages, working toward the cool night.

The group walked for fifteen minutes, past the old airfield.

"Is it much farther?" asked Reece.

"Fifteen more minutes," said Afewerki.

"Oh," the group responded in unison.

The wide path narrowed. Everyone had to look down due to the sharp rocks. The fading light took on a blue. Reece thought about a disco song that had lodged in his head back in the '80s. "You can ring my bell" was the chorus.

Soon, the man pointed at a hut. "Just there," he seemed to say. He looked frightened at what might have transpired in his absence. His first wife had died in childbirth.

Gudmunder let Svana go in first. She was a labor and delivery nurse back in Iceland. The hut was too small to hold them all. A loud voice crying for help.

Svana entered, and a woman stood there. She seemed to be a ghost, swaying from side to side. Beneath her was a huge puddle of drying blood and fluid. Her eyes seemed vacant. She had her arms outstretched as if in a trance. Svana approached. "Ishi, ishi," she said. She took the woman by the hand and tried to have her sit. She looked around for a baby. Nothing. "Afewerki!"

Afewerki ducked inside.

"I need her to lie down."

Afewerki spoke to the woman. The husband entered.

The woman looked wild. Svana decided to lift her long green dress. The woman smelled of sweat and fear. Svana kneeled and drew up the dress. From between the woman's legs protruded one limp leg.

"Down, get her down!" said Svana.

With much confusion, the woman finally squatted and leaned back against the wall. She was confused, mumbling.

Svana palpated the woman's abdomen. The baby was breech, but with only one leg out. She slid her hand into the woman's vagina. The other leg was bent toward the baby's head. This was something new. What was she to do? "Gudmunder!"

Gudmunder entered, stooping. Svana explained the situation. "Push the leg back in," he said.

Svana dissociated herself from her hands. They worked independent of her mind. She bent the leg at the knee and pushed. The knee, with some force, fit back inside the birth canal. Now she had a butt to grab and pull, which she did. "Tell her to breathe deep and slow!" With both hands inside the woman's vagina, she pulled. "Tell her to push!" She pulled the legs gently but firmly. Nothing seemed to be happening. "Push!" The woman groaned. She seemed on the verge of passing out.

"Stand her up," said Gudmunder.

Afewerki shouted the order. The husband and he grabbed the woman's limp arms and, yelling for her to stand, pulled her upright. Svana pulled gently, and out the baby came, face to knees, into her arms. Overwhelmed, she turned and saw Eydis. She handed the baby to her. The woman slid down the wall, unconscious but breathing, as the baby screamed. In the light of a small kerosene lamp, the room looked like a butcher shop. Blood covered Svana's arms.

TEN

The next day, Reece and Afewerki decided to hang out at the government clinic and do interviews with patients after Berhanu had treated them. The building was oblong with a creaky tin door and two windows to let in light. There was nowhere for the patients to sit, so they made a line squatting on the ground outside, the warm morning sun breathing down on them.

Two posters in Amharic graced the clinic: "One Syringe, One Needle" and "Getting AIDS is not just the end of sex. It's the end of life. AIDS will kill you." Reece knew that Berhanu reused needles. Inside smelled of dust and sweat.

The first patient that day was being treated for malaria. He had recently traveled into the kolla, the low zone, and had most likely been infected there, as mosquitoes could not survive at the altitude of Gwar. He had a chill and shivered from head to toe. The one thing Berhanu had in abundance was chloroquine. Reece imagined that he would perhaps like to be a nurse or doctor and work in a rural clinic like this one.

The plan was to interview patients as they left the clinic, but the man with malaria hurried away. So, they sat nearby in the shade of the fence.

"Why don't you have a girlfriend?" asked Reece.

"Oh, the womans are spiteful," said Afewerki.

"What about sex, though?"

Afewerki frowned and shook his finger no, no, no. He would not do that unless he were married.

"What do you think of Eydis and Svana?"

"Svana is very strong. She is a good storyteller." He paused. He imagined blonde Eydis. "Eydis is, is, is..." He searched for the word.

A purple juwa bird chased another, running across the grass like a chicken, its vestigial third wing flapping uselessly.

"Eydis is hot," said Reece. He made curvy lines in the air.

"Hot?"

"Gorgeous, pretty. I'd love to see her naked."

"Oh, my goodness." Afewerki viewed Eydis as a kind of angel. "You must not think such things."

"Why not?"

Afewerki made a face. "It is not right."

"Ha, do you like her?"

Afewerki blushed. "She is good person."

"I agree," said Reece. "But I bet she can be a bad girl."

"No. That is not possible."

"You really do like her," said Reece.

Afewerki cleared his throat. He frowned. Did Reece want to fight?

"Let the best man win," said Reece.

"Win?" asked Afewerki. He stood. An elderly man stepped down from the clinic. He wanted to be interviewed. Did they want to come to his house for talla?

"Back to work," said Reece, convinced that Afewerki had a crush on Eydis.

That night, the group gathered for dinner. The Icelanders had returned from Sokol. It was as if the enclave was about to implode from neglect. Everyone had worms. No one had enough to eat. Gudmunder had diagnosed two cases of hepatitis. Their prognosis was not good.

Reece had started a fire, having bought another load of firewood that day. He blew on the tinder, making it roar and then fade until the larger sticks caught. Eydis clapped her hands. She could see Reece's crack and wanted to ride him like a wild horse.

Gebremariam walked over, cradling his rifle. He spoke to Afewerki and pointed toward the fence gap.

"It is a little girl," said Afewerki. "She is begging. She wants to sing for us."

Svana said, "Oh, that is very sad. Tell her to come inside."

"She will come every night," said Afewerki.

"Let's hear her sing," said Gudmunder.

Reece had the fire going. He tossed on more wood.

The little girl followed Gebremariam into the compound. Perhaps eight years old and with her mother, she wore a long dress of dirty, green, and patched cloth. Two tight braids hung to her shoulders. Looking down, she sauntered toward the fire.

"This will be her debut concert," said Eydis.

"She is adorable," said Svana.

The little girl twisted a sash around her dress. She looked like a miniature of her mother, standing outside in the path.

"Afewerki, ask her to sing," said Gudmunder.

Afewerki did, and the little girl fidgeted. She looked at the ferenji and began. She sang a children's song about a crocodile and a monkey who became friends. The first notes sent a chill through Reece. Her voice seemed to come from a place deep in the earth. She sang from the bottom of her heart, bringing Svana to tears. The song had four stanzas.

By the third stanza, everyone was transfixed, including Afewerki. The little girl had the voice of a professional adult singer.

A gunshot. A scream. The group stood. The little girl turned toward the fence. Through the broken fence stepped the Snake, followed by two of his colleagues. He staggered and waved his Makarov pistol like a bubble wand. The little girl ran toward the fence and her mother. The Snake blocked her way, and wailing, she ran back and hid behind Svana.

"What the hell!" said Reece.

"Wait," said Afewerki. "Let him come to us."

As if on command, the Snake weaved his way toward the fire, drawn like a moth. He stooped and picked up a piece of wood and threw it toward the fire, but missed. He let his pistol dangle. He pointed at Gudmunder with his left hand.

"You were told not to go to Sokol. They are hyenas! They will give us buda. You must be punished. You are under arrest." He motioned for his minions to take Dr. Thorsonn. Both were carrying AK-47s.

Afewerki stepped forward. "No, you may arrest me. He will not understand."

"You then tell him what I say," said the Snake.

"Does he want me?" asked Gudmunder.

"He can take me," said Reece. He clenched his fists. At that moment, he felt invulnerable to bullets, as if he were a traveler from another dimension, another universe.

Afewerki argued with the Snake in Amharic. In the cook house, Abebe watched from the doorway. Dinner was ready. She needed to leave and see about her children. She despised the Snake. He would have tried to rape her by now, but she owned an old rifle and had bought a WWII vintage hand grenade for five birr.

The men with AK-47s moved toward Gudmunder. They got behind him and nudged him forward.

"So, this is it?" he said. "What a huge disappointment."

Afewerki translated, and the Snake laughed. "Your mother is disappointed." He laughed and put his hand on his thigh, taken with his humor.

"If you take him, you have to take me," said Reece. "Afewerki, tell him."

"No, that is bad," said Afewerki. He thought about having Eydis to himself.

Reece took a few steps toward the Snake. "Shoot me, you son of a bitch." He gestured with his arms.

"Reece, please," said Eydis. "Stop."

"I suppose it's just the black spot on the sun," said Reece.

Svana stepped forward. "Take me too."

"And me," said Eydis.

They all joined hands, the Snake in front of them, the minions behind them. The little girl ran toward the fence. The Snake turned, nearly fell, beading his pistol on the little girl. He turned back to the group and laughed. What was he to do now? The ferenji confused him.

Gudmunder felt the tips of the AK-47s in his kidneys. The early stars were out. He imagined the universe as cotton candy and turned with care. The barrels now pointed now at his belly button. He wanted to reach, grab their heads, and crash their skulls together. He looked from one qat-addled face to the other.

"Did you hear the little girl singing?" he said.

Afewerki interpreted.

They laughed.

"Afewerki, bring back the little girl and let her sing."

"Bring her to sing again?"

"Yes. They need to hear her sing."

"Ishi."

Afewerki returned with the little girl in front of him. Her name was Mariam. She looked at the ground, her body shaking. Afewerki whispered into her ear. He said that he would give her breakfast, lunch, and dinner.

At those words, Mariam lifted her head. She began in a whisper, but soon began to sing at full volume, raising goosebumps on the arms of the Snake. Mariam sang a simple peasant's song about the joy of enjera. She belted the tune. She went low and then she went high. For a moment, Reece felt as if he was lifted from the earth.

Mariam sang loud and hard. The AK-47s drooped. The Snake's face was a morass of confusion. He was moved, but why? Why not just execute this foreigner with hair the color of orange Fanta? Why not just shoot them all? He could have sex with the women as they lay dying.

Mariam worked to the finale. Her voice rose and fell, modulating. Bats flying overhead seemed to be dancing in response. She had crushed the will of the Snake.

The Snake spat onto the ground. "Give me your katika-la, and you are free."

Gudmunder went to his tent. He presented the Snake with a full wine bottle of 120-proof katikala. "Bucka," he said. "Enough. Finished."

To prove a point, the next day, everyone visited Sokol. Afewerki would interpret as needed for Gudmunder, Eydis, Svana, and Reece. He was frightened, though, worried that he would succumb to the evil eye. He did not want to turn into a hyena and scavenge the dead bodies of humans at midnight. Eydis had promised to give him a foot massage. He worried that his feet were rough and smelled like fish.

The group of five walked the narrow, rutted lane to Sokol. Thorn bushes lined the way with the occasional towering fig tree. Afewerki held Reece's red tape player, playing traditional Amharic music. They passed a rocky field being plowed by two oxen and a tenacious farmer. From a distance of one hundred feet, Reece could see a plaque of eczema on the man's legs. There seemed to be more rocks than dirt, but the sorghum and teff would grow nonetheless.

When they arrived in Sokol, a crowd of fifteen soon gathered. Most had already been treated by the Icelanders and were thus assigned to the health survey of Reece. He began to belch rotten eggs. "Shit." The night before had been dorowot, the spiciest of spicy dishes.

Reece and Afewerki entered a crumbling hut with half a roof. An ancient dog, scarred and blind, wandered around inside. Piles of shit littered the floor. Reece couldn't breathe. He asked the questions, and he struggled to write down the answers. He thought about his grandparents back in Alabama. They were probably asleep, dreaming of the old days. He was trying very hard not to throw up. He thought about the jokes that his grandfather Chester loved to tell. He thought about squash frying on the stove. At some point, Afewerki reached and shook Reece's shoulder.

"She says that she has no compound. The only animal is the dog, and they cannot to eat the dog."

Reece shook his head. He felt dizzy. He started to think about fifth graders making out at the skating rink in Fort Knox, Kentucky. He had hated the skating rink. He had hated everything about Fort Knox except the George W. Patton Museum and the library.

"How much energy do you have every day?"

The young woman said, "I feel very weak, especially when I have hip pain."

Reece wrote Afewerki's words. He felt he was working at an ice cream stand at the North Pole. He suddenly doubted the existence of God. How many hours were there in a day? Twenty-four, three hundred? Did it matter? Later, he would determine that forty-two percent of his respondents had to travel up to ten thousand meters for water, usually down a steep incline. He remembered receiving a train set for Christmas when he was seven. His dad had set it up and then insisted on playing with it.

"Where is your latrine?" The woman just shrugged.

After analyzing the data, Reece would discover that eighty-eight percent of his respondents did not have a latrine in their compound. So, you just went where you had to go. The long dresses of women were a specific benefit in this regard. They could squat most anywhere and relieve themselves. The men, with their wide-legged short pants, could do the same when urinating.

A clucking rooster ran into the decrepit hut, turned, and bolted. The dog looked dead, lying against the cracked wall. They finished the interview within thirty minutes, and the woman posed outside for her photo. In the sun and smiling, she was attractive but had that starved look in her eyes.

Just down the lane, the Icelanders had set up shop beneath a tall eucalyptus tree, stripped of its lower branches. A dozen little boys and girls ran in circles, playing, wondering at the whiteness of the ferenjis' skin. One little naked boy sported a large erection. Reece laughed.

"Afewerki, come," said Gudmunder. "I need your help." His patient was an old woman with a giant goiter, the size of a football. She was talking nonstop.

Eydis and Svana were huddled around a bony teenage boy sitting on a biscuit tin. He had epilepsy and had fallen into a fire the previous night, burning his arm badly. With a gloved hand, Eydis spread silver sulfadiazine cream over the sloughed skin onto the pink meat of his arm. He winced and moaned. Svana wrapped the forearm with sterile gauze.

"Afewerki?" said Eydis. She looked at her tennis shoes, coated with dust, and battled with flies, trying to get at the moisture in her eyes. She wanted to tell the boy to come to their compound every day to change the dressing.

Afewerki was telling Gudmunder that the old woman said she urinated when she sneezed, and she was having terrible gas. Her throat burned when she lay down. A mist clouded her eyes, and she had no blanket, leaving her very cold at night. He stepped away to let Dr. Thorsonn digest the information and went to relay Eydis's instructions to the burn victim and his mother, who squatted nearby.

Reece stood with Gudmunder. "She has many problems," said Reece. The old woman was tiny. The goiter was huge. "She's not complaining of her goiter, though."

"Yes, quite large. I think we can give her some antacids and tell her to avoid spicy food for now." He listened to her stomach with his stethoscope. Bowel sounds were hyperactive. He looked back and called for Afewerki.

By lunch, Reece had interviewed five people, and over thirty patients had been treated, three being travelers passing by. Afewerki said that they were shifta, bandits, who lived in the Wenchit River Valley. All three had rotten teeth, which needed to be removed. He had each one rinse their mouths with hydrogen peroxide, but they balked at the foam and taste. Afewerki said that they thought the doctor was trying to trick them, and that they wanted injections. He drew up 10 ccs of sterile saline and injected each one in their skinny hips. Afewerki was relieved when they left, worried they might try to kidnap Eydis or Svana.

"What a hell," said Afewerki as they left.

ELEVEN

The next morning, Abebe awoke later than usual. She kissed each of her children and scurried to work. She would need to start a fire from scratch, so she stopped first at Afewerki's compound to receive a hot coal from his mother. Barefoot, she tossed the coal back and forth between her hands until she reached the cold cook house. Within minutes, a hot fire spewed smoke. She boiled eggs for the team's breakfast. She had purchased wheat rolls for three cents each to go with the eggs.

Gudmunder stretched and touched his toes. The others were still in their tents. Gebremariam was coming with the teakettle. Over the top of the fence, Gudmunder could see a man approaching on a mule. It was the Snake, wearing a green military uniform. He dismounted and tied his mule, which he had commandeered, to a post.

Into the compound, preceded by the same two young men with AK-47s, the Snake entered, flashing his smile and gold teeth. He walked up to Gudmunder and held out his hand. Gudmunder took the sweaty hand and shook it.

"You will be going to the jail with me," he said in Amharic. He removed his dark shades. His eyes were streaked with red. He wore his pistol in a holster.

"Ai yi," said Gebremariam. He went to Reece's tent and mumbled.

Abebe was washing the dishes from breakfast. She had packaged the uneaten eggs in a cloth packet. Boiled eggs would last for a month. She stood just inside the doorway, watching. She hated the Snake.

"You are a thief, no? You have taken the tabot from the church in Alem Ketema, no? I am arresting you."

The two guards moved toward Gudmunder. He stood still. He had recognized the words Alem Ketema and thought the worst.

"Plus, you disobeyed me and went to Sokol once more. You are a very dangerous man. Where are your workers? Are they fucking the hyenas?" The guards laughed.

Reece unzipped and stepped out of his tent. He knew there was trouble. *Shit.* It was the Snake. *What's going on?* He hoped that Eydis and Svana would stay in their tent.

"What is it? said Svana. She had poked her head through the tent flap.

"Just stay inside," said Gudmunder.

"Oh, it's the pretty ladies," said the Snake. He walked near the tent and scratched the fabric with his nails. "Won't you come out? I would like to see you. Are you sucking each other's tits?"

Reece saw Afewerki run into the compound.

Afewerki slowed. He had to be careful, but he was angry. He asked the Snake what was going on. He interpreted for Gudmunder and Reece. "He is arresting you," he said. "He is accusing you of stealing the tabot in Alem Ketema. One person has seen you there stealing it."

"Dear God," said Gudmunder. That was the last thing he wanted to hear.

Svana emerged quickly from the tent, fists clenched, her black hair twisted from sleep. "If you arrest him, you will arrest me as well!" She pointed her finger at the Snake. "Afewerki, tell him what I say."

The Snake grinned. "It would be my pleasure to arrest

you. Perhaps the tabot is in your tent? Search the tents," he said to the guards. "I will watch the good doctor."

"You don't have the authority to come here and search our tents," said Gudmunder.

The guard poked his AK-47 into Eydis's tent. He ordered her out. She was wearing blue flannel pajamas. He went to his knees and crawled in halfway. He touched the silky sleeping bags. There were so many things to see. He saw a cigarette lighter and put it in his pocket. There were clothes, a bra. He had never seen a bra but imagined what it was for. He smelled it.

The Snake said something to the other guard.

Afewerki said, "No!" and moved toward Eydis, but not quick enough.

The guard grabbed Eydis's pajama top and ripped down, breaking the buttons, exposing her breasts. She yelled and hit the guard, not caring that she was half naked. He shoved her with one hand, angry. "Farðu til helvítis!"

"You bastard!" yelled Svana.

Reece moved in, but the other guard had emerged and fired a round into the ground. The shot thundered. Everyone flinched, including the Snake.

"Goddamn it," said Reece. He thought about the pistol that Gudmunder kept in his tent.

The Snake ordered the guard to search the other tents, and then they would search the little house where they kept their supplies.

Eydis covered herself and growled.

From Reece's orange pup tent, the guard emerged with a bar of chocolate and a pair of Reece's socks. "Caramella!"

he said. He loved candy. He crawled into Gudmunder's tent and marveled at the ornate book. He could not read it. There was a tape player, a glass IV bottle with water in it, a warm coat. Too many things to count, but no tabot. He pocketed some loose change.

"Yellum," he said to the Snake.

"Okay, arrest me, but leave the women alone," said Gudmunder.

Afewerki translated. He had seen Eydis's breasts and so had Reece. She stood now with her arms crossed, talking coarsely to the Snake.

"Perhaps they, too, should be arrested for returning to Sokol," said the Snake. "They may have been cursed. I wouldn't be surprised if they turned into hyenas and ate the dead."

Afewerki let the Snake talk. "He is only bragging," he said. "And now they must search this one." He pointed to the little square house that held supplies."

Gudmunder protested. "They will steal if they go inside." He walked toward the gap in the fence, a guard behind him.

"Afewerki, go with him," said Reece. "I'll stay here. Come back and tell us what happens." He reached into his tent and grabbed a scrub top for Eydis.

The guard yelled that he needed a key for the padlock on the door. Gudmunder kept the key in his pocket.

Having knocked the lock from the door with an ax, the guard began his search for the tabot in the little house. Boxes of IV bottles and shelves of medicine filled the room. The floor was slanted and uneven. Afewerki stood in the doorway, watching.

"Do you think we should go out today?" asked Eydis. She spat toothpaste into the grass.

Svana smirked. "Hmph. He does not scare me. We will do our work." She had a plan. She brushed and spat, rinsing from an IV bottle. There were still lots of children to be weighed.

Two women with clay pots of water entered the compound and emptied the jugs into the water barrel. They were paid weekly by Afewerki. Inside the cook house was the gravity-feed ceramic water filter. It was Abebe's job to filter water for the ferenji.

With four boiled eggs and brown bread rolls, Eydis and Svana gathered their backpacks and prepared to leave.

The Snake stood with his hands behind his back, beaming at them.

"Are you leaving?" asked Reece. "Maybe you should stay for the day until things settle down."

"No," said Svana. "We will work and not be intimidated."

"That's not a good idea, I think. Maybe I should come with you?"

"No, we are fine," said Svana.

"Eydis?"

"Oh, we will be fine."

The skinny bodyguard yelled out. He had found something. He sounded angry.

Gudmunder walked into the jail compound, which shared a fence with the government compound, the Snake's building. On the other side, Afewerki's family's compound shared another fence with the jail. Every day, his sister would sell bread over the fence to the prisoners.

Afewerki followed Gudmunder in to explain the jail. It was easy to escape, but he would be shot if he tried. The jail was a one-room rectangular house made of poles and mud. The roof was tin. Inside was dark and smelled of urine. One man sat alone against the wall. "He has killed a man," said Afewerki. The only beds were stacks of old grain bags on the dirt floor. "You will get the lice here," he told Gudmunder.

"Excellent news, huh?" asked Gudmunder. "What will happen next? Is there a lawyer?"

"Only God knows. We must send to Addis Ababa for help."

"Hmm, there is a man there, Dr. Guthrie. He is a veterinarian with the Baptist Mission. He sends the vaccines. Can you send word to him about what has happened?"

"I will try," said Afewerki. "Shall I take the jeep to Alem Ketema, or shall I wait for Andreas to come with the helicopter?"

"Go ahead and take the next jeep. Have Svana or Eydis give you money. I wonder if Reece should go with you? No, that's not a good idea. The ladies need him here."

"But who will interpret?" asked Afewerki.

"Ah, you are right."

"Perhaps Reece shall go, and I shall stay."

The man in the corner cursed them and told them to go outside.

"What did he say?" asked Gudmunder.

"Nothing. Let us go outside."

In the dirt and rock courtyard, they stood.

"Yes, Reece could go. But you will need to stay in the

compound with Eydis and Svana. You can sleep in my tent."

Afewerki thought of Eydis, of being near her while she slept. He had seen her breasts. And Reece would be gone for at least five days. "Okay, I will tell to him."

The bodyguard emerged from behind a stack of boxes holding a magazine. It was a magazine of naked men and belonged to Gudmunder. The guard was angry and shouting through the door. He held it out for Reece to see. Reece turned his hands palms up. What was he supposed to say?

"What is it?" asked Svana. "What has he found?"

"A magazine, with nude men."

"Nude men?" asked Eydis. "Oh, it is belonging to Gudmunder."

"Doctor, busheti?" The guard was putting two and two together. He had once heard that gay men had the red hair. He had to get out of there and warn the Snake. The doctor could have HIV. He threw the magazine to the ground and trotted away.

"What is happening?" asked Eydis.

"I really don't know. It seems he connected the magazine with Gudmunder and ran off." Reece wondered if they would shoot him. "I'll go to the jail and see what's going on."

Svana said for him to be careful. Eydis touched his arm.

Reece stepped into the lane. He navigated the curving paths, passed Afewerki's house, and then came into the town square. It was Tuesday, market day, and vendors crowded the shady areas. He stepped on a man's foot. "I'm sorry. Mi dispiace." He had taken Italian for two years in college. He looked over the fence and saw Gudmunder. *Where is Afewerki?* "Hey!"

Inside the Snake's dank and dusty office, a huge snake-skin nailed to the wall above his desk, were the Snake, the guards, and Afewerki. One guard was talking frantically. Reece walked in.

"Afewerki," said Reece. "What's going on?"

"Is it true?" asked Afewerki. "This man is finding a busheti magazine in the house? It is belonging to Dr. Thorsonn?"

"It has nude pictures of men, yes. I think it may be his. What's the big deal?"

"Well, they say he will have the HIV."

The Snake looked genuinely worried. He could not have a busheti in his jail. It was too dangerous. He spoke to Afewerki. "You must take him out and back to your compound. He is still under arrest. He must not leave the compound. He will be spreading sickness to the people. Oh, God. He will be shot if he leaves. Go!"

"Come," said Afewerki. He did not like homosexuals but had never met one. Gudmunder did not seem like a homosexual. Had he not been married?

Reece followed Afewerki into the jail's courtyard.

Gudmunder was surprised to see them. "Will you bring me lunch?" he said.

Reece explained the situation. "No, we must go. You are free to leave the jail." He looked at Gudmunder. His ear lobes were creased. He was more complicated than he had imagined, a genuine good soul, and now this.

"Dear God," said Gudmunder. He had forgotten about the magazine.

Afewerki and Reece went through the gate. Gudmunder hesitated, remembering that he would be shot if he tried to escape.

Back at the compound, they gathered. They all thought it funny that the Snake was now afraid of Dr. Thorsonn.

"What a fool," said Svana.

Afewerki cleared his throat. He thought about how he had planned to sleep in Gudmunder's tent.

"Reece," said Gudmunder. "I think you need to go to Addis and find some help. I am still a prisoner here. You should see Dr. Guthrie at the Baptist Mission. He will know what to do. There is no embassy for Iceland there. Do you have money?"

Reece contemplated the journey. Would it really be the best thing to do?

"Yes, you must go," said Afewerki. I will work with Eydis and Svana. The Baptist Mission is in neighborhood of Mekanisa. The taxi driver will take you there."

"Is there an address for this Baptist Mission?" He looked at Eydis. Maybe she could go with him?

"Just to say Mekanisa and the taxi driver will take you there."

Reece put his hands in his jeans' pockets. It would be an adventure. "Should someone come with me?" He looked at Eydis.

Gudmunder spoke. "Hmm, I don't know."

"That is a bad idea," said Afewerki. "Who will help Svana to weigh the children?"

"You could," said Reece.

There was silence. Abebe was watching from the cook

house. She had decided to stay because so many interesting things were happening. It seemed that the doctor was a homosexual. She'd had a brother who was homosexual and who became a priest. He lived in a cave by himself. She wanted to visit him, but the travel was too dangerous to reach him.

"Yes, I will help. I will translate," said Afewerki.

"But they normally do not have a translator. The mothers know what to do," said Reece.

Gudmunder said, "I will decide this. We need Afewerki here to translate. Eydis, it is your decision if you want to go with Reece."

All eyes turned to Eydis.

Eydis looked at the ankle-high grass. "I should stay. I think. I think Svana will need me." She glanced at Reece with his hands in his pockets and felt a pang of guilt.

TWELVE

Gudmunder paced inside the perimeter of the old Baptist Mission compound, which measured roughly thirty meters by twenty meters. Eydis and Svana had decided to go and weigh children, and Afewerki was with them. Reece was waiting for a jeep at the foot of the road that led into Gwar. It could be an hour or days before a jeep came.

Reece sat through lunch, hungry. He carried a bag, packed with some clothes, a toothbrush, a comb, and condoms. He always traveled with condoms because one never knew. He'd met an Ethiopian Airlines stewardess on his flight into Addis Ababa. He had been sick on the flight, and she had visited him in his hotel room, bringing him medicine. He had her phone number.

A farmer walked by, his head wrapped with a dirty shamma. The farmer stopped and questioned him. Reece just said, "Ishi. Chicorilla." The farmer smiled and moved on. An hour passed and then two. He walked uphill to the former Baptist warehouse compound where the helipad was. Below it were mounds of rocks, graves of typhus victims from the 1980s. From his survey, he knew that the most feared disease in Gwar was typhus, which was spread by lice.

He walked in circles. A man beating a donkey passed. The donkey dug in every few meters. The man blasted its side with a wooden staff, and the donkey moved forward again. Reece could not watch and walked downhill.

In the distance, he thought he could hear an engine noise. He ran back to his bag by the road. Suddenly, there appeared three others, running down the hill. He would have to fight for a seat in the jeep.

The engine became louder, and he glimpsed a vehicle on a loop of road in the distance. The others gathered near him. They smelled of smoke and sweat. Around a bend and up the rocky road came a diesel Mercedes dump truck. There would be plenty of room. The truck passed them and stopped. Ten or so men and women piled out of the back and dispersed. The truck pulled into the former Baptist compound, turned around, and stopped again.

The others began to run up the hill, and Reece followed. The driver sat counting the money he had earned for the trip, about two hundred birr. He decided to visit the teahouse before returning. A prostitute he liked worked there. He swung down and began walking.

"What the hell?" asked Reece. He fell in behind the others and followed the driver uphill. They walked into the village center. The driver entered the teahouse, and the others sat down outside.

Reece didn't know what to do. Should he wait? Should he go back to the truck and just get in the back? He peeked inside. The driver had taken a seat and was being served. He was short and very light-skinned. He wore a mustache, which seemed unusual. Reece went inside and took a seat. He ordered tea as well.

Eydis, Svana, and Afewerki took a narrow trail out beyond the old Polish airfield. Afewerki had told them of a church being built into the rock that was in the area. They soon came across a collection of four compounds, two sharing a common fence.

"Ferenj!" came the cry of a child.

Soon, a dozen adults and children had gathered. Eydis removed the sling and scale from her backpack. The people knew what to do and gathered the children to be weighed and measured. They assumed that food relief would result. As usual, a few with some medical complaints gathered as well.

One young woman seemed especially agitated. She grabbed the hand of Svana and pleaded with her eyes.

"Mendeno?" asked Svana.

Using a cable, Eydis set up the scale and sling.

The woman poured her heart out to Svana, telling her that a neighbor had cursed her, and what could she do?

Afewerki shook his head. "She has been cursed by one with the evil eye. A ghost will live in her body."

"Oh," said Svana. "Shall we pray for her?"

Afewerki knew that was a ridiculous solution. "Of course. I will tell her."

The woman listened with wide eyes and began crying.

Svana took the woman's hands and closed her eyes. "Dear God, please bless this woman. Do not let the curse affect her..." She prayed for a minute or more.

The frightened woman had calmed. "Amenseganalo," she said, thanking Svana.

"Chicorilla," said Svana.

Eydis called for Svana. "Look how fat this baby is."

Svana couldn't believe her eyes. The baby was not so much fat as swollen.

The truck driver, who had just paid off the investment in his truck, left two birr on the table and walked downhill.

The prostitute was not in and could not be reached. Like children, everyone followed, including Reece. A small boy took his hand along the way.

The crowd following the driver had grown to eleven. Reece surveyed his fellow travelers. Most were wearing crazy combinations of Western shirts and pants with patches. One man wore a shirt made from a quilt. Another wore a Ted Nugent t-shirt with a huge tongue on it. Only the two farmers in their ragged green shorts and tire sandals seemed of the place.

Reece wore loose jeans. Already, he had lost ten pounds. His shirt was the only button-up he had brought. It was a dull green, and he wore it untucked. He had his expensive Italian hiking boots on, but they were a half-size too small and were uncomfortable, although rugged. *I should have worn my tennis shoes.*

At the truck, a struggle took place over who would sit in the cab. Two men pushed and climbed their way to victory, leaving two others shouting insults. The dump truck was bright red. The cab was square, and the dumper in back of the truck deep. Reece paid twenty birr to the driver and waited his turn to climb up the ladder on the side of the truck. He slung his bag over his shoulder and first stepped up onto the tire. He had to drop into the dumper, which was higher than his head. The bed was clean except for some gravel.

Reece stood until the truck roared to life, turned around, and began the forty-kilometer journey to Alem Ketema. The driver tried to avoid the biggest rocks and potholes, but the road was very rough, and Reece bounced on his butt. There was nothing to hold on to. The sun was still warm, but he could feel the coolness of the afternoon turning to evening. He hoped to arrive in time for dinner at the hotel in AK and avoid any trouble like the last time. He wondered if Lebna would be there.

Afewerki said, "Tsk, tsk, tsk," appraising the frightful state of this swollen newborn. He knew it would die soon.

"Is it a boy or girl?" asked Svana.

"It is a boy," said Afewerki, translating.

"May I hold him. He's so tiny but so puffy. How long has he been like this?"

"One day since birth," said Afewerki. "He is ten days old now."

The infant's breaths were noisy. Where Svana pressed her fingers, deep indentations were left. "Such a severe case of edema."

"And the lungs are very wet. We can hear it without the stethoscope," said Eydis. "Gudmunder should see this child."

"But he is under arrest," said Afewerki. "He cannot come here."

"Perhaps the mother can bring the baby to him," said Svana. "Ask her." She placed the infant in the sling. "Nine point one kilograms. He is twice the weight he should be with this fluid. Is he breastfeeding?"

"Yes, but he has stopped by one day. He is not urinating."

"That's very bad," said Svana. She handed the infant back to the barefoot mother.

"She says she will come to see the doctor," said Afewerki. He could not get the image of Dr. Thorsonn as a busheti out of his mind. Should he tell this to the mother? Everyone probably already knew. But Gudmunder was so healthy. And the rumor of him stealing the tabot was known to all. Someone could try to kill him.

"Eydis, I will take the mother and child back to see Gudmunder. You will be okay to weigh the children with Afewerki?"

Eydis agreed and indicated for the mothers to make a line.

Back at the compound, Gudmunder lay in his tent. He was thinking of the "Lost Saga," of Gaukur and the Ark of the Covenant. A lone fly tormented him. He put on his glasses and focused on snatching it from the air. The fly eluded him. He sat up, took off his sandals, and slapped them together, killing the black fly. "Jesus Christ," he said.

In the cook house, Abebe had just arrived. It was close to four p.m. and time to begin dinner. She looked around for the doctor, assuming he was in his tent or the shintabet. She knew that he was a prisoner inside the compound. After dinner, she had invited a group of her friends to hear the story of what had happened that day. She would charge ten cents to each person for her tale.

She found a red coal in the ashes from lunch. She slipped a dry corn husk beneath it and blew. A curl of smoke and then a tiny flame. She held another corn husk above the flame and then began to add twigs. There was some charcoal, but she would use mostly wood.

Gebremariam returned to the compound just as Svana returned with the mother and the swollen baby. He could not give up his job with the Icelanders, but he was now afraid of the doctor. He was a busheti, and he had stolen the tabot from the church in Alem Ketema. Everyone was talking. Some had seen the American Reece leaving the village in a truck and were wondering what it meant.

"Hallo!" said Svana. She led the mother to a biscuit tin to sit on. She was tiny and wore a shawl over her head.

"Svana?" Gudmunder unzipped the tent and, on his hands and knees, peered outside.

"We have a patient for you to see, an infant."

He reached back inside for his stethoscope and emerged. "What do we have?"

"The baby is retaining fluids."

Gudmunder sat beside the mother holding the child. "Tenesteling."

The mother whispered.

He held the baby's swollen feet. He looked at the swollen arms. The stomach was swollen, as was the head. He listened to the heart. There was a terrible murmur. He could hear blood backwashing from the mitral valve. He also suspected a hole between the ventricles. He listened to the lungs, which sounded very wet, crackling like wadded plastic. The neck veins were distended. The baby would die soon if not treated.

"Is the baby urinating?"

"No, said Svana."

"She will need to go to Addis immediately, to Black Lion Hospital, if she can. This child will most likely need open-heart surgery to live. If only Andreas were coming soon with the helicopter."

Svana squatted beside the mother and held her hand. "Addis Ababa. Hakim."

A tear came to the mother's eyes. She whispered that she could not go to Addis. That she had four other children. There was no money. Svana and Gudmunder could not understand her without Afewerki but guessed at her response.

"Take her back and have Afewerki explain the situation, okay?" Gudmunder stood. *I am a prisoner. The people think I am gay. Someone believes I stole the tabot from Alem Ketema.*

Svana led the woman from the compound, as she cradled her swollen baby. Svana waved at Abebe in the cook house, stirring topless over the pot of bugwot, a spicy stew made with sheep. There was an entire leg nailed to the cook house wall, covered with just a few flies due to the smoke.

Back at the compounds beyond the Polish airstrip, a fifteen-minute walk, Svana found Eydis and Afewerki weighing children. She asked Afewerki to explain what Gudmunder had said to the frail mother.

The mother told him she could not go because of her children. She could not neglect four because of one.

Afewerki nodded. He knew that it was true. The child would die. There would be a funeral.

"What if the helicopter could take her to Addis Ababa?" asked Svana.

"We do not know when Andreas is returning," said Afewerki. "The child will die before then."

Svana was frustrated. Something had to be done. Lasix, but they had no Lasix, surgery, something.

Three men had returned from the fields, followed by a session at the tejj bet. They squatted nearby and watched.

They were hungry, and their wives should be cooking, not weighing the children.

Eydis recorded the weight of a skinny three-year-old in the sling. He wore a charm around his neck on a dirty string. Eleven kilograms. She measured his height and plotted his height/weight percentile on the yellow card. There were five more in line. Her stomach rumbled.

Svana was reaching. "Maybe she could take the jeep to AK and then Reece could take her to Addis?"

"He does not know she is coming. They will not find each other," said Afewerki.

Svana shook her head. She looked over to the mother, who was trying to breastfeed the child. It would not take the nipple, a blank look in its eyes. It was not even crying as if it had given up. "Fuck," she said.

THIRTEEN

Thoroughly jolted and bruised from his ride in the back of the dump truck, Reece wandered in a daze to the Beselfui Hotel. Two young boys carried his light bag, just the stuff sack for his sleeping bag. His feet hurt, and he was hungry, especially since he had missed lunch.

He didn't know if a bus would arrive and depart for Addis. He hoped to find someone who spoke English. The air was cooling, and a large pink sun was setting in the east, disappearing behind a distant amba. A few calls of ferenj! came from doorways as he walked. One little girl, about eight years old, her father having been a Polish soldier, called out "Stashu!" the name of her mythic father. Reece knew about the famous Stashu and said, "Yellum."

He arrived at the hotel. It was five birr per night for ferenji and three for Ethiopians. The owner greeted him with a loud voice and took his money. She said, "Amist," and he knew that his room was number five. Lebna would be happy to see him, she said. She called him "beefcake." Reece couldn't understand what she was saying.

His plain room held a single plank bed. That was it. There was no chamber pot as before. The floor was of cement, and the pink painted walls of mud. He did not have his watch but guessed that it was around six p.m. He wondered what was for dinner.

Reece walked outside. He closed his door. There was no lock. The courtyard held three tables, empty. The power would come on at seven. The doors to a few of the rooms were open. Bats circled overhead. There was a steady breeze, which sent a light chill through him, and he wondered how the others were doing in Gwar.

He wanted to eat, but felt it was too early. He looked inside the bar and saw no one, and decided to take a walk. The wide path led to a road that wound along the cliff's edge. Alem Ketema was exposed on a high, flat, and rolling plateau. The view tumbled thousands of feet to the dry kolla below. In the distance, he could see the shine of a river. Near the edge of the cliff line, the wind blew inward with unusual strength. An old Nissan truck passed him, going very, very slowly. He waved, and they waved.

He had thoughts of his grandparents back in Alabama. He wondered what they were doing. It was around six in AK, which meant it was eight hours behind in Alabama, around ten a.m. His grandmother was probably washing clothes. His grandfather might be outside, working in the garden, chatting with his neighbor, Elbert, resting in the shade of a black walnut tree. He thought of his parents in their pink brick home before they were killed. It had been four years. His mother had kept the windows shaded night and day. It had been so dark and depressing inside.

He walked and met a group of barefoot boys. They grinned and began to follow him. He just walked and let them follow. A very bright shooting star streaked across the horizon. It startled him, and he turned to see if the boys had noticed. *Apparently not.* Should he make a wish? *Why not?* And he did. Eydis was so pretty. She was strong. He felt awkward about asking her out. But, he decided, he would as soon as he returned. They could go to the teahouse. What was wrong with him?

The dusk of evening began to fall, and Reece turned

back. Only three boys followed him now, each wearing what looked to be a wool hat. He was cold and wanted to be warmed by hot food and warm beer. By the time he returned to the Beselfui, it was dark outside and really dark inside. There was a squeal, and Lebna ran outside to hug him.

FOURTEEN

Svana, Eydis, and Afewerki returned to the compound. Gudmunder was glad to see them. He had bathed, shaved, and combed his unruly red hair. They were just in time for dinner as Abebe brought out the platter of enjera with the bugwot ladled in four portions. Steam rose from the pot.

"I wonder how Reece is doing?" asked Eydis.

"He is fine," said Afewerki.

"Ha!" said Gudmunder. "Of course he is."

They began to eat. Each had an IV bottle of filtered water. The bugwot was spicy as usual, but not as spicy as the dorowot.

Svana took a scrap of enjera and folded it around a bit of the wot. "Mmm," she said. "Abebe is a good cook."

"She is divorc-ed," said Afewerki.

"Does that matter?" asked Eydis.

Afewerki struggled with his reply. "She is a good cook," he said. "Delicious."

Gudmunder laughed. He wondered again if Afewerki was attracted to Eydis. He wondered how he could not be. She was blonde and shapely and smart as well. Had he been younger, he would have pursued her.

"So, tell us about this stealing accusation," said Svana.

Afewerki cleared his throat.

"Yes, what does it mean?" asked Eydis. "We know that you did not steal anything, but why would they say so?"

"I don't know," said Gudmunder, "other than I have visited the churches. They say they have a witness who saw me go inside. That it was the ferenj with red hair. I never did that. I always left money in the offering box."

"Many years ago, the tabot from Gwar was stolen," said Afewerki. "He was a missionary like you. The people are remembering."

"But the real tabot is in the Ark of the Covenant in Axum, right? The others scattered around the country are just replicas," said Gudmunder.

"Yes, but the Ark is sometimes to move from place to place," said Afewerki. "During the war with EPLF and TPLF, many think that the Ark was hidden, perhaps in Gwar, perhaps in Alem Ketema. The Ark is mov-ed many times."

Gudmunder thought about this. "So maybe whoever stole the tabot actually stole the real tabot from Mt. Sinai, depending on the real tabot's location at the time."

"Yes," said Afewerki. "But not just anyone can touch the tabot and live. You must be a son of God."

Gudmunder laughed. He remembered the tale of the "Lost Saga," of Gaukur Trandilsson, who traveled from Iceland to Ethiopia to take the Ark. He had left without it. The Ethiopians at the time had thought him a son of God.

"If I am a son of God, why are they arresting me?"

"Because they think you have taken the tabot. No one is knowing if it is the true tabot. They are replicas, as you say. The true tabot is in Axum."

"Unless it has been moved," said Gudmunder. Maybe he was a son of God. Why not?

"Yes," said Afewerki.

Eydis spoke. "He has not stolen a thing. He is only here to help."

"I believe this thing," said Afewerki. He wanted to.

"But…"

Svana drank water. "But what?"

Afewerki seemed embarrassed. "What of the maga-zine?"

"That? What is the word they are calling me?" asked Gudmunder.

"Busheti," said Afewerki. "The busheti have AIDS."

"That's utter bullshit," said Gudmunder. "Some do, but not all. Plus, I'm not 'busheti' as you say. If anything, I am asexual. I'm beyond sex. Sex ruins many sacred moments. Yes, maybe I was bisexual when I was younger, but now I have more important things to do than sleep with a man or a woman."

Afewerki bristled. He was not quite sure what Gud-munder had said. "You are not busheti?"

"No, but if I were, I would say it didn't matter. Jesus Christ, gay people must go through hell here."

"There is no homosexual in Gwar," said Afewerki. "It is forbidden."

"Afewerki, how do you know that?" asked Eydis. "There are homosexuals everywhere, even in Gwar."

"We do not know that," said Afewerki. "God is our keeper."

Gudmunder decided to end the conversation. "If it helps, I am not a busheti as you say. I am not a homosex-ual, okay? Will you let people know? Including the Snake. Tell him that the magazine was here when we arrived. I'm worried that our work here will be interrupted for no good reason." His serving of wot was untouched.

"You must eat," said Eydis.

Afewerki was happy to hear Gudmunder's words, but would anyone believe him?

FIFTEEN

Reece let Lebna hug him. He looked at her tightly braided hair. She smelled like cloves and smoke. Why not branch out?

Lebna took his hand and led him inside the bar. Reece sat at a small round table with two chairs.

"E'rat?" asked Reece, meaning dinner.

"Ishi," said Lebna. "Birra?" she said.

"Ow," said Reece. "St. George."

Lebna exited through the rear of the building to fetch a platter for Reece from the cook house.

Reece looked around. He recognized one man from his earlier visit. Two women were playing checkers and drinking beer, which seemed odd to him. He felt his pocket for the folded money there and wondered about the missionary shot many years before in Gwar. Anything could happen, he supposed.

Lebna returned with a metal platter. On it were two folded triangles of teff enjera and a meaty-looking wot. He thanked her and began to eat. The meat was soft but firm and had a metallic spicy flavor. It was gubet, sheep's liver, and a bit of spleen. Reece hated liver but did not know what he was eating. He was hungry and finished his plate within ten minutes. He drank his warm St. George beer. It was so dark that he could only see five feet in front of him. The radio played Amharic music from Addis Ababa.

He pushed his plate to the center of the table. He needed another beer and then a shot of Johnny Walker. Lebna was servicing the crowd, which had grown quickly in the past half hour. Suddenly, the light came on, blinding Reece. It was just a single bulb. Lebna hurried to the cassette player and popped in a tape. It was country music. Reece could have sworn that it was Jim Reeves, and it was.

The night wore on. Jim Reeves was replaced by another country band that Reece did not recognize. He was on his second serving of Johnny Walker Red and feeling very good. Lebna was looking more and more attractive as were the two women who continued to play checkers, although they were no longer drinking or eating.

A man walked in, the town administrator. The only empty chair was at Reece's table. He walked over, put his hand out, and sat down. Reece recognized him and said, "Tenesteling." Reece fiddled with his glass of whiskey. He didn't know what to say. The man began to speak. He looked Reece in the eye and spoke at length, perhaps ten minutes. He was there to sleep with Lebna. She was his regular.

Lebna brought the administrator an open bottle of white Awash wine without asking him what he wanted. She smiled at Reece.

Reece thought about burning down his grandfather's barn when he was a kid. No one had ever accused him of the crime, but their behavior suggested they knew he did it. He had been smoking a cigar in the hayloft with his friend Bob. He puckered his mouth, worried that his thoughts would suddenly start broadcasting on the tape player.

Lebna brought the administrator a box of vanilla cookies. The administrator held out the box and offered him one. Reece took one and chewed it slowly. His stomach gurgled, but he didn't want to lose his place at the table. The room was packed.

An hour passed, then two, and then, without warning, the light went out. Lebna scrambled to light the candles as a hush came across the room. She turned on the battery radio. The AM station yawned a weirdness into the Amharic music.

The bar owner, the only person in the region who could be described as fat, came into the bar. She spoke with Lebna. Lebna delivered two more bottles of beer and left through the back entrance. The town administrator, who had just finished his last glass of wine, reached over to shake Reece's hand and leave.

Reece discovered that to get another drink, he would have to go to the bar. The owner did not come to the tables. He thought a beer should do it. Just one birr. He went to the bar and stood behind a drunk man. He was holding the shoulders of the person in front to keep from falling. The man stepped back onto Reece's foot. Instead of saying he was sorry, he looked back at Reece and snarled.

"Doma ras," he said loudly, meaning dumb ass. He didn't like foreigners, especially Americans. When he was a child, an American had circumcised him and cut too much skin away. Now his erections were painful.

Reece went on guard. He tensed and stepped back. He did not want a fight, but if pushed, why not? He changed his mind about the beer and decided to have another whiskey. He had an idea. He would buy the drunk's next drink. That would settle things. The man was now speaking loudly, none of which Reece understood. He smelled of intense body odor.

The man grabbed the bar for support and ordered a glass of katikala. With a blank face, the bar owner poured from a large glass jug. The price was fifty cents. Reece came around and placed a birr on the smooth wooden counter. He pointed to the man's drink. "Chicorilla," he said.

The owner took the bill and returned fifty cents.

The drunk man took a while to process what was going on. Was this foreigner shitface trying to buy him a drink? Was he wendegered? Did he think he was a busheti? He roared that Reece was a fucking disgrace. He turned and punched Reece in the stomach. Reece doubled over. He felt like he was going off a diving board. The man sprawled on the ground and tried to stand. The room was spinning.

For Reece, time stood still. He could not hear the laughter or the bar owner yelling at them. He wanted to kick the man in the face, to break his neck. His mind swam. He stood over the man, waiting for him to stand. That was only fair.

Lebna rushed in through the back door. She went to Reece and pushed him backward. "Yellum!" she said.

Reece moved back. Someone helped the drunk man to his feet and led him outside. The room was full of murmuring and the fading in and out of the radio. Lebna led him back to his seat and sat in his lap for a moment. She was rubbing his privates through his jeans and asking if the doctor had really stolen the tabot.

SIXTEEN

The day would be clear and hot, as roosters crowed around Gwar. Juwa birds scratched their claws on the tin roof of the supply house. Eydis rolled into Svana, waking her up. "Ah, I was dreaming!"

Gudmunder was up, pacing. He felt the victim of a colossal misunderstanding, that he was the focus of the entire world. How could he continue his work here if the people were against him? Gebremariam emerged from the cook house with the teakettle. He wore a piece of cloth over his face. He walked slowly, as if about to fall into a great hole.

"Good God," said Gudmunder. He had his cup ready.

Gebremariam approached, said good morning, and poured the tea.

"Amenseganalo," said Gudmunder. He smelled the strong, spiced tea. It was refreshing.

Eydis crawled out of the tent, her pajamas rumpled. Abebe had sewn the buttons back onto her top. Her breasts swung beneath the thin fabric as she stood. "Svana, dear, it is teatime!"

Afewerki strolled into the compound. He stuck his head in the cook house and greeted Abebe.

Svana groaned from inside the tent. She sat up and ran her fingers through her hair. She thrust her cup through the tent fly. "Grazie," she said, hearing the pour and feeling the weight of her cup grow heavy.

Gudmunder was deep in thought. Perhaps he should strike up a relationship with Svana or Eydis? Maybe they would play along. But how to get around the accusations that he had stolen the tabot? They had said that a ferenj with red hair had been seen entering the church late at night. Did not Reece have red hair? No, it was more of a mahogany, but close.

Abebe came with a platter of eggs and bits of meat and torn strips of enjera. Even though she had four children, she was still young and attractive. She had lovely, rounded hips and large breasts. Gudmunder thanked her and watched her walk away. He had to act quickly. Gebremariam brought the IV bottles of water.

Gudmunder went to his tent and retrieved a fifty-birr note, a full month's salary for Abebe. "Afewerki?"

"Abet?"

"I want you to give this money to Abebe, for her children tell her."

"Ishi," said Afewerki. He was stealing glances at Eydis in her pajamas. He waited for just a moment before standing.

Svana spoke. "Oh, I see your plan. Are you sure it is a good idea?"

"She is single, no? And she must take care of the children." Gudmunder felt his heart skip a beat. He wanted time to speed up. "And is it a good idea for you to get drunk and sleep with the men here?" asked Gudmunder

"Oh," said Svana. "But no one is accusing me of stealing."

"For us all, even Abebe," said Eydis. "Let Gudmunder do this. No one will be hurt. Just don't tell her you love her. And you can't have sex with her. Just court her."

"You are as crazy as he is." Svana looked at the ground.

She ate another bite of enjera and walked away.

Afewerki returned. Abebe was waving from the cook house with a big smile on her face. Gudmunder stood and waved at her. Should he go to her?

There was a pounding on the fence, and in walked the Snake wearing a pair of latex gloves, his gold teeth visible from thirty feet.

SEVENTEEN

Reece awoke with a headache. He opened his eyes and tried to remember the night before. Had he had sex with Lebna, or was it just a dream? She had insisted on coming to his room. She had pulled her dress top down and shown him her breasts, placing his hand there. She had reached for his other hand and pulled up her dress. She'd had no underwear on. By the light of the candle, he could discern her pubic hair.

She had wanted to give him a blowjob. He had almost let her, but decided against it. He checked his bag. He had three condoms, and they were still there. He decided that he definitely had not had sex with Lebna. He was relieved but hungover. Had he given her money out of guilt? He couldn't remember.

"Oh God," he said, remembering that he needed a ride to Addis. He rushed to get his things together, but he needed to eat. His stomach trembled, and a sharp pain ripped through his gut. "Fuck," and he trotted to the nasty shintabet for a session.

With his bag, he walked to the town circle, the roundabout with the low wall. He knew it was too late to catch the bus. It left very early before sunrise. There were no jeeps in sight, and he walked to a tiny grocery stand. Hanging from the wall were the little boxes of vanilla crème cookies. He took his cookies and sat on the dusty stone wall, thick clouds curdling in the sky. A warm wind whipped his shirtsleeves.

A young man, a teenager, approached him. Reece recognized him from the hotel. He was a relation of the owner and spoke a little English.

"Kindly sir, you must pay amist birr for the hotel. You were to forget?"

"What? I paid when I arrived. Five birr. I paid in advance."

The teenager laughed. "Yes. But kindly sir, you must to pay amist birr."

"Huh?" He had a ten birr note and gave it to him. "I need change. Five birr?"

"Yes, I will come again."

Reece walked around the barely used traffic circle. There were footprints in the rocky dust, but not a tire mark to be seen. If there were no jeep, he would have to go back to the hotel for another night. He still couldn't believe that the drunk guy had punched him. He felt his heart rate increase and a pressure build behind his eyes.

Looking at the sun high overhead, Reece determined that it was noon. He was hungry but mostly thirsty, and he had to use the restroom. The cramping had subsided, but he was belching. In fact, now that he thought about it, he was constipated, not having gone for three or four days. He suddenly felt bloated and mildly sick. Back in the States, he was never constipated. He thought about his grandfather using Fleet's enemas on occasion.

He walked back to the Beselfui Hotel. A young boy approached, wanting to clean his sandals. He carried a little wooden box with a cloth and a brush. "Yellum," he told the boy. The boy frowned, cursed him, and ran away.

Not thirty seconds later, the strap on his sandal broke.

"Dammit." The sole flapped, making it hard to walk. He felt that the world was conspiring against him. Back at the hotel, he looked for the teenager who had not brought him the change from his ten. Mariam, the owner, was not there. Five men sat inside eating shurowot. There was another woman, plumper than Lebna, with a round face, serving customers. Reece sat at a table.

The waitress seemed to be ignoring him. Reece waved at her, and she came. "Ah, shurowot," said Reece. "Fanta, arancia."

The waitress nodded with a blank look and walked away. It took five minutes for the orange Fanta to arrive and ten more minutes for the shurowot with a fold of enjera. Reece felt that everyone was looking at him, and they were. There were so many rumors going around. The lentils were spicy with berbere and paired perfectly with the tangy enjera. He ordered another Fanta. He was sitting just inside the open door and saw a man with a duffel bag trotting down the road, nearly running—jeep!

EIGHTEEN

The Snake was alone. His compatriot duo with the AK-47s had preferred to stay outside the compound. He was high on qat and waved at the group in a friendly fashion. His mouth looked wet and bitter.

"Salaam! I see that our prisoner is still here. Very good." The Snake patted his pistol.

Afewerki translated.

"So, what is next?" asked Gudmunder. "My former wife, back in Iceland, will be very worried when she hears of this."

"Oh, so now you have a wife."

"Yes, he was married," said Eydis in an angry tone. She suddenly felt naked in her pajamas and went into the tent.

"She is a pretty one," said the Snake. "And you too." He nodded toward Svana and tried to whistle. He laughed at himself. "So how does that explain the busheti magazine?"

Svana was weary of the busheti talk. "It belonged to a woman. The woman who lived in the little house."

"Oh, really? How do you know?" He wavered from side to side.

"I met her in another universe. We are friends there. She told me where the magazine was hidden, and I found it between the plastic and the wall. Only women like to look at nude men. Everyone knows that." Svana was breaking a twig into small pieces.

Afewerki left out the part about the universe.

"The doctor is not busheti? He is not wendegered?"

Gudmunder held his tongue. He wanted to take the

Snake's pistol and push it down his throat. This was ridiculous, the games being played, but Svana was convincing.

"No," said Svana. "But does God not love everyone?"

"You will have to ask the priest," said the Snake. "Well, still, he is my prisoner. Soon he will be taken to Alem Ketema to face his accuser." He turned toward Gudmunder. "Maybe you will spend many years in the jail?"

"Dear God," said Gudmunder. "This is a nightmare."

"What does he say, this one?" asked the Snake.

"He says to go and have a good day," said Afewerki.

"Well, how nice. I think I will do that." He had plans to drink katikala with his guards. He turned and stepped through the fence.

"I appreciate you playing along," said Gudmunder.

"No worries," said Svana. She fixed a small plastic plate of fit-fit. Her appetite had returned.

"Eydis, come and finish your breakfast," said Gudmunder. "The Snake has left us."

"Yes, please to come," said Afewerki.

Eydis emerged and stood, wearing aqua scrubs from her hospital back in Reykjavik. "Do you think he bought it?"

"What is he buying?" asked Afewerki.

"No, do you think he believed what Svana said about the magazine?"

"It is true, no? She said it. The nurse told her where to find it. I did not know this."

"Okay," said Gudmunder. That was a good sign if Afewerki believed the story.

"No, she was lying, but for a good reason," said Svana.

"Eydis!" said Svana.

"Oh, Svana is not truthing?" Afewerki was confused.

"What Svana said is true," said Gudmunder. "That is settled." He changed the subject. "Let's give Abebe the morning off. We can wash our own dishes today. How about it?"

Svana said, "Sure," and Eydis rolled her eyes.

"Who is this?" asked Gudmunder. A tall farmer in shorts and tire sandals had entered the compound. He took off his hat and was holding something.

"It is Mulu," said Afewerki with a definite frown. He glanced at Svana who had slept with him.

NINETEEN

Reece knocked his empty Fanta bottle off the table, and it broke on the cement floor. "Shit." He would have to pay for the bottle. The barmaid came over and frowned.

"Sentino?" asked Reece. The jeep would fill up fast.

"And birr," she said.

He handed her a twenty, and she frowned. She went to the till and fetched his change, all in ones. He didn't bother to count it and handed her a birr for a tip. Her face lit up.

Out the door, he went in a slow run. He was really full but still thirsty. His head itched of a sudden, and he felt as if something was in his hair. He reached up to feel with his left hand and knocked off his glasses. "Dammit to hell!" In the distance, he could see an old yellow Land Rover surrounded by a crowd of people.

He reached the Rover, and the driver was directing people where to sit. Two women were wearing their finest dresses with sashes. The driver ordered them into the very back, a cramped space behind a second-row bench seat. He then seated the men, four in the second-row seat and two in the single front seat beside him. On top was being loaded luggage, a bag of charcoal, and a load of sugarcane. A young boy grabbed Reece's bag and threw it up top before he could react. Where would he sit? Ropes were thrown over the baggage and tied to the rack.

After taking $20 from him, the driver motioned for Reece and another man to get up topside. Reece hesitated. All of this because of Gudmunder? He could be thrown from the top and killed. What if the Rover rolled over? The other man climbed up and over the tire on the back. He extended his hand to Reece. Reece gave way to his fate, and up top, he couldn't decide where to sit. Everything was hard and lumpy. He finally mimicked his fellow rider, pushing his feet against the front of the rack and holding onto the side. He searched with his free hand and grabbed a rope. The jeep lurched forward. Already, the speed was enough to make him cringe. He felt as if the jeep was tipping over and closed his eyes, and there was itching on his scalp again. With the wind in his face, his eyes began to water. The bumps in the road jolted him, and he held on for dear life. The punishment would last for one hundred and twenty kilometers, seventy-five miles. His companion just laughed and waved as they passed farmers and children along the road.

TWENTY

Mulu walked farther into the compound and then stopped as if waiting for instructions. He nodded to Abebe, who was going to get the dishes. Afewerki grabbed her arm and told her that Dr. Thorsonn had given her the morning off.

She protested. This was her job. She needed the money. What did it mean to take the morning off?

Mulu, nodding his head with a sheepish grin, walked closer to the group by the fire pit.

Afewerki put his hands up. "She does not want to take off this morning," he said.

"No, she must," said Gudmunder. He was eying Mulu's legs. He seemed to have some psoriasis there, a shiny patch of skin, or perhaps ringworm.

Mulu saw Gudmunder looking at his legs. He cleared his throat. Svana was just there, sitting in a chair. Mulu watched her stand. He approached with his gift. The gift moved inside the burlap.

Afewerki shifted his focus from Abebe to Mulu. Mulu had a wife, for god's sake. He reluctantly translated. "He says he has bring to you a gift. He wonders if you will come again to the tejj bet."

Gudmunder had wandered to the cook house and taken Abebe's hand. "Chicorilla," he said.

She withdrew her hand, angry at being denied her work.

Svana stared at Mulu. He was handsome, of course, but she had not meant to sleep with him. This happened when she drank. "Gudmunder! Abebe does not want to take the day off. Listen to her, for God's sake."

Mulu untied the bag and revealed a blue and orange rooster. It crowed in fear. He brought it from the bag and dropped it onto the grass. Immediately, it ran and then began pecking at the ground.

"Is for your dinner," said Afewerki. "To make the dorowot."

Svana was embarrassed but touched. "Amenseganalo," she told him.

Mulu gripped his hat as if it weighed many kilos.

"Oh, okay," said Gudmunder. He let go of Abebe's hand. She seemed to be far too upset.

"What a hell," said Afewerki to no one.

"Eydis, we must get ready to weigh the children," said Svana. She said goodbye to Mulu and went to the tent.

Mulu looked sad, and Afewerki said that he could go. Mulu put on his hat and left, muttering to himself. It looked to Mulu that Svana must be sleeping with Afewerki. He gritted his teeth, angry.

The Rover struggled along, mostly going downhill. Reece held on and could hear the engine groaning with the load. It had been nearly an hour, and he was exhausted. He didn't know if he could hold on any longer. His companion seemed unfazed, with a steady stream of comments in Amharic. They turned a bend, and there was a mini-bus stuck. It had rained, and the mini-bus had slid into some mud. Everyone was waving for them to stop. The driver emerged and, with the help of the mini-bus driver, attached a steel cable between the two. He put it into reverse, and the Rover bucked as the mini-bus spun its wheels, sliding farther off the road.

The driver stopped and turned the Rover around. He hooked the cable to the back and tried again in low gear, all-wheel drive. It was hit and miss, but the mini-bus spun its way free to many cheers.

They were on their way again, bucking and rocking in an immense valley of rolling hills. There was not much to see other than a gray-scale toucan, which flew alongside the jeep for nearly a minute, much to Reece's delight. It made him think of the Fruit Loops he ate as a child.

The highlight, as usual, was the climb from the desert valley up the escarpment via a winding, death-defying road. Reece closed his eyes, feeling like he was drunk. Once at the top, another hour later, the Rover passed through Lomi and then stopped in Mookaturi for tea and bread. Reece climbed down from the roof, hoping that someone had died inside the jeep so he could take their place. His legs felt wobbly, and his arms strained as if turning heavy screwdrivers. His eyes hurt from the wind, and he felt that his face and neck were seriously sunburned.

The collection of huts and square buildings with tin roofs seemed just a breath away from falling over. Inside, the teahouse was relatively bright with numerous open windows. Reece drank his tea from a fragile cup with a rose on the side. He thought they would stay for a while, but the driver slurped down his tea and made the call for all aboard in less than ten minutes. Some had not yet even ordered their tea but had managed to buy buns outside.

Reece climbed back up top and gritted his teeth. He had no idea that they would stop again within the hour, but was grateful when they did. This time it was for coffee in Choncho. The driver liked his caffeine.

TWENTY-TWO

The Snake had received orders from the kebele court in Alem Ketema to bring Gudmunder there. Most likely, though, the theft of the tabot would be considered a state issue and placed under the jurisdiction of a first instance court in Addis Ababa. The Snake stood outside the jail compound talking to Gudmunder through the fence opening. Gudmunder had his arms folded across his chest, listening.

"Afewerki, tell him again that I had nothing to do with the theft. Please. I have work to do here. This is ridiculous."

Afewerki told the Snake. The Snake asked Afewerki why he did not fear the busheti doctor. Afewerki replied that it was not possible, that he had been married in Iceland. The Snake began to wonder if it was really true. And what was the significance of the fereni, Reece, leaving for Addis?

"He is going for help for us," said Afewerki.

The Snake had not considered that possibility. The doctor was a wise man, no doubt, and had a plan. "Perhaps this Reece has the tabot and will sell it in Addis?"

Afewerki explained to Gudmunder.

"No need to cast doubt on Reece. This gets worse every minute." Gudmunder had an idea. "Afewerki, will he have dinner with us tonight? He needs to be our friend and not our enemy."

Afewerki's eyes opened wide and then relaxed. "This man is stealing from us. He has arrested me. He has arrested you. If we let him, he will rape the nurses." Afewerki, just that morning, had seen the Snake force a pregnant woman from her mule so that he could ride it to buy qat.

"Maybe we can change that. We should love our enemies. As the Bible says, no?"

"What of Eydis and Svana?"

"They will understand. Ask him."

"He fears you are homosexual," said Afewerki.

"Remind him that I was married. Tell him that I do not wear my ring any longer because I am divorced. Tell him that I have my eye on Abebe, and I do."

Afewerki chuckled. Working with the ferenji was always interesting. "Perhaps you are cutting your own throat?"

Gudmunder paused at that one. "Or I get sent to prison for stealing a national treasure and possibly executed. Who knows what they will do? I do not want to risk it. They could accuse you of helping me, you know. Anything is possible."

Afewerki spoke to the Snake in a low tone. Would he have dinner with them?

The Snake laughed. He couldn't stop laughing.

The Rover ground up the hill to the inspection station at Entoto. From there, it would be a downhill drive into Addis. A big bus, a mini-bus, and a taxi idled in front of them. Reece watched as the occupants piled out and headed toward several little girls selling tea, coffee, cakes, and rolls. He felt frozen in position. His companion jumped down. Reece stood and went to his knees as his back cramped.

"Ah!"

He crawled down instead of jumping. He was definitely sunburned. He felt for his wallet, and it wasn't there. His stomach went hollow. It was in his front pocket. "Jesus Christ." He walked slowly, stretching. Men in green fatigues with berets and pistols were inspecting luggage. At the lift gate, a man stood with an AK-47, a new one. Reece wanted water, but there was none for sale. He contemplated a warm Coke and opted for a cup of sweet, spiced tea. He gave the girl thirty cents. She tried to give him change, but he refused. Little pins of cloves floated in the green plastic cup, which he had to return.

Standing there, he gazed around at the vegetation, the grass, the patches of dirt. He felt like a foreigner. He was exposed. How could he ever explain how he felt at that moment? *I am a speck of dust. Blown into another dimension.* He returned to the Rover. Everyone seemed to have a travel document of some sort, and passports, too. He began to worry.

A soldier approached. He opened the door and looked inside. He opened the glove box. He eased into the back seat and opened a bag there. He looked into the back and emerged. Reece did not make eye contact and drank his tea. The soldier asked for the driver's papers. He looked at them, silent, and returned them. He turned toward Reece.

"Who is this?" he said.

The driver hesitated. "Ah, he is a man of God. He is here to study the church, to find the real God." He looked serious.

The soldier nodded. He checked the documents of two more people. He scrawled on a pad, gave the driver a copy, and moved on to a jeep that had pulled up behind them.

Down into the bowl of Addis they descended, threading through donkeys, goats, and the humanity. Reece tried to remember the name of the neighborhood that Afewerki had told him to tell the taxi driver. It started with an M. Was he near there now? Should he get off? Where exactly was the Rover headed?

From his perch, Reece watched as children waved at him and laughed. He felt like a country bumpkin coming to town for the big dance and reminded himself why he was there: to find Dr. Guthrie and bring help for Gudmunder. He shook his head. Why the hell would Dr. Thorsonn steal a religious artifact? Yeah, there was the story of the Lost Saga, but the hero had decided not to steal the tabot, or was it the whole Ark, after seeing it in Axum, or was it somewhere else? "Must find Guthrie," he told himself.

The Rover merged into a two-lane, which became a four-lane, or was it a two-lane? He couldn't tell. The driver turned onto Haile Selassie Street, near Addis Ababa University, and stopped with full traffic behind him. Horns blared, but the driver remained nonplussed. He waved traffic around. Reece hurried down from his perch with his bag. The driver took him by the hand and pointed to a restaurant that was just on the other side of the sidewalk. "Amarinia food. Very tasty," he said. "You go there, no?"

Reece decided it was best to say yes and did so. He was hungry, but the business of the roads and the crowding made him anxious. What was the name of the neighborhood? "Baptist Mission?" he said to the driver, who only shrugged.

A policeman had appeared to ticket the Rover. The driver abandoned Reece and began yelling at everyone. He scrambled to the top and began untying the ropes. He did not want to have to bribe this policeman.

Reece shouldered his light bag. He walked to the restaurant and looked inside. A pretty bronze woman motioned for him to come inside. *Why not?* He stepped in, and the smells of fantastic spices greeted him. He could see large portions of meat being grilled. The woman, perhaps nineteen, led him to a table in the window. She handed him a menu. "Coming soon," she said.

Reece nodded. He looked for the alcoholic beverages. He needed at least wine. There was beer, wine, and some liquors. He calmed, anticipating the warm feeling. The wind of the ride had chilled him to the bone, even though it had been warm. His skin felt tight and tired. He was lucky it had not rained.

After a few minutes, an old man, stooped over, came to take his order. He spoke in Amharic. Reece pointed to an item on the menu. It seemed to be some sort of tibs, a meat dish. He was pretty sure it would be goat. He pointed to the wine. It was in English and Amharic, a white wine. He hoped it would be chilled. The old man scribbled on his pad and nodded.

Reece crossed his legs and folded his hands in his lap. He looked out the window at the endless traffic. *It must be rush hour. Ore di punta.* He glanced back at the chef in a white uniform and hat, rushing from one stove to another. The restaurant was somewhat crowded, a good sign.

The pretty hostess brought the wine, an entire bottle of Awash white wine with the plain yellow label. It was served in the bars of Alem Ketema and was not a bad choice. The bottle looked warm, and it was. Nonetheless, the first glass he gulped, enjoying the rush of alcohol. *I must be dehydrated,* and he was.

He thought it must be six p.m. or so and sipped his second glass of wine. Thoughts turned to Eydis. He imagined her bent over a child, her blonde hair falling into her face, her breasts surging against her bra. He imagined bringing her to the States and meeting his grandparents. His grandmother would be coy and perhaps say, "You sure are a pretty thing. What country are you from?" His grandfather would be interested in her history. He would say, "Are there any Myers in your neck of the woods?" Reece smiled and sipped the warm wine.

He uncrossed and recrossed his legs. He watched the traffic. Numerous taxis were passing. It wouldn't be that hard to find Guthrie, would it? He went back to Eydis. He wished she were there with him, sharing the wine. He wondered about Afewerki. He seemed to like Eydis as well.

The old man returned. He wore a green jacket and a white shirt. He placed on the table a steaming plate of meat on the bone. There was a half loaf of what looked to be Italian bread. He bowed and filled Reece's glass with wine.

"Amenseganalo," said Reece.

"Minem aydelem," said the old man.

Reece faced a dilemma. He looked around at others eating. Should he use the fork or pick up the meat with his hand? The right hand for sure. Everyone seemed to be using their forks, so he did the same. *But what is the name of that damn neighborhood that starts with an M?*

TWENTY-FOUR

Eydis and Svana walked uphill. It was so steep that they could reach out and touch the ground. In their backpacks were empty IV bottles of water, the sling and weight gauge, and supplies they had not used. They had walked toward the river, farther than ever. Walking with them was a woman, thirty or so in age, who had been to the river to wash her dress. She did this once per year. She kept her pace slow to stay with the Icelanders. Who knew? Shifta could attack at any moment.

Svana's hair was a muddle, a series of cowlicks. "Do you think Gudmunder will escape this mess?"

Eydis plodded along. She pushed the straps of her backpack with her thumbs. "Can this even be? The Ark of the Covenant is ancient history. I don't understand. Maybe he should not have visited the church."

"But somebody stole it while we were in Alem Ketema."

"Somebody, but who? I do not think he would do such a thing. It's unbelievable. Aren't you supposed to die if you even see it?"

"I think so," said Eydis. "But this is folklore."

"Maybe Gudmunder is a son of God. Ha!"

Eydis looked back at the strong woman following them. She felt safer. "And you are the daughter of Satan."

Svana laughed. "I do feel like the daughter of Satan sometimes, especially when I drink."

"Gudmunder was drinking that night. He says that he visited the church, that he left money there." Eydis breathed hard. Sweat burned the corners of her eyes. The altitude gain was steady and relentless as the cool of evening descended.

"Ah, but we did not know he was a homosexual until yesterday!" Svana laughed and then coughed.

Eydis laughed. She tried to imagine Gudmunder cradling another man.

A column of dirt jumped into the air, followed by the sound of a gunshot.

"Fuck!" said Svana.

"Ai yi!" said the woman behind them. She spoke in Amharic. "The young men are playing at target practice. Just go on. They will shoot again."

"Let us walk quicker," said Svana. There was nowhere to hide. They were being fired at from the rim of the canyon near the former Polish airfield. The young girls who carried water were their favorite targets. They didn't try actually to hit them.

Another shot, and Eydis went down.

TWENTY-FIVE

Reece paid the pretty bronze woman, leaving a nice tip. He'd had a whole bottle of wine and was feeling pretty good. The air smelled of diesel. A shoeshine boy wanted to clean his hiking boots. He had changed from his broken sandals. *Why not?*

The boy, dressed in torn pants and a tank top, went to work. He scrubbed the split-grain leather and Gore-Tex fabric with a stiff brush. He took a mouthful of water and sprayed both shoes, buffing with a dirty cloth. Reece handed the boy ten cents, twice what was requested.

A woman in a long dress approached him, holding out her hand and touching her mouth. It had to end somewhere, and Reece forged ahead to the street. He held his hand up as taxis passed by. Finally, one stopped. He slid into the front seat of the heroic blue and white Lada. The middle-aged man seemed to be nearly unconscious.

"Baptist Mission?" asked Reece. He wanted to add, "Dr. Guthrie."

The taxi driver looked at him as if he were two people. He spoke, but Reece could not discern what he said. Reece realized that this was a trip to nowhere and said, "Bucka," enough. "Sentino?"

The driver stopped in the middle of traffic. Horns blared. Reece had been in the taxi less than sixty seconds.

"Amist birr."

"Chicorilla," said Reece. He handed the driver five birr and jumped out. Traffic flowed around them, and he sprinted to the sidewalk. A man was defecating in an alley there as evening ratcheted down.

There was not much more to do than try another taxi. Without hailing it, a blue and white Fiat pulled alongside him. "Inside!" said the man. He had dreads and looked Rasta, which was good. Reece opened the door with some difficulty and fell into the tiny front seat. Yellow shag carpet covered the dashboard. A photo of Haile Selassie swung from the rearview. The taxi smelled of sweat and something sweet.

"Where to, mahn?" asked the driver. He was Sebastian from Liverpool, England. Hardcore Rasta.

Reece assessed the situation. "Baptist Mission?" He threw up his hands.

"Ah, yes. Mekanisa," said Sebastian. The taxi belonged to another man, an Ethiopian, and he was driving for a twenty-five percent take of the profits.

Reece nearly fell over backward. "Yes, Mekanisa!"

The radio played Amharic music, women serenading, calling out lyrics in somewhat of a yodel. Lots of accordion, drums, and the single-stringed masinqo. The route took them past Black Lion Hospital and through the immense Meskel Square. Reece imagined there must be twelve lanes of traffic there. Sebastian asked why Reece was in Ethiopia.

Reece thought. He didn't really know. To do a health survey?

"To do a health survey in northern Shewa, in Gwar," he said.

"Ah, you are a doctor, no?"

"Right, no. I'm a student. I study public health."

"Yes, God will bless you, no?"

"Well, I guess," said Reece. He only wanted to help people, but was he?

"Yes, I know the Baptist Mission. My friend Tesfaw works there. He has had some polio when he was small."

"Do you know Dr. Guthrie?"

"No," said Sebastian. Tesfaw bought ganja from him. He used to be Rasta, many years ago. "Do you like Rasta holiday?"

"What is that?"

"Ganja and reggae, mahn." Sebastian laughed. His mouth missed several teeth.

Reece had smoked weed on occasion. It didn't seem to do anything for him. Reggae was okay. "Yeah, ganja is okay. The ladies seem to like it."

That made Sebastian happy. "My brother," he said. "Yes, to fuck the ladies, you must have ganja and reggae."

"Four twenty," said Reece.

Sebastian was *driving*. He streaked across a lane. He was on Roosevelt, heading to Mekanisa. Reece wanted to roll down the window, but knew that was taboo. Traffic slowed, and a slew of beggars dispersed. Two little girls came up to Reece's window. They touched their stomachs and mouths. Reece nodded, not sure what to do.

"You can give them money," said Sebastian.

Reece felt in his pocket for change. He had eighty cents. The window had no handle.

"Just open the door, mahn."

Reece opened the door. He gave one girl thirty cents and the other fifty. The girl with thirty cents cursed him. "Tebeda!" She ran, not looking back.

Sebastian laughed.

TWENTY-SIX

The Snake showed up early for dinner. He wore his military finest: crisp uniform, shined boots, and a brimmed military hat with gold braids. He was high on qat but not yet drunk. Abebe looked out of the cook house and shook her head. What would happen next?

Gudmunder greeted him at the fence and shook his hand. Afewerki had the day off, but was supposed to return for dinner.

"Tenesteling," said Gudmunder.

"Salaam," said the Snake. He wanted liquor.

Gudmunder wanted liquor. He had three-fourths of a bottle of Reyka vodka from home. He led the Snake to the cold fire pit and offered him a folding chair.

The sky held a single blue streak of cloud. The high moon was at the quarter mark. Two juwa birds fought midair, falling to the ground inside the government clinic compound next door.

On seeing the fancy bottle of clear Reyka vodka, the Snake smacked his lips. This was going to be special. He wished for a real glass, and the Doctor did not disappoint. The only better thing would be to have sex with one of the nurses.

Gudmunder poured two generous glasses of vodka and handed one to the Snake. "Cheers," he said.

"Tchirz," said the Snake. He took a swallow. Strong. He approved and raised his glass again.

Gudmunder drank as well, appreciating the clean taste. He held his glass and looked at the Snake. Gudmunder suddenly thought of music. He should bring out his tape player. He made a motion for the Snake to wait and went to his tent.

Where were the nurses? The Snake relaxed. This would make a good story for his grandchildren. He'd lost track of how many he had.

"Music," said Gudmunder. He placed the red tape player on a biscuit tin. It was the Sugarcubes with Bjork.

The Snake listened. The music was horrible. What the hell? He liked Amharic music.

Svana and Eydis stepped through the fence and saw the Snake. They paused. The Sugarcubes were singing "Birthday." They'd just been shot at but not hit.

Gudmunder stood. "Come in. We are having dinner together. It is for the best. Wash your hands and join us, please."

They said nothing, still in shock, and went to the water barrel. There was a bar of soap in a dish there, and they washed their hands, pouring water for one another. "What is this?" asked Svana.

"I don't know," said Eydis. She hated the Snake more than Svana. His minion had torn her pajama top. "Let's just eat. I'm starving."

Afewerki appeared. He'd been at the teahouse with friends. "Hallo!" He saw the Snake and walked over to him. "Hallo," he said.

The Snake stood and shook Afewerki's hand. He said that the ferenj's liquor was delicious.

Afewerki went to the cook house and spoke with Abebe. He was surprised to see the carcass of an entire goat. Gudmunder had paid to have a goat slaughtered. Entrails were boiling in one pot. He knew the ferenji would not eat that. He questioned Abebe. There would be others who came for the tasty bits.

"Ishi," said Afewerki. He hoped Gudmunder would get the Snake drunk enough to fall into the fire.

TWENTY-SEVEN

Sebastian negotiated the rough road past Awash Winery. The smell was unbearable, like shoving your head in vomit, and Reece held his breath. He didn't know that most taxis would not venture into Mekanisa due to the holes in the roads.

Reece held onto the door handle to keep from hitting his head on the ceiling. The taxi slowed, pushing through a wave of people who parted like a school of drugged fish.

"Soon," said Sebastian. He drove with both hands, avoiding the yawning holes. "Do you need ganja?"

Reece thought. He wasn't sure what the drug laws in Ethiopia had to say about pot. "Is it legal?"

"Ha ha," said Sebastian. "No way, mahn. But even the soldiers buy from me. It is okay."

Reece wondered if Eydis liked ganja. "How much?"

"For you, just a few birr, ten birr. To make your lady happy happy."

That seemed reasonable. "Okay."

Sebastian reached under his seat and pulled out a battered manila envelope. It was stamped with the Catholic Relief Services logo and address. Driving with one hand, he withdrew a smaller envelope and handed it to Reece. "You can smell. Excellent ganja from Shashamane."

Reece unwound the string from the paper coin and looked inside at the deep green buds. He smelled. It smelled like pot. "Okay, deal."

The taxi slogged along through the thickening crowd of people and animals on the road. Several people pounded on the hood, giving glares. The cab passed shacks and rickety fences made of corrugated tin. There was a concrete block structure with a dog lying in the dirt.

Within ten minutes, Sebastian pulled up to a high metal gate. Reece could read the sign, "Baptist Mission of Ethiopia." Dusk was settling. He wondered if he could spend the night there.

"Okay, mahn. Fifteen for all."

Reece fumbled for his tiny travel wallet. He gave Sebastian a twenty and took his change in coins and ones, handing back two birr. He reached to grab his bag from the back seat and couldn't reach it. He stepped out and opened the back door.

"Okay, thanks," said Reece. He turned away.

"Hey, mahn, you forget something." He held out the envelope of ganja over the back seat and beeped the horn twice.

"Yeah, thanks again." He was about to put the envelope in his bag when the gate swung inward. A guard with a shamma wrapped around his neck and shoulders stood there.

"Abet?"

"Dr. Guthrie?" Reece peered inside. The compound was deep with several small buildings.

"Ah, okay," said the guard. He led Reece inside and closed the gate. There was a white house with a front porch, and the guard entered. Reece could hear machinery working inside the building. It vaguely reminded him of a printing press, and it was.

The guard came back outside and motioned for Reece to stay and wait. He stood there beside Reece as if waiting for something to happen. There were two other houses, American-style houses. In the back of the compound was a small white guest house.

It took a few minutes, but a man wearing a purple suit emerged. He used crutches to walk. One of his legs seemed to be withered.

"You must be Tesfaw," said Reece.

Tesfaw looked very, very surprised. He gazed at Reece carefully. "Yes. You want the Dr. Guthrie? He is looking for you?"

"Oh, Sebastian, the taxi driver mentioned you."

Tesfaw's eyes widened just a bit. "Yes, the world is a small place. Dr. Guthrie is not inside this place. No one is to answer the phone. His house is just nearby. You can walk. You must go into the road this way." He indicated left. "His house is on this side, very close. Do not take pictures of the people. They will anger to you. Okay?"

"Yes sir. No problem," said Reece. He had not brought his camera.

The guard opened the gate again and patted Reece on the back as if to wish him luck. It was getting dark.

TWENTY-EIGHT

Abebe made three dishes with the goat meat: tibs, a wot, and a plain stew of the succulent parts, such as the tongue and head. Everyone had their own IV bottle of water.

"Birra?" asked the Snake.

"He wants beer," said Afewerki. The food was delicious, and he hated that they were wasting it on the town administrator.

"Yes, beer," said Gudmunder. He had not thought of that. He had four bottles in his tent. He fetched them and placed all four beside the Snake. He took his Swiss Army knife and popped the first brew.

"Mmm, delicato," said the Snake. He knew a little Italian. He guzzled half the bottle and resumed eating, but not so fast as to lose his buzz.

Eydis and Svana sat back from the small fire that Gebremariam had built. They were hungry and annoyed that the Snake was there.

"Are you from here?" asked Eydis. She knew he wasn't. The rumor was that he had been sent to Gwar as punishment for being incompetent.

"Oh, can you not see my dark skin?" he said with a slight laugh. "I am from far away in Jimma. "Are you from here?"

Afewerki wanted to eat but had to translate.

Eydis smirked. "Yes, I was born here. Tell him."

Gudmunder said, "Eydis."

Afewerki hesitated but told him what she had said.

The Snake was in the middle of swallowing his beer and spewed it onto the ground. He laughed and laughed.

He slapped his leg. "She is so pretty and with a sharp tongue, no?"

"You are pretty and have a sharp tongue," said Afewerki. He fished for the tongue in the stew. He was beginning to see this as a game. He held up the gray tongue. "For my brother." He stood and fed the tongue to the Snake, who received it with a slurp.

"Xavier meskin," said the Snake, a lilt of sarcasm in his voice.

Gudmunder spoke. "Ato…" He referred to the Snake as sir. "What is the hardest part of being the town administrator?"

"Ah, yes," said the Snake. "Each day is difficult. The peasants are very ignorant. They do not follow the law. They are always fighting and killing."

"Why do you mistreat women?" asked Svana.

"Svana," said Gudmunder.

The Snake did not laugh. Did she really ask that question? Svana to him looked like trouble. "God made the woman to give birth. That is all."

"Do you like to have sex with women?" asked Eydis.

Afewerki hesitated. He modified her question.

"Yes, I very much like the meat of the goat. Is delicious, no?"

Afewerki said, "Yes, he likes to have sex."

"No doubt," said Eydis. "But who would want to?"

Afewerki did not translate.

The Snake, on his second beer, wanted to know what she said.

"She has said that Abebe cooks very well."

The snake responded. "That one is a naughty girl. Perhaps I shall teach her a lesson one day."

"He has said that Abebe must be a good mother to her children."

Gudmunder could tell that Afewerki was bullshitting. Maybe it was for the best. He poured two glasses of vodka. "Anyone else?"

The Snake moaned with pleasure. Gudmunder thought that he was enjoying himself. Sitting there with him, the Snake did not seem so evil. Years earlier, he had shot and possibly killed a Baptist worker, it was rumored. But no one had seen him do it.

The Snake downed the vodka in two gulps. He was humming to himself. "Ato doctor, come and drink with me at the tejj bet some day soon."

"Of course," said Gudmunder.

The Snake put down his plate on the grass. He opened a bottle of beer with his teeth. He was a sponge.

Svana and Eydis stood and took their plates to the cook house. They washed the grease from their hands. "Let's go for a walk," said Svana. "Okay," said Eydis. "Let me get my sweater." They walked to the tent.

"Are they to leaving?" asked the Snake. He frowned. "We have much drinking to do." He'd seen Eydis's tits, and he wanted to see Svana's.

Afewerki intervened. "They must walk to digest their food."

"No, they must stay." He pulled a liter of katikala from inside his vast jacket.

"You must stay."

"To hell with him," said Eydis.

Afewerki let the cards fall where they may. "To hell

with you.”

The Snake stood, undid his leather holster, and pulled out his Makarov.

TWENTY-NINE

Reece took his bag and entered the wide dirt lane. Huge puddles of mud littered his way. He fell into a weave of bustling souls and kept pace with its forward progress. Ahead was a tractor-trailer coming down the road slowly. The driver was flashing his lights. Reece felt almost like a balloon floating down a shallow creek. He looked to his left for the house of Dr. Guthrie, afraid he would miss it.

From ahead, the crowd had changed shape. There were cries. The flow slowed. The tractor-trailer had stopped. Reece moved ahead through the crowd. Something was calling him. People streamed onto the road from shanties. A woman was screaming. Reece drew forward. He pushed his way through. He could not see his feet. The people were so thick. Piercing ululations. A man was dragging the driver of the semi through the window.

A thick circle had formed on the left side of the road. Desperate, Reece pushed through. At some point, the people noticed his approach, and a narrow path opened in front of him. Walking on marshmallows, he drifted forward. There, in the road, beneath the trailer, lay the body of a young girl. She had been crushed. Women wept and cried, but no one was helping. Reece floated to the girl's body. He knew CPR. She was maybe twelve and dressed in a long maroon dress. Blood surrounded her head and shoulders. *Open airway and give two rescue breaths.*

Reece knelt in the blood. Her eyes were half closed. Her mouth seemed full. He checked her carotids. Nothing. He opened her mouth, and it was crowded with blood and lung tissue. He tried to breathe for her, but the lungs and airway had been crushed. He remembered that next came the chest compressions. It was futile, wasn't it? He compressed twenty times and checked the pulse. Nothing. He forced open the mouth again and gagged. There was nothing he could do.

Reece stood. A large circle had formed around him. He could not remember which way to go, so he just began to walk. The crowd parted for him like magic, as if he were the girl's spirit walking its way to heaven. The faces he saw showed shock and surprise. He looked to the left for Dr. Guthrie's house. He kept walking, glancing to the left. He looked back and saw the end of the truck, realizing he was going in the right direction. He spotted the house, an American ranch-style. There was no doorbell. He could see light coming through the curtains. He knocked.

A man in a short-sleeved shirt answered. He looked at Reece. Blood circled Reece's lips, smeared his hands. His knees were stained dark red as well. "Great God Almighty!" said Dr. Guthrie. "Who are you?"

THIRTY

The Snake fired a single shot into the air. He just wanted to have fun, and that was all. Why must he always be rejected? His father had beaten him until he was sixteen, when he had run away from home. He hoisted the katikala and took a slug. Svana and Eydis had stalled at the gate.

"Great God," said Gudmunder.

Afewerki had predicted the dinner would be a failure. "What shall I tell him?

"Eydis and Svana, please come back," said Gudmunder.

"He will shoot us all," said Svana.

Gebremariam was hiding in the cook house with his rifle. He would come if called, but would rather not. Abebe had left. A small crowd was gathering at the hole in the fence, peering inside.

"Come back, and we will drink. You can drink as much as you like. I think the Snake will be a happy drunk. Let's find out," said Gudmunder.

"Hmm. What do you think, Eydis?" Svana liked the idea of getting drunk. It had been a trying day.

"Well, let's go and buy a bottle of katikala or have Afewerki go. There is not enough to go around. He will drink it all."

"Okay, but he must apologize to Eydis for the behavior of his guards," said Svana. She and Eydis came back to the fire.

Afewerki translated.

A spread of relief crossed the Snake's face. This would be a night to remember. "Yes, I am very sorry. They are only young men. They have only been taught to fight, that is all."

Eydis nodded. Svana nodded. "Afewerki, can you fetch another bottle of katikala for us?"

"Ishi," said Afewerki, sure that it was an unwise thing to do.

"No, we should go," said Svana. "We know the way."

"Thank you, ladies," said Gudmunder. He threw two more heavy sticks onto the fire.

"Cheers!" said Gudmunder.

"Tchirz!" said the Snake.

Afewerki sipped from his IV bottle of water. He supposed the next thing would be to celebrate the Snake's birthday.

"I was very glad to hear about your wife," said the Snake.

"Oh, yes," said Gudmunder. "She was beautiful, like the nurses." He paused. "But she was always nagging, no? Do you know what I mean?"

Afewerki laughed.

"Of course, my brother. My sisters know only how to nag. My mother, she nagged my father. That is why he was so mean to his children, of course. We are the same age, no?"

"I am forty," said Gudmunder.

"Yes, you are older. I am thirty-five." The Snake drained his third beer. He reached down to fumble for his glass. He started to open the loosely corked katikala, but Gudmunder produced the vodka, one stiff glass remaining.

"So, you used to be in the military, I hear," said Gudmunder.

"Yes, I am fighting for many years in the north. I kill-ed many men." His gold tooth seemed bronze in the light of the fire.

"I have never killed a man. I am a doctor, so I help them."

"You must kill a man, no? To be a man." The Snake drained his vodka and coughed.

"Is this true in Ethiopia?"

"Yes, of course it is true. There are many bad men who must be kill-ed. It is our duty."

Afewerki was counting shooting stars as he translated.

"So, do you sleep with the nurses?" asked the Snake.

Gudmunder thought. "I want to, but it's best that I do not. I do not want to be ruled by the pussy."

The Snake roared. He laughed and started choking. Gudmunder thought he was in distress and stood. The Snake slowly recovered, his eyes wet with tears. "You are a good person!" he said.

THIRTY-ONE

Reece put out his hand and realized it was red with blood. "I'm Reece Myers. I'm in Gwar with the Icelanders."

"What's happened?" asked Dr. Guthrie, Norbert to his wife and friends. He was the Baptist Mission's veterinarian.

Reece explained the accident on the road, the dead girl.

"I'll have to go and see. That's sad. A little girl?" He wondered if he knew her, if she was the daughter of the many herdsmen he knew. He would pay for the burial if so. "Come on in. You need to go to the bathroom and clean up."

"Thanks," said Reece. Inside, he felt like he was back in the States. The kitchen held a narrow table. The living room had a vaulted ceiling. Bookshelves lined the walls. There was a fireplace and mantle. A woman emerged from the hallway leading to three bedrooms.

"Livvie, this is, uh, Rice. He's up at Gwar doing work." The shooting there came to mind, and this guy Reece looked very much like Bobby, who had been shot in the head.

Livvie was stunned at his appearance, and Dr. Guthrie explained the accident on the road. "Oh, my goodness. I've always been afraid that would happen with those big trucks." She guided Reece to the bathroom.

Reece looked at himself in the mirror. The O of blood around his mouth, he could taste it. He held up his hands, dark with the dried blood of a dead girl he did not know. Perhaps if he'd been ten minutes sooner, the girl could somehow be alive. He looked around the bathroom and marveled at the toothbrushes, the soap, the towels, the shower curtain, and especially the commode. It had been nearly a month since he'd used a commode.

Free of blood, except for the stains on his knees, Reece came into the living room. The walls were paneled. There was a warm, cozy feeling.

"Have a seat," said Guthrie. He fell into an orange recliner.

Reece sat on the edge of the couch. Anything could happen.

"You look awfully familiar," said Norbert. "Where you from?"

"Alabama, Birmingham."

"No kidding." Bobby had been from Alabama. "You're not a nurse, are you?"

"No, a public health student. I'm doing a health survey in Gwar. I'm camping out with the Icelanders. I really had no idea they would be there. So, you know them, I'm hoping."

"What school?"

"Yale."

Guthrie whistled. "Yankee school. How'd you wind up there?"

"I just applied."

"Several years ago, 1985 to be exact, we worked with another Icelandic team in Gwar. They were like our first responders. We didn't pay them, but we supplied them with medicine and supplies. They got into some trouble, though. We wound up setting up a feeding station and clinic there. You remind me of one of the nurses, Bobby

Hartwig."

Reece knew of some Hartwigs back in Birmingham. "So why did the Icelanders come back? They're great people."

"You know, I'm not sure. They just showed up and asked for our help. I'd worked with Icelanders before and thought it was a good idea to see how Gwar was doing after we shut down the operation there."

"Well, they're why I'm here to see you," said Reece.

"How so? You had dinner?"

"I'm good. I'm still full. So, Gudmunder, Dr. Thorsonn, has asked me to come and see you. He's been arrested."

"Oh Lord. It has to be that damn Snake character. Pardon my language," said Guthrie.

Livvie came in with a tray of homemade crackers with deli cheese slices. "You men need some nourishment." She set the tray on the coffee table between them.

Reece couldn't resist. "Yep, the Snake."

"Why did they arrest him? Is he in jail?"

"They say he stole the tabot from the church in Alem Ketema, AK. He's not in jail, but is under house arrest. He can't leave the compound. There was a bunch of nonsense about him possibly being gay and they didn't want him in the jail. Anyway..."

"Stole the tabot? That's unbelievable. Why would he want to do that under any circumstance?" asked Guthrie. He nibbled a cracker with cheese. "And homosexual?"

Reece ate a whole cracker. It was crisp. "I know, right? He's not in jail, but they want to take him to Alem Ketema to face trial. He sent me here to see if there was anything you could do to stop the process."

"Why in the devil do they think he stole a tabot?"

Reece noticed the ancient console television. He wondered if it worked. "Well, he's always talking about the Ark of the Covenant and visiting the church in Gwar. Someone in AK says they saw him go inside the church. He says he visited the church, but only to leave an offering."

"Where were you when this happened? Why was he in AK?"

"We were there for a mini-vacation of sorts. Things had gotten heated with the Snake." Reece felt thoroughly at home. "I was in the bar at the hotel with Eydis and Svana. Gudmunder went for a walk and visited the church."

"Yeah, I've met the nurses. Are they behaving? The other Icelandic nurses we worked with were a handful, a little on the wild side."

"Svana gets in trouble, drinking. Eydis is very, uh, headstrong. But they're good people."

The doorbell rang. It was the driver who ran over the girl. He had been beaten and needed help.

THIRTY-TWO

Svana and Eydis returned with two bottles of katikala. They were determined to get the Snake snockered. He was already well on his way.

Gebremariam hung back, afraid of the Snake but wanting to protect the team. He wandered over and stoked the fire, bringing it full blaze.

With the vodka gone, a bottle of katikala made the rounds, with Afewerki abstaining. Gudmunder was peaking at his alcohol limit, but he drank on. He began to tell the story of Gaukur Trandilsson and the Lost Saga and its bearing on the Ark of the Covenant.

"Yes," said the Snake, "the Ark has been brought to Ethiopia by Menelik. He is the great son of Solomon. Sometimes it has to be mov-ed. Many want to steal it."

Gudmunder nodded. "Gaukur was the first European to visit Africa," said Gudmunder. "He came alone around 1,000 AD. He is said to have visited the Emperor Jan Seyum, bringing a gift of gold with him to Lalibela."

"Should you be talking about the Ark, since you have been accused of stealing the tabot?" asked Eydis. She sat with elbows on knees until she realized that the Snake was looking down her scrub top.

"I hadn't thought," said Gudmunder. "But what is done is done."

"What does that mean?" asked Svana.

Afewerki kept silent.

Gudmunder poured himself a drink and passed the bottle. "Gaukur was allowed to see the Ark."

The Snake drank. "This story is new, no? A man with red hair like you and the white skin was allowed to visit the Ark? It sounds like a lie. He would be kill-ed by its power."

"Maybe he was a blond, like Eydis. I do not know the color of his hair. It is not a lie. It has been written as Icelandic history." Gudmunder felt his face getting red. The small fire chewed holes in the descending shadows.

Svana and Eydis murmured with one another, taking small sips of liquor.

Afewerki spoke. "Yes, it is a strange story. No one is allowed to see or touch the Ark except the priest. This person you speak of will die."

"Ah!" said Gudmunder. "Gaukur was special. He was a son of God. The Bible speaks of this. The angels came down and took wives. Their children were giants."

"Are you sure you're not talking about aliens, Gudmunder?" asked Svana.

"What is alien?" asked Afewerki.

"Beings from other planets, from other worlds, other universes," said Gudmunder.

Afewerki chuckled and relayed the information to the Snake.

"Maybe the doctor is crazy," said the Snake.

"You are crazy," said Afewerki.

Gudmunder was a bit woozy. "Who is crazy? How does he know there is not life on other planets?" He started to stand. He had only said sons of God because he knew the Snake, and now obviously Afewerki, would not otherwise understand.

"The Bible does not speak of such things, this alien,"

said Afewerki.

"Yes it does," said Gudmunder. "It just uses a different language."

Eydis sighed. "I did not know you have been reading the Bible."

"So, everyone!" said the Snake. "This talk is old. Is there some music? To drink and have music is good, no?"

Svana thought the Snake was sounding more rational than Gudmunder. Maybe he would be cleared of the charge by reason of insanity. "I'll turn on the radio."

Gudmunder threw sticks onto the fire. He wished he were a son of God, then he could travel to other dimensions, other worlds. Perhaps he could meet Gaukur there and travel with him to find the Ark. He poured more katikala into green cups as the radio played, accordion music fading in and out.

THIRTY-THREE

The driver's face was bloody. He could not stand straight, having been kicked in the ribs. Behind him was an angry mob, shouting that he should be killed. One man held a long knife and approached the steps. The girl was his niece, he said.

Norbert brought the man inside and stepped out. He spoke Amharic forcefully and asked the crowd of twenty or so to remain calm. He would call the authorities, and they were welcome to call them as well. "God is watching," he said.

"God is watching, but the little one has died," said the uncle.

Guthrie was at a loss for words. "You can wait here if you like. This man may need to go to the hospital before he can be arrested." He decided he should go to the scene of the accident. Perhaps they would follow. He called back inside to Livvie and said that he would return shortly to lock the doors.

In the living room, Livvie didn't have any paper towels. She found a clean rag, wet it, and washed the man's face. He wore black pants and a white, bloodstained shirt, reeking of body odor. He said his name was Mesfin and that he was from Addis, leaning over to breathe. Livvy raised his shirt. Reece looked and could tell that ribs had been broken.

"How did it happen?" she said.

He struggled to talk in broken English. "I do not know. I am driving so slowly. She is wearing the long dress. Perhaps she is caught into the wheel."

"Would you like some water?"

The man asked for liquor of any kind, but water would be fine otherwise.

She went to the kitchen.

Reece sat. The man's swollen right eye was shut. He was thin and perhaps twenty-five. The man cried. His life was ruined, he said in Amharic.

Reece didn't know what to do, so just sat there and watched tears run down his face. He thought about the dead girl, about how she had possibly exsanguinated her entire blood volume. He imagined her mother was standing there now, wailing, and he was right. It wouldn't surprise him if the girl had no father, and he was right again.

Dr. Guthrie returned. He had seen the corpse of the little girl, and she was indeed dead. He had given the mother of the girl a hundred birr as a gift of condolence, and she had dropped to her knees. "Tough scene out there," he said. He picked up the phone and dialed 991 for the police. "Hey, Livvie. Just in case, would you get the pistol?"

She gave Mesfin a glass of water and went to the bedroom.

THIRTY-FOUR

Afewerki and Gebremariam had to walk and half carry the Snake to his tin-roofed house. The Snake was very happy and sick at the same time. Inside was very dark. They laid him on an old bed slung with leather straps to support a homemade mattress. Afewerki noticed several blankets, relics of the famine years before. The Mennonites of Canada had sent them over. The room was very tidy.

"What a hell," said Afewerki.

Gebremariam just nodded, not understanding the English.

The next morning, Saturday, market day, everyone slept in. The late rains, the meher, which normally fell between June and September, had been late in arriving, just a shower here and there. Without thunder or lightning, the first downpour since April flooded the village. The water barrel connected to the tin roof of the cook house boiled over with water.

The tents began to flood, and one by one, Svana, Eydis, and Gudmunder fled to the cook house. Abebe was not there, being Saturday. They shivered in the sudden cold.

"Damn," said Svana. "My sleeping bag is soaked." Her head ached.

"Let's build a fire," said Gudmunder. His head ached as well.

"Yes, go ahead, doctor. Build us a fire. Maybe you can run and get the chairs?" She laughed. The rain was like a curtain of water, the wind blowing it into the cook house door.

"We'll squat like everyone else," said Gudmunder. He needed to pee. Like Svana and Eydis, he was barefoot, except in soggy socks that were soaking up the dirt floor. He knelt beside the fire ring and held his hand over it, feeling for the heat of a coal. Nothing. He poked his finger into the ash. It was warm, just there. He brushed the ash back and blew; a few black slivers of charcoal glowed orange. He raided Abebe's hoard of twigs and corn shucks and soon had a small fire going. He laid more sticks and then a couple of larger ones. Smoke filled the cook house, and everyone coughed and moved to get away from it. "Come down like me," said Gudmunder.

They squatted as best they could below the collecting haze.

"I wonder how Reece is doing," said Eydis. "I miss him."

"He is very sweet, no?" asked Svana. "He will stick his tongue down your throat if you will let him."

"Shush," said Eydis. "You will stick your tongue down that farmer's throat, Mulu."

"I already did," said Svana. She moved closer to the fire. It was getting warm.

"I need the 'hair of the dog,' as the English say," said Gudmunder.

"What do you mean by hair of the dog?" asked Eydis.

"He wants to cure his hangover with alcohol," said Svana. "Sounds like a good idea, but we have no more beer or katikala."

"I have some mouthwash," said Eydis.

No one laughed.

The fire reached a size that was perhaps too large for

the cook house. The poles nearest the fire pit were steaming. The smoke was getting hot.

"What shall we eat?" asked Gudmunder. "Svana, check the enjera basket."

"There are many breads, but no wot. I wanted to eat at market." Svana felt like eating goman, greens with enjera. The rain thundered on the tin roof, flooding the compound. They had all given in to sitting on the dirt floor and stared at one another.

"Why again are we here?" asked Svana.

"Because we thirst for adventure," said Gudmunder. He had organized the trip and recruited Svana and Eydis. He knew that Icelanders had been in Gwar before, during the famine a few years back. It was enough to secure six-month visas and establish a relationship with the Baptists, enabling them to supply vaccines, supplies, and medicine. Dr. Guthrie had been key in obtaining the permission of the Snake, who welcomed foreigners for their money. The Snake had known that two of them were women, and that had also played a key role.

"But you are under arrest, no?" asked Eydis. "Is that part of the adventure?"

Gudmunder thought. "Yes, I think so." He added more fuel to the fire. The cook house was getting cozy.

THIRTY-FIVE

The police never arrived, and Mesfin snuck out of the Guthrie's house around three in the morning. The pale green moon lit his way. He climbed into the rig, still in the middle of the road. The keys were gone. He sank, but then remembered his spare. Someone was coming down the road. He opened the door, swung out, and reached behind. There was a magnetic key holder there. He grabbed it. The person coming down the road had a shotgun.

He didn't bother to close the door and struggled to get the key from the box, which seemed to be rusted. He realized the cab light was on and shut the door. He locked it. He turned the key to on. The gunman stood in front of the rig, pointing the gun at the window. He turned the key and held it for ten seconds, but nothing. The gunman was banging on the side with his fist. He turned the key again, and it cranked. There was a gunshot, deafening.

Mesfin flinched and threw it into low and jolted away. Right away, he realized that the flatbed had been disconnected from the rig. "Tebeda!" but he kept going, fearing for his life.

The next morning, Dr. Guthrie figured out what had happened. He saw the flatbed in the road and laughed at the ingenuity of the people. Someone would have to come and get it.

"Well, Reece, you arrived in high fashion," said Guthrie. They drank hot coffee. Livvie was cooking biscuits and frying thick rounds of beef salami.

"I apologize, sir," said Reece. "It just happened."

"I can't get over how much you look like Bobby Hartwig, not to be morbid at such a time. Where did you go to church back in Birmingham? I've been to all of them, doing the missionary circuit."

"I didn't really go to church. When I visited my grandparents, I would go with them sometimes. Palmerdale Baptist."

"Oh yeah, Palmerdale. Been there. Small brick church with a handicap ramp up the side."

"Yep," said Reece.

"Not to worry. Good people are good people." Guthrie's chest strained against his button-up shirt.

"What about Dr. Thorsonn? Can you do anything?" He was thinking about Eydis, her rosy cheeks as if she was always blushing.

"Gosh, I don't know. Tesfaw over at the compound has some legal experience. He would be the first person I ask. It's sad, but sometimes the quickest way to do business is to pay the right person. I'd suggest that you take that route in AK. A hundred birr should do it. If that doesn't work, then send word back to me and I'll see what I can do."

Reece felt like he had wasted a trip. "A bribe, really?"

"Yes. Works like a charm."

Reece drank his coffee. "Would US dollars work?"

"Hmm, not in the countryside. You'll need birr, preferably five twenties. In fact, I can loan it to you."

"That might be best. I don't have five twenties. Gudmunder might, but not sure." He thought about the envelope of ganja. "Sure, I'll just trade you the birr in dollars if that's okay."

"We'll walk over to the compound after breakfast." He smelled smoke. "Livvie?"

THIRTY-SIX

The inside poles of the cook house were on fire, but no one noticed. The thin fire licked gently the grain, spreading up toward the pole rafters.

"It's very hot in here," said Gudmunder. He was tired of sitting and stood, being enveloped in a scorch of heat and smoke. He coughed and stepped through the doorway into the pouring rain. "Oh shit. Fire!"

Svana crawled out on her hands and knees, followed by Eydis. Water was everywhere, but there was no bucket. Gudmunder ran back inside. There was a pot. He dipped water from the rain barrel and ran back inside, throwing the water onto the wall. Back and forth he went as the nurses stood beneath the roof overhang, ready to run. He was breathless, but his senses on full alert as he doused the wall. He realized the fire on the ground needed to be put out as well. He poured water on it, and a great cloud of steam enveloped him, burning his face and hands. He dropped the pot and ran outside. Svana ran inside, grabbed the pot, and continued splashing water until there was only smoke and no flames.

"Jesus Christ," said Eydis. "Are you okay?"

Like magic, the rain abated into a light drizzle. Gudmunder's face and hands were red, mildly burned. "I'm okay."

Smoke continued to pour through the door, cracks in the wall, and the space between the walls and the roof. Svana slowed but continued to throw water on the wall and fire. The enjera in the basket was ruined, and Abebe would be furious, no doubt.

Gebremariam walked through the gap in the fence. He had gone to purchase more sugar. Behind him came Afewerki, wearing a jacket with the collar turned up. Both surveyed the bedraggled Icelanders.

"Mendeno?" asked Afewerki. He smelled fire and looked inside the cook house. "Oh my goodness."

"We have nearly burned the cook house," said Gudmunder. He looked like a lobster with his first-degree burns.

Gebremariam was alarmed and worried they would be angry with him for leaving. Afewerki told him what had happened.

"Ishi," he said, and inspired deeply, expressing regret.

"Chicorilla," said Gudmunder. He was just glad that everyone was okay.

"I was coming to see if you would have breakfast. My mother has invited you," said Afewerki. He said mother as muzzer.

That sounded good to everyone.

THIRTY-SEVEN

The salami smoking, Livvie pulled the skillet from the stove. She pushed out the rounds onto a plate, a little crisp but not burned.

Reece cut his salami with a fork, and he had to keep from moaning when he took it with a bite of biscuit. "Damn. I mean, wow, this is good."

"Well, thank you," said Livvie. "More coffee. Plenty to go around."

"Sure thing," said Reece. The coffee was the best he'd ever had, except for the coffee in Gwar. But this was black coffee. He never thought he would like black coffee.

"I may have some good news for you. The Helimission copter is in Addis and may be headed to Gwar with a stop in Alem Ketema. You met Andreas?"

"Yeah, I've met him. That would be great."

"I think he's sweet on Svana, the nurse," said Guthrie. "He wanted to know if she had a boyfriend, and I told him I didn't know. Anyway, that's good luck for you. He would probably not go there otherwise, unless he had a delivery."

"Yeah, sure, that's good, I guess."

"You'll need to ride over and hang out at Helimission 'headquarters' and get a ride to the airport with him."

"Where is headquarters?"

"It's actually a small hotel in the Mercato, the big market. Next to a coffin factory. He likes to live slim and on the edge. I've got the name, somewhere. Oh yeah, it's called the Crocodile. No electricity, just a candle. Any taxi driver worth his salt will know where it is."

Reece sensed a small adventure in the making. "Okay, sounds good." He ate a third biscuit layered with salami and sipped his coffee. "Man, this is good eats. Just like home."

"Well, if you don't go home now and then, you're likely to lose your mind."

Reece nodded. It was true.

Inkolal was breakfast. Scrambled eggs with chopped peppers, mild and spicy, onion, and lots of butter served with warm enjera. Drying quickly in the high altitude, still wearing their wet clothes, the Icelanders oohed and aahed over Afewerki's mother's breakfast. They sat in Afewerki's little square house, crowded around a tiny table that held an ancient metal platter. The only problem was that there was nothing to drink except birzz, honey water, which was very sweet.

"Please tell your mother many thanks," said Gudmunder. Eydis and Svana seconded. The rain had dissipated, and it looked like market day would be in full swing, although muddy. Vendors often walked twenty kilometers to sell their wares. Afewerki's wet white hen poked her head inside and clucked.

"Shall we go to market like this?" asked Eydis. Her pants were muddy, and her shirt smeared. She imagined she looked a wreck.

"You must change the clothes," said Afewerki. "The people will murmur against you."

"Really?" asked Svana.

"We do look a mess," said Gudmunder. He took another bite of eggs and enjera. There was plenty left over for Afewerki's two younger brothers. They always ate last.

"I wonder how the Snake is feeling this morning," said Svana.

"Let's not talk of him," said Afewerki. "I am not inside his house before and do not wish to go again."

"But he will become our friend," said Gudmunder. "We must try to work with him."

Afewerki frowned. He glanced at Eydis, who was stretching her arms over her head.

"Let's get cleaned up," said Eydis. "We need to hang our bags up to dry as well. That was the hardest rain we have had."

"Yes, the long rains are coming. It will rain much more," said Afewerki. He wanted to suggest that Eydis could sleep in his house. She could have his bed, and he would sleep on the floor.

"Perhaps," said Gudmunder, "we should begin sleeping in the supply house. It's crowded but dry."

"The man Bobby Hartwig was kill-ed inside. We believe his ghost is there," said Afewerki.

"Ooh ghosts," said Svana. "Let's do it." She rubbed her hands together.

"This is a bad idea," said Afewerki.

"I disagree," said Gudmunder. "We'll be flooded every day otherwise. I think we will be safe."

"I think Gudmunder is right," said Eydis. "I'm ready."

The Icelanders walked back to the compound. Abebe was there. Everyone in the whole village already knew about the fire.

"Tsk, tsk, tsk," she said with arms folded.

"Oh, we are so sorry, Abebe," said Svana.

Abebe nodded and began to salvage what she could from the enjera basket.

They each dragged out their wet belongings and hung them on the fence. The sky was still cloudy, but the sun would be intense that day.

"Ugh, such a mess," said Eydis. The area around the tents was muddy.

"My book is saved," said Gudmunder. It had been in his backpack.

"I'm just going to change out here," said Svana. "The tent is too wet." Without further ado, she dropped her pants and pulled off her shirt, standing there in her underwear.

Gudmunder chuckled and got an eyeful.

"Me too," said Svana. She stripped down to her underwear as well, bikini briefs and a sports bra.

Gebremariam watched, amazed. Wait until he told Afewerki. Abebe did not approve, even though she often cooked topless. She mumbled to Gebremariam, saying that the nurses would be raped if they weren't careful.

THIRTY-NINE

Reece stopped in at the Mission and spoke again to Tesfaw. He supposed he was going to try to bribe the right person in AK, as suggested by Dr. Guthrie, but first, he had to find Andreas in the Mercato. The day started off bright, but a light rain moved in.

As instructed by Tesfaw, he would walk east, looking for Egypt Street. There was a bus station there, Sarbet, and he could catch a taxi or mini-bus to the Mercato. The guard opened the gate for Reece. Reece drifted onto the dirt road, joining others with dirty pieces of plastic over their heads. A few had umbrellas. He had been walking for five minutes and saw one of the dark baby-blue mini-buses, known as blue donkeys. He trotted ahead. The side door was open. Inside were four people. One lady was brightly dressed in gold and yellow. There was a case of Coke bottles in her lap.

"Mercato?" asked Reece. He smelled the humanity.

"Ishi." The driver motioned for him to take the front seat beside him.

Reece held his backpack in his lap. The driver was waiting on something. A boy in tattered pants and a dirty ballcap hopped in and shut the door. The mini-bus, like a large mini-van, careened down the mud-sheened street. The radio played Amharic music. A zebra-striped cloth covered the dashboard. The mini-bus soon turned onto Egypt, Reece assumed, passed a bus station, hit a roundabout, and continued straight. He saw little shops and houses made of plastic sheeting and scraps. Horns blew aplenty. They drove past a long, high wall.

The street changed to Roosevelt, and soon they were circling in the chaos of Mexico Square, a massive roundabout. With horns blaring, the driver pulled over to the sidewalk. The young boy opened the door, jumped out, and took the case of bottles from the woman. She emerged and took her bottles, and they were off again.

Just as they crossed Burundi Street, the mini-bus slowed and shoved its way into a morass of vehicles. It was another bus station. Everyone piled out. Reece looked at the driver. "Mercato?"

"No, no. Mercato..." The driver pointed with his finger. "Taxi, Mercato."

"Oh, huh. Sentino?"

"Sost birr," said the driver.

Reece peeled off three birr. He had a fifty-cent piece and gave that as a tip.

"Amenseganalo."

The boy opened Reece's door for him and held out his hand. Reece fished out ten cents from his pocket, and the boy frowned. The bus station was chaotic, noisy, and reeked of diesel. Taxis and mini-buses clogged the street. He approached a small Lada taxi. A woman stepped on his foot and kept moving.

"Mi scusi, Mercato?"

The driver nodded and reached and pushed open the squeaky door. On the windows were Ethiopian flag stickers. A photo of Haile Selassie was fixed on the dashboard. The seat sagged. It felt like he was sitting on wires. He thought about the marijuana in his bag. The driver was chewing something.

The driver drove carefully and slowly. There was no meter as usual. Reece watched the people cutting through traffic to cross the street. He saw a group of children in a vacant paved area. One boy, who had no legs, was pushing himself on a homemade skateboard of sorts. Within five minutes, the taxi stopped. Reece saw a mosque.

"Mercato?"

"Ow, Mercato."

Reece thought. "Crocodile Hotel?"

The driver looked surprised. "No, no. No go Crocodile." He made motions with his hands. Reece did not know what he was trying to say.

"Sentino? How much?"

"Hulet birr."

Reece gave him two birr and got out. He had to find someone who would take him to the Crocodile. The rain started again.

FORTY

Roosters crowed, purple juwa birds tussled in the trees, and the black spot on the sun seemed to blink. In the flat area that was once the feeding/clinic compound, dozens of donkeys and brightly dressed mules waited for their owners. Teenage boys were paid to watch over them, which they did with an iron fist and whips. A few cows stood still, each hobbled with a leg tied to its body.

Eydis and Svana passed down and around to the village center, where the market took place. Afewerki had said he would go with them, but they decided not to wait. They passed two men with carbine rifles walking uphill and a woman carrying chickens upside down by their feet. Gudmunder had stayed behind, unsure if he was still under arrest. The Snake was busy collecting one birr from every vendor in cash or in goods. It was a small amount to pay. He would net fifty birr, more than a farmer could make in a month, plus limes, chickens, sugar cane, and other goodies.

"You know the tejj bet is open today?" said Svana.

"Svana, can we not think about alcohol?"

"But it is safer to go in the daytime."

"True," said Eydis. "But still."

They wandered to the fringe of the crowded, muddy market. A woman was selling okra.

"Oh, what is that?" asked Svana.

"Is it an insect?"

"Bamiya." The wrinkled woman held up a pod.

"Maybe not," said Svana. "Let's buy some potatoes for

Abebe to cook." They would have to search to find them.

Afewerki ran from the compound to the market to find Eydis and Svana. Where were they? He searched the crowd for the blonde hair of Eydis. She was wearing a brown long-sleeve sweater with jeans that were very tight. He waded through the masses selling peas, ginger, and teff. He asked a friend if he'd seen the Icelanders. Of course, but they were gone now.

He stumbled through the tire sandals and past the hand-forged plow points. "Oh, my goodness," he said. He saw them buying potatoes.

He worked his way up to Eydis. "Eydis!"

Eydis turned. "Hey. What is wrong?"

"They have taken Dr. Thorsonn to Alem Ketema. Two with rifles. The Snake has allowed this thing. He only wants to drink with you and not Gudmunder. He is evil."

With their potatoes, they worked to extricate themselves from the tight knot of people, trying to make a path. It took a few minutes, but they reached a clearing near Afewerki's parents' compound.

"They may execute him if he is guilty," said Afewerki.

"What? That is crazy?" asked Svana.

"It is true, or they may shoot in the butt, to teach a lesson."

"Where are they now?" asked Svana.

"I do not know. They have gone down. Perhaps there is a jeep. We must see."

"Lead the way." Svana carried the potatoes, gathered in the tail of her scrub top.

They walked downhill, slipping in the mud. Svana lost a potato. "Shit." They saw a jeep, stuck in some mud, and slowed.

"He is here," said Afewerki. He ran forward, careful not to get sprayed with mud. Gudmunder sat in the jeep with his two captors. Three mud-covered men were trying to push the jeep free. "Wait!"

Svana ran with the potatoes held to her belly with one hand. She slid and slipped and grabbed the ladder on the back of the jeep. Fuck the potatoes, and she let them fall into the black mud.

The jeep slid back into the mire. Afewerki approached the passenger side. The door opened, and he spoke in low tones to the man with a rifle. He wore no uniform, but was from the police in Alem Ketema. The other man was just helping out. Gudmunder sat in the back, silent as they talked.

"They must take him to the jail in Alem Ketema. The kebele court has ordered it, and the Snake has approved it." Afewerki said this with an I-told-you-so inflection.

"I will go with him, then," said Svana.

"No," said Eydis.

"Yes," said Svana.

"It will be okay," said Afewerki.

"What does that mean?" asked Svana.

"If you must go..."

Gudmunder spoke up. "No, Svana, you stay here with Eydis. Maybe Afewerki can come with me."

"Then there will be no one to translate," said Svana. "I will come. Tell them to wait. No, I am ready just as I am. I have money and am warmly dressed. Eydis, you will stay here with Afewerki."

Eydis thought about it. "Okay. If Gudmunder approves."

Gudmunder said, "Okay, fine. What a mess."

Svana opened the passenger door and climbed in back with him. "Together as one!"

FORTY-ONE

Reece spotted a blue-and-white truck taxi. It had two bench seats in the truck bed with a white overcab and a door in the back. There was one woman inside. Reece walked to the driver's side. "Hotel Crocodile?"

The driver looked at him for a moment. "Azo?"

Reece stared at him. "Azo?"

"Azo, crocodile," said the driver.

"Yes, Azo Hotel," said Reece.

"No, Crocodile Hotel," said the driver.

"Okay," said Reece. He walked to the back. A teenager was barking up riders. Reece stepped in, stooped over, and sat on the bench facing the woman. It was very hot and humid, and he began to sweat. He put his bag between his legs. The woman smiled and then looked at her feet.

It took fifteen minutes, but the taxi filled, five people facing five people. The teenager stood on the bumper, holding onto the ladder to the roof. A woman sitting by the door was reaching when the door slammed. It caught her finger, and she let out a low moan. Everyone looked, and her finger was smashed, bleeding heavily. The taxi entered the road and began a very bumpy ride. No one spoke to the woman, perhaps worried that her bad luck would rub off on them. She began to weep.

Across from Reece sat a middle-aged man in a too-small suit coat. Beside him was a teenage boy wearing plain black pants and a ripped tie-dye shirt. Bouncing, Reece tried to keep from landing in his neighbor's lap. Out of nowhere, the man across from him half stood and punched the boy in the face. Blood streamed from his nose. The boy cried out and cringed. The man reached for his wallet, seeing if it was still there. The boy wailed. The man continued to curse him.

Next to Reece was a young woman with an automatic mini-umbrella. The taxi lurched and sprawled across holes that could swallow a man. Reece kept leaning into her and the young man to his right. He worried that someone would punch him in the face. Of a sudden, on hitting a pothole, the woman pressed the umbrella button. Instead of opening, the whole thing fired like a rocket, hitting the pugilist in the forehead across from her. For a brief moment, there was silence. Someone laughed, and soon everyone, including Reece, was laughing.

The taxi stopped and two got out. Soon, Reece was the only one left. He'd paid three birr in advance. He was getting hungry and eager to get out of the cramped space, having to stoop over even while sitting. The taxi stopped, and the door opened. He watched his fingers and jumped out. He looked around at the signs in Amharic. The taxi pulled away, leaving him standing amid a busy crowd of thin people.

FORTY-TWO

The journey from Gwar had taken two and a half hours with one flat tire. The jeep pulled up near the administrative compound, which had mud-and-pole walls with a tin roof. A small crowd gathered, and news spread like wildfire that the ferenj who stole the tabot was in town. One threw a rock.

Gudmunder's guards took him inside. There was no one there, so they led him into the jail, which had no lock on the door. Inside the muddy courtyard, sitting on rough stones, were two seedy characters, frequent inmates. Eydis had followed him inside.

"I will stay with you," said Eydis.

"No, you must take the hotel," said Gudmunder.

"Be quiet. I will stay."

The guard in uniform took Svana by the arm. She had to leave.

Svana resisted and pulled away. "Go to hell."

The guard was perplexed. What should he do? He had the authority to shoot her if need be. In the leg, then the butt, and then the head. He gripped her wrist with the intent to hurt her.

Svana reached back and struck the guard as hard as she could in the face. She caught him in the jaw, and he nearly passed out from the impact. He let go, recovered, and then grabbed Eydis and threw her to the ground, putting his knee on her back. Gudmunder grabbed him in a choke-hold from behind. The other two prisoners sat dumbfounded.

The guard let go of Eydis, being choked by Gudmunder, who also suddenly let go, afraid that he would kill him.

The guard looked around for his rifle. He had left it in the open area, the office. This was bad. The doctor from Iceland would pay severely for his crime. He berated the doctor and then closed the door, leaving Svana inside as well. He was shaken. These were white devils. Where was the administrator? Probably drinking or fucking, or most likely both.

FORTY-THREE

Reece didn't know if he should be looking for a hotel named Azo or Crocodile. He turned in a circle three times before he saw a wooden carving of a crocodile. The flies were thick. He swatted.

He walked to the hotel, a collection of a dozen rooms in an L-shape. He smelled food cooking and entered the office, which was also a bar. A young girl was standing in a chair adjusting a black-and-white TV. There was a sign with prices, but he couldn't read it.

"Tenesteling," he said to the young woman behind a kind of wrap-around counter.

She had a bright smile. She explained they had a room, and it was six birr per night.

Reece sort of understood and gave her a ten-birr note. She gave him change and led him to the room, number twelve.

"Andreas? Helimission?" asked Reece.

The woman's smile flattened. "Andreas?"

"Ow, Andreas."

"Okay." She walked and pointed at number six, a dark green door. She'd about had enough of Andreas. He was shorter than she was and would not sleep with her.

First, Reece put his bag in his room. He had a key to the padlock on the door. He walked to number six and knocked. Nothing. He knocked again. There was a window with a screen. The door opened.

"Andreas!"

"Hello, is it Rice?"

"Yeah, Reece. Dr. Guthrie sent me."

"Nice to see you. You need a ride up country, no?"

"Yeah, how did you know?"

"Oh, I know," said Andreas.

"I'll buy you dinner and drinks," said Reece.

"Yeah, no problem. I'm going to Alem Ketema, Gwar, and then into Wollo tomorrow."

"Sounds good. What time is it?"

"It is 3:20." Andreas smoothed back his short black hair. "Let us rest until six." He paused. "Maybe you need a haircut and shave?"

"What?" asked Reece.

"Scissors and razor. I know a good place. You will feel nice. The ladies will like it."

"Okay. Now?"

"Sure. Meet me in front of the office."

Reece stepped back into his room. It had been a couple of months since he'd had a haircut and three days since he'd shaved. He tested the bed. The mattress was very thick, unusual. Dried candle wax flowed down the headboard. The walls were a bright green. He'd heard that the Mercato was dicey and worried about having his passport or wallet stolen.

Andreas wore his shades, making him look exotic. "Yesterday was fasting. I had soup. Something more filling today."

"Sure," said Reece. He was ready to eat raw shark.

"Come." Andreas walked to a barbershop. The signage was in Amharic. There was a tiny window and an open door.

All three chairs were open, but only one barber. He led

Reece to one chair and then Andreas to another. Reece could tell that they knew one another.

The barber leaned Andreas back, his head cradled by a cushion. He took a kettle of water from a charcoal stove and saturated a small towel with the nearly boiling water. The barber draped the towel across Andreas's face. He flinched.

Likewise, the barber laid a hot towel across Reece's face. Reece sat up, feeling that he was being burned. The barber laughed and pushed him back into the chair. It did feel good, and Reece relaxed. He took a deep breath and imagined Alabama, grocery stores with frozen lasagna that was pretty damn good. The barber stepped away to tend to Andreas.

It took more than an hour, but the two walked away with haircuts and shaves for three birr each. Reece felt like a new man. The barber had trimmed his hair as if initiating the sequence to a nuclear war, very methodical.

FORTY-FOUR

Gudmunder and Eydis remained in the jail, even though the door was unlocked. They feared being shot. This was more like a jail, a single large cell attached to a fenced courtyard. There was a bucket tin which to pee and defecate, but no toilet paper. There was enough bench for them and the two other prisoners who wore tire sandals, rough shorts, and dirty shamma wraps.

"Tenesteling," said Gudmunder.

"Hello," said the taller of the two. He spoke some English. He stood and looked down at Gudmunder. "What is it? Why you are here?"

"They think he stole something," said Svana. She stood.

"You are very strong woman." He introduced himself as Omar. He wore a black string around his neck. "Ah, yes, you are the ferenj who has taken from the church, no?"

"No, I did not," said Gudmunder. "It is a lie." He couldn't believe that he'd tried to choke the guard, but what else was he to do?

Omar laughed. "They accuse me of stealing a sheep, and also I say it is a lie." He laughed again. "I tell them to check my shit and see if it is true."

"Yes, but he is telling the truth," said Svana.

"And I am telling the truth," said Omar. "Do you have some foods?"

"No," said Svana. She wished that she had taken a hotel room. Omar was a bit creepy. He had a pointy, scraggly chin beard. A deep scar over his left eye made him look surprised, and he spoke in a low, gravelly tone.

Omar introduced the other man, who stood and gave his hand to Gudmunder. His name was just Brother, Wendim in Amharic. He seemed harmless. He was short but thick. "He has killed a man who killed his brother," said Omar. "He is very strong with his hands. He is safe here. He will be killed if he is set free."

The worried look on Wendim's face seemed to confirm this.

The guard was back. He could not find the administrator. He was definitely sleeping with a woman somewhere. He entered the dank, dim room and tried not to breathe in the piss smell. He glared at Svana, his jaw still smarting, and spoke. She did not move. She ruffled back her jet-black hair. She looked like she was ready to go to a punk show in Hell's Kitchen. Omar translated.

"Go with him, he says. You are not to be here with the men."

"Yellum. I stay with the doctor."

The guard was wearing his rifle and carrying a wicked-looking baton. He wasn't taking any chances this time.

"Come with me now!" he said.

"Fuck you!" said Svana, not understanding him.

Gudmunder stood, getting between them. "Svana. It's okay. Omar, where will they take Svana?"

"She will go to the hotel and stay there. She will pay for her room and food. She cannot leave. She will be charged for hitting this man."

"Svana, what do you think?"

"I think this is bullshit."

"Do you have any money?" asked Gudmunder. "Here, take this." He pulled eighty birr from his pocket.

"You are rich," said Omar. "You can send to buy us some foods, no?"

Svana frowned and took the money. She would buy a gun.

The guard shouldered his rifle and motioned for Svana to come through the door. He kept his distance.

"Okay, Gudmunder. I will be back tomorrow to check on you. "Shall I bring you dinner?"

"They will bring if there is money," said Omar.

"No," said Gudmunder. "I'll send for everyone to have some dinner. Bring me some bread in the morning. I'll be fine."

"Maybe we should tell them you are a homosexual," said Svana in Icelandic. She smiled.

"No, no, just go and be safe. Reece should be back soon. He will come through AK."

"Nah!" said the guard.

"Bite me," said Svana.

Svana was gone. Gudmunder was gone. Reece was gone. To keep a sense of normalcy, Eydis went with Afewerki and bought some oranges and more potatoes. She walked, looking at everything for sale. There was a pretty basket that she bought to keep her stethoscope in. A little boy, covered in mud and pushed by his mother, approached Eydis. The mother whispered.

"There is a wound on his leg. She wants medicine," said Afewerki. So many people wanting so many things.

"Let's look. Oh my," said Svana. A deep gash festered on his calf. Pus ran down his leg, mixing with mud.

"His brother has crack-ed him with the whip. Is very dangerous. There is some bone in the whip." Afewerki made a face. He did not like to see such things.

"Okay, let's go back to the compound. I'll treat him there."

"We must tell him to go there alone. If they see, many others will come."

Eydis knew it was true, but didn't care. "Just let us go."

Afewerki frowned. "Okay. Come, mamoosh." He had ideas of taking a long walk with Eydis. He also wanted to lunch with her at his house.

At the compound, it didn't take long for Eydis to express the pus and disinfect the wound with hydrogen peroxide. She told the mother to keep it clean and apply antibiotic ointment, which she gave her. The woman, moved to tears, feared that perhaps her son would lose his leg.

"No tears," said Eydis. She noticed others had gathered

at the gap in the fence and were questioning the mother as she left with her son.

"What a hell," said Afewerki. He did not want to work on his day off, but was happy being with Eydis.

Within minutes, an impromptu clinic began, the most serious case being a woman who was seriously dehydrated and jaundiced. For her, Eydis started a jugular IV and dripped in nearly two liters of fluid over four hours. Whereas she had been lethargic and unable to walk, the woman was now responsive and limping on her own. Eydis did not know why she was jaundiced, perhaps a case of hepatitis. After five hours of working and treating twenty-five patients, without stopping for lunch, the line was finally finished except for a group of women requesting lotion for their hands.

"They use for sex," said Afewerki. He made a sour face. "I will tell them to go," and he did.

"Well, that was unexpected," said Svana. "I think the Baptists should reopen a clinic here."

"It is possible," said Afewerki, "especially if they are giving away foods. The people will come each day and stand in line. Let us wash our hands and go to eat. My mother will make for us some dorowot."

Eydis knew she would get heartburn from the volcanic wot but said okay. "Let me wash up and I'll come to your compound in half an hour."

"Oh no, I shall return. The people are murmuring. They know that Dr. Thorsonn has been arrested. They may think that you have also some work in this."

That alarmed Eydis. "Really? That is disturbing. I can't believe the Snake let them take Gudmunder after we fed him, and he drank all of our alcohol."

"He is nasty man," said Afewerki. "God will punish him." He had bought some cologne at the market, a half-empty bottle of Old Spice.

FORTY-SIX

After their haircuts and shaves, Andreas took Reece by the coffin factory, which was next to a bar. There was no building, just stacks of wood and finished coffins in all sizes, including coffins for infants. Several young men stood in the mud, sawing and hammering.

"There are two ways to leave Ethiopia, the people say. Ethiopian Airlines and in a coffin." Andreas threw up his hands as if to say, "What can I do?" He led Reece around a deep, black puddle. A used syringe floated there.

They walked into a narrow one-way street clogged with big trucks. It smelled of rotting vegetable matter. Vendors lined the way. Some had crude awnings covering their goods. There was a huge pile of red potatoes, a wooden box of tomatoes. Two men sat sewing old grain bags. A woman with a purple shawl sold big cabbages. A man wearing a straw hat sold green peppers laid out on burlap. The rain from earlier in the day had stopped, but the puddles were everywhere. Two men passed, weighted down with refrigerator-sized bales of cloth.

"Just here," said Andreas. "We can drink." He pointed to a tin shack with an open blue door.

"It seems we're in the countryside and not the city," said Reece. Most of the women were wearing traditional clothing, their heads covered with scarves. It was the sprawl and crowding that made it different.

Andreas grunted.

"Why not drink back at the hotel bar?"

"They have only Johnny Walker," said Andreas. "I drink

that in the rural areas. Here they have Jack Daniel's. Do you like?"

Reece said, "Sure." He liked whiskey. "Do they have ice?"

"Ha!" said Andreas. "You must go to the Hilton for ice."

Inside was empty. There was a tiny bar and three tiny tables with rickety chairs. The floor was dirt. The owner came from behind the bar, smiling.

"Hallo, Mr. Helicopter Pilot. How is it today?" He wore a blue jacket with the cuffs upturned and a gold chain around his neck.

"Is good, very good. Ato Shimellis, this is Rice."

Reece stood halfway and shook Shimellis's hand. "It's Reece. Nice to meet you."

"My pleasure," said Shimellis. "What shall you drink today? Jack Daniels?"

Andreas nodded. "Hulet Jack Daniel's, doubles please."

"My pleasure. Do you need to order some food?"

"Just drinks are okay," said Andreas. He pushed his sunglasses onto his head.

"So, are you from Switzerland?" asked Reece. He tested his chair and decided it would be too risky to lean back, which he was wont to do.

"I am from Hamburg. Germany. I have lived many places. Do you know Hamburg? The Elbe River enters to the sea."

"No," said Reece. "When I was young, I lived in Augsburg."

"Ah, your father was in the American military?"

"Yeah. We moved quite a bit. I also lived near Stuttgart when I was in first grade."

"I have been to your country, to New York and Texas."

Shimellis brought real glasses, filled halfway with Jack Daniel's.

"Amenseganalo," said Andreas.

"Minem aydelem."

A beggar peeked his head into the bar. The beggar always pretended to be blind. Shimellis quickly intercepted him and shoved him outside, threatening to shoot him. He kept a pistol for such occasions.

They sipped their whiskey. "Why are you in Addis?" asked Andreas.

Reece explained the situation with Gudmunder and the accusation that he had stolen the tabot. That Dr. Guthrie had basically told him the best way to solve the problem was with a bribe.

Andreas looked puzzled. "That is crazy? Why would Gudmunder do such a thing? But it is very serious, I think."

"He's under house arrest." He explained the whole farce of Gudmunder being homosexual and having AIDS.

Andreas laughed. "Oh, that is a good one. I do wonder about him, though. Why does he not sleep with the nurses?"

Reece felt uncomfortable. "I guess he just wants a working relationship."

"Yes, but fucking is more important. Svana is nicely built, and Eydis is very beautiful, I think. What do you think?"

Reece thought about it. "I like Eydis. She is very pretty and kind. Svana is attractive but very rough. She could eat me for breakfast."

"I like that, eating for breakfast. Do you think Svana

will like me? She is taller than me, no?"

"I don't know." Reece leaned back in the chair. A loose leg snapped, sending him to the floor. "Fuck!"

Shimellis ran over to Reece, who was already standing.

"I'm okay," said Reece. He felt bad. "How much for the chair?"

"It is no problem," said Shimellis.

"No, I want to pay." He pulled out his wallet.

"Please, no."

Reece took a ten-birr note and handed it to him. Andreas was amused.

"No, chicorilla," said Shimellis.

"No, I broke your chair. I must pay." Reece felt himself getting angry. He didn't know why.

"Okay, okay," said Shimellis. He took the bill. Ferenji were crazy.

FORTY-SEVEN

Svana understood she could leave her room, but not the hotel. The owner of the Beselfui had been thrilled to see her. If anything, people would want to come to the bar to see the woman who was associated with the church thief.

The next morning, the first thing Svana did was to leave the hotel, buy six warm wheat buns and a bottle of Ambo water, and then walk to the jail. She entered the front office and met a man she did not know. The man seemed nervous, so she just walked past him into the back, where the holding cell was. The door was closed, and she knocked. "Why I am knocking?"

She opened the door, and Gudmunder was not there. No one was there. She thought the worst, that he had been taken to Addis Ababa and executed.

The man in the front office, a deputy of sorts, knew she was looking for the thief of the tabot. He approached Svana with caution and motioned for her to follow him. Outside, he walked, and Svana followed. They headed toward the town square, the roundabout where people waited for jeeps and caught the bus that came once a week or so from Addis Ababa.

Carrying the buns and Ambo, she could see the low circular wall at the center of the roundabout. Gudmunder was there. She passed the deputy, breaking into a trot. "Fokk!" Gudmunder was tied to a chair, as were the two other prisoners. Each had a sign on the back of their chair, indicating their crime. On the back of Gudmunder's chair was "leba," the word for thief. Many people were lingering, talking with covered mouths.

"What is this?" She was out of breath. "Gudmunder?"

"Svana, give me some of that water. They brought food last night, but nothing to drink." He blinked in the blistering sun, sweating.

Svana opened the carbonated water, and it spewed. Gudmunder was loosely tied, a rope around his chest. "Careful, there is a guard just over there." He nodded toward a jacaranda tree where sat the jailer with his rifle. Gudmunder drank from the bottle. The other two prisoners mumbled. Svana handed a bun to them, which they took. Omar said, "Thank you, madam."

"I'll have a word with him," said Svana. A fly was trying to crawl up her nose.

"No, Svana. He does not speak English or Icelandic. You know that." He took another drink of water.

"Omar, what is this?"

"We are being punished, no?"

"How long does this last?" asked Svana.

"Who is knowing?" asked Omar. "Perhaps until noon." Svana was livid, shaking. "Dammit!"

"Svana, it's okay, maybe this is just for one day. Perhaps Reece will come today or tomorrow. Listen for the helicopter. I am okay."

"Are you kidding me? I will find the town administrator. I will bring him here." Svana felt her legs shaking.

"Ferenj!" came the shout of a child.

Svana frowned but then remembered that she was a guest in another country. She looked at a group of children who were staring and waved at them. They giggled. "Caramella!" shouted one. She wanted candy.

There was a grocery stall near the circle, and Svana bought a box of cookies. The children gathered around, and she passed them out one at a time. She looked back at Gudmunder and wished she had a camera. She remembered that she would buy a gun.

FORTY-EIGHT

With an IV bottle of filtered water, Eydis walked with Afewerki to his parents' compound near the town center. He smelled like Old Spice, sweet and strong. The early stars were out. She thought about the last man she had dated in Reykjavik, a nurse with big biceps. He had been a good lover, but had latched on too quickly and made her uncomfortable.

Afewerki's two younger brothers were bringing in the goats and the oxen, penning them inside circles of brush and thorns. The hyenas in Gwar were no joke. His father slept outside with a rifle beneath the hut's overhang. Smoke leaked through the center of the tukul's steep roof.

Afewerki poked his head inside. He told his mother to prepare dinner for two. His father was at the tejj bet. Eydis looked in and waved at the middle-aged woman stooping over the fire. The hut was neat, smoky, and cozy, with daubed rock sides up to the roof line.

He pushed in the door to his small square house with a tin roof. Inside was the plank bed and a small homemade table with two three-legged stools. His heart raced, and he searched for words. It would be about half an hour before his brother brought in the food. He held out his hand as if demonstrating that there was a God and that He was good. "Inside?" he said.

Eydis wore a loose red shift and white wool stockings as the evenings cooled quickly. "Thank you. This is very nice."

"My father has built for me. I give to him some money." He walked inside. His white hen hopped over the door stoop and clucked.

"This is the chicken's house?" asked Eydis. She stepped in. The space was tiny.

"Yes, she must sleep inside." He pointed to the rafter over his bed. The chicken strutted back and forth, then made the leap, flapping, landing on a horizontal pole.

"Very sweet," said Eydis. "She sleeps the whole night?"

"Yes, she wakes very early."

"What is her name?"

"Name?" Afewerki worried that she expected the chicken to have a name. "Eydis." He wanted to shoot himself in the head.

Eydis laughed. "Really? That is sweet." She smoothed down her dress and looked at the pages from magazines pinned to the mud walls. Her arms felt chilled. She wondered how Reece was doing, when he would return. "It looks more like Svana, though."

Afewerki laughed. Should he laugh? "No, no, it is a chicken. It is disease-resistant, from Germany."

"So, am I disease-resistant?" asked Eydis. Her cheeks blushed. She felt hot and cold.

Afewerki was horrified. "No! The chicken is imported to breed with the local chickens, to decrease the influenza."

Eydis was having fun at his expense. She bumped into him, looked him in the eyes, and stepped back outside. She needed a drink, something substantial. "Do you have some alcohol?"

Afewerki felt like kicking himself. He had not thought of buying alcohol. Maybe his father had some stored beside the tukul. "Just wait." He stepped outside and went to his father's raised bed beneath the eave. He searched and found a bottle half full of clear liquid. He smelled, and it was katikala.

"Oh, you found?" asked Eydis. *Thank God.*

"Katikala." He took two green plastic cups and poured two healthy servings.

Eydis took her cup. She sipped and coughed.

Afewerki was sweating. The katikala burned his throat, and he coughed as well.

Eydis laughed and took a large swallow. She knew she would be eating soon. She would excuse herself when they were through eating. In the early evening light, Afewerki's skin looked soft. The cows lowed. The goats nipped at one another's heels. The smell of fresh dung and smoke. "Are you a virgin?" asked Eydis.

Afewerki choked.

FORTY-NINE

After two doubles of Jack Daniels straight up, Andreas and Reece floated to a nearby restaurant called Medre Genet, Heaven on Earth. Mostly men seemed to crowd the sidewalks and streets. Men held hands with men. Women walked hand in hand with women. They passed a white VW Beetle that looked to be in excellent shape. A young man was grooming himself in the side-view mirror. The restaurant was pink with a windowed front.

Smells of what seemed to be fried fish and tomato sauce, and Reece was intrigued. Andreas spoke to the hostess. Her face was young and pretty. She wore a dark green dress with a beige sweater and a white headscarf. She seemed European.

"You like?" asked Andreas.

"Sure," said Reece.

They took a table in the narrower back part of the café. Reece needed the restroom. There was a single bathroom with a broken toilet. He held his breath and urinated. No way to wash his hands. He zipped and opened the door with his pinky finger.

Andreas had ordered two St. George beers.

"Thanks," said Reece. "What's good here?" There didn't seem to be a menu.

"We must ask?" asked Andreas. "It is different each day."

"I'm hungry," said Reece. Posters depicting singers plastered the narrow space. Light streamed through the front window. The table was a tiny square. He had a sudden vision of Eydis and wondered what she tasted like, all over.

He thought about Nick Cave in *Wings of Desire.* He wanted to arm wrestle Andreas or body slam him on the wooden floor. He sipped his beer.

"Ethiopia makes one hungry," said Andreas.

"Why are you flying up country? Are you delivering supplies?"

"Of course, delivering vaccines. I will drop an RRC man in Gwar with you. You will have to sit on the floor behind the seats."

"No problem," said Reece. "What is RRC?"

"Relief and Rehabilitation Commission. He is interested in the work of the clinic in AK and data regarding hunger.

"Gudmunder would be glad to meet him. They want their findings to result in grain for the area."

"Maybe," said Andreas. "It is possible, depending on the data. I have seen some fat ones in Alem Ketema, though."

"From what I've read, famine can occur at twelve thousand feet and not at seven thousand feet, just a few miles away. Agro-ecological zones."

"Perhaps," said Andreas.

The hostess came by. She said they had spaghetti Bolognese with bread. Other than that, it was fried fish left over from the previous day. They both nodded to the daily special.

"Do you have brothers or sisters?" asked Reece. He was interested in family constellations, how birth order figured in one's relationships.

"I am an only child," said Andreas.

Shit, thought Reece. "Me too." Eydis, he knew, was the youngest of three sisters, a perfect match for an only child.

The spaghetti came in large white plastic bowls, soaking in a thin tomato sauce sprinkled with a bit of ground meat. Reece twirled a bite and blew on it. It needed salt, but was tasty. Andreas did the same, except he cut his spaghetti with his knife. Reece watched the hostess walk away. He imagined her curvy hips beneath the heavy dress. It had been six months since he'd had sex. He tried to remember why he was in Addis and had to think for a moment.

FIFTY

Svana didn't know where to buy a gun, so just asked a teenage boy working in a fruit stand. "AK-47?" she said. He sold bananas, limes, and oranges. In a whisper, he pointed to a scrappy-looking building just across the way. Beside it was a petrol station with two hand-pump gas dispensers. She bought an orange for ten cents and walked across to the tin-roofed shack.

Svana entered, and a man was sitting behind a metal desk on a concrete floor. The desk was empty on top. Against the wall leaned a few rifles. There was a Lalibela travel poster tacked to the wall, and an Ethiopian calendar. The man was misshapen, leaning to Svana's left. She thought about scoliosis.

"Mendeno?" asked the man.

"AK-47," said Eydis. "Bullets."

The man looked surprised. In Amharic, he asked her how much money she had. Svana somehow understood his question. She pulled a twenty-birr note from her pocket. She thought she'd start low.

The man's expression did not change. He opened his desk drawer. Something was there. He pulled out something silver and shiny.

Svana had to study it for a minute before she realized it was a hand grenade. The spoon was down. There was a pin with a ring pull. She didn't know it was from World War II, an Italian product. It was pretty and called to her. She didn't like guns anyway. She could hide the grenade in her pocket, a bag, or even her bra, and handed the man the twenty. He stood and presented her with the shiny hand-bomb. He mimicked pulling the pin and throwing it, put his hands over his ears, and laughed.

Svana nodded. It was too big for her pocket. She slid it into her bra through the neck of her scrub top. It was cool and very heavy, and she hoped it wouldn't fall out. She went back, told Gudmunder to hang in there, gave him more water, and walked toward the hotel feeling very powerful. To calm her nerves, she went to the bar and ordered a grape Fanta. Lebna was on duty. She brought the drink and spoke at length, none of which Svana understood. When she had finished, Svana pulled down her top, reached in, and exposed the hand grenade in her bra. Lebna's eyes grew wide.

FIFTY-ONE

Afewerki did not respond to Eydis's question about his virginity. Why would she ask such a thing? Just then, Afewerki's brother brought in the platter of enjera garnished with two mounds of dorowot, chicken, and boiled eggs dyed red by the berbere pepper. There was plenty of clarified butter in there. The top of Eydis's head, beneath her washed blonde hair, broke into beads of sweat. She anticipated the burn. The katikala had given her a nice buzz, and now it was going to be killed.

They ate slowly, taking small bites. Afewerki had begun to feel drunk and was glad to slowly begin feeling normal. Dorowot was his favorite, the hotter the better. He worried, though, that it was too hot for Eydis. He imagined her as living a charmed life, as a kind of princess protected from the evils of the world. Why had she come to Ethiopia? Had she come to find a husband?

"Do you think Gudmunder is okay?" asked Eydis. The silence was bothering her, and she feared the chicken in the rafters would poop on her.

"He is strong," said Afewerki. "And Svana is stronger. She will keep him from trouble." He glanced into Eydis's light blue eyes. He had never seen such a thing before her.

Eydis laughed. "I wonder how Reece is doing." She wiped sweat from her eyebrows and guzzled her water.

"He will come back soon. I do not think Dr. Guthrie will help him, though."

"Why not?" asked Eydis

"What can he do? He is powerless for such things." He

bit an egg in half.

"Maybe he can send a lawyer, one who knows the law."

Afewerki was looking at her hair. Their knees nearly touched around the side of the tiny table. It was getting dim inside. "Hmm?"

"A lawyer." Eydis took a last bite of plain enjera. She could not eat any more of the flaming wot. In the distance, she could hear the hustle and bustle of loaded donkeys, the end of market day.

"Ah, is best to settle this matter in the countryside," said Afewerki. "Addis will swallow him like the whale."

"Is there anyone who can advise us here in Gwar? I know the Snake is useless, or is he?"

Afewerki smirked. "He is like the sleeping hyena. But there is a man. He is digging a church into the rock. He is the Abba Paulos. He is very wise. He is said to cure the evil eye."

"Is he a priest?"

"No, he is like a holy man who lives alone. He is monk," said Afewerki. "Perhaps he can tell if Dr. Thorsonn is lying."

"You think he is lying?" asked Eydis.

"Oh no, but he can tell the people the truth, and they will listen." He imagined her breasts beneath her red dress. He had seen them just briefly when the Snake's guard had ripped her blouse. They were white, just like the rest of her.

"Even the people in Alem Ketema?" She felt Afewerki's gaze. She drank the last of her water.

"Yes, the Abba is very famous. We will go to see him tomorrow. He is digging each day except for Sunday."

"Well, sounds like fun." She thought about how she would have to sleep alone without Svana. Gebremariam would stand guard as usual, she hoped.

Afewerki's youngest brother shyly knocked on the open door. He wore a long brown sweater with sleeves much too long. Afewerki handed him the platter of soaked enjera.

"He is cute," said Svana. "He doesn't look like you."

Afewerki did not know how to respond. "He is my brother. He is twelve. Shall I build the fire for you?"

"At the compound?" asked Eydis. "Sure. Can we stop by the teahouse? I would like some tea, and then we can drink the rest of the katikala."

Afewerki grinned. "No problem."

FIFTY-TWO

Andreas asked Reece if he wanted to play Uno, but Reece declined. He was tired, and he didn't care for games. He returned to his bright green room. There was enough candle to read for perhaps half an hour from a tattered copy of *Fathers and Sons* he'd picked up in the Mercato for a birr. Outside, the guard was whistling. He whistled all night long, keeping Reece awake.

The next morning, Andreas knocked on his door. They would have coffee and buns and then catch a taxi to Bole Airport. It was Sunday, but still the Mercato was hopping. As they walked, Reece watched two young shoeshine boys drying their rags in the exhaust of a diesel mini-bus. An old woman was begging with one hand and picking her nose with the other. Reece fished out twenty cents. The woman nodded.

They navigated their way to a two-lane road. The sun's light seemed plastic to Reece. He let an old man with a white skullcap and a cane pass in front of him. A huge white goat stood on a pile of broken sidewalk. Several blue-and-white Ladas and Fiats lined the street, some piled with goods on their roof racks.

"Let us try this one," said Andreas. The taxi was parked in front of a community school that was set behind a stone wall that reached above Reece's head.

The road was dirt, but the taxi gleamed as if it had just been washed. They squeezed into the back seat. Reece held his bag in his lap. The inside smelled like ripe leather.

"Bole Airport," said Andreas.

"Ishi," said the driver. Wiry and hunched over the wheel, he drove methodically, steering around the giant mud holes and threading through the human traffic. It took ten minutes to wend their way out of the Mercato and then another five sprinting through the sprawling Meskel Square.

"Usually, I fly from the old airport at Lideta," said Andreas. "But I am in RRC space for my passenger."

Reece nodded, not sure what he meant.

The taxi headed down Cameroon Street. Andreas directed the driver to the east end of the airport. They turned right and stopped at a guard shack with a manual lift gate. The guard carried an AK-47. Reece could see fuel tanks to his left and a collection of buildings to his right. The taxi was not allowed to enter, and they had to walk in after showing their passports. Andreas had a standing in-country travel permit adorned with numerous purple stamps. They walked beside an enormous building filled with equipment and passed between two large buildings that reminded Reece of Quonset huts. Near a large tent filled with medical supplies headed to various parts of the country was their passenger, Ato Kifle of the RRC.

"Hello, my friend!" said Ato Kifle. He shook Andreas's hand and then Reece's. He would be inspecting the government health clinic in Alem Ketema and examining their patient log. He wore pressed slacks and a blue shirt. They would need to wait for a shuttle to take them to a small-craft area in the middle of a dirt field near a small hangar. An Ethiopian Airlines 747 took off headed northeast, roaring down the far runway. Reece had to pee.

Svana wasn't quite sure what she would do with the hand grenade, but by noon, everyone in Alem Ketema knew that she had one hidden in her bra. There was no real rule against having a hand grenade, and it did command respect.

Against her house arrest at the hotel, she left again to check on Gudmunder. From a distance, she could tell he was no longer sitting in the sun tied to a chair. She backtracked and stopped at the jail, stepping into the front office. A different jailer was there, sucking on a lime as he ate shurowot. He did not stop eating and glared at her.

Svana held up her hands. "Ferenj?" She pointed to the door leading to the courtyard.

The man wiped his mouth on his sleeve. A carbine rifle with a folding stock leaned against the wall. He imagined he could see the outline of the hand grenade beneath her yellow print shirt. "Ow." He spoke further, but Svana could not understand. She wished Afewerki were there.

"I need to see him," said Svana.

The jailer figured the best approach was to just say no to anything she suggested. "Yellum."

"Yellum? Why?" Svana put her hands on her hips.

"Yellum," said the guard. He stood and yelled at her. He was trying to eat his lunch. Could she not see that? Plus, she was supposed to be at the hotel. He could shoot her and probably should, but he was eating.

"Gudmunder!" She listened for a response. She realized she should go outside and yell over the wall. This guy was getting her nowhere. He just kept eating.

Outside in the bright sunshine, she walked around the corner to the middle of the dull corrugated tin wall. Just beyond was the courtyard. She peered in through a crack in the fence seam. "Gudmunder!" She knocked on the wall.

Gudmunder recognized Svana's voice. Just then, a military jet flew overhead. Probably a MiG. "Svana!" He excused himself from his conversation with Omar. They were talking about the Ark of the Covenant. He walked to the fence and rapped. Soon, Svana was opposite him on the other side.

"Gudmunder?"

"Svana? How are you? You are supposed to be in the hotel, no?"

"Fuck that," said Svana. "Are you okay?"

"Yes. I'm okay. It will make an interesting story."

That made Svana angry. "They will release you soon."

"How do you know?"

"I will force them." She felt the grenade in her bra. It was making a bruise on her breast.

"No, Svana. Be patient. Let's wait for Reece to return. Perhaps Dr. Guthrie will come with him."

"Oh, I am so angry."

"Svana, just relax. It will be okay. They will discover who stole the tabot. I am innocent, but we must be patient."

"Agh! Do you need lunch?"

"They have brought lunch. It is very good, only two birr. Perhaps buy a bottle of Awash wine and have it sent to us for dinner. Omar is very interesting. He is a real criminal!"

Was he having fun? "Okay, Gudmunder. I will send the wine."

"Send two bottles. There are three of us."

"Chicorilla," said Svana. A fly flew up her nose. "Hell!"

FIFTY-FOUR

While Afewerki was building the fire, Eydis became sleepy. The teahouse had been crowded, and they had returned to the compound. The stars were brilliant in the evening sky. She imagined her mother back in Iceland, drinking icy Brennivín. Her father had died of brain cancer when she was just seven. She tried to remember his face.

Afewerki sat on a biscuit tin, poking the fire. He sensed the evening was drawing to a close.

"I am feeling sad," said Eydis. "I am thinking of my family. I think I will go to sleep soon."

Afewerki nodded. He couldn't imagine traveling to Iceland, and Eydis seemed a thousand kilometers away. "Yes, okay." He threw his stick into the fire and wished that the others were there to prolong the evening.

The next day was sunny without rain. Eydis woke up sore as usual. There were so many small rocks beneath her tent. She lay on her back in her sleeping bag, a fleece blanket inside. The dark green tent admitted little light except through the window. She could nearly stand inside. She looked over at Svana's sleeping bag and missed her with a pang. They would be friends for life.

Slowly, she roused and dressed in clean underwear, jeans, and a light yellow sweater. She needed to wash her bra. She remembered Afewerki was taking her to see the monk carving a church into the rock. That should be interesting. To mask her unwashed hair, she put on a white bandanna and then pushed her feet into her heavy tennis shoes. She knelt and unzipped the tent flap. Abebe would cook breakfast, but that was all on Sunday. It definitely felt like Sunday. Like a marshmallow.

"Good morning," said Afewerki. He sat in Gudmunder's chair near a small fire.

"You have been here the entire night?" asked Eydis.

"Yes. To watch the compound."

But that was Gebremariam's job. She did not see him. "You were worried?"

"Just to be safe. Chicorilla."

Eydis crawled out of the tent. She stood and stretched, exposing her midriff. "You are a good man."

Afewerki was so glad that the long night was over and that Eydis was awake. "Maybe Reece will come today?"

"It will be best when we are all together again," said Eydis. "We are a team." She walked behind Afewerki and put her hands on his shoulders. She kneaded the muscular flesh and then kissed the top of his head.

Afewerki felt paralyzed. "Oh," he said.

"Shall we see the monk today?"

"Yes, Abba Paulos. Today." He pointed to the cook house, meaning to indicate that Abebe would cook breakfast first.

"I am hungry. What is she cooking?"

"I will see." Afewerki stood. His blood pressure dropped, and he was dizzy.

"You okay?"

"Ow." He walked to the cook house, the early morning light brighter than it should be. Abebe was crouched, making the fire into coals. Breakfast would be fit-fit. She was also roasting coffee beans.

FIFTY-FIVE

Andreas circled Alem Ketema, zoning for the helipad of rocks at the former Baptist Mission compound. The blue fuel bladder, empty, was still there. He had just enough fuel for Gwar and Wollo and a return trip to Lideta in Addis.

A small crowd, mostly young boys, greeted them as usual. Svana had heard the helicopter beating the air, but the landing site was too far away. She held her ground at the Beselfui Hotel.

The helicopter landed. Andreas did not shut down the engine. He intended to head straight to Gwar and pay a visit to Svana. Maybe he would spend the night in Gwar if he was lucky.

Reece and Ato Kifle exited the helicopter, bent over in the downwash. They straightened and waved goodbye to Andreas in his jumpsuit and sunglasses. They knew it was fruitless to resist the boys' efforts to carry their bags and surrendered right away. The road to AK was less than a kilometer, and they started walking.

There was minimal conversation as the two walked. Reece was thinking about the plan to bribe the town administrator. Dr. Guthrie had made it seem so simple. He wanted to discuss it with Ato Kifle, but it didn't seem right. At the health clinic/hospital, the two said their goodbyes.

Reece had no idea that Gudmunder and Svana were in AK. Out of habit, he made his way past the town square toward the Beselfui Hotel. He waved at the children peering from doorways, yelling, "Ferenj!" He approached the administrative compound walking with purpose.

"Reece!"

He looked around.

"Reece!" There was a pounding on a tin compound wall. He wasn't sure. He walked over, stepping over rocks.

"Dr. Thorsonn?"

"Reece, I am in the jail here. On the other side."

Reece found his way to the voice. "I thought you were in Gwar? What happened?"

"The Snake betrayed me and sent me here. I think there will be a trial."

"Are you okay? Are they feeding you?"

"Yes, I am okay, but I have work to do. What did Dr. Guthrie say?"

Reece looked behind him, and a dozen people were standing there, along with the boy holding his small bag. He gave the boy a birr. "Let me come inside. Hold on." He walked into the open door, and the jailer was there. "Ferenj?" He pointed at the door.

The jailer looked displeased. He stood, opened the door, and motioned Reece through. "Five minutes," he said in Amharic. He held up five fingers.

"Amenseganalo," said Reece.

"Ah, Reece, good friend," said Gudmunder. He introduced Reece to his two cellmates, Omar and the man who had killed another man. They nodded.

"So, did you come here in a jeep? Did you walk?" asked Reece.

"In a jeep. We had a feast with the Snake with plenty of liquor. Within a day, I was brought here to face charges. They do not listen that I am innocent. So, how was your trip to Addis? I heard the helicopter and waited for you to pass.”

Reece contemplated his journey. “It was a good trip. Andreas flew me back here.” It suddenly hit him that Andreas was flying to Gwar and that he had expressed an interest in Eydis, or was it Svana? Being away from Eydis had magnified his like for her. “I found Dr. Guthrie. There was an accident, though.”

“An accident?”

“A girl was crushed by a large truck. I tried to do CPR.” He could see the girl’s mouth. “It was just outside his house.”

“I’m sorry,” said Gudmunder. He sat on the bench, and Reece joined him.

“I stayed in the Mercato with Andreas at a hotel. We had shaves and haircuts. There was Jack Daniel’s.”

“Yes, you look nice. But what did Guthrie say?”

“He said to bribe the town administrator. It will be the quickest way. You do not want to be subject to a first-instance court or any court. If you are found guilty, then what?”

“A bribe?” asked Gudmunder. “Okay, let’s do it. What time is it?”

Reece didn’t have a watch. He looked at the sun. It was near noon. “Probably eleven.”

“Did you see the administrator in his office? It’s inside this building as you come in.”

“No,” said Reece.

“Damn,” said Gudmunder. “You can probably catch him at the Beselfui for lunch. Svana is there.”

“Svana?”

"She is now under arrest, too. She has to stay at the hotel as she punched one of the jailers."

Reece laughed. "Really?"

"Yes, she did. We may have to make several bribes if what Guthrie says is true."

Svana was in the bar, drinking warm beer. She looked around at the men being served lunch, bugwot. Everyone seemed tense. Why didn't women eat lunch out? The beer foamed in her mouth. She tried to tame her restless leg from bobbing up and down. In walked a white guy.

"Reece!" She waved him over.

"Hey, Svana!"

She stood and gave him a friendly hug. He was surprised at how soft she was.

"I just saw Gudmunder, and he told me you were here." He pulled out the chair and sat. Sweat dripped from his nose. The tin roof creaked with the noonday heat.

"I am under arrest."

"I hear, for punching someone?"

"Yes. My hand is hurting still." She showed him her blued knuckles.

"Yikes. Well, I told Gudmunder that Dr. Guthrie recommends we bribe the town administrator to drop the charges, but we'll have to figure you in, too. You're dangerous."

"Hell yes," said Svana. "I bought a hand grenade. It's in my bra."

"What?"

She patted her chest. "Just in case. The jailer was getting rough with me after I hit him. Next time, I will take one of his legs."

"You really bought a hand grenade? And it's in your bra?"

"Yes. It's hard to show with this top."

"That's okay. Be very careful, though."

The town administrator, wearing knit pants and a button-up, purple, short-sleeve shirt, walked into the bar. He let his eyes adjust and took a table against the wall on the other side of the room with his back to them.

"That's who we need to bribe," said Svana. "But he doesn't speak English. Omar, a prisoner at the jail, speaks English. It's perfect, no?"

"Do you think we'll have to bribe Omar, too?" This was getting complicated quickly. He thought back to Yale. He'd been offered a prime-paying internship at Greenwich Hospital that summer, but had chosen the community health survey in Ethiopia instead, and at his own expense. Where would the madness end?

"We might as well eat lunch," said Svana.

Reece didn't have the best appetite at the moment. "Yeah." He just wanted to see Eydis.

FIFTY-SIX

Filled with fit-fit and fresh coffee, Eydis and Afewerki left the compound, headed to visit the Abba Paulos. Eydis wondered what sort of advice he could have regarding Gudmunder. He sounded interesting, though.

They passed Afewerki's compound, headed toward the Polish airstrip. The day was dry thus far, but Afewerki had warned her it was likely to rain in the afternoon. They passed a mother, who was loaded with firewood, several feet above her head. She was so stooped that Eydis worried her back was breaking. They took a path that dropped below the cliff line, descending steadily, somewhat west. The slope led up to their right and down to their left.

The bright cloudy sky was brilliant. The rocky path required one's eyes down to keep from stumbling. After thirty minutes, Afewerki scanned to his right for a scramble that led up and over the lip of a ledge, which would place them in front of the holy place. He stopped, listened, and continued.

Eydis followed closely. Afewerki was nondescript from behind in his generic jeans and a t-shirt advertising "Antartica!" missing a c.

Afewerki turned right and began the hand-over-hand climb. The top hold was blind, and he threw his hand there, searching. Nothing, and he jumped back and fell the few feet to the ground. "Shit."

Eydis laughed. Her legs were scuffed from the brush. "You want me to try?"

"No, no," said Afewerki. As if on steroids, he climbed up

and over the lip of the ridge. From there, he could see the opening to the church in the rock. He almost forgot what he was doing. He turned, and Eydis was already halfway up. He squatted and then went to his knees, ready to pull her up, but she hit the handhold and pulled herself up on the first try. He stood, impressed. "Very good," he said.

Eydis brushed the dust from her shorts and stood.

"Just here," said Afewerki. He glanced at her legs. The whiteness of her skin still amazed him. He pointed to a black oblong hole in the rock, fronted by a green door that was open. There was a faint tapping.

"Wow," she said.

Afewerki led the way to the opening. He called, "Abba Paulos!" The sound reverberated from within. The *tap tap* stopped. He stepped in and motioned for Eydis to follow him. Together they stood inside a chamber that was twenty-four feet square with a ceiling of fifteen feet.

"Abet!" came the voice.

Eydis focused over Afewerki's shoulder. There was a central pillar in the room. Against the wall was a crude ladder. There was a wooden wheelbarrow with an iron wheel. A figure was approaching them, the Abba Paulos.

"Xavier meskin," said the Abba. He put down his wood-handled pick. He was supposed to be resting on the Sabbath. Dust filled the air.

For a full five minutes, he and Afewerki exchanged greetings and news. Eydis wandered from wall to wall, wondering at the work required. How did he do it? Who cooked for him? Did he have a wife?"

Afewerki motioned to Eydis. The Abba responded with a blessing, wishing it upon her many children. He wore a long, tattered robe and a gold skullcap. "He is saying welcome," said Afewerki.

"Amenseganalo," said Eydis. "I am privileged to be in his church. When will it be finished?"

Afewerki translated.

"It is finished each day," said the Abba. His forearms looked like steel cables.

Eydis tried to remember why she was there. It was cool inside the cavernous space. She wanted to sit, but there was no chair or bench.

To begin, Afewerki produced a ten-birr note. He presented it to the Abba. "We have come to receive advice," said Afewerki.

"Yes, I know," said the Abba.

Afewerki cleared his throat. He told the story of Gudmunder and the accusation of stealing the tabot in Alem Ketema. "What should be done?"

The Abba said that he knew of the theft. The thief would be caught soon, and it was not the Icelander.

"What shall we do?" asked Afewerki.

"The thief will be caught, but for now, you must buy innocence. In Spanish, it is called the little bite, the mordida."

Afewerki translated. He was amazed at the monk's knowledge. "We must bribe for innocence," he told Eydis.

Eydis took a deep breath. She wanted to laugh, but maybe that seemed to be the best answer.

FIFTY-SEVEN

The town administrator's name was Dingil. He was tall and thin, with a receding horseshoe-shaped hairline, and was a high-school graduate. He knew that Svana had a hand grenade in her bra and occasionally glanced back. He enjoyed his bugwot and beer but not as much as usual. He was the only person drinking beer for lunch other than Svana and the ferenj.

Svana let Reece know that the administrator was leaving. They stood and followed him outside. He turned and addressed them. They had no clue what he was saying.

"Omar? At the jail?" asked Reece.

Dingil shrugged his shoulders.

"Nah," said Reece, remembering the word for come. He motioned for the administrator and Svana to follow him.

They moved as a group, passing a young boy with a herd of goats. The jail was near, just two hundred feet from the Beselfui. Svana entered the jail office. Reece and Dingil followed.

"Omar." She pointed at the door.

"Ah, Omar," said Dingil. He thought he understood. This should be good. He pushed the door open and held it for Svana and Reece. Omar was there with the other man. Gudmunder was in the courtyard.

"Hello," said Omar. He stood, insinuating his sudden importance.

Svana shook his hand. "Omar, this is Reece—he must explain something."

Reece shook Omar's hand. He explained the bribe

scheme to Omar.

Omar smiled and nodded. "Shall I be free as well?"

Svana looked at Reece. "Sure," said Reece. "Let's see what can happen."

Omar began by noting that Svana had a hand grenade in her bra. He then explained the bribe scheme to Dingil. One hundred birr for Dingil to drop the charges.

Dingil's eyes brightened. He needed cash to pay his meal tabs at the Beselfui. One hundred birr, though, seemed insufficient. And what about the priest at the church? It would cost several hundred birr to replace the tabot. The new tabot would have to travel to Addis Ababa and be consecrated by the Abuna there.

"And eh sheek birr," he said.

"One thousand birr," said Omar. He smiled. He could smell a deal for his release in the works.

Reece thought. *One thousand birr.* That was ten times what Dr. Guthrie had suggested. He did the math. And what about the hint of cash for Omar? At eight birr to the dollar, the total price was US $125. That was a cheap way to avoid trial, but someone would have to return to Gwar to retrieve the dollars, which would be traded for birr in AK. Reece volunteered. He had about three hundred dollars in twenties and fifties in his orange tent.

Reece and Svana spent another half hour with Gudmunder and left. They walked back to the Beselfui, which Svana was not supposed to leave, and sat at the table outside.

"Do you think a jeep will come today?" asked Svana.

"I should go to the square and hang out, just in case," said Reece. "It seems too late, but who knows?"

"Right," said Svana. She was tired of the grenade in her bra, went to her room, and hid the shiny bomb under her pillow. She was ready for another beer and wished she could lock the door from the outside.

"The helicopter is coming," said Afewerki. He and Eydis were making their way up the path that climbed the sloping escarpment, returning from visiting the Abba Paulos.

Eydis paused, listening. Just barely, she could hear the distant chatter. "Maybe Gudmunder is returning?"

"Maybe," said Afewerki. He didn't think so, though, and wondered why Andreas was visiting. He had recently delivered vaccines. There must be some news or a special delivery.

They reached the town center and kept on toward the helicopter landing site, the muffled sound becoming crisp and loud. The red, white, and blue helicopter was visible, perhaps five kilometers away and closing fast. They stood with shielded eyes, waiting for Andreas to land.

As Andreas approached the initial slope up into Gwar, he could see two people at the helipad. He circled. He wasn't going to land there, though, and picked out the large, mostly empty compound of the Icelanders with the tents and hovered his way to a landing at the end of the fenced area. He wouldn't have to worry about the helicopter if he spent the night. The downwash from the rotors pummeled the tents. Reece's orange tent collapsed, held down by stakes. Ash from the fire pit exploded into the air.

Puzzled, Eydis and Afewerki walked back to the compound. A small crowd of children stood at the gap in the fence, laughing and playing. Gebremariam was trying to shoo them away. Out of the cook house came Abebe, topless, waving at Andreas. She was making enjera for the week over the fire. The turbine was cycling down with Andreas still inside.

"Why he is landing here?"

"Maybe he wants us to wash the helicopter," said Eydis.

Afewerki looked puzzled. "Why he would want such a thing?"

"I'm just kidding." She waved at the helicopter. Afewerki waved at the helicopter. Everyone at the fence was waving at the helicopter.

The rotor continued to slow, and Andreas waited until it was completely stopped before jumping out. He would change out of his flight uniform into something more comfortable. He grabbed his bag and closed the door.

Eydis smoothed back her blonde hair. "Hey!" She thought Andreas was cute, but he was an inch or two shorter than she was.

He gave her a strong side-hug and shook Afewerki's hand. "I brought some medicine and some food for the people, famine biscuits!"

"Oh, yum," said Eydis. "It's good to have at the weight clinics. The children like them very much. So, why are you landing on top of us?"

There was a commotion at the gate. Afewerki said, "Damn," and walked that way.

"I thought that since the cats were away, the mice would play." He grinned.

She didn't quite get his drift.

"Reece is in Alem Ketema. I thought maybe you and Svana would need some company. But I see you have Afewerki." He laughed. He put his hands in his pockets.

"Svana and Gudmunder are in AK," said Eydis.

"Really?" and she told him why.

At the gap in the fence, a man was holding a black goat, yelling at Afewerki, who told the man to wait and jogged back to Eydis and Andreas. "There is problem."

"What?" asked Eydis.

"The helicopter has frightened a donkey, which has kicked the goat and broken its leg." He pointed back at the man. "We must buy the goat and slaughter."

Andreas didn't seem too upset. "Well, goat for dinner is good."

"He is demanding sixty birr."

"Is that a fair price?" asked Eydis.

"Yes," said Afewerki. "Shall we pay him?" He looked at Andreas.

"Okay, okay. I can do that. No problem. As you say, chicorilla." He fished for his wallet and gave Afewerki sixty birr.

"I will go for the man to slaughter the goat. It must be done quickly." He ran back and gave the man the money, who bowed his head in thanks and gave the goat to Afewerki. He brought the goat into the compound and let it go near the cook house. It bleated in pain, dragging the broken leg.

"So sad," said Eydis. She wanted to berate Andreas, but held her tongue. She went to pet the goat, but it hopped away from her, bleating and bleating.

FIFTY-NINE

Reece leaned back on his arms, sitting on the low wall of the town circle, waiting for the possibility of a jeep. The sun burned his head. For less than sixty seconds, hot drops of rain pocketed the dust of the road. He stood and walked around. The sky was empty. He laughed. Svana was a handful. He wondered who would be lucky enough to tame her. He thought about his grandparents and imagined his grandmother putting a chocolate cream pie on the table.

He wondered what time it was. *Probably two or so.* The strap on his sandal was broken. A shoeshine boy was eying him from across the road. He motioned for the boy to come over. The boy, eight or nine, gathered his wooden shoeshine box and ran across to Reece. Reece took off his sandal and showed him the broken strap.

The kid nodded as if securing a government contract. From his box, he pulled a leather punch. He took the sandal and, with some pushing and pulling and a round of thick thread, restored the sandal to its former glory. Reece was astounded.

"Sentino," said Reece.

"And birr," said the boy.

Reece was elated and decided to give the kid five birr instead of one.

The kid was beside himself and offered many thanks in Amharic.

"Chicorilla," said Reece. He wanted to pat the boy on the head, but that didn't seem right. He stood and tested the repaired sandal. Good as new.

An hour or so passed, and Reece decided to go back to the hotel. He could use a Johnny Walker Red. But then there was the unmistakable sound of a jeep grinding its way up to AK. He thanked his lucky stars.

The jeep, a blue 1965 Toyota, motored its way to the circle. Reece stood. He watched, and sure enough, a handful of would-be riders appeared from nowhere. He would have to fight for a spot in the jeep, and he did, scoring the outside of the front passenger seat, sharing it with a young man wearing a Citgo ballcap.

Within an hour, the jeep began its ascent from the Jara River in the lowest gear and four-wheel drive. Reece estimated that he would arrive in time for dinner. He wondered how Eydis was doing without Svana and Gudmunder. He saw her as innocent, tough, but willing to be delicate. Her smile was killer, accentuated by her perpetually rosy cheeks.

The jeep took a hairpin turn, rolling over rocks in the road. Reece sat hip to hip with his seat partner, who smelled a little like milk. His back hurt. No one was speaking, the windows were rolled up, and it was just the tearing noise of the engine and the squeak of the suspension.

SIXTY

Eydis went behind the supply house and put her fingers in her ears when the goat was being killed. Andreas and Afewerki looked on from a distance. It was over very quickly, and the offal shuttled out of the compound to be cooked right away by Gebremariam's wife. The man skinning the goat took the hide and a front joint of meat for his trouble. At Abebe's request, he roughly quartered what was left and nailed each piece to the inside of the cook house wall, except for the ribs, which she was going to stew for the ferenji's dinner.

Eydis lingered at the fire pit. "Oh, it tastes so good, but I cannot watch."

"It is the way of the people," said Afewerki. Goat meat was his favorite. He studied Andreas gazing at Eydis.

"Is there anything to drink?" asked Andreas. "Alcohol?" He had definitely decided that he was spending the night.

"No, but we can get some. Afewerki, is it possible to buy some katikala?"

"It may be too late," said Afewerki. There were two places close by that he could check.

"But can you try?" asked Eydis.

"I will give you the money," said Andreas.

"I will need ten birr." He sighed. So much drinking. He took the money from Andreas and walked off on his mission.

"He is a nice guy," said Andreas. "He was here working with the Baptists many years ago."

"Yes, he is a great guy. I think he may be religious. He

does not like to drink."

"Perhaps. You would like a fire?"

"Yes, of course," said Eydis. Fires were magical, especially as night fell and the air quickly cooled.

Andreas stood and adjusted his pants. There was no kindling, just a vast pile of rock-hard branches the diameter of his narrow wrist. He looked around for dry grass.

"Do you need some help?" asked Eydis.

"I am fine." He picked up one of the sticks with the idea of breaking it. He put his knee into it, and nothing happened. He held one end to the ground and pushed his foot into it. Nothing.

"Reece!" Eydis jumped up and ran to the fence.

"What?" said Andreas. He turned, on his hands and knees, and Reece stood there with his bag.

She gave him a big hug. "Did you have success? In Addis? How are Svana and Gudmunder? Did you see them?"

Reece was stunned. He patted Eydis's back as if she were his sister. "A long story. I'll tell you everything." He yelled hello into the cookhouse. Abebe was tending a very hot fire, boiling up the ribs. "Smells good."

"Andreas is here," said Eydis.

Reece fully recognized that the helicopter was inside the compound. "Whoa, that's new. Hey, Andreas."

Andreas stood and shook his hand. He cleared his throat.

"Starting a fire?" asked Reece.

"Yes," said Andreas.

"Need any help?"

"No," said Andreas.

"It would be easiest if we took some coals from Abebe,"

said Eydis.

"I can do this. I have a lighter," said Andreas.

"Not the same as hot coals," said Reece.

Andreas went to the small tree on the other side of Gudmunder's tent and broke off the tips of branches. He had a copy of *The Ethiopian Herald* in the copter. He went to fetch it.

"So, tell me about Gudmunder and Svana," said Eydis. "They are okay?"

"Gudmunder is in the jail, and Svana is under house arrest at the hotel. Svana bought a hand grenade."

Eydis took Reece by the arm and made him sit in a folding chair. She pulled her chair next to his. "A grenade? But why?"

"To frighten," said Reece. He laughed.

"She must be careful. She should come back so that I can keep an eye on her."

Andreas returned with the paper and twigs. He crouched at the fire pit.

"She is safe with the grenade for sure. Gudmunder is okay. He's made friends with two prisoners. One is Omar, and he speaks English. But they did tie him to a chair in the sun." He explained the surreal scene.

"That is terrible," said Eydis. "We have to bring him back. Did Dr. Guthrie have any advice? What are we to do?"

Andreas flicked his lighter several times. The altitude wasn't helping.

"That's why I'm here. We're supposed to bribe the town administrator in AK and also pay some money to the priest for the stolen tabot. Dr. Guthrie says it's the quickest way."

"You're kidding. Afewerki and I went to visit a man here, a monk, and he said the same thing."

"Really? Well, twice is nice, I suppose," said Reece.

Andreas crouched over balls of burning newspaper. He put the twigs on the fire.

Ten minutes passed. The stars were out with the fading of last light. Afewerki stepped through the fence carrying a clear liter bottle and a clay jug. It took him a moment to realize that Reece was there. "My brother!"

Reece stood and shook Afewerki's hand. "What do you have? Join us."

Afewerki presented the bottles to Eydis. "One of katikala, and one of areke with garlic."

Andreas lifted his head. "Areke? We shall enjoy." He blew on the fading balls of fire. The twigs were not catching.

Afewerki determined that the fire would not succeed and went to the cook house for some coals.

"Shall we drink now or wait until we have eaten?" asked Eydis. The food would kill the buzz.

Andreas was anxious for a drink. "I'll have one now." He stared at the pile of burned paper.

"Let me get cups," said Eydis.

"Maybe a drink before dinner would be nice. Maybe we could just skip dinner?" asked Reece.

"Oh no," said Eydis. She told him the story of the donkey and the goat. Abebe had been cooking nonstop. They had to eat.

"Hallo! Here we come!" said Afewerki.

He was followed by Abebe, who juggled two hot coals back and forth.

"Shit," said Andreas.

Abebe dropped the coals into the fire ring and wiped her hands on her dress. Afewerki had a handful of dry twigs and corn husks and handed them to Andreas. Within five minutes, a small fire was licking the ends of three ragged sticks. Within ten minutes, a bright, cheery fire was growing.

SIXTY-ONE

Restless, Svana drank a warm beer as slowly as she could and then took a short walk around the hotel. She wondered what the alcohol content of St. George beer was. Not enough. She checked her watch, three p.m. She would wait until five to have a shot of Johnny Walker Red. The administrator Dingil was older but not bad-looking.

The cook house was a long room attached to the back of the bar. She peered in. There was a little naked boy with an erection chasing a little girl in a dirty dress. Two women were squatting, cooking. Svana said, "Hallo." They put their hands to their eyes as if looking into the sun. Svana took it all in. The toe next to her big toe on her right foot was aching. She remembered sailing fjords with her father. She moved on.

She walked back to her room and opened the door. Something was wrong with her toe. She took off her tennis shoe. It looked as if a thread had been tied around it. It was swollen. Puzzled, she rubbed the toe. She caught something. It was a hair wrapped around the toe, constricting it. She yanked it off with immediate relief. "Goddamn," she said.

The hotel seemed empty, very quiet. It *was* Sunday. Svana rose from the bed, having rested there for two hours. Time for a serious drink. She wondered how Gudmunder was doing. He seemed to be getting along very well, making friends with the prisoners. She would visit him again in the morning.

The bar was empty. She was the first customer of the

late afternoon, and Lebna was sweeping with a gnarled broom. She smiled at Svana.

"Johnny Walker," said Svana.

"Ishi," said Lebna. She swept a pile out the front door, looked at the descending sun, and sneezed twice. She poured out the whiskey and brought it to Svana.

"Amenseganolo," said Svana. She sipped at first and then downed the shot. She appreciated the warm burn. "Radio, music?"

Lebna understood "radio." She turned it on. It was a gospel song.

Svana nodded. She would prefer something by the Electric Prunes or Annie Lennox, but the Amharic music was strangely transfixing. Lebna brought her another shot of whiskey. This one Svana sipped. She was beginning to feel good, upbeat. She took in the earthy smell of the bar, the pool of light coming in through the front door. There was work to do, and she was doing it.

A man, a traveler, entered the bar. He was light-skinned and had a goatee. He stopped and stared at Svana. What the hell? The last thing he expected to see was a white ferenj in a bar. He sat at a table, facing in her general direction. This would make a good story, no doubt. He nodded at Svana, who returned with a nod of her own. He spoke just a little English. He assumed she was an American. His name was Teka.

Before she got too tipsy, Svana decided to order food. She motioned for Lebna.

"Abet?"

"Enjera b'wot?" asked Svana.

"Ow." Lebna inspired.

Svana couldn't help noticing the newcomer watching her. He was dressed business casual and was definitely not a farmer.

SIXTY-TWO

Eydis, Afewerki, and Andreas devoured their ribs and enjera with fresh pepper and onion. A great pile of greasy bones lay on the platter. Eydis needed to wash her right hand and worried that her face was stained with the rib juice. There was meat trapped between her back teeth, which made her uncomfortable. There was no dental floss in Gwar.

Andreas figured that it would be at least thirty minutes before he could feel the effects of his liquor. "Delicious," he said. He loved spicy food.

Eydis sensed that she was being "observed" by Afewerki and Andreas. Reece was less obvious. He was more aloof, and that was the most interesting. She was on her period, though, and they were all out of luck. She laughed to herself. She supposed she could have anal sex, but that was not her thing. She saw Andreas as the most likely "back door" man.

"It will rain tomorrow," said Afewerki.

"Will it?" asked Eydis.

"It is the time of the long rains," said Afewerki.

Reece hated the rain and fog. He needed the crazy hot sun.

"The rain is bad for flying," said Andreas.

Gebremariam had returned and called to the group to let them know that all was well.

Eydis looked up at the starry sky. It was there always. "Do you fly at night?"

"Oh no. Depth perception is not useful at night. And

what if there is fog? There would be a crash, and no one would live."

"Ah," said Eydis. She supposed that it really was harder than it looked.

"In Alabama, the trails glow at night. Fool's gold in the dirt. The moon makes it glow," said Reece.

"I would like to visit Alabama," said Eydis.

Reece felt he had scored a point. "Sure. If you come, I'll take you on a tour."

The fire burned brightly, illuminating faces in oranges, reds, and blacks. The inky night sky seemed to move with the stars.

"Do you think that one day mobile phones will work in Gwar?" asked Andreas.

"That would be freaky," said Reece.

Afewerki did not know what a mobile phone was.

"The day will come," said Eydis.

Andreas tended the fire as if it were a baby about to die. The night cooled quickly, and then quicker. It always caught Reece by surprise. He had not re-pitched his collapsed tent. The helicopter glowed in the starlight.

There was a flashlight at the gap in the fence. Gebremariam recognized the Snake and one of his minions, cradling an AK-47. He said good evening.

The Snake stepped into the compound as if he owned it. He had one thing on his mind and surveyed the large compound, the shadows. He focused on the fire. Eydis would be near the fire. He was cold. He was stoned on qat.

"Who the hell is that?" asked Andreas.

"Jesus, it's the Snake," said Reece.

"What a hell," said Afewerki.

"Shit," said Eydis.

The Snake staggered into the compound. He'd had sex three times that day. His guard held back a few meters. The Snake was more trouble than he was worth. He made his way to the fire, dizzy, and tried to focus. Which one was Eydis? He widened his eyes to try to make sense.

"Tenesteling," said Reece.

"Tebeda," said the Snake.

Afewerki whistled and squatted before he spoke. "Today is the holy day. Tomorrow will begin the new week."

There was silence.

Eydis stood from her chair. She went to the Snake and put her arm within his arm. By the light of the fire, she looked into his eyes.

The Snake looked into her eyes. The steam from his kettle settled. He relaxed. "You make me think of my mother," he said in Amharic.

Afewerki translated.

"Oh, that's sweet," said Eydis. She held up the bottle of katikala. Did he want a drink?

SIXTY-THREE

Teka was married, but wasted no time getting to know the ferenj. He had Lebna take Svana a shot of Johnny Walker Red. She seemed to glow like a light bulb, sitting at the table alone. He was fascinated with the way she ate her enjera. She seemed to labor over each bite as if it were her last.

Svana acknowledged the drink by smiling. She set it aside for when she was through eating. Her parents had split up when she was twelve, but it had been for the best. Her dad had taken an apartment very close by and often cooked dinner. He was fond of his vodka, and her mom was a closet smoker. Svana ate slowly, enfolding each tear of enjera with a bite of wot. There were denich and goman, potato and greens. The tastes were so agreeable. She craved seafood, but this was a second best. The salty liquid of the greens was prime.

The radio played. Svana ate and assessed her position in life, occasionally glancing at Teka. She was young and on a grand adventure. The world was her oyster, as they said. Her work in Gwar was rewarding. It seemed that the area needed food relief based on the number of underweight children they were discovering. It wasn't a famine scenario, but still, the people needed to eat. The man with the goatee was coming over with a beer in his hand.

"Hallo," said Teka. He waited for Svana to invite him to sit down.

"Hallo," said Svana. Other men were trickling in, filling the tables. The only other woman was Lebna. "Thank you for this." She pointed at the whiskey shot.

"Minem aydelem, no problem," said Teka. He glanced around. Everyone was watching him. "Uh, you are married?"

Svana said, "No. Are you married?"

He stumbled for a second. He hadn't expected that. "No, no, no." He laughed and stroked his goatee.

Svana knew he was lying. He was wearing a brass wedding ring on a string around his neck.

Teka, embarrassed at having to stand, just pulled out the chair and sat down with Svana. Her black hair was thick and short. He wanted to touch it. He had never touched a ferenj's hair.

Svana said nothing and continued to eat. She chuckled to herself. "Are you traveling?"

"Yes, I am traveling to Menz. We have sent many seeds there, and I must check the people to see that they are not selling them."

"What kind of seeds?"

"Oh, teff, sorghum, corn, peas, and lentils. Many seeds."

"Do they ever eat the seeds?" asked Svana.

"Yes, when there is no food, they will do this."

"Hmm," said Svana. She finished her meal and sipped her beer. She watched Dingil, the town administrator, step into the bar. He was wearing a suit without a tie. In the dimness, he pretended to gaze around the room. Lebna greeted him.

Dingil approached Svana and Teka. He wondered who the man was, an official from Addis Ababa, no doubt. He had planned on buying Svana a drink. He saw that she had whiskey and a beer. He fumbled for an English word in his head. "Ah, thank you," he said.

Svana laughed. "You are welcome."

Dingil laughed. He was missing several teeth in the back of his mouth. He came around and put his arm on Svana's shoulder. She let it stay there for a moment, but then brushed him away.

Teka said something in Amharic. Dingil frowned. His plan of seducing the ferenj was falling apart.

Svana was not amused but did not want to lessen Gudmunder's chances of getting out of jail. She told Teka to tell Dingil that she would speak with him later, perhaps when the generator came on.

Teka relayed the message, hoping to get rid of him.

Dingil wiped sweat from his brow and frowned again. He needed a drink right away. He called Lebna and ordered a beer for himself and a shot of whiskey for Svana. He'd heard that she liked to drink. He took a small table by himself. He appeared to Svana to be moping.

Lebna brought a St. George to Dingil and then delivered the whiskey to Svana. So, now she had two shots.

"So, what is your wife's name?" asked Svana.

Teka almost blurted it out. "No. No wife."

"I think you are lying. You have the ring."

Teka's eyes widened. Had she called him a liar? He wanted to slap her like he would his wife. He was beginning to see that this woman was unreasonable. "Will you dance when the light comes on?"

Svana rolled her eyes. Maybe she would. Maybe she wouldn't.

Teka held his tongue. He looked around the room and decided to sit with the town administrator. At least they could talk about seeds.

SIXTY-FOUR

The wood of Gwar was as hard as a rock but burned slow and long. Ever since he had failed to get the fire going, Andreas was forever poking it and adding a stick or two when needed. He was beginning to think that he should have left.

The Snake drowsed, sitting on a biscuit tin. His guard stood nearby, cradling his AK-47. The Snake had tried to get Eydis to sit in his lap. She'd told him no, that they would fall into the fire.

Eydis sat between Reece and Afewerki in the most comfortable folding chair. Her blonde hair looked golden in the fire's light. They were trying to tell jokes, but it wasn't going very well. Reece could only think of really dirty jokes. Against his better judgment, he decided to try one. The joke involved a daughter giving her father a blowjob. No one laughed. Reece decided to drink a bit slower. The katikala was gone, and they had started the infused areke, which was in a clay jug.

Eydis sipped the areke. "Oh God, the garlic is powerful!" She smiled, surrounded by a cadre of admirers. She felt warm and safe, even with the Snake there. "So, Afewerki. Tell us about the worker who was killed here. He was young, no?"

Afewerki had had a shot of the katikala and wasn't feeling well. "Yes, very young, perhaps twenty-two."

Reece took another draught of areke. He breathed in deep. "Who killed him?"

Afewerki looked perplexed. He put his finger to his lips

and pointed at the Snake.

There was a collective gasp from Eydis and Reece. Andreas thought he already knew that from Dr. Guthrie.

"But it was never proven," said Afewerki.

The Snake suddenly came alive. He fell from the biscuit tin onto his back and cursed. The guard rushed to help him up. The Snake stood and surveyed the group as if choosing who to execute next. He pounded his chest with his hand. "I am the administrator!" He sat slowly on the biscuit tin. "Why I am sitting on a fucking can!" he shouted in Amharic. He looked around for the bottle.

Afewerki offered to change places, and the Snake agreed. He was now next to Eydis. Andreas took the jug and held it out to the Snake. His hand shook as Andreas poured.

Reece wanted to hear more about the volunteer who was killed. He knew it had been about eight years ago and that the Baptists had withdrawn soon after. "So, it was a gunshot?"

The Snake knew no English other than profanities.

"Yes, one gunshot that is hitting him in the head. His name was Bobby. Everyone liked him. He was inside this house." Afewerki pointed to the supply house. "He was died instantly. The other nurse was Emma, and she tried to save him, but he died soon."

"I had no clue," said Eydis. "That's why you have been so against him. And here we are giving him free alcohol."

Afewerki continued to remember that night. "The bullet was coming through the wall. It passed into the head and did not come out. There was much blood." A tear threatened the corner of his right eye. In the distance, he saw two shooting stars.

"And *he* did it?" asked Eydis. She held out her cup to Andreas, who was pouring. She suddenly felt there was a trapdoor beneath her chair that would open at any moment. The thought of dying in Ethiopia had never crossed her mind. "Wow, just twenty-two."

The Snake put his hand on Eydis's knee. She pushed it away. He realized she was looking him in the eye. Very few did that, and certainly not women. He settled down and drank more areke. He turned to his left and saw Reece. The Snake was sitting between two ferenji. He laughed to himself and cursed. What was next, pigs for dinner?

Andreas stood, anticipating a confrontation. He wanted to hit the Snake in the face. Hell, he wanted to hit Reece in the face. Eydis was talking to him as if he were the only one there. What the hell? The fire was burning his leg, and he moved back.

SIXTY-FIVE

The generator had been on for two hours, one hour to go, powering the single light bulb and the tape player. It was Ephram Tamiru, modulating his voice in that Amharic way. Saxophone, drum, and an electric guitar, Svana was dancing, sweating, and swaying. The square room seemed to have no walls.

In front of her was Teka, and behind was Dingil. They looked lost as Svana rubbed against them and ran her hands across their shoulders. She seemed very near to entering a trance, and both feared that she might be afflicted with the evil eye.

Svana had lost track of how many whiskies she'd had. She was chasing them with beer. Her parents had separated right as she got her first period. Each month, she was reminded of the family's split. God, she was horny. Even when the tape stopped and Lebna had to flip it over, Svana continued to grind and sway, swigging beer. Men packed the bar, all speculating on who she would sleep with that night. If she passed out, maybe they could all have a go at the ferenj?

Lebna dashed madly to keep up with the drink orders. The enjera b'wot had sold out an hour ago. The hotel owner popped in as usual and was very happy to see the place packed. The ferenj was good for business, but she needed to be careful. She did not want a rape to occur at her hotel, especially with a foreigner. She caught Lebna and told her to keep an eye on the ferenj. There was a pistol behind the bar, in case things got too crazy.

Svana continued to dance. She felt fantastic. Time seemed suspended. The tape stopped again, followed by a squealing noise and a *chk, chk, chk*. Lebna hurried over as quickly as possible. She had a mixed tape of ferenji music. She thought that maybe it would bring the energy down a notch. The first song was "Silver Bells" by Bing Crosby.

Svana recognized the tune and burst out laughing. Christmas music! She reimagined it as death metal and thrust her hips even harder. She didn't notice, but the room had gone quiet. Everyone watched the crazy ferenj gyrating, expecting her to either explode or shoot through the roof.

Fuck, living in Ethiopia, in the countryside, without running water or electricity was fucking hard! But the people were so beautiful, like the men she was dancing with. Svana opened her eyes. She was the only one dancing. Teka stared at her with a lost look. She turned, and Dingil had his hands in his pockets to cover a giant erection.

"Silver bells, silver bells, it's Christmas time in the city..." sang Bing.

Svana slowed. Everyone was staring at her. Lebna rushed around the room. It was standing room only. A few were outside the door, peering in, and then the light bulb went out. It was pitch dark. Lebna yelled for people to get out of her way as she felt her way to the bar.

Svana felt hands on her body, grabbing and squeezing. She kicked and punched. Her blouse was tearing. She felt a hand at the front of her jeans. Lebna lit a candle and then another. Svana fell and looked up at the hungry eyes staring down at her. Teka had a room at the hotel. He yelled for everyone to stand back. He whispered to Dingil, who helped Svana to stand. Suddenly, she was very drunk and dizzy. "God help me," she said. Dingil and Teka were leading her from the bar through the tense crowd.

The cool air hit her. "No," she said, being carried along. She could no longer stand on her own.

Lebna fought her way through the crowd, yelling at them. They had to take her to her room and leave her alone. Dingil agreed. "Which is her room?"

"Arat," said Lebna. She feared the worst, but had to run back inside to guard the money and liquor.

Svana staggered along with Dingil to her left and Teka to her right. She doubled over and vomited her entire stomach contents. They dragged her along as she gagged, gagging with her. A small light went on inside her head. She felt like she was going to have diarrhea. She would shit on them, rub it into their eyes.

Teka pushed open the door to Svana's room, number four. A bright moon sent light through the door. A crowd followed. Dingil closed the door but opened the rough window, pushing it out so people could watch. Teka forced her onto the bed. Svana felt as though she was rolling down a hill, unable to gather her bearings. She lashed out as best she could.

Teka grabbed her blouse and pulled it up around her neck. He ripped her bra off and was momentarily stunned at the sight of her breasts.

Svana rallied and reached beneath the pillow. She had the grenade. She focused. Teka grabbed her arms, trying to twist them and make her drop it, before she pulled the pin. She let out a blood-curdling scream.

SIXTY-SIX

The Snake wanted to play Russian roulette with his pistol. It was clip-fed, but he couldn't remember if there was a bullet in the chamber.

"No, no, no," said Afewerki. He felt like a father scolding a small child.

"Jesus Christ," said Reece. "He can play by himself."

Eydis was comfortably numb. "Yeah, he can stick it up his asshole." Everyone laughed except the Snake. He wanted to know what she had said.

Afewerki said that Eydis wanted to dance. He then wondered why he said that.

"Oh, let's dance," said the Snake. He tried to stand but couldn't. He felt that he weighed as much as a tank. His guard, hopelessly bored, had left, hoping to send someone else.

"He wants to dance," said Afewerki. The night was going badly. It was cold. He needed to pee.

"We need music. The radio." She stood and nearly blacked out. She stumbled to the tent.

Reece was buzzed with a heavy garlic smell to his breath, which was making him sick. At home in Alabama, when he'd had too much to drink, he would sit in the shower and let cool water drench his body.

Andreas had just about given up on connecting with Eydis, but dancing opened up the possibilities. Who knew, maybe she would get naked. He added six large sticks to the fire, which glowed a hot red.

Eydis returned with her black radio. The speakers were

detachable. She knew there would be nothing on the FM dial, so she started to search on the AM. Weird squeaks and outer space sounds. She hit something, French, a pop song in French, and she turned up the volume. The station was broadcasting from Djibouti.

As if by magic, everyone except the Snake stood and began to slow dance with themselves. The moon cast the dancers in a weird light.

Eydis danced, drawn to Reece. She took his hand. They drifted away from the fire pit toward the cook house, into the ankle-high grass. Spontaneously, Reece said the Amharic for tapeworm, "Kosa." Eydis responded with the Amharic for roundworm, "Wosfat." She wanted to kiss him as they laughed at one another.

Andreas was done. He would sleep in the back of the helicopter. He had everything he needed.

Afewerki stared into the blazing fire. The next song was Dire Straits with "So Far Away." He knew the lyrics by heart and felt very sad as he watched Reece and Eydis dancing together.

Sixty-seven

Teka held down the arm with the grenade. Dingil had the other arm, pinned above Svana's head. There was shouting from outside, the small crowd in a frenzy. Svana remembered her parents. They were fucked up, but she loved them. She twisted and bit the hand holding her arm above her head. Dingle yelled and cursed, letting go.

Svana punched Teka in the right eye as hard as she could. For a brief second, he let go. Svana pulled the pin on the grenade and let it drop. Time stood still, as everyone knew the grenade would explode if she let go of the spoon. Teka backed off, eager to be a thousand miles away. Dingil, breathing hard, retreated to the door and opened it. He had no desire to be shredded.

Lebna fought her way through the crowd. She had been raped many times and felt bad for the ferenj. Svana was lying on the bed, gripping the hand grenade. Lebna pulled down her blouse and motioned for Svana to stand. Svana was dizzy. She felt like she would shit herself. There was a live hand grenade in her right hand. The sight of Lebna encouraged her. She sat up, clinging tightly to the grenade. Lebna motioned for Svana to follow her.

Svana put her feet to the floor. She almost vomited. Lebna helped her stand, encouraging her in Amharic. Lebna was wearing a soccer jersey. What to do with the grenade? As soon as Svana let it go, it would explode within five to seven seconds.

Lebna had one idea. She encouraged Svana to follow her. They exited the hotel room, parting a crowd of thirty, all men. Lebna had never felt more powerful, although she was abandoing the bar. She held Svana's left hand and led her away from the hotel down the road that led to the former Baptist Mission station.

Down the road, they walked in the moonlight. Svana was clueless, but she followed nonetheless. Behind them, a small crowd followed. She thought about her parents again. Had her mom kicked her father out of the house or had he left of his own accord? It wasn't clear. The notion of a mutual agreement did not render finality. Wasn't someone supposed to be wrong and someone right?

The rocky road caused them to stumble many times. The night sky was perverse with stars. Lebna could only think about God. He wanted to protect this ferenj. She was a stranger. She should suffer no harm. Perhaps one day she would visit the ferenj's homeland. The thought made her trip. She would have to fly on a plane.

The pair walked, but Eydis was nearly done. She felt that she was walking to the end of the earth. She looked at her hand interlocked with the hand of Lebna. Her gaze traveled to Lebna's face, a tranquil but steadfast visage. This was necessary.

It took ten more minutes of vigorous walking, but soon they approached the cliff line of Alem Ketema. In the distance was only air. Lebna left the road with Svana in tow, sauntering. Beside a large boulder, she determined that they were at the edge of the abyss. She grabbed Svana's right hand. Keeping the spoon depressed, she took the grenade from Svana.

SIXTY-EIGHT

The Snake was asleep in his chair. A new guard, who had arrived minutes earlier, whispered to Gebremariam to help him. He then shook the Snake. "Let us go now." They both lifted him by an arm. He mumbled and swayed as he stood. Half carrying and half dragging him, they stumbled through the fence to carry the Snake to his house.

Eydis sat beneath a blanket between Reece and Afewerki. The radio station had faded, and now the only sounds were the subtle hiss of the fire and dogs fighting in the distance. The jug of areke was empty.

"So, Reece, why are you here?" asked Eydis.

Reece thought about saying, *To meet you.* "I think it all started back in Texas when my parents were killed. I felt so helpless..."

"Oh my, I didn't know this," said Afewerki.

"That is terrible. I'm so sorry," said Eydis.

"No worries...It was thirteen years ago. We were at a restaurant called Luby's in Killeen, Texas, which is beside Fort Hood. This guy ran his pickup truck through the front glass. I watched it happen. It was crazy. And then there were loud pops. I saw a man fall backward. He was a veterinarian. I thought the tires were exploding on the truck. But then the driver got out, and he had a pistol in each hand. He was shooting people, coming right at us."

"Dear God," said Eydis. "But you lived?"

"And that's part of the problem. There was nothing I could do. He shot them. I went back to Alabama, moved in with my grandparents, and went to school there. I just wanted to help people, even then. It's all pretty simple but complicated too."

"What a hell," said Afewerki.

"We have many guns in Iceland, but never such violence as that," said Eydis. "America is a very violent country." She shivered beneath her blanket. She looked at Reece's face in a new light. He often had a somewhat blank look, a faraway look. His face looked younger than thirty-two, but his eyes seemed much older. She reached over and squeezed his shoulder.

"Yeah, I'd like to visit Iceland someday. So, why are you here?"

"The government of Iceland works closely with the United Nations to help other countries. I found out about this through Dr. Thorsonn. He recruited Svana as well. You know, there have been many Icelandic medical teams to visit Ethiopia."

"I didn't know that," said Reece. He leaned forward, letting the fire warm his face.

"I have met them many years ago," said Afewerki. "I was very young. The bottles for the water are from that time."

"The old IV bottles," said Reece. "I love those. From Iceland, huh?"

"Now we use only the bags," said Eydis. "So, I am here just to be helpful, like you."

"You worked in a hospital?" asked Reece.

"Yes. In Reykjavik. It's very nice, but I admit that I was bored."

Afewerki had worked with many ferenji volunteers. "You were needing for adventure?"

Reece laughed. He knew that restless feeling.

"Yes, I think so," said Eydis. She had a headache. "Is it late?"

Afewerki was the only one with a watch. "It is ten-thirty. Reece, you must fix your tent. Shall I help you?"

"I can do it," said Reece. While they were dancing, Eydis had invited him to her tent. She'd said, "No fucking, though."

"Okay, good night," said Eydis. She ruffled Reece's hair and walked to the shintabet.

SIXTY-NINE

Lebna motioned for Svana to move away from the cliff line. She threw the grenade and ran back toward Svana, pulling her to the ground.

The grenade sailed downward, hit a rock, and exploded with a loud report. White smoke drifted in the breeze back up and over the cliff edge. Svana thanked Lebna and hugged her. The wind blew very cold. In the moonlight, she paused to inspect herself. Her blouse had been torn, and her bra was undone and askew, which she refastened.

With a clearer head, Svana replayed all that had just happened. Should she report the assault to the authorities? But it was the town administrator who had held her down. Nothing could come of that. She walked side by side with Lebna, shivering in the frigid breeze.

They approached the town center with its roundabout and passed the jail. There were very few people out. Should she go back to the hotel? Was it safe? She didn't know. At least she'd had the grenade, but that was gone. God, she just wanted to be back in Gwar, weighing the children with Eydis.

Lebna led Svana up to the hotel. Holding her hand, she looked into the bar lit by candles. Dingil wasn't there. The other man wasn't there either. The bar would close at midnight. She motioned for Svana to enter the quiet bar. Several patrons had served themselves, and Lebna had to go around and tally up what each person owed.

Svana sat alone near the bar. She sensed that Lebna had a plan, that she was safe for the time being. Lebna brought some cold enjera soaked in a mild wot, and a bottle of orange Fanta. Svana nodded. She felt bad that she had drunk so much. She would have to be more careful. She was not in Iceland. She was in a bar with only men in a rural area of Ethiopia. Maybe she had a drinking problem? Perhaps the assault was her fault. A chill went down her spine, reliving the scene in her hotel room. Her hand hurt from punching Teka.

Lebna turned the radio on, tuning to an Addis Ababa station. There was significant static, but the music added a surreal note to the bar, shadows licking the walls. Svana ate the enjera, enjoying the rush back to normalcy. The Fanta was warm but refreshing. She thought about asking for a beer, but did not. Lebna had saved her, or had it simply been the grenade? Probably both. She watched Lebna work the room in her long dress and soccer jersey. She was very good at what she did.

The bar closed, and Lebna went around collecting the tabs, wondering if the ferenj would mind sleeping on the floor of her tiny house.

In walked Dingil, just as she was preparing to blow out the candles. He came in just a few steps, keeping back from Svana, who was glaring at him. He spoke in a low voice to Lebna. He wanted to have sex after the bar was closed, and she was obliged.

Lebna sighed and made a growling noise. But it was true. He owed money to the bar but paid her in advance for sex. What to do with the ferenj?

Svana felt that she was on the edge of attacking. She did not break her gaze with the town administrator. Something was going on between Dingil and Lebna. What it was, she did not know. Where would she spend the night, in her hotel room? There was no inside lock, not even a latch. She glared.

Lebna extinguished all but two candles, tossing the room into deeper shadows. She approached Svana and spoke from her heart. Svana did not understand what she said, but trusted her, nonetheless. "Nah," said Lebna, motioning for Svana to come.

Dingil stood aside as they passed. Lebna had keys on a ring. They passed into the night and walked to Svana's room. Lebna explained that she would padlock the door from the outside so that no one could enter. She would come in the morning and take off the lock. Svana did not understand until they were at the room, and Lebna mimed putting the lock on. What if there was a fire? What other choice did she have?

"Ishi," said Svana, and she entered her dark room.

SEVENTY

Andreas awoke inside the helicopter very early, a rooster, many roosters, invading his overhung sleep. He'd had to pee three times during the night, which aggravated him. He dreaded seeing if Reece's tent had been fixed or not. There was a thick fog just overhead. He looked, and the tent was still flat on the ground. *Shit.*

He walked to the dead fire and held his hands over the ash. A steady heat was there. There was enough wood for a small fire. He knelt and blew away ash, finding the hot orange coals. He arranged a few sticks and blew on the coals beneath, yielding thin wisps of smoke. It was the act of others watching that made building a fire hard.

He eyed the empty jug of areke. The thought of it made his stomach turn, and he needed water. He went into the cook house and checked the gravity-feed filter. It was empty. He looked around for a clean pot. He chose the cleanest and dipped water from the barrel outside. It would take a few minutes for the water to percolate through the ceramic filter. He dared not drink it otherwise. Where was Gebremariam?

As if on command, Gebremariam appeared, wrapped in a shamma. "Dehna," he said, greeting Andreas.

Andreas nodded. He walked back to the smoldering fire, went to his knees, and blew on the coals. A small fire appeared. He paced around the fire, thinking. What would he do when both Eydis and Reece emerged from the tent together? He would look foolish. He decided to take the bull by the horns and wake them up.

"Hallo! Anybody home?" He scratched on the tent fabric.

Inside the tent, Reece sat up. He could see the shadow of Andreas. Reece was shirtless and suddenly chilled. He looked at Eydis beside him, lost in her slumber. Even while sleeping, her cheeks were rosy. She'd let him give her a back massage. She'd smelled like hot metal, and her skin was oh so soft. "Abet?" he said. Eydis roused just a bit and smiled. She was topless as well, her arms crossed across her breasts beneath the sleeping bag. Reece felt guilty, but somewhat triumphant, as he put on his shirt. "Hold on!" he said.

Reece unzipped the fly. He was about to stand. Andreas swung at him, hitting him in the jaw. On instinct, Reece dove for the legs in front of him. He'd wrestled in high school. He took Andreas down, his head in Andreas's stomach. Andreas rabbit punched his head. Reece reached and hooked Andreas's head. He had his head and legs. Slowly, he brought Andreas's head to his knees.

Eydis was awake now and confused. What the hell was going on? She thought of dogs fighting. She put her head through the tent flap. *Oh my God.* Reece had Andreas on the ground, squeezing him into a ball. She turned and found a scrub top.

"What the fuck?" asked Reece. He was sweating and winded.

"Let go," said Andreas. "I...can't breathe."

Reece saw Eydis. He grinned through the sweat in his eyes. Andreas rolled and broke free. He jumped to his feet, ready to fight.

Reece stood more slowly. "That's a nice way to wake

up," he said. "What is your problem?"

"Maybe you," said Andreas. His face was red.

Eydis stood, amazed. What was going on? She saw Gebremariam at the fence. He looked frightened. "Am I dreaming?"

"Why don't you take your fucking helicopter and leave?" asked Reece. He realized his hands were in fists and let them relax.

"That's the last ride," said Andreas. He felt like going crazy. Like smashing a rock into Reece's skull.

Reece tried to calm himself. He realized that Andreas had feelings for Eydis. "Whatever I've done, I'm sorry."

Andreas looked from Reece to Eydis. He looked back at Gebremariam. He tried to slow his breathing. "No problem," he said. He extended his hand.

Reece still felt like fighting. He grabbed Andreas's hand and went in for a leg sweep. He was laughing. Andreas was down.

Andreas was on his back. He began laughing as well.

Eydis was stunned. *What the hell?* She decided that it was best to laugh. Everyone was laughing except Gebremariam.

SEVENTY-ONE

Surprisingly, Svana slept well, although she had a long nightmare about being abducted by aliens. Out of bed, she couldn't open the door, it being padlocked from the outside. She swung the small window open, welcoming the birds and the sunshine. She stood there waiting for Lebna.

She reviewed the previous night's events and shook her head. She supposed she would have great stories to tell her children one day. A covey of doves landed on the metal roof, sliding and scratching their nails. She took a shoe and threw it against the roof's underside.

Lebna left her tiny room, part of a six-room house. She was about to lock the door and realized she had left her ring of keys inside. She retrieved it and hurried to the Beselfui. They didn't serve breakfast, but she had to clean the rooms and empty the chamber pots. She worried that she had not locked the bar the previous night. So many things had happened.

Svana was standing in front of the window when she saw Lebna and waved. Back in Iceland, Lebna would be recognized for her vigor and salt. She was a prize. The door opened. "Lebna!" said Svana.

Lebna looked exhausted. The goddamned town administrator had not been able to come. She'd had to jack him off with a wine bottle in his ass.

The two embraced. Svana smelled the sweat of sex. Lebna smelled the sweat of fear. Quickly, Lebna took her leave, having many chores.

Svana decided to walk to the town's water distribution center. Six faucets tapped into a well some hundred feet down. It had been engineered by the Baptists many years ago. She only wanted to wash her face and hands. She passed the jail along the way and walked along the perimeter of the road-facing wall. She knocked on the metal sheeting. Nothing. Gudmunder must still be inside, asleep.

She arrived at the faucets, three deep with young women waiting to fill water pots and plastic jugs. She took her place in line, smiling at her compatriots in life.

Inside the jail, Gudmunder stood. He'd spent the best part of the night sitting with his face in his hands, listening to dogs fight in the distance. He was getting progressively more tired with each passing day. He thought often of his children, two girls, one married and one not. They were more real in Alem Ketema than they had ever been in real life.

Omar and the other fellow were asleep. He went to the wall fronting the road and looked through a seam. A young boy was moving goats along with a whip. He thought about Gaukur and the lost Icelandic saga. Gaukur had been to Ethiopia. There was an Ark of the Covenant, and it was in Ethiopia. Gaukur had come to steal it, but the Ark belonged in Ethiopia. There were higher powers at work.

Svana waited. The morning was bright and quickly warming. The young girl in front of her had filled her clay pot and hoisted it onto her back with a rope. Svana let the water trickle as she washed her face. She wet her hair as well with cold water. Water dripping down her face onto her scrub top, she stood. She felt reborn.

What next? She decided she would go inside the jail and wake up Gudmunder. If Dingil were there, she would confront him. Maybe, though, she should eat first. She was hungry.

She walked to the jail and went along the outer wall.

"Svana!"

"Gudmunder," said Svana. "Are you well?" She could see one of his eyes through the crack.

"I am okay, but tired of having to shit in front of strangers. How are you?"

"I'm okay. There was some trouble last night. I'll tell you later. Do you need food?"

"I'm okay. A woman brings bread and bottles of Ambo. I have money," said Gudmunder.

"I will go eat and come back," said Svana. "Okay?"

"When will Reece return?"

"Maybe today?" asked Svana. "You shall be free today. I guarantee it."

"Ha," said Gudmunder. "I appreciate it." He noted his body odor. It was strong. He needed a bath.

"I will come again at noon," said Svana. She left Gudmunder and headed toward the Beselfui. She would have a nice breakfast, perhaps buns and tea. It was her right as a human being. She felt confident, although she missed her hand grenade.

SEVENTY-TWO

Monday was go day. Time to work. Eydis prepared to venture out on a child-weighing expedition with Afewerki. Andreas had lifted out of the compound, headed back to Addis Ababa, waking the entire village. Reece stood, waiting for Afewerki. He was sore from having wrestled with Andreas. There had been a connection, though, something like friendship. Why were women always the subject of fantastic emotions? He watched Eydis brushing her teeth. What else was worth dying for?

Gebremariam came through the hole in the fence with a kettle of hot spiced tea. Reece went to his collapsed tent, poked around, and found his green plastic cup. Gebremariam poured. He looked at Reece as if he were a new person. He then moved on to Eydis.

Eydis had to rummage a bit before producing her own cup. The steam from the tea made her yawn. "Amenseganolo."

"Yiqirta," said Gebremariam. This was the first year he was relying on someone else for his income, the Icelanders, and it made him very nervous. The other men were out plowing. It felt wrong somehow.

"I'll need to get back to AK today," said Reece.

"Yeah," said Eydis. She wondered if he liked Svana.

"Maybe Gudmunder will be free today." He wished Andreas had waited to take him to AK, but his punishment was worth it.

"Well, if the bribe works." She looked around, took Reece by the hands, and brought him close. She kissed him.

A full minute went by.

"Jesus," said Reece. He was in love.

"Eat breakfast and get a jeep," said Eydis. She looked like a high-school girl in her torn pajama top. There was a distinct V leading down.

"Jesus," said Reece.

"Is that all you can say?" She laughed and brushed the hair from her eyes.

"Oh, no problem, sorry," said Reece. "You're just so... pretty." That last word had taken his breath away.

Eydis smiled. She felt like slapping him to break him from his reverie. She would marry him. She would have his children. The world was cruel; the world was a blessing.

Below Gwar, just near the former Baptist Mission warehouse and clinic, Reece waited on a jeep. He squatted, building the muscles in his thighs and buttocks. After a minute or so, he had to stand. He wondered about his grandparents. He imagined them watching a VHS tape of a Billy Graham crusade. Chester loved to garden, and Dora loved to gossip on the phone. She was hilarious. Both Chester and Dora had grown up in rural Alabama. The whole world was either black or white. That was it. No Chinese or Russians. Just black and white. African-American and Caucasian.

Reece stood, his legs cramping, and walked uphill back to the compound. "Ferenj!" came the usual cry. He waved and continued. He thought back to his first love, a woman named Kristin. She'd stolen his heart. It had all seemed so perfect. But it didn't work out, and he wasn't exactly sure why. He supposed that at any given moment, there were a million women he could fall in love with. Was it all up to chance?

SEVENTY-THREE

Svana bought a six-inch white candle and paid ten cents. She'd had a wheat bun for breakfast. She walked to the jail. Dingil was not in his office, which was probably for the best. She had some choice Icelandic words for him. The jailer, recognizing her, frowned and let her in.

"Gudmunder?" He was inside the dark cell, which surprised her.

"Svana!" Gudmunder was sitting in a corner on the floor, relaxing his back. He stood with some pain. He looked tired and haggard, not having shaved for three days.

"Hallo!" said Svana. They did not embrace but rather stared at each other as if meeting after a long absence.

"Good God, what has happened?" asked Gudmunder. Svana seemed compromised.

Svana searched for words. "There was some trouble last night."

"What about the grenade?"

Svana yawned. "The grenade is gone now. No problem." She decided to spare him the story of the night before.

"That's good to know. Do you think Reece will return today?"

"I don't know. Hopefully." She wondered if her jeans were too tight, too revealing. She'd never had that thought before.

"You need to be very careful," said Gudmunder. "If Reece does not return today, you should return to Gwar. There is Gebremariam there. You need to be safe. This is not Iceland."

"I understand," said Svana. "Shall I bring you lunch?"

"No, but...You could bring me something sweet, some cookies perhaps."

Omar stood. "You are brave woman."

Svana assumed he had heard about the attack.

In walked Dingil. He yelled at the jailer, who retreated into the front room. He continued to rail.

Omar translated. "Wicked women will be punished."

Svana felt her blood pressure rise. *Why the hell was Gudmunder so compliant? They could just walk out. Let them shoot!* She doubted if they were brave enough, though. Her heart raced seeing Dingil there. "You should be arrested!"

Omar was translating.

Dingil put both of his hands to his head. "If you do not leave, I will place you in the jail!"

"You, you, bald fuck freak," said Svana.

Omar was laughing. Svana pushed Dingil through the door. She was heading outside, but he grabbed her arm and spun her around.

"Svana!" yelled Gudmunder.

"Into jail!" Dingil motioned for the guard to help him.

Svana angled for the open front door, but the guard blocked her way. He looked shocked.

Dingil grabbed her from behind. Svana let out a roar, throwing her elbows into his ribs.

Suddenly, Gudmunder was there. He punched Dingil between his shoulder blades as hard as he could. He'd never hit anyone before. Svana was free and going for the jailer's rifle, an AKM. The guard was trying to get a bead on Gudmunder. He was trying to escape, and orders were to shoot first in the leg.

The rifle fired.

SEVENTY-FOUR

Reece entered the compound. The jeep coming was a gamble, but he wanted to see Eydis again before he left. She was not there. Abebe was washing clothes in a bucket. She smiled at Reece, and he waved. He returned down the hill, careful of the rocks. A gray sky looked fat with rain. He could smell it. He hated that there was no thunder or lightning with the rain.

On his way down, a woman approached him. She took him by the hand and began to lead him toward her humble hut. She was single with four children, the oldest being eight. He could feel the calluses on her hand. She wore a long, ragged dress with a twisted sash around her waist. Her face was thin, her hair shoulder-length and turned up at the ends with beads. He expected the worst. The children peered out from the hut with eyes wide.

First, she dipped him a plastic cup of talla from a barrel cut in half, floating with gesho leaves. Reece took the cup. He really didn't like the smoky talla. It was too weak, tasted like smoky beer water. What was going on? She took him by the hand and led him inside the dark hut with the steep-sloped roof of straw. She was talking in Amharic.

Mesmerized, he stepped inside and sat on the mud bench built into the wall. He sipped the warm talla and made a face. A red hen hopped into the hut, looking this way and that, clucking. The woman approached him. She lifted her dress. She took his hand and pressed it to her vagina.

Reece suddenly snapped from his reverie. He was being seduced as children looked on. He stood and put his hands in his pockets. He put down his talla. He didn't know what to do. He pulled out his small wallet. Did she want money? He held out a five-birr note.

She slapped him and began to yell. Reece seemed to wake from a dream. He felt danger and left the hut, walking backward. She berated him, shaking her finger. *What the hell?* The kids were laughing. "Ferenj!"

Reece walked into the lane and downhill, confused. Had he met the woman before? Rain was falling, and he had not noticed. The drops were large and shot into the dust, creating puffs. He focused on the steep path, holding back to keep from breaking into a run. Back at the old Baptist warehouse compound, he stopped. Three others were there, waiting on a ride, young guys in Western clothes. One had an umbrella, which he was sharing with the others.

The rain progressed into a flood. Water ran down the steep lane, a muddy torrent. Reece was soaked. The others left, but he waited another half hour. Freezing and walking in circles, he thought about Eydis. Surely, she wasn't out weighing children. It seemed they would have to move into the supply house during the rainy season. If a jeep didn't come within half an hour, there was no use waiting.

Svana and Afewerki weighed and measured ten children in an open field, using a small tree before the rain started. Afewerki was sure that the rain would last for several hours and convinced Eydis they should head back to the compound. They sloshed into the flooded yard and stepped inside the cook house. Wet laundry hung on a makeshift clothesline. There was nowhere to sit, and they entered the supply house, where there were blankets.

"Such a rain," said Svana. She grabbed two blankets.

"It is the time of the long rains," said Afewerki. He draped himself in a single handmade blanket. "Is good for planting."

"I guess that's good," said Svana. She thought about her younger brother, who was afflicted with cerebral palsy. He was bound to a wheelchair. He was exceptionally intelligent but hindered by his physical limitations.

The rain pounded the tin roof. Eydis looked around at the boxes. One was stamped "U.S. Government Property, Commercial Resale is Unlawful." It was a case of MREs, meals ready to eat. Svana opened the box. "Spaghetti with meat sauce. Chicken stew. Are they good?"

"I do not like," said Afewerki.

"Huh, I'd like to try it. But we're having more goat for dinner, right?"

"Yes, we have much goat to eat." Afewerki felt a distinct notion of being alone with Eydis and her rosy cheeks. He wanted to touch her blonde hair, let his mind wander, and bit his lip. He didn't like the local women because they never bathed, plus they were so stubborn. But how often did Eydis bathe? He had no idea.

The crack of the rifle. Silence. Gudmunder put his hands in the air. Svana was livid, panting. Dingil panted. The jailer had the AKM pointed at Gudmunder, motioning him backward through the door. He pointed it at Svana and then back to Gudmunder. Gudmunder retreated through the door into the cell and then into the open air of the courtyard with Omar. Omar saw the jailer with the rifle and scurried beyond the doorway to the cell. The gray sky opened with rain.

Dingil was confused. What had happened? He made sure that Gudmunder was secure. He should jail this Svana, but she was trouble. He'd never met the likes of her. He remembered the money that Reece was bringing. He decided to double the bribe to two thousand birr. Otherwise, the doctor would remain his prisoner. But he gave up the idea of having sex with Svana. God, she was a bitch.

Svana walked outside. She felt angry but lucky. No one had been shot. Gudmunder had saved her. She went to the fence of tin sheets. "Hey! Gudmunder." The rain was steady and cold.

"Svana, please go back to the hotel and wait for Reece. You are in danger." Gudmunder put his eye to the fence, watching Svana's reaction. She had her hands on her hips. She seemed winded.

"Maybe I'll buy another grenade," she said.

"No, Svana. Go and have a beer. Relax. Reece will be here soon with the money. Just stay focused. It's raining."

Svana looked around. The path was deserted. She

wanted to crawl into a hole. She wanted to rip somebody's head off. "Okay, I will go and wait."

"Thank you, Svana," said Gudmunder.

Svana hurried back to the hotel. What if she ran into that other fucker, Teka? She was running in her tennis shoes, passed into the hotel yard, and ducked into the bar. She needed a drink. Where was Lebna? What time was it, maybe ten? Two men played checkers, drinking tea and eating dark sorghum buns. Both examined her. No music played, just the drum of rain on the roof. She looked into the cook house attached to the back. An old woman stirring a pot. A tiny snotty-nosed girl standing by the fire.

Like she'd seen others do, Svana helped herself. She chose a bottle of Awash wine. She wanted whiskey but decided to hold back. How to open the bottle? There was no corkscrew. The rain poured. She stood at the bar for a minute, waiting for Lebna to appear. There was a knife. She began to dig out the cork.

"Abet?"

Svana jumped. Lebna was taking the bottle from her, shaking her head no. Lebna pulled a black corkscrew from an apron pocket. Svana had made a mess of the cork. She managed to pull out most of the cork, but several bits floated in the bottle. She said, "Tsk, tsk, tsk."

Svana was amused. She watched Lebna open a bottle of Coke. Before she could react, Lebna poured the Coke into the wine bottle. *What the hell?* She watched Lebna brush the resulting foam aside. The foam had brought the bits of cork out of the bottle. She poured in more Coke. Svana put her hand over the top of the bottle, laughing. What was next?

"Ishi, ishi," said Svana. She poured a cup full of the white wine, now flavored with Coke. She tasted. Not bad.

"Dabo?" asked Lebna, asking her if she wanted bread.

Svana thought about how the morning had gone thus far. "Yellum." She needed the buzz of the wine as quickly as possible.

An old red Land Rover arrived at the last minute with six passengers. Reece got in without asking any questions. He just assumed that the driver was headed back to AK. The driver pushed a button that blew a makeshift horn. Reece knew that he was waiting for more riders. The horn bleared over and over, but no one came.

"Dollars?" asked the driver. He wanted dollars. "Assir dollars."

Reece thought. Assir was ten. That was eighty birr. Usually, he paid twenty birr for the trip. "No, birr," said Reece. "Haya birr."

The driver was very young. He made a sour face. He knew the ferenj needed a ride badly. "Salasa birr."

That was thirty birr. Reece frowned but agreed. He pulled out thirty wet birr and handed it to the driver, who blew his horn one last time.

He was headed uphill. The wheels spun. The Rover fishtailed. Reece noticed that the windshield wipers were not on, broken. The driver reversed and then began the downhill journey to the river.

The rain abated halfway into the journey. The Rover jounced through mud holes, the sludge turning from red to orange. Reece had to hold on with both hands to keep from being thrown like a beanbag. *Shit,* he'd forgotten his backpack. He shook his head. He'd have to wear his underwear again.

The Rover ground its way up draining roads of mud, the

engine groaning and whining. The sun had reappeared, making the landscape surreal with clarity. The dirt and rocks would be there a million years from now. Reece had forgotten there was a driver, imagining his forward progress as magic.

Arriving in AK, the driver pulled into the town center and stopped. Reece jumped out. The air was electric with positive ions, or so he imagined. It felt pure. He walked in the mud toward the Beselfui. He passed the jail and walked into the courtyard of the hotel after scraping his shoes. He was cold and wet from the rain. He wanted hot food.

Svana saw the shadow in the door and knew that it was Reece. She took a sip of wine and went to meet him.

"Svana!" said Reece.

"Hey, you," said Svana. They hugged and went back to the table. "Wine?"

"Hmm, maybe just some food and hot tea for now." He looked around. Lebna came out of the back. She greeted him with a big smile.

"Dabo?" asked Reece. "Chai?"

"Ishi," said Lebna. She wanted to touch his hair and did just that, laughing.

"Okay," said Reece. "How is everything?"

Svana thought about where to start. "Well, the administrator and this other guy tried to rape me, but I had a hand grenade." She chuckled as if trying to believe her own story.

"What?"

She filled him in on the details. "This morning, I went to the jail, and I got in a fight with the administrator, Dingil. Gudmunder came to the rescue but was shot at by the jailer."

"What?" said Reece. "So, everyone is okay?"

"I think so. Did you bring the money? The bribe?"

"Yeah, but I forgot my backpack. Oh well. Should we go now?"

"No," said Svana. "Eat some bread. I have this wine to drink."

Lebna appeared just then with the roll and the teapot. Reece ate the roll in four bites and drank the sweet, spiced tea. Being chilled had made him hungry. Svana had another cup of wine and decided to save it. "Let's stop by my room."

After dropping the leftover wine in her room, Svana and Reece walked to the jail. Large puddles filled the road. Mud was everywhere, but the air smelled clean. Inside, the jailer was not there, but Dingil was in his office. He frowned at the sight of the ferenji.

"We need Omar," said Svana. "He speaks English. Omar?" she said to Dingil. He pushed away from his desk as if he had not slept in a week. He returned with Omar in front of him.

"We have the money," said Svana.

Omar interpreted.

"You have two thousand birr? It is now two thousand." Dingil resumed his place behind his blank desk.

"Two thousand?" asked Reece.

Svana spoke. "You said one thousand. We have one thousand."

"The price has changed my bold ferenj," said Dingil. "You should be in jail with Omar and the white devil!"

"I hate you!" said Svana.

Reece sighed.

The rain lasted and lasted. Outside the tiny square house, the rocky dirt was sponging the water and shedding the excess to the river far away.

Afewerki thought if there were music, maybe Eydis would want to dance. There was no radio inside, though, and he didn't know how to dance. They were just sitting there, draped in blankets. Eydis was thinking about Reece. Maybe they should have had sex. Perhaps he would have been okay with her being on her period. At least she wouldn't have gotten pregnant. She thought about having a chocolate baby with Afewerki. The possibilities were unlimited.

Eydis opened the chicken stew MRE. She looked at the various components and pulled out a packet of sweetened cocoa. "Oh, chocolate," she said. "Let's try it." She tore the foil pouch and stepped outside beneath the roof overhang. She held the pouch out and let it fill halfway with water.

Afewerki opened the utensil packet and handed her a plastic spoon. The chocolate powder was what he liked best about the MREs.

"You want to try?" asked Eydis. Her feet were wet and cold inside her tennis shoes.

"No, it is for you."

Eydis let the blankets slide from her shoulders onto the chair back. "Oh, it's very sweet. Mmm."

"Do you have the black men in Iceland?" asked Afewerki.

Eydis laughed. "Not so many," she said. "We have some

people from the Philippines. They are brown, no? We have some people from Poland, too."

"They are very white like you," said Afewerki.

"Yes, white like the snow." She savored the liquid chocolate in her mouth.

The rain lessened as they talked, but still it came. Afewerki was desperate to make some claim to Eydis to draw closer to her, but he was in knots. His stomach hurt. He had an idea.

"Let us go to the tejj bet. What do you think?"

Eydis thought about drinking the honey mead in the afternoon. "It will be crowded with the rain, no?" She remembered sitting in Afewerki's lap, being very drunk. And Svana had slept with a man that night.

"Well, let us see." He hoped the Snake wasn't there. Eydis was thinking the same thing.

SEVENTY-EIGHT

Reece discussed it briefly with Svana. He had the two thousand birr but in dollars, and Dingil was agreeable. Reece wanted a thousand to go directly to the church.

Dingil shook his head no. He would personally give the money to the church.

"You will steal it," said Svana.

Omar did not translate.

"Svana," said Reece.

Dingil took the bills. He counted one bill at a time, holding some up to the light. A fifty-dollar note with tape on it, he rejected.

"Really?" Reece traded him a different fifty.

Dingil called for the jailer in the adjoining room.

"Abet!" The jailer came as soon as called, holding his rifle. Anything could happen with these ferenji.

Dingil told him to bring the ferenj prisoner. He was being released.

"So, he's free?" asked Svana.

"Yes, free," said Omar. "Shall I be free as well? You have promised." He looked at Reece.

"Damn," said Reece. "I guess I did. Why are you in jail? You didn't kill anybody, did you?"

Omar laughed. "Some are saying that I steal a sheep. That is all."

Reece had another US fifty. "How much for Omar to go free?"

Dingil had seen the bill.

"He is saying fifty American dollars," said Omar.

"Damn," said Reece. He looked to Svana, who was frowning.

Reece folded the fifty and laid it on the dusty desk. He expected to receive some kind of purple-stamped documents, but there were none. The deal was done. Gudmunder stepped into the room and hugged Svana. He was dirty with sweat and grime.

"You need a bath," said Svana. She ruffled Gudmunder's red hair.

"We should go," said Reece. He shook Gudmunder's hand.

"Good work," said Gudmunder. "My first time ever in a jail."

"Ah, but you are trouble," said Svana. She shook her finger at him. It was raining again.

They stood in the doorway, waiting for the rain to settle, but soon decided that it was best to just go and get wet. They took off, sloshing through muddy water. Omar followed them with a big smile.

Into the Beselfui bar they went, all four of them. They received gazes from everyone. It was just about lunchtime, and a few patrons sat at tables. By now, everyone in Alem Ketema knew that the red-haired ferenj had stolen the tabot, so why wasn't he in jail? And why were they hanging out with the town thief?

Lebna entered through the back. She saw Gudmunder and slowed. She saw Omar, and she smirked. Should she serve them? She caught Reece's eye and smiled. He smiled back. The plump owner of the bar came in through the front door. She folded her dripping umbrella. She spied Omar from behind and began to shout.

"Get out of here, you dirty beggar!" she yelled.

Omar turned and cringed. He looked to Gudmunder for help. Gudmunder was confused. Was she yelling at him? The owner stood over Omar, cursing and pointing to the door. He owed the bar money. He was a thief. "Get out!"

"What is she saying?" asked Reece. He wanted to give Omar some money, but had none.

Omar stood. "Nothing. I must go. You are in danger." He touched Gudmunder's shoulder. "I will wait for you on the road?" He turned and slipped out the front door into the rain.

"I think Omar may be trouble," said Gudmunder. "He was helpful in the jail, though."

"He's certainly not welcome here," said Svana.

SEVENTY-NINE

Afewerki and Eydis stepped quickly through the rain and puddles. A heavy fog, the clouds really, hovered just above their heads. Eydis followed Afewerki as if it were night. They passed a man hurrying in the opposite direction and exchanged quick greetings with him.

At the tejj bet, the door was open. Black flies clung to the doorpost, unmoving. Afewerki entered, followed by Eydis. It was very dim and not too crowded. The radio played an AM station, Amharic music. Afewerki murmured, and a man in rough shorts and tire sandals scooted down the bench to make room.

"Is that your new wife?" asked a man from across the room. The other men laughed.

"What did he say?" asked Eydis.

"Just nothing." He frowned and called out an order to the short barmaid. She had finely braided hair and smelled of rancid butter. She wiped her hands on her dress, pulled down a clear bottle of amber tejj and two green plastic cups, yanked the corncob cork, and placed the cups and bottle on the low, narrow table. The rain pecked on the tin roof.

Eydis poured for both of them. The smell was of honey and spice. She sipped. It was warm and sweet. She was hungry, and the alcohol going into her body felt good. "Drink," she said. "Soon we have to eat."

Afewerki took a big swallow and made a face. "My goodness."

Eydis laughed. She crossed her legs, but her jeans were

too tight or too wet. She wore a long-sleeve light wool sweater with a collar. "Let's see how fast we can drink the bottle," she said. She filled his cup and refilled hers. She saw a middle-aged man across the room wink at Afewerki. He wore one of those hats made of scraps and was missing several teeth up front.

"Do you think Dr. Thorsonn is in the jail?" asked Afewerki. He caught a fly in mid-flight, shook it, and threw it on the dirt floor. He stepped on the fly and took another swallow of tejj.

"Maybe he is free by now," said Eydis.

"Yes, thanks to God," said Afewerki. He searched for something to say.

"Are you a virgin, Afewerki? You never told me." Eydis drank, smiling. She knew she was making him uncomfortable.

"Oh, such a question." He started to stand and walk away, but caught himself. His face was hot. He drank. Why did she keep asking?

"I'm sorry." She took another drink and put her hand on his. His hand was warm. Hers was cold. She was feeling peppy from the early buzz.

"Chicorilla," he said. He'd never had sex. He was shy and tongue-tied around women and girls. They made him nervous. He did not want a wife or baby as they were too expensive. Plus, the local women were bitchy. But Eydis was different.

In walked the Snake. He waited for the room to go quiet, except for the radio. No one was smiling now. He wore his pistol, but was alone. He zoomed in on Eydis. Hadn't she disrespected him? He couldn't remember if it was her or the black-haired woman. He decided to sit across from Eydis. He tipped his camouflage ballcap. The barmaid brought him a bottle and a real glass. "Amenseganolo," he said. His gold teeth flashed. He'd had sex with the barmaid plenty of times.

Eydis downed the entire cup of tejj. The Snake made her sick to her stomach. She glanced at him but otherwise looked away toward Afewerki.

"Shall we leave?" asked Afewerki. He was ready to go.

"No, we shall drink," said Eydis. "Drink more."

Afewerki drank some more. He was feeling a bit intoxicated, and he didn't like it.

"Who likes to fuck?" shouted the Snake. He stood and raised his glass to fucking.

There was a titter in the room. One by one, the farmers with their cups nodded the affirmative, mumbling like little boys.

"What did he say?" whispered Svana.

"He says to remember those who have died."

"I don't believe you."

"It is true."

The Snake sat and poured more tejj. He was lonely and looked forward to his drinking sessions with the farmers. The white girl, though, had disrespected him. She should be home with a baby on her tit, not drinking with real men in a bar. He drank. He spat on the dirt floor.

"I've seen your tits, you whore," said the Snake. He stared at Eydis.

The atmosphere in the bar turned electric. The Snake grabbed his bottle and drank straight from it.

"Oh oh," said Afewerki.

Svana said, "What? What?" She too felt the change in the air, as if something bad was about to happen.

Afewerki held up his hand to her. "He is crazy," he whispered. "Better not to drink more. We must leave."

Eydis looked across the table at the Snake. She picked up her cup and drank and, holding his gaze, felt sick. She should be back in Reykjavik, partying with her girlfriends. She hated the Snake. She picked up the tejj bottle and took a big swig. There was murmuring in the room and then laughter. Eydis was winning.

"Dear Jesus Christ," said Afewerki. He had to pee. Everything seemed askew. The donkey his father had bought had died in the night.

The Snake stood. He stared at Eydis. He would humiliate her. No one would ever forget it. He undid his belt. He unbuttoned his military trousers. On the radio was traditional music, the yiqirta and an accordion. He turned, dropped his pants, and mooned Eydis. The room erupted in laughter.

EIGHTY

Lebna and the bar owner were whispering. Lebna seemed reluctant to come to their table. The bar owner was dusting the bottles of wine and Johnny Walker Red.

"As soon as the rain stops, we should leave," said Reece. "There will be a jeep, maybe to Gwar."

"But it's Sunday," said Svana. "Do you think—"

"Let's relax," said Gudmunder. "All is well. I am free."

"Precisely," said Reece. "But maybe you were safer in jail."

"That is ridiculous," said Gudmunder. "I am here to help the people. They know that. I do vaccine clinics!"

Svana motioned for Lebna. It was close enough to noon for whiskey.

"You stole the fricking tabot," said Reece. "People think that."

Gudmunder flushed. "Do you believe this?"

"Gudmunder, no, we do not believe it," said Svana. Gudmunder was cute when he was angry.

Lebna came to their table. Was she shaking?

"Johnny Walker, sost," said Svana, ordering for everyone. She wanted to say doubles but didn't know how.

"Ishi," said Lebna. She was a devout Orthodox Christian. Stealing from the church was worse than murder.

Reece looked around. Everyone seemed to be on pins and needles. "The people know. You could never do this in Iceland or, what, Belgium?"

The mention of Belgium made Gudmunder laugh. "Chocolate," he said. "Is it Thursday?"

"Is it Tuesday?" asked Svana

"Oh, yes," said Gudmunder. "Tuesday."

Reece was lost. "What?"

Dingil was at the door to the bar. He was going to pay his overdue bar/food tab. He ignored the Icelanders and Reece, taking a table on the other side of the room. He was fucking rich. Two thousand birr. He made ninety birr per month as the town administrator. The government was two months behind in paying his salary.

Lebna scurried to his table before he could sit. He always drank grape Fanta at lunch. He saw that the ferenji were drinking whiskey. He ordered a double of Johnny Walker. "What is for lunch?"

"Shurowot with fresh peppers and onion," said Lebna.

"Perfect." He told Lebna to spit in the ferenji's food. She nodded and retreated backward. She had two children. Her mother took care of them. Why was life so hard?

An older man glared at Gudmunder between sips of his tea. He had a gray goatee and wore shorts with a short-sleeved purple shirt. He put his thumbnail to his tooth and flipped the doctor. Basically, a "Fuck you!"

The tension in the room ratcheted a notch. Everyone was watching everyone.

"Maybe you are correct, Reece," said Gudmunder. Something was not right. Usually, he felt completely at ease in the bar.

Reece nodded. "You and Svana go to her room. I'll go to the town center and wait for the jeep. I'll have him drive down to pick you up."

"Maybe we should eat first," said Gudmunder. Lebna had delivered plates to two customers, Dingil being first.

"I'm not hungry," said Reece. He finished his whiskey. He was ready to fight if needed. He was ready to give birth to triplets. "Go ahead and order without me."

Svana looked back and forth between Reece and Gudmunder. "Knock three times," she said, "on the ceiling if you want me."

"Will do," said Reece.

EIGHTY-ONE

Eydis was stunned. She stared at the ass of the Snake, his balls hanging down. She turned to Afewerki. He was laughing! Everyone was laughing except the barmaid. She was behind the bar, looking at the ground, fearing the worst.

The Snake pulled up his trousers and refastened his belt. He'd never felt better. He didn't know what to say, though. He felt accepted and momentarily forgot about Eydis. Were his eyes misting? "Long live international proletarianism!" The room dulled a bit. They didn't get the joke, like someone from the city would. The Marxist military government had fallen, replaced with a more democratic transitional government. Everyone had hated the Russians.

With his moment vanquished, the Snake sat on the bench and focused on his bottle. He glanced at Eydis and saw that she was drinking, that she looked afraid. He laughed.

"We shall go," said Afewerki. He felt that the crisis was over, but what would happen next?

"No. I will not run from him," said Eydis. "I can drink more than he can. Pussy."

Afewerki thought about his little house with the soft bed. He wished he were there. Eydis was going to get them in trouble.

Eydis put her hand on Afewerki's leg to calm him. The gesture was not unnoticed. The radio played, weirdly suffusing the alarm and laughter. She drank, and the bottle was empty. She held it up for the barmaid to see.

"Dear God," said Afewerki. "We will be late for dinner." Thoughts of sleeping beside Eydis in her tent had fled. He only wanted to get her out of there.

The Snake continued to drink and settled down. His smile faded to his usual frown. The room was getting lively, conversation flowing, as if everyone was waiting for part two of the show to begin. The Snake's mother had raised him and four others, his father having been killed by wild bees. She had been cruel, beating him when he did not beg hard enough. She was still alive in Nazret, living in a shack, and would probably never die.

The barmaid shuttled back and forth, taking empty bottles and bringing new ones. She was the only one sweating in the warming room. She wished to be far away, if not for her children. Someone slapped her behind, and she turned and barked a warning. "Bucka!" The guilty party laughed and said something nasty to his neighbor.

Eydis poured from the new bottle. Who knew that a Sunday in rural Ethiopia could be so much fun? She glanced at the Snake, but he seemed to have forgotten about her. She supposed that they were somehow even, and that made her angry. Everyone feared him because of his guns and power. He raped disabled women. He had mooned her in public.

"The Snake should be punished," said Eydis.

"What?" asked Afewerki. He had stopped drinking and was wringing his hands. Maybe his best chances were with Svana. She had slept with one local man. But what did he really want? He looked at Eydis. Her skin must be so soft. Her blonde hair was exotic. Why had God sent her to Gwar? Why did God put within him such a yearning for her?

There was a noise at the open door. A young woman leaned her head inside. She was yelling and pointing at one man. She held a child in one arm, had another on her back, and two clinging to her filthy dress.

"What is it?" asked Eydis.

Afewerki seemed to cheer up. "This woman is angry at her husband for drinking. Their roof is broken, and the rain is coming inside. There is no money for food."

The guilty man sat with his head in his hands. He was thirty-three and muscular and just beginning to get drunk. He peered at her through his hands. She did not stop, shouting over the radio and the patter of rain on the roof. The children looked terrified. Suddenly, she stopped. The room was silent. The barmaid had turned off the radio, adding to the dramatic tension. She wiped her hand on a dirty cloth, commiserating with the mother.

The man stood and shouted at his wife. He told her to go to hell. There was some laughter. He took his bottle of tejj, tilted it to his mouth, and drained it. "I'm going for a walk," he announced to the room.

The barmaid said that he owed five birr. The man searched his pocket and came up with three. He laughed. He looked to his wife and asked for two birr.

She slaughtered him with language, stomping her foot. The baby in her arms began to cry.

"Go," said the barmaid. She would put it on his tab.

"Ishi," he said, humbled. He raised his chin and waited for his wife and children to clear the doorway before heading into the growing afternoon.

"Ha!" said the Snake. "He is a warrior!" There was a smattering of laughter.

Briefly humored, Eydis glared at the Snake. She was going to punish him.

EIGHTY-TWO

Reece stood in the light rain, waiting for a jeep. He walked around the circle, over and over. His feet were soaked and cold. His hair clung to his head. He could only think of going back to the bar and having another shot of whiskey to warm himself. He thought of the Jack London story "To Build a Fire." He didn't want to make the same mistake, run out of matches and freeze to death.

Instead of retreating to the room, as Reece had suggested, Svana and Gudmunder had ordered lunch: shurowot and enjera. The tension in the room had abated somewhat as the crowd grew, some out-of-towners unaware of the stolen tabot. But still the old man glared at them, muttering. He had told Lebna to tell the ferenji to leave or else, but she had refused. He would have to do it himself.

They were about finished eating when the man stood and approached them. Svana's heart caught. She had been watching him. He carried a doolah, a heavy stick with lead wrapped around its end. He stood back from their table and spoke in a loud voice. The room slowly went silent as he roared in Amharic.

"You have stolen the sacred tabot! You will be punished! The bribe has set you free, but the people will punish you." He pointed his finger at Gudmunder, his eyes on fire.

Flummoxed, Gudmunder somehow understood the man. What to do? "That is a lie. I did not steal the tabot. It is a lie!" He spoke in Icelandic. He lowered his head.

"Someone should shoot him," said the man. "Or I will

strike him dead."

Svana triggered into action. She stood, taller and meatier than the old man. She put a hand on his shoulder and spoke at length, denying the charge. The doctor was only there to help. He was a friend.

Lebna and the bar owner watched along with everyone else. The bar owner intervened. Somehow, she understood the plea of Svana. She asked the man to back away, to let God punish those who were guilty. The man replied that God seldom visited Alem Ketema and that it was up to the people to punish the thief. The bar owner shrank, wondering what to do next.

A horn blared from outside, and Reece appeared in the doorway. "Come!" he yelled.

Svana and Gudmunder edged around the old man and headed for the door. The jeep was there. Svana decided to leave her bag in her room.

EIGHTY-THREE

The radio was back on, a traditional song.

"What are you doing?" asked Afewerki.

Eydis had taken a long drink from the bottle instead of using her cup. She was standing.

"Eydis, it is dangerous," said Afewerki. "We must go." He stood.

Eydis turned her back on the Snake. She unbuttoned her pants. She slid down her pants and mooned him.

A loud groan of confusion emanated from the room, followed by laughter and lewd comments. Afewerki was dumbfounded. Had she really done that?

Eydis zipped up and turned around. She stared at the Snake. He looked as if he had been immersed in ice water. He would kill the ferenj bitch. He stood and drew his pistol. She was just a few feet away. The men jumped to their feet, a few running from the square shack. The barmaid screamed. The Snake aimed at Eydis's head. Afewerki wrapped his arms around Eydis, hovering over her, his eyes closed.

"I will shoot you both if you do not move!" said the Snake. Never had he imagined he would be insulted in such a way. He pulled the trigger, and a loud shot went through the tin roof. Right away, rainwater began to drip.

"Eydis, we must run," said Afewerki. "Let us go." Their backs were to the Snake.

The Snake watched them, his pistol trained on Afewerki's back. They crept around the table toward the door. They were at point-blank range.

Suddenly, they were outside in the rain and dim light and running, splashing through puddles, tripping on rocks. The Snake staggered outside, aiming at the moving figures. He fired.

Instead of going to the compound, Afewerki led Eydis to his little house. They passed through the gate and entered, soaked. His two brothers were out gathering a lost goat. The white chicken was already roosting over his bed.

"He will kill us," said Afewerki. His heart was racing.

Eydis sat on the edge of Afewerki's bed. God, when would it end? "He is crazy. Do you have a gun?"

"No, my father has a rifle," said Afewerki.

"Will he come here?" asked Eydis.

"My father?"

"No, the Snake."

"No, no. He will not enter this compound. "But he may go to your compound. He will be angry."

"Jesus Christ, he was going to shoot me."

"He is a dangerous man," said Afewerki.

"I am shaking inside. Can you rub my shoulders?"

"What do you mean?" asked Afewerki.

"Here, just put your hands here." She turned sideways on the bed, sitting on half of her butt.

Afewerki did as he was told. Her hair was in the way, so he moved it. It was surprisingly stiff. He put his hands on her shoulders and froze.

"No, let me show you. Sit."

Afewerki sat on a biscuit tin. Eydis went behind him. She put her hands on his shoulders and kneaded the muscles there, working her way up to his neck. A thrill and warmth went through his body. Time slowed.

"Now me," said Eydis.

Afewerki was briefly stunned. "Oh, yes." He stood and put his hands on her warm neck, doing his best.

"That is nice," said Eydis, and it was.

Afewerki was having trouble breathing. He crossed his legs and kept massaging. He could do this until Christ returned. The thought made him grin.

"You have strong hands," said Eydis.

"It is from plowing," said Afewerki. He felt that he had the world in his hands.

"Mmm, will Abebe cook dinner if we are not there?"

"Yes, she will cook." He looked down at the top of her head. He could see the whorl at the center of her hair. He wondered if Reece had done such a thing with Eydis. It was getting dim. He needed to light a candle.

"I should probably go home," said Eydis. "Maybe soon."

The half-loaded jeep slipped and slid its way to Gwar. Svana paid the driver. They stood at the bottom of the hill leading up to the village. It had taken over two hours and was getting dark. The old Baptist warehouse compound was to their left. The rain had abated to a light sprinkle, and everyone was cold.

Gudmunder led the way uphill. He felt like an imposter. Would the people of Gwar trust him? Svana followed, then Reece.

At the top of the hill, they turned left, weaving their way to the compound. Inside, Gebremariam was there with his rifle, sitting beneath the overhang of the cook house. He jumped up, bubbling with enthusiasm. There was a trickle of smoke from inside. Abebe was cooking dinner, goat with fiery berbere peppers.

They surveyed the area. Reece's tent was still down. There seemed to be no one else around.

"Where are they?" asked Reece.

"It's too wet to weigh the children," said Svana.

"Let's go inside the supply house," said Gudmunder.

And they did, except for Reece, who went to fix his tent.

Afewerki and Eydis entered the compound. Reece's tent was up. Gebremariam told them that everyone was in the supply house. The door was open. Tipsy, Eydis and Afewerki approached. They could hear talk from inside.

"Reece!" said Eydis. She rushed him, hugged him, and kissed him on the cheek.

Reece was a bit stunned. He hugged Eydis, feeling her firm breasts against his chest. He went to Afewerki and shook his hand. There was a brief silence.

Gudmunder filled in Afewerki and Eydis on the events in Alem Ketema. They, in turn, recounted that day's encounter with the Snake.

"Sounds like our backs are against the wall," said Reece.

No one quite understood what he meant.

"We are in trouble," said Reece.

"Perhaps just me," said Gudmunder.

"No," said Eydis. "We are under attack. But, what to do?"

Afewerki cleared his throat. "You must go to Addis. The people will forget."

"Is it that simple?" asked Reece.

"But we have work to do," said Gudmunder. "The vaccines are here to give."

"What of our safety?" asked Svana.

"The Snake is an idiot," said Eydis. "He would shoot a baby if it shit."

"The Snake will shoot in the head," said Afewerki. "You must go to Addis." He was hoping they would invite him as well.

The supply house was small, and they stepped outside into the fresh air. It was only misting now. The group walked to the fire pit and took their usual but wet seats. "Can we have fire?" asked Svana.

"Sure," said Reece. "Coals from Abebe."

"The wood is very wet," said Afewerki.

Reece went to the cook house. Abebe was there, sweating over a large metal pan frying goat meat. Reece waved, walked out, and then realized he'd come for coals. He felt silly. He went back inside and looked around. There was dry wood and some corn husks. He went through the motions.

Abebe did not wholly understand. She spoke to him at length, none of which was understood. She took her time, her breasts swaying. He picked up a small stone and tossed it from hand to hand. Ahh, she understood. She took a stick and isolated a fiery coal. She picked it up and tossed it back and forth as she hurried to the fire pit.

The late afternoon was raw, like a peeled onion. Gudmunder was thinking of soup with parsnips. Reece was on his knees, blowing on the coal covered with twigs and corn husks. Smoke swirled.

"Good to be back," said Gudmunder. "I thought the end was near."

"Ha," said Reece. His nose was full of smoke. "Sounds like we've initiated the end of the world."

Svana said, "I could use a drink."

Afewerki frowned. Wasn't alcohol part of the general problem?

"Me too," said Gudmunder. "What do we have?"

"Nothing," said Eydis.

"Shit," said Svana.

"Dear God," said Afewerki.

"Katikala?" asked Reece.

The others, except for Afewerki, gave the affirmative.

"The Snake will come, and we must be prepared," said Afewerki.

"Fuck the Snake," said Svana.

"Afewerki, just this time," said Reece. "Two bottles of katikala?" He reached for his wallet. "I'm broke." He pulled a single birr note. "This is all I have."

"Ah," said Gudmunder. He pulled a ten-birr note from his large wallet.

Afewerki sighed. He glanced at Eydis. It seemed as if she had not had a single drink. He thought she must be very strong. He took the ten and trotted out of the compound.

"He's a good man," said Gudmunder. He wasn't necessarily in need of alcohol, but needed affirmation. "What about dinner?"

As if called, Gebremariam approached with a platter of enjera and fried goat. He wasn't sure if they wanted to eat outside or in the house.

Reece had him balance the heavy platter on an empty biscuit tin near the fire. The fire was small, six or so sticks crackling.

Eydis hated to relinquish her buzz, but the meat looked amazing. She was the first to indulge in the morsels of steaming goat.

The Snake, after vomiting, had come straight to the compound of the bitch named Eydis. She wasn't there, and he went back to the tejj bet. He wanted to suck her tits and fuck her cunt; she was a grade-A whore. He thought about his mother sleeping with half the men in his home village. And then there was that goddamned story about the Americans landing on the moon. *Fuck that shit.* Back at the tejj bet, he sat there, his neat hair touching the rim of his new cup of honey wine. The damn radio was playing ferenji music. His leg moved up and down.

Reece waited for Eydis to take the first bite before folding the meat inside a wad of enjera. He broke into a sweat, as usual, just smelling the pepper.

"Well, we are together," said Gudmunder. "Many things have happened. Let's hope we have some peace." In the distance, he could hear the *pop, pop, pop* of the engine that ran the grain mill.

"There will be trouble," said Eydis. She faced the gap in the fence, watching. She had a feeling that Afewerki would be willing to die for her. What about Reece? "This time it is my fault. I'm sorry."

Svana laughed. "You mooned that asshole! I wish I had been there. I cannot believe it."

They ate, speaking gravely in one instant and laughing in the next. The enjera and meat were just about gone when Afewerki returned with the katikala. He hadn't seen the Snake. "He will come this night," he said. "I will stay tonight. Gebremariam must not sleep."

Gebremariam came to check on the platter. Afewerki asked him to bring more enjera and meat, and pulled him aside, telling him that the Snake was coming and to shoot him if necessary. The color drained from Gebremariam's face. *Really?* He trotted back to the cook house, where Abebe was putting things away. He told her about the Snake, and she jumped into high gear. He was the last thing she needed.

Reece watched Eydis. She was tougher than he'd imagined. He looked away when her gaze met his, and he wondered about her life in Iceland. He would love to hang out with her in Reykjavik. He imagined that her mother must be very pretty. Why wasn't Gudmunder interested in her or Svana? He wondered if Svana and Afewerki could possibly hook up.

"Oh, I can't eat any more," said Eydis. Her buzz was gone, and she was becoming increasingly worried. "Look, the bats have come." She pointed to the sky just above them, a dozen bats dipping and swirling. The sun was setting, but it was still a dull shade of bright amid the shadows. She had a hangnail, and it hurt.

Preceded by his two goons with AK-47s, the Snake stumbled through the fence. Gebremariam made a stand, his rifle in hand but pointed at the ground. The Snake told his companions to continue. He looked at Gebremariam and smirked. Qat packed his lower lip. Everything was crystal clear. He put one foot in front of the other, making his way closer and closer to the fire. He could see Eydis. The others were there as well. Perfect. They could watch her die.

He spoke, but nothing made sense. His guards looked confused. He tried again. "Bitch, no one. You die. When do you, bitch?" The ground seemed tilted. He leaned the wrong way and fell. One of his pals ran to help him stand.

Afewerki stood. He spoke. "She is apologizing. It was the alcohol. She is very sorry for her actions. She asks forgiveness."

Had Eydis known what he was saying, she would have had a seizure. She was ready to go head-to-head.

The Snake held onto his guard. "I must knock the stone from her shoulder." He was feeling out of touch with the earth. He didn't think he could remain standing even with help.

"Ishi," said Afewerki. He picked up a small stone. "Come," he said to Eydis. "Quickly."

"What?" asked Eydis.

"You must kneel with the stone on your shoulder. He will knock it to the ground. This is the way of forgiveness."

Eydis thought about it. The Snake was drunk out of his mind, but how could she refuse? She looked at Gudmunder, Reece, and Svana. She went to her knees on the soggy ground, her jeans' knees absorbing water. Afewerki placed the stone on her shoulder.

The Snake tried to walk forward and tripped. His minion caught him. The Snake focused on the rock. Perhaps this was the beginning of a meaningful relationship. He laughed to himself, caught his reaction, and slightly urinated in his trousers. *Fuck.* He reached and slapped the stone from Eydis's shoulder. It was official. All was even.

He mumbled to his guards, and they turned him around and led him from the compound.

No one spoke for a moment.

"Thanks to God," said Gudmunder. He had not completely understood what was going on.

Afewerki looked as if the Earth had been lifted from his shoulders. "Tonight is very lucky," he said. "If he wakes, he may return."

"Jesus Christ," said Reece. Tension cramped his back, and he stood and stretched. In the distance, dogs snarled wickedly.

"Should I have done that?" asked Eydis. She scratched her arms. They were dry, and she needed lotion.

Svana was perplexed. "Well, it made him leave. So there is that. I thought we were fucking going to die. I need a drink."

Reece held up a bottle of katikala. "I think we have that covered." He, too, felt somewhat lucky.

Afewerki was astounded. He considered his options. Maybe it was best to have a drink. He had thought Eydis would be shot. He had considered dying to protect her life. Less than three months ago, his world had been limited to Gwar. Now it included Iceland and the United States. Was the reaction of the Snake to Eydis in any way a message to him? He wasn't sure.

"Pour me," said Gudmunder. "I think that I am dreaming."

"Me too," said Svana.

"What the hell is next?" asked Reece.

"Only God knows," said Afewerki. "What a hell!"

EIGHTY-FOUR

Monday was Monday. Reece awoke to roosters crowing. His tent was soggy. His sleeping bag was warm but wet. He would move into the supply house that day. It had rained for hours during the night and looked like rain again. He emerged, cradled his hot, sweet tea from Gebremariam, and walked the perimeter of the slushy compound. Perhaps they should consider getting a goat to eat the grass. It was ankle-high.

Gudmunder's head popped out from his tent, his red hair a royal mess, curled and folded from sleep. He was on his hands and knees, having trouble standing. "The girls are lazy today."

Reece laughed.

"Afi minn fór á honum Rauð." Svana was singing a children's song from the tent.

"My grandfather went on his red horse," said Gudmunder. His eyes brightened.

Eydis was the next to emerge. Reece watched her stand, stretch, and touch her toes. She wore her tight jeans and a brown t-shirt. She had mooned the Snake and was still alive. Reece imagined telling stories to his grandparents. They would be horrified, and he couldn't wait. Would they ever meet Eydis? He wished he could magically return to Alabama and then back to Ethiopia.

"Good morning," said Reece.

"Yah," said Eydis. Had she dreamed the previous night? She wasn't sure. She wanted a big glass of orange juice, thirsted for it.

Reece circled the dead fire pit. He kneeled, put his fingers over the ash, feeling for heat. He blew, looking for an orange glow. *Just there.* He walked to the cook house. Abebe was not yet there. He took some corn husks and a few twigs. Within ten minutes, an intense but small fire licked, releasing heat and smoke. Strangely, he felt like having a shot of katikala, which seemed always to bring things to closure.

A rooster crowed, and Afewerki entered the compound. It was as he expected, and made him feel that all was well. He felt lucky to be alive, to be a friend of the Icelanders and Reece. Now for breakfast.

"Hallo, y'all!" said Afewerki. Reece sometimes said y'all.

"Hello, brother," said Reece. They shook hands. "You're in a good mood."

"I am happy to be alive. I was fearing, especially for Eydis."

"That is sweet," said Eydis. "I think it is Reece's turn to get in trouble." She wanted to oil him down and give him a massage. He could do the same for her. A little thrill shot through her stomach.

"We must behave from now on," said Gudmunder. He laughed, but realized the danger they had been in. Was the Snake really satisfied by knocking a stone from the shoulder of Eydis?

Gebremariam emerged from the cook house with the kettle of tea. He was so thin and dark brown and always cheerful. He had told the story to his wife, and she had scolded him for approaching the Snake the previous night. After all, they had five children to take care of. He shivered thinking about it. It was tough to dig a grave in Gwar, and she would have to pay a large sum, perhaps twenty birr.

"Chai?" he said, and everyone scrambled for their green plastic mugs.

"Everything is so damp," said Svana. She stood from the tent, stiff and stretching. Her black hair was twisted. Her stomach rumbled and squawked. She'd been uncomfortable since midnight and belched.

"The frog is here," said Eydis. She laughed, but then watched Svana lean over, hands to knees. "Are you okay?"

Svana said nothing. She felt like she was inhaling car exhaust. She sat in a chair. Gebremariam walked over, concerned. He held forth the teakettle. Svana shook her head and then leaned over and vomited into the fire pit. Gebremariam did a one-eighty. What to do?

"Shit," said Reece. "He jumped up and put his hand on her shoulder." The vomit was slick with thick mucus.

Eydis squatted beside her, rubbing her back. Svana tried to laugh, but felt too sick.

Gudmunder stood near them. "You will need to rest, my dear. No work for you today."

Svana rubbed her face and looked up. "I'm fine." She stood. Her blood pressure dropped, and her vision went black. She could only taste the spicy katikala from the night before. She groped in space and nearly fell. Reece caught her and eased her into a chair. She wanted to kneel beside a porcelain toilet bowl.

"I wish we had beds in the supply house," said Svana. "The floor is very hard."

Abebe arrived. She surveyed the scene. Was something amiss? She decided she should get to work cooking and hope for the best.

Svana made a pallet in the supply house and lay as still as she could. She wanted to listen to an Icelandic radio station. She thought of home, her mother baking rye bread, rúgbrauð. She felt sicker and tried to think of something else, baby powder, whatever. The ceiling was an inverted V. She took comfort in that. Her stomach gurgled.

Eydis took the backpack, which contained the scale and the height/weight cards. She was heading beyond Aferbiny with Afewerki and Reece, a twenty-minute walk. It was overkill, but she was thrilled to have their company. Gudmunder was taking the day off, hanging out with Svana in case she needed anything. He was just a bit hungover anyway.

"Off to work we go," said Reece.

"Like a dwarf in *Cinderella*," said Eydis.

Reece laughed at her mistake. He looked at his hands. The skin was dry. He pinched the skin on his right hand, and the skin tented for a moment. He was dehydrated from the alcohol of the night before. In his backpack, he carried two of the old Icelandic IV bottles of water with red rubber stoppers, along with a bottle of hydrogen peroxide and tubes of antibiotic ointment. He'd laced his hiking boots too tight.

They passed several locals on the narrow footpath. An old woman carrying a mammoth bag of charcoal approached, moving like a tortoise. The burlap bag seemed about to crush her. Her son made the charcoal, and she was carrying it to the jeep stop. From there, the charcoal would make its way to Addis Ababa.

Reece glanced at the sun. He was chilled but warmed

up with the uphill and downhill hike. He hoped it wouldn't rain. A drop of rain hit his nose. He watched Eydis's ass in front of him. Her thighs did not rub. He imagined her bending over.

Afewerki led the way. He felt strong, virile. He glanced back at Eydis and Reece, both looking at the ground. How had God led them there? He continued, taking long strides without breathing hard. He thought about the Bible. Some had memorized numerous verses of the Bible. He only knew one from the book of James, chapter two.

The first tukuls appeared, ancient-looking, round mud-and-stick huts with steep straw roofs. There were very few signs of life outside the compounds. "Ferenj!" and that was enough to mobilize a line of twelve women with their children. It was still cool, but the day would soon grow warm.

Gudmunder had eaten a large breakfast of spicy fit-fit. He still felt very full an hour after the meal. Svana had to make half a dozen trips to the shintabet. He felt sorry for her, but what could he do? He offered to go and buy bananas. She had told him no way.

He walked brisk laps around the inside of the compound for exercise. The altitude quickly raised his heart rate to 130. He thought about his baby sister, Rosetta. She had died when he was six, drowned in a bucket of mop water. He shook his head. He stared at the ground. He stared at the sky. *What the hell?* There was definitely not a God. He tried hard to think of something else.

Gaukur Trandilsson. Why had the tabot in Alem Ketema been stolen? What if it had been the original tabot of the Ark of the Covenant? But it was deadly. It killed anyone who touched it, except the one blessed and protected by Jehovah. However, the Ark was occasionally moved. Maybe it had been moved to Alem Ketema and then secretly whisked away. *Who knows?* He felt a tiny bit sick, nauseous. He reflected. He'd been arrested but had bribed his way out of jail. Would his family understand? Did he understand?

He continued his pacing, nodding to Gebremariam at the hole in the fence as he passed. He thought about fellow Icelandic doctor Sigmundur Benediktsson, who had died near Axum. Should he try to visit the unmarked grave that held the doctor's legs? What about the church in Gwar? He had yet to see inside. He only wanted to glimpse the maq'das, to be near a replica of the holy tablets. He felt that perhaps time would stop, that the meaning of life would become clear. Gaukur Trandilsson would be proud. He burped, emitting a foul smell, reminiscent of boiled eggs and methane. *Dear God.*

Svana lay on her back. She was cold, although hot and sweaty just a few minutes before. The floor was hard through the layers of grain bags and her sleeping bag. Maybe the wet, rocky ground was better. She wanted a cup of hot coffee. She wanted a soft bed, to be waited on by her mother. She was weighing children in a rural area of Ethiopia. Would her efforts make a difference? Was she merely chasing rainbows? She shifted onto her left side, pulling up her knees.

Within a few minutes, Dr. Thorsonn was disabled. He sat in a chair near the fire pit, his head in his hands. He felt that he would lift from the ground and explode. The essence of his experience was in his head, but tied to his stomach. He felt that he would lift, *float,* and *then* explode. The feeling hesitated for a few seconds, but then returned. He again feared that he was lifting from the ground. He was dizzy and stumbled to the shintabet.

Gebremariam helped Abebe with the chores, bringing in the cups and platter, which she washed. He was confused. Why were the ferenji always sick? Would everyone become sick? Was their God weaker than his own? He sat in one of the folding chairs and began to clean his rifle with a stained cloth. At least that was reliable.

Achtung baby. Where had he heard that before? Reece racked his brain, but nothing would come. They had to find a tree to hang the scale and sling. They walked beyond the tukuls, skirting gesho bushes, heading for a shady jacaranda.

Eydis led the way, being the expert weigher and measurer. Plump drops of rain splattered on her face. Just a drop here and there, but enough to raise a smell of wet earth.

They gathered beneath the tree, the trunk twisted like a tornado. There was a sturdy branch that reached out five meters or so. It was just out of reach.

Afewerki assessed the situation. Eydis could sit on his shoulders and reach the branch.

"Afewerki," said Reece, "you can sit on my shoulders."

"That's a good idea," said Eydis.

Afewerki grunted. Reece was skinny and taller. "Ishi."

"Hmm, how do we do this?" asked Reece. "I'll squat down and you step over my shoulders, if you can." He squatted.

Eydis began to laugh.

"Abet?" asked Afewerki.

"Oh, nothing," said Eydis. She stifled her laugh. Suddenly, everything was funny.

Afewerki stepped over. Reece's neck was between his legs.

"Okay, here we go." Reece tried to stand, wobbled, and went to his knees, skinning his hands. "Shit."

The group of women and children laughed, covering their mouths with their hands. "Ferenj!"

"Oh, look," said Svana.

A young boy had climbed up. He scooted along the limb a few feet from the trunk.

"Bataam taruno!" said Afewerki. "Give to him the rope."

Within minutes, the scale was ready, and weighing and measuring began, with everyone smiling.

Gudmunder met Svana in the shintabet. He recoiled as if bitten by a snake and retreated a few meters to give her some privacy. His stomach boiled. He sat on the ground, holding a roll of Ethiopian toilet paper from Addis Ababa that cost ten birr at the market, fearing that he would shit himself. He thought he actually did. Why not just squat right there and let it rip?

In the shintabet, Svana squatted over the toilet seat cemented into the floor, a kind of joke. Flies attacked her face and anus. She couldn't be still. She wanted to vomit. She looked through the cracks in the shintabet, bits of blue sky. An occasional drop of water hit the tin roof. She smelled smoke and gagged. She smelled her body odor and gagged. *Jesus Christ.* She imagined Christmas in Iceland. The thirteen Yule Lads. Trolls. A smile crept onto her face. Her legs were going to sleep. She needed water. Gudmunder was waiting, but the urgency was relentless even though nothing was coming.

Gebremariam continued to clean his gun. Abebe finished the dishes and began work on the laundry, heating water in a pot. She took the box of Omo and shook a handful of flakes into a halved steel barrel. If she had a husband, she could get rich working for the Baptists, but everything was on her shoulders. She said a quick prayer.

EIGHTY-FIVE

The weight clinic went well. They measured and weighed eighteen children. The rain had held back with only one sustained shower of ten minutes or so. Time seemed to pass slowly. Eydis had a routine: introduction, explanation, request for permission, and then a minute or so warming up the child. The mothers generally tolerated their children's screams and fought them into the sling. There was that magic moment when all hands left the sling and Eydis stared at the scale, turning quickly to write down the weight. The measuring of height was no less dramatic in many cases, the children grabbing their mother's legs. Reece thought that an extra inch or two should be added to every child's height.

"I hope Svana is well," said Eydis.

They were on their way back uphill to Gwar. Everyone had muddy shoes and socks. It was past lunch, perhaps two in the afternoon. The locals estimated time by how many hours had passed since the sun rose.

"Dr. Thorsonn will take care of her," said Afewerki.

"Her personal physician," said Reece.

Eydis laughed.

They worked their way uphill, the wide road narrowing to the lanes that wound among the compounds. A dog slunk by, and Afewerki picked up a rock. The mongrel ran before he had a chance to throw it.

"Oh, poor baby," said Eydis.

"It will bite," said Afewerki. "Very bad."

"Maybe they just need love," said Reece.

Afewerki stopped in his tracks for a second. He wanted to laugh. What did Reece mean? "You are joking?"

Reece thought for a moment. "I don't know. It's just that everyone needs a chance."

Afewerki did not know what he meant. "They will bite. They have the rabies. You know rabies?"

"Yeah," said Reece.

"Maybe he's right," said Eydis. The dogs frightened her. The way they fought at night was murderous.

Afewerki swelled with the approval of Eydis. "We have many dangers in this place."

"What is the worst danger?" asked Reece.

Afewerki did not hesitate. "The buda, the evil eye."

"Really? I know it is a serious thing, but you believe it?"

"Of course," said Afewerki. "It is a curse."

"Wow," said Eydis. She was ready to believe anything. Ethiopia had turned her world upside-down. "They turn into hyenas at night and eat the dead?"

"It is true," said Afewerki. "We must be careful to not speak of these things."

"Can a ferenj have the buda?" asked Reece. He could feel his heart beating. The altitude still affected him.

"Oh, yes," said Afewerki. "We suspect this."

Eydis turned and stared at Afewerki with bug eyes.

Afewerki stopped in his tracks. "Oh no! You must not."

Eydis laughed.

"This is not the joke," said Afewerki. His face was blank.

They began the even steeper uphill climb into the heart of the village. A group of boys, popping toy whips, stopped and ran toward them. "Ferenj!"

Afewerki shooed them away. "Hidu!" But both Eydis

and Reece wound up with one on each hand. Reece could only imagine the filth on their hands, but what could he do?

"I guess they like us," said Eydis. She liked the attention, the physical contact. Their little hands were so rough.

A man in tattered shorts and shirt was coming downhill. He approached Reece and held out his hand for Reece to shake. Reece didn't want to let go of the boys' hands. The man was grimacing and insisting, talking loudly.

Afewerki intervened. "Why you will not shake his hand? he is saying."

"I'm busy," said Reece. He looked the man in the eyes.

Afewerki told the man to be on his way.

The man cursed, calling Reece the son of a pig. Who gave him permission to come to this place? Was he better than the local people?

Afewerki murmured and shook his head. "He is crazy."

Reece considered his options. He liked crazy people. He pulled his hands away from the children and held them out.

The man sneered and walked away.

"What the hell?" said Reece.

"Chicorilla," said Afewerki. "He is gone."

They reached the compound, let the children go, and passed through the gap in the fence. It would be two hours before dinner. No one seemed to be around.

"Hungry?" asked Eydis.

"Let us look," said Afewerki.

In the cook house was a large pot of cold shurowot. "The wot is cold. You like?" asked Afewerki.

Both Reece and Eydis said yes. Before they ate a cold

meal around the cold fire ring, though, Eydis checked on Gudmunder in his tent and Svana in the supply house.

"They both have diarrhea and vomiting," she said.

"Hell," said Reece. "That sucks. What can we do? Nothing?"

"Just to filter water," said Eydis. "To keep them hydrated."

That seemed counterintuitive to Afewerki. They should drink less to decrease their diarrhea. "They must rest," he said.

Eydis could only think of dancing. If everyone were healthy enough to dance, then all would be well. "Let's have a dance."

Reece and Afewerki were silent for a few seconds. Reece looked at the sun, shading his eyes with his hand. He couldn't dance, but he would like to try with Eydis. "When? Maybe next Saturday. Everyone should be well by then."

"Sure," said Eydis. There was a fluttering in her stomach. She monitored the beat of her heart in her throat. It seemed rather strong and a bit fast.

Afewerki brought out the cold shurowot and a platter of cold enjera, one of his favorite meals. He only lacked for fresh onion. He loved the crunch. The three gathered around the cold fire and ate, drinking water from the old Icelandic IV bottles.

That night, Reece, Gudmunder, and Eydis moved into the supply house with Svana, placing their sleeping bags between stacked boxes and rickety particleboard shelves. Abebe had come, but no one was hungry, so she left, happy to have the evening off. Outside, beside a small fire,

Gudmunder and Svana sat, wrapped in blankets around their shoulders. They stared into the fire as if it were medicine. Reece was standing, and Eydis and Afewerki sat in chairs. There was an early moon just above the horizon.

Afewerki wanted to take Eydis to the teahouse. Perhaps Reece would not want to go. He sat silent, crafting his words. "Who would like some hot tea?"

Svana groaned. "No." Gudmunder was hunched over and did not respond.

"Hot tea!" said Reece. That sounded nice, especially since they'd had an early dinner. The evening was coming. It was the perfect time to fish for bass back in Alabama, the sun setting, the moon rising.

Eydis pondered hot tea. It would be very sweet. She needed something dry, some alcohol. "How about some katikala?" Sitting in a tukul drinking Ethiopian vodka sounded like a nice end to the day. What else was there to do?

Afewerki leaned back in the chair, his legs crossed. "Oh, oh." He feared the drama that alcohol brought, but if she wanted katikala, what was he to do?

"You sure?" asked Reece.

Eydis imagined going out with her friends in Reykjavik. It was usually vodka shots in a favorite bar. There was a giant steel fishhook in the middle of the bar. Icelandic vodka was best, followed by Russian, and then Swedish. The Ethiopian vodka was smoky, very different, but the results were the same. She was lost in her thoughts.

Svana stood and, with the blanket over her head, headed to the shintabet. She belched rotten eggs. "Oh, God."

Reece felt bad about wanting to go out while Svana and

Gudmunder were sick. "I'm flexible."

"It is Monday, and the katikala may be gone from the weekend," said Afewerki.

"We just need a bottle," said Eydis. She needed to feel balanced, and alcohol was the best remedy. "The bats." She looked up.

"Please be careful," said Gudmunder, feeling useless. He was a doctor, but felt like a water balloon. "The Snake is alive and well."

"Yes, the Snake," said Afewerki. Perhaps that was enough to dissuade them.

"The fucking Snake," said Reece. "I'll buy him a drink."

Eydis laughed. "Is he not, how do you say...ridiculous with his gun? Does he take a bath with it?"

"He does not take a bath," said Afewerki. He smiled.

Eydis needed a drink. It would help her sleep on the hard concrete. "Let us go. Afewerki, lead the way. Reece?"

Svana stumbled back to her chair.

"Svana, we are going for *hot tea,*" said Eydis.

"Yes," said Svana. She wanted to lie down.

Eydis stood and rubbed Svana's neck for a moment. "We will be back," she said to Gudmunder. "No worries."

Reece led the way through the fence but let Afewerki take over. He knew where to go.

There were a few people out, men coming from the tea and tejj bets, young boys bringing home the goats and sheep. Afewerki headed for the Polish airstrip and the enclave of divorced women living there. Most of their income came from katikala and talla. The path was relatively dry.

Afewerki approached one of the houses where Reece had conducted interviews. There were six rooms, three on each side. The doors were open, with children playing in the dirt.

"Ferenj!"

They followed Afewerki around back to the middle room. "Ciao!" he called. A woman met them at the door. She was distilling katikala at that moment, a thick smoke filling the room. A fire burned beneath a metal pot, sending vapors of alcohol up a metal tube. Reece thought the woman said, "Entre nous." She was young and wore a tight black cloth over her head like pantyhose. Two small girls clung to her dirty dress.

In the dimness, Reece could see one middle-aged man sitting against the wall with a green plastic cup. The hostess scurried. She threw back a grain bag that concealed three Ambo bottles of katikala. She was open for business, desperate for business. There was no enjera in her basket, and she needed to buy from her neighbors. She then surprised everyone by bringing out a tape player and motioning for them to sit. She inserted a tape and hit play. It was Black Sabbath's *Paranoid*.

"Holy shit," said Reece. "War Pigs." He nodded his head.

Afewerki made a face. "What is it?" It sounded like an announcement of death to him.

Eydis vaguely recognized the song and just nodded her head along with Reece.

Their reactions pleased the hostess. She'd found the tape in the pocket of a coat that she'd received many years before during the famine. She hurried to fill three cups with katikala and wondered who would be paying. Another man appeared at the door. A banner night!

"This is fantastic," said Reece. He sipped and made a

face.

The smoke, heavy metal, and alcohol made Afewerki uncomfortable. He would have preferred traditional Amharic music and tea.

"What the hell is this music?" asked the newcomer. He was not happy.

The hostess told him it was ferenji music. She knew he wanted to get drunk and told him basically to relax and drink.

Afewerki laughed. He wondered if he really wanted to go to the United States. Sometimes he did, but right now he didn't.

They sat on the dirt floor, holding their cups of katikala.

"Perhaps tomorrow will be a better day," said Afewerki. He wondered why he said that.

"Today was good, no?" asked Eydis.

"It's turning into a very nice day," said Reece. He took a shot of his liquor from the green cup. It burned and coated his stomach with warmth. "Paranoid." He was ready to die and go to heaven, except he wanted to have sex with Eydis.

The newcomer was still complaining about the music. The hostess was placating him. She promised him a free shot. Did she not have Jim Reeves like the teahouse?

Eydis stood. She reached down for Reece's hand. He stood, and she began to close dance. Reece danced without moving his feet. He sipped from his cup, finishing his ample portion, and put his cup on the ground. The hostess came over and refilled his cup, then returned to her seat. The heat of the fire muddled the room.

Afewerki frowned. He did not like katikala. The music was terrible, and now Eydis was dancing with Reece. He imagined Lake Tana, drowning in it. He looked down at the floor between his feet. *What to do?* He stood and stepped outside into the cooler air. Instantly, he felt better but empty. He drained his cup, gagged. *What a hell,* and he went back inside.

He joined Eydis and Reece. Eydis took his hand, smiling. He tried to dance. He watched Reece and imitated his swaying and weird arm movements, feeling better.

"Dance, baby," said Eydis.

A little drunk, Reece was irritated to see Afewerki dancing with them. He looked at the ground, moving to Sabbath.

Eydis enjoyed being courted. The grind of Iommi's guitar was growing on her. She danced and twirled, nearly dropping her cup. She realized it was empty and stopped. The hostess was quick to refill.

"Tebeda!" said the newcomer. He stood, already drunk from talla, and joined the dance party. His wife was pregnant with their fourth child. One of his sons had epilepsy and had fallen into the fire. The ferenj was pretty. Her blonde hair seemed a million miles away. He wanted to suck on it.

The four swayed. Eydis was amused. She knew that she was the center of attention. She liked oral sex. She wondered if that was common in Ethiopia. Reece seemed like he would enjoy that. She wanted to explore his body. She sipped from her cup.

The four came together, grinding on one another. Afewerki suddenly realized what he was doing and withdrew. His heart was beating nonstop. He put his hands on his knees. They were still dancing. What should he do?

The newcomer moved in closer, pushing Reece. He put his arm around the waist of Eydis and drew her close. "Planet Caravan" bled into "Iron Man." The heavy guitar energized Reece. He pushed back against the newcomer. Eydis smelled like carbon dioxide.

The newcomer punched Reece in the neck. Reece recoiled and spun. He threw himself at the newcomer and both fell close to the fire. The hostess bellowed in alarm. The newcomer was on top of Reece, throwing and missing punches. Reece spun to his stomach and covered his head. He threw back his head and stood with the newcomer, falling to his knees. He kicked backward and connected with his nose. "Aaagh!" The newcomer jumped to his feet and began circling with Reece.

"Please!" said Eydis.

Afewerki was stunned. What should he do?

Reece swung, taking only air.

The newcomer caught him on the upper lip. Reece didn't feel it. He stepped back, angry. He punched the newcomer in the cheek.

"Yellum!" said Eydis. She tried to intervene.

They exchanged blows back and forth without seeming effect. Both were bleeding, Reece from his mouth, the newcomer from his nose. The hostess sat beside the fire, quiet, guarding her still.

Afewerki swept the legs from the newcomer, sending him to the ground. Everyone froze as if waiting for further instruction.

EIGHTY-SIX

"Tomorrow is a better day," as Reece's grandfather liked to say. Reece wanted to get up but struggled. Why not sleep more? His back ached. He needed to pee. There were the interviews. He tried to piece together the previous night, but fell short. Had he been in a fight? He had, and he felt dizzy. He craved cranberry juice. Where was Afewerki? Were Svana and Gudmunder better? He lay on his back staring at the corrugated tin ceiling. Purple juwa birds slid their talons down the metal. His head did not ache, and he wondered why. His lip and neck hurt, though. Supplies crowded the room.

Gudmunder was feeling better. He sipped water from an IV bottle. He'd checked on Svana, and she was still nauseous. He would give her an injection if she would let him. He greeted Reece. "Hallo."

"Hey," said Reece. "Is she better?"

"Yes, I think so," said Gudmunder. "Maybe some chloroquine will help her."

"Sounds good," said Reece. "She's really sick."

Svana lay in her sleeping bag. She heard them talking about her. She had to go again and crawled out. She squatted then slowly stood. She was dizzy but made her way out of the supply house to the shintabet.

"My God," said Gudmunder. "There she goes."

"Perhaps she'll be better today," said Reece.

Eydis rolled from her bruised left side to her right. She wanted them to be quiet, just for a few more minutes.

There was a knock on the door. It was Gebremariam

with tea.

"Damn," said Reece. He needed water, not hot tea.

"Abet?" asked Gebremariam. He looked puzzled. Couldn't the ferenji afford to have beds off the floor?

"Ishi," said Reece. He reached for the teapot.

Gebremariam was reluctant to hand it to him. Pouring tea was his job.

"Amenseganolo," said Reece. He took the teapot. He only wanted to sleep, but it was Tuesday, time to work. He had sixty-three more interviews to go.

"Tea, anyone?" he said.

"No," said Eydis. Reece had fought for her. She wondered that he was standing and awake. He had been a bit punch-drunk walking back, his mouth bleeding. She'd wanted to drink more, but the fight had ended the night.

"I will try some tea," said Gudmunder. Reece found an empty cup and filled it for him.

"Thank you."

"Chicorilla," said Reece. He poured himself a cup, steam wafting. He smelled yellow sugar and cloves and handed the kettle back to Gebremariam, who was a bit upset. Reece was still wearing his clothes from the day before. He rummaged in the suitcase next to his sleeping bag and found a clean t-shirt. It was too small, and he hadn't worn it since arriving in Ethiopia. There was a rich smell of laundry detergent. He inhaled. His apartment back in Birmingham had come with a washer and dryer.

There was a knock, and it was Afewerki. The ferenji were wearing on his nerves, especially when they drank and got into fights. Could they not see the trouble they were causing? "Salaam," he said. He did not enter. How could the men and women sleep together like this?

"Hey," said Reece.

"Your lip is big," said Afewerki.

"Huh, I guess it does seem tender." He made bug eyes.

Afewerki looked away. "You are well, praise God," said Afewerki to Gudmunder.

"The rest has helped." Gudmunder sipped his tea. "I need to get some fresh air." He stepped outside and watched Svana making her way back to the tiny house.

"How is it? Your diarrhea?" asked Gudmunder.

"Worse," said Svana. Her shock of black hair looked like it was twisted with a hundred bread ties. She leaned against a pole supporting the overhang.

"Will you take the injection? And an IV? You must."

"Yes, to be well," said Afewerki. He was back outside, unable to watch Eydis lying in her sleeping bag.

"I don't think so," said Svana. She put her hands on her knees, dizzy.

"You are dehydrated," said Gudmunder. "Everything is here, so get ready. No complaints."

"No," said Svana.

"Ah, she is stubborn." Gudmunder laughed. "Go lie down. I am starting an IV."

Svana was an expert at starting IVs, but was afraid of needles. "Whatever." She staggered into the doorway. Afewerki helped her step up.

"Okay, let's do it now," said Gudmunder. He went to the shelves and retrieved an IV start kit and IV tubing. "Reece, can you draw up two hundred milligrams of chloroquine into a ten-cc syringe?"

"Nooo!" said Svana from the floor. "Only Eydis can start

the IV. Not you."

"Oh, don't be a child," said Gudmunder. He inserted the tubing into the thousand-cc bag and let the saline run through. "Here, hold this," he said to Afewerki. They were bumping into one another, trying not to step on Eydis.

"Eydis, you are needed," said Gudmunder.

"I am so uncomfortable. I can't stand this hard floor," she said. Huffing, she rolled out and stood. A drop of sweat dripped from her hairline onto her neck. "Ugh!" She wanted to scream.

She took the IV kit from Gudmunder. "I need alcohol wipes and a tourniquet."

"Ishi," said Afewerki.

"Oh, baby, here I come," said Eydis. God, she was sore, and her head hurt from the katikala.

Svana groaned. "Do it quickly."

Eydis squatted and put on the tourniquet. She slapped the pit of Svana's arm with her fingers, trying to raise a vein. "You are very dehydrated, my dear. Make a fist."

"It hurts," said Svana.

"I feel something, but cannot see it. Let's try the other arm. Scoot over."

Gebremariam peeked in the door and shook his head, laughing. It was standing room only. He whispered to Afewerki. Afewerki shushed him.

"Okay, this one," said Eydis. She palpated a thin blue vein, rubbed it with alcohol, and pulled the plastic cap off the IV needle with her teeth. "A little stick."

"Ah," said Svana. "Goddamn. Is it in?"

"Am I killing you?" Blood pushed back, and Eydis popped the tourniquet. "There. Tape! Somebody."

"Excellent," said Gudmunder. He'd been holding his breath and took a deep gulp of air. "Now for the injection."

Eydis finished the tape job. "Give to me. I will do it. She is my patient, right? And you hold the bag." She had Eydis turn around and lower her pants. "Ok! Done!" She withdrew the needle and rubbed the area with an alcohol wipe.

"I have to shit," said Svana. She went to her knees. The IV pulled against the tape.

"Be careful!" said Eydis. Blood was backing up in the tube.

Reece held the bag higher and increased the drip rate. She needed the fluid. Just then, heavy drops of rain pelted the roof. Svana stood, clutching her stomach.

"Svana, stop!" said Gudmunder. He was holding the tape.

Svana held out her arm, the IV catheter slipping back.

Gudmunder slapped another piece of tape across the antecubital fossa. "Be still!"

"I cannot wait," said Svana.

"I want my mother," said Eydis, heading out the door, bent over with Reece shadowing behind her, holding the bag of IV fluid high in the air, trailing after Svana.

"What a hell," said Afewerki.

The sky opened, dumping buckets of rain.

"Shit," said Svana.

"Hell," said Eydis.

"Goddamn," said Reece.

After the chloroquine, Svana had chilled and sweated so violently that Gudmunder thought she was seizing. She'd been thinking of making a last will and testament. Now, suddenly, she had an appetite, but she still waited another day before she and Eydis went out to weigh the children. She and Eydis had decided that it was a good idea to travel with Reece and Afewerki. The Snake was in the back of their minds, especially since Eydis had mooned him at the tejj bet. While the guys did surveys, they could weigh the children. Gudmunder was back doing vaccines with the government clinic, but spent most of his time diagnosing patients and instructing Berhanu on how to treat them.

The Snake listened to the creaking of the metal roof. He sat at his wooden desk. Five of the seven drawers were missing. The gloom oppressed him. He didn't feel like drinking, but he might as well get high. He called for his associate to bring him some qat leaves to pack into his bleeding gums. The white boy, Rice, was fucking the white nurses, no doubt. The older man, the doctor, seemed somewhat out of the picture. But why wouldn't he fuck the nurses? Certainly, he had power over them. The Snake wanted to see Eydis naked. He'd seen her breasts *and* her goddamn ass, but what did her pussy look like? He sat like a zombie, arms straight. His guard threw down a bundle of leaves still on the stem. One by one, he put the leaves into his watering mouth, chewing slowly. Pussy from what, Ice-land?

The group had walked east of Gwar, taking a new path, weighing and measuring as they went. Svana and Eydis occasionally worried that they were weighing the same children more than once, but took the possibility as inevitable. They never went to the same place twice, but people moved around.

They came to an overgrown field where a large tree grew near the path. It was a clear day, the sky spotted with clouds.

"The people will come here," said Afewerki. It was a natural gathering place. Plus, there was shade. He'd spoken to two women they'd passed, telling them where they'd be and to spread the word.

"The branches are too high," said Svana. She looked thin after her bout with death's-door diarrhea.

"I will hold the scale," said Afewerki. He was tired of interpreting for Reece and wanted to work with Eydis and Svana. "No problem."

"Okay," said Eydis.

A woman was approaching, her wrap covering the child on her back. Soon there were nine women, all with children, and one very simple man, the brother of one of the women.

Reece sat on a low stone, watching Afewerki hold the scale, struggling with the larger children. He guessed that some of the children weighed forty pounds or more. He waited nearly half an hour before Afewerki was free to help him with the interviews.

"My turn," said Reece. "Afewerki, ready?"

Afewerki, sweating, cornered their first interview and went through the motions, confirming consent. Reece sat ready with his pen, waiting for the responses.

The first interviewee was young and pretty. She smelled of smoke and spoke urgently to Reece, as if he could understand her. Reece looked to Afewerki.

"She is pregnant by an angel from God," said Afewerki.

"Really?" asked Reece. "How?"

Afewerki spoke to the woman. The woman mumbled a reply, and he interpreted. "The angel came in the night. He was a giant with golden hair. This happens many times in this place."

Reece thought. "It's happened before?"

"Oh, yes," said Afewerki.

"What do the children look like?" asked Reece.

"They are golden, light-skinned."

"Do you believe this?" asked Reece.

"Of course. The Bible talks of this."

"Wow. Tell her that we wish her well. That when she gives birth, we would love to see the child."

Afewerki translated. The woman nodded, a serious look on her face. Was she ready for the interview? She replied no, that she had to return home and tend to the fire.

"Well, damn," said Reece. "Who's next?"

"Reece? Can we borrow Afewerki?" asked Svana.

"Jesus. Let me get one interview done," said Reece. It was all give and no take. At this rate, he'd be in Ethiopia until he died.

"Okay, settle down," said Eydis.

Afewerki motioned for the next in line to come and sit. The woman had a broad face and smile. Her son was three and clung to her dress with terrified eyes. She spoke at length.

Reece looked to Afewerki. "She says she is poor, and what can she do?" said Afewerki.

Reece coughed. He motioned for Afewerki to begin the interview. He could feel the life draining from his bones.

On the upside, Reece managed to do thirteen interviews, even though it took all day. Svana and Eydis had left after three hours, with no children left to weigh.

One woman was remaining. She had high cheekbones and had been weaving a basket while she waited. Reece couldn't stomach doing another interview, asking the same damn questions. He wondered if he was wasting his time, their time, Afewerki's time. He told Afewerki to tell the woman to come to the compound at nine the next morning. It was the best he could do. He fumbled in his pocket and came up with three birr. He gave it to the woman, who at first looked alarmed.

Afewerki intervened. The money was for her children, their dinner. The woman relaxed and said she would come the next morning. Reece nodded. He felt blank, expended. He was sitting on the stone. His right butt cheek was asleep. He looked up to the clear blue sky. What did the rest of the day hold beyond dinner and banter?

EIGHTY-SEVEN

The group gathered back in the compound. Smoke poured from the cook house. It would be dorowot, but with only hard eggs and no chicken. Abebe was economizing. It was expensive to feed the ferenji, but she did her best to be fair. She poured in a bit of clarified butter, feeling generous, removed the lid from the enjera basket, and layered the serving platter. She needed to make more money. She was afraid of Afewerki, worried that he would fire her. If only she could speak English or the other language of the doctor. Afewerki had tried to explain to her where Gudmunder was from, but she had not understood. A land of what, ice? Where were the female nurses from? She wasn't sure.

Gudmunder sat in his folding chair beside the cold fire ring. Reece was building a fire there. Gudmunder had watched Berhanu give two injections with the same needle that day. It had seemed like slow motion, and he could not stop it. His only recourse was to give him half of the needles in the supply house.

Reece and Afewerki stood with Eydis in front of the dining hut. She'd changed from her scrubs to tight jeans and a long-sleeve light sweater that outlined her figure. Already it was cooling from the high of seventy-eight degrees that day.

"So, what do you do for fun, back in Reykjavik?" asked Reece.

Eydis looked brilliant, her blonde hair golden in the late afternoon sun. "I have girlfriends. We drink and dance."

"You are a good dancer," said Afewerki.

"Thanks," said Eydis. She felt pretty, wanted.

Svana emerged from the supply house *cum* sleeping quarters. She'd bathed with cool water and cheap soap and felt like a million dollars.

There was a commotion at the fence. The Snake. He tried to step through the gap in the fence and fell forward, running to keep from falling.

Unbalanced, he ran nearly ten meters before he could stop himself. He was alone. He needed an injection. The dripping of his penis was back, and it hurt like fuck. Was he standing straight? He prepared to fall over and spit green from the qat. He felt cold air being piped through his insides.

Svana felt her sweet soap smell go out the window. She joined the others around the fire pit. Reece was standing watch over a small fire of kindling.

Gudmunder stood. He went to greet the Snake, extending his hand.

"You are arrested," said the Snake. He reached for the pistol on his hip, but couldn't get it out of the holster. He shouldn't have drunk after the qat and felt that he was floating in a river.

"What?" asked Gudmunder. He looked to Afewerki.

"He says you are under arrest." Afewerki rolled his eyes.

"Again?"

"For what?" asked Eydis. Amused, she imagined she could push the Snake over with a finger.

Afewerki queried the Snake. He searched for four-leafed clovers in the grass. He'd learned that from a Polish soldier.

Afewerki interpreted. "Because you are trying to steal from the people, from the church. The same things. But he is dripping from his penis. He needs an injection."

Gudmunder paused. "But I've already been arrested for that and released. In Alem Ketema. Dripping?" That changed the tone of the conversation.

Without a word, the Snake unbuckled his belt and let his pants fall for all to see.

Unperturbed, Gudmunder leaned over for a look. The head of the Snake's otherwise healthy penis looked reddened and moist. He looked into the Snake's pants and saw a sticky mess there. Had he ejaculated in his pants?

There was another visitor at the gate, the blind woman from the airfield who lived alone. The Snake had raped her. The tall woman, who resembled a pirate with her head wrap, stood behind her. Eydis went to see what the matter was. The air was cool and fresh.

"Does he think he has gonorrhea?" asked Gudmunder. It certainly smelled like it. He tried to swallow and gagged just a bit.

Afewerki translated. "Yes. He needs the injection."

"Pull up your pants," said Gudmunder, "and follow me." He walked toward the supply house.

Svana followed Eydis to the fence and the two women there. The blind woman was weeping and pleading. Eydis hugged her and stroked her hair. "Mendeno, mama?"

The pirate, beautifully sculpted, looked angry and impatient. She was talking to Gebremariam, and he was going "tsk, tsk, tsk."

Svana walked back to the supply house. Afewerki was telling the Snake to prepare for an injection of penicillin.

The Snake wanted to see the bottle to see if the medicine had expired. Gudmunder let him examine the tiny print. The Snake tried to read it but could not. He handed it back and dropped his pants again. He leaned with both hands against the wall as if about to receive a terrible beating.

"Afewerki, can you come to the fence? A woman is there."

"Ishi." He left Gudmunder in charge of the Snake and the injection. He felt like a yo-yo.

He recognized the blind woman and sighed. Her friend spoke loudly, saying that the woman was pregnant and that the Snake was the father, that it was like having the devil's child, and what could be done?

"What does she say?" asked Svana.

There was a blood-curdling scream from the supply house.

"Jesus Christ," said Afewerki. He paused. "The Snake is raping her, and now she is pregnant. What will she do? She is blind. How will she care for a child? The child will die."

Both Svana and Eydis grumbled. "Can she have an abortion, perhaps in Addis? We will pay for it," said Eydis.

"Oh no," said Afewerki. "It is a sin."

Svana shook her head. "Ask her anyway."

Afewerki asked her about an abortion.

"Ow, yes, anything!" the woman pleaded. "But how, where?"

Afewerki was shocked. Women who had abortions in Gwar often died. It was a punishment from God.

"What does she say?" asked Eydis, still holding onto her. Thick white cataracts clouded the woman's eyes.

"She wishes for the abortion," said Afewerki.

"No doubt," said Svana, arms folded. She hoped that Gudmunder had injected the Snake in his dick. "What is her name?"

Afewerki didn't know. She was simply the blind woman. He asked.

The woman whispered, "Mengesha."

Svana wanted to say what a pretty name, but it wasn't. It sounded like a town in hell. She took Mengesha's hand and held it.

Out of the supply house, the Snake staggered. The knot on his buttock was cramping his leg. He was furious that the injection was so painful. "Kularas," he said, calling Gudmunder a dickhead. He limped into the yard, needing a stiff drink. He saw the scene at the gate and muttered. He should just pull his Makarov and blow them all away, goddamn whores.

As if she sensed him, Mengesha tore away from Eydis and Svana. She lumbered into the yard, going left and then right. She was wailing, calling him a child of the devil. Her friend followed and grabbed her from behind. Mengesha surged forward, strengthened by the ferenji. She called the Snake, wusha, a dog, and said that he would burn in hell for raping her. She was blind! She could not protect herself! And now she was pregnant. She collapsed in a heap at her friend's feet. There was silence. The whole village was listening. Everyone was stunned. He would kill her, no doubt.

Svana thought about getting Gudmunder's pistol from his tent and shooting the Snake. Reece was standing by the fire. He walked to Svana and Eydis, who were helping

Mengesha from the ground. "She should stay here from now on. I've seen her hut. It's cold there with no protection from the wind. He will kill her otherwise."

Eydis felt a surge of love for Reece.

"Good idea," said Svana. "She will sleep here, perhaps in the cook house."

Afewerki made a face. He was torn. What to say? He wanted to avoid trouble. This would put the ferenji in danger. What would happen next? Would the sky split in half like the curtain in the temple?

The blind woman, Mengesha, set up her pallet in the cook house. The smoke didn't bother her, and she enjoyed talking with Abebe, an old friend from elementary school. She was basically useless in terms of chores, so she stayed out of the way, careful not to annoy Abebe. No more being raped at night. She was ecstatic and wandered the compound during the day, just walking from fence to fence, gaining her strength, talking to herself. She tried not to eat too much but was always famished. She thanked God several times per day.

Reece and Afewerki walked in the cool of the morning toward a new gathering of huts west of Gwar, another day of interviews. He had forty-one to go, perhaps two or three days, maybe four. The day was real, sunny, but with clouds threatening rain. Reece's mind was always on Eydis. He had developed a desire to travel with her back to Iceland—the thermal springs, the glaciers, the vodka. But first, there were the people of Gwar to whom he felt an allegiance. He owed them something intangible, perhaps his life, and it brought tears to his eyes. How to explain?

Reece wore a plaid, brimmed hat that he'd unearthed from his luggage after moving into the supply house due to the rains. Did he look like a carny? Oh, and the ganja he'd bought in Addis. Did Eydis do weed? He'd forgotten about it, searched his bag and tent, and couldn't find it. He followed Afewerki, looking forward to the discovery that awaited. It was all about the human experience, right? If everyone accepted their place in the drama, the show would always go on. Freddy Mercury. *Right?*

Silent, Afewerki plodded along the path. He could easily walk around the earth. No problem. *Chicorilla.* Afewerki stopped in a high place that was open, a meadow with tall grass and a bedena tree. Small yellow fruits hung from the branches. Afewerki picked one for himself and one for Reece. Reece made a face but ate it, spitting out the seed. It reminded him that he was thirsty. He needed to drink more water, especially since he was drinking so much alcohol at night. He wondered how long until his next shot of katikala or areke. It made him feel good and usually without a hangover. But there was the trouble that happened in the evenings. Perhaps if he had children…

"I would like to come to the United States," said Afewerki. He was wearing his Exxon ballcap and cheap sunglasses.

The grass grew to their waists. "No problem. I will help you." Reece nodded his head. It was the least he could do. How he would do it, he had no idea, but he would try. "Sure."

Afewerki was speechless. He imagined flying in a plane with ferenji across the oceans. "Yes," was all he could say.

Reece wondered if he was being rash. *What the hell?* It

would be a social experiment. The details would take care of themselves. "Right on," he said. He put his hand out and shook on it with Afewerki. Done deal.

Afewerki felt ten million meters high. His life had new purpose. Working with the ferenji was worth it, despite their love of getting drunk and fighting.

EIGHTY-EIGHT

Reece threw in an extra survey question just for fun. "What is your favorite fruit?"

Afewerki replied that the woman's answer was pawpaw.

Reece was stunned. Pawpaw, a fruit from Alabama? "Papaya?"

"Pawpaw, large and green, very sweet." Afewerki had never tasted it, though.

Reece accepted his explanation. "Okay. Is her favorite marsupial the 'possum?"

Afewerki did not respond. He was comfortable in the thin shade of the tree, thinking of his mother making enjera. He would miss her when he traveled to the U.S. with Reece. Could it actually be a real possibility? Reece had said yes. A toe on his left foot hurt. He needed new shoes.

Reece was thinking of hot dogs, the boiling water. Hot-dog-flavored water sounded tasty. And sauerkraut. He loved sauerkraut. Afewerki had the woman stand so that she could have her photo taken by Reece. She looked down at the ground.

"Have her look up and smile if she would," said Reece. He suddenly realized how frail the woman was, belied by her strong voice. Her husband worked in a fishery on Lake Tana. She had not seen him in over a year. She had three boys and took care of her sister's children as well, since her sister had broken both of her collarbones and could not use her arms.

The woman laughed and covered her mouth. She'd never had her photo taken. She arranged a cloth over her head and pressed her lips together, a reserved smile in the background, playing at perhaps toughness. *Click. Click.*

"Ishi, bataam taruno," said Reece.

"Amenseganolo," said the woman. She stood there transfixed, not knowing what to do next.

Afewerki laughed and told her they were finished.

"But where is the photo?" the woman said.

Afewerki explained that the film would have to be developed with a machine. Reece would send back the photo, and he would bring it to her.

The woman nodded, gathered her long dress, and drifted away, the last interview of the day. Reece looked to the sky, perhaps three o'clock.

Down the path was coming someone, in a slight hurry.

"Oh, oh," said Afewerki. He recognized the schoolteacher. She was short and plump and wore a combination of Western and local clothes, bright colors, twenty-three, and never married.

"What is it?" asked Reece. "An interview?"

"No, no."

The woman waddled up to them, huffing and puffing, sweating. She grabbed Afewerki's hand and spoke at length, locking eyes with Reece. A farmer with his long plow on his shoulder veered from the path around them. Reece nodded to the old man. The old man grinned and spat.

"I have promised to her that we would have dinner at her house. She is ready for us to come."

"Right now?" asked Reece.

"Yes, we must. I have promised."

"Should we let Abebe know we won't be there for

dinner?"

"We will send word," said Afewerki.

"What is her name?"

"It is Abebe."

"So many Abebes."

Abebe was now holding Reece's right hand in hers and looking at his chest. "Come, come," she said, practicing one of the English words she was familiar with. She released Reece's hand and turned for them to follow her.

"I am to be sorry," said Afewerki. "I did not think she would cook. She has promised many times to cook for me, and always I say yes. She has no husband."

The heat of the day had peaked, and it was beginning to cool. They were heading toward Gwar, which was a good sign to Reece. He walked behind Afewerki, who walked behind Abebe. Every now and then, she would turn and babble in Amharic. They approached the village proper and continued through, going from east to west, greeting many people along the way. The women smiled, and the men laughed.

"Is it near?" asked Reece.

"Very soon," said Afewerki. He felt silly. Smoke rising from every compound, dinner in the making.

They trudged on, passing through the market area, past the jail, and up toward the Orthodox Church where the land was exposed and the wind blew. Reece looked down across the many compound fences and could see smoke rising from their cook house. *One Abebe, two Abebe, three Abebe, four.*

They veered right and descended, coming to a grouping of three compounds, all walled with green desert plants growing between a circular arrangement of denuded poles. Two shy girls stood nearby. "Ferenj," one whispered. The other smiled.

"Are we here?" asked Reece.

"Yes, we are here."

Talking rapidly, Abebe motioned them to sit on the ground and hurried into her large hut. Reece squatted and leaned back against the smooth, hard exterior. He really wanted to be back at his own compound, relaxing with the others, perhaps having a drink.

"Is there something to drink?" asked Reece.

"Oh, we must not ask," said Afewerki.

"Okay." Reece pulled up his knees and squinted at the sky above the fence. He watched Abebe hurry through the gate. "Where is she going?" He swatted at the flies.

"I think to buy some salt and some meat," said Afewerki.

"Look, a cat." A skinny yellow cat was peeking its head out of the hut.

"Ah, it will bite," said Afewerki.

Reece struggled to stand and called for the cat. He liked cats and had not seen one in Gwar. "Kitty, kitty." He walked toward the door, and the cat ran back inside. Reece peered inside the hut. There was no fire. A large sagging bed sat against the wall. He noted a pile of cat poop on the floor.

"Reece! You must not look inside the house," said Afewerki.

"Right," and he sat back down in the shade. A light breeze blew, and he was hungry. "How long will this take?"

"Only God knows," said Afewerki. "But she has invited us." He took his hat off and batted at the flies, resigned to his fate.

"There's not even a fire inside," said Reece. He shifted from one hip bone to the next.

"I think I will need to study in the U.S., but to get the visa...is very hard to leave this country," said Afewerki. "There is Abrehem. Another nurse is helping him, and he is studying in U.S."

"Yeah, a student visa," said Reece. "I'm not exactly sure how it works."

"It is called the I-9 visa," said Afewerki.

"You know more than I do." A bearded vulture dipped its wings overhead.

"I must pass the TOEFL exam to study there," said Afewerki.

"An English test? Your English is pretty good."

"Thank you, I have studied hard in school."

"When will Abebe be back?" Reece's back hurt from sitting on a rock during the interviews. Flies dive-bombed his sweaty head. He imagined Gudmunder pulling out a secret stash of beer.

"Perhaps soon." He was grinning, thinking of leaving this small town, the adventures he would have.

Reece stood again. He saw Afewerki's father walking by with a long knife in his hand. He waved. "Afewerki, it's your dad."

Afewerki stood and talked to his father through the gate. He was going to have the knife sharpened. Abebe came up, swishing her dress and holding a live hen upside down. The hen was trying to squawk but couldn't. Not wanting to get involved in killing the chicken and to be on his way, Afewerki's father hurried off. The last thing he wanted was to get tangled up with the schoolteacher.

Abebe let the hen run loose in the enclosure. In a shawl around her waist were six eggs and a cloth of rock salt. She trotted across the way to borrow her neighbor's pot to cook the wot and to buy a few folds of enjera.

The cat slunk from the hut, and off went the hen, exploding in a swirl of feathers, hitting the fence. Reece dove for the chicken, which ran straight back at the cat, which turned and ran back into the hut. Afewerki circled to help him catch the hen. In a mighty effort, the hen leaped and flew over the fence into the vast expanse of brush, dirt, and rocks behind the compound, squawking.

"Oh, hell," said Afewerki. He took off after the hen, which was running for its life, lifting and sailing. Reece started to follow, then stopped. He hoped it would get away.

Reece lingered behind the compound, watching Afewerki get farther away. He shaded his eyes and walked back to the dirt path, wondering when Abebe would start cooking. Something caught his eye. Was he seeing things?

"Hello!" He walked toward a young girl standing at the gate of the next compound.

"Hey," said the girl. She was white with long brown hair. She had an American accent.

Reece walked that way, twenty feet or so, like a magnet was drawing him. She looked very familiar. She wore what seemed to be pajamas. "What's your name?"

"Mia."

Afewerki had climbed back up the incline, his shoes dusty and full of hitchhiker burrs. The hen was gone. He saw Reece and the young girl. So, the rumor was true.

"Reece," he said.

Reece vaguely heard his name. The girl's hair had a tinge of red to it, a ginger. Her nose was defined, and she had a curious look in her eyes. The girl stood with arms folded, as if holding back. Was she starting to cry?

Reece completely forgot about dinner with the schoolteacher. Here was a little girl who could be any little girl back in the States, and her name was Mia.

Reece looked at Afewerki with surprise. "Where are your parents?" He turned to Afewerki. "Do you know who this is?" He turned back to Mia. "Do you live in this hut?"

"I live in Kentucky," said Mia as if stating the sky was blue. "My parents are there. I don't know how I got here, and I want to go home. Enjera makes my stomach hurt."

Reece had a thousand questions. "So, you are here alone? How can that be?" He looked to Afewerki for help."

"The monk, the Abba Paulos, has found her," said Afewerki.

"The guy building the church into the cliff?"

"Yes, he has found her and brought her here to his sister's house. He cannot to take care of a girl."

"Of course not," said Reece. "How did you get here?" He was squatting and feeling unbalanced. His legs were going to sleep.

"Dahlia kidnapped me. I don't know how I got here. I miss my mom and my dad. I really have to find them," said Mia. She was digging her toe in the dirt and swatting at flies.

Abebe called for them to come inside. What were they doing? Hadn't they heard about the little white girl, and could Afewerki start a fire?

"Can you come with us?" Reece pointed to Abebe's compound.

"You look like my dad," said Mia. She glanced back at a frail woman standing in the hut's doorway and waved.

The woman came to the gate. "Yellum, nah!" She motioned for Mia to come back.

"Afewerki?" Reece looked around, and he was gone.

Mia spoke to the woman. "It's okay. He's okay. I'll come back."

The woman looked worried. She'd promised her brother, the Abba Paulos, that she would look after this little girl. Could the schoolteacher and this ferenj be trusted?

Mia took Reece's hand and led him into the schoolteacher's compound. "You look younger than my dad. I'm glad that you came. Did the chicken get away?"

Reece was dumbstruck.

"Can you take me home?" asked Mia. She sat and leaned against the hut.

"Well, I'm here doing some work. I just don't understand how you got here. Your parents didn't bring you here? They're in Kentucky?"

"Yeah. I was sleepwalking, then I was in my mom's bed, and then she took me. It was Dahlia. She called herself Charlotte at first, but Dad called her Dahlia. She came to our new house and pretended to want to be friends. We played hide and seek. She came back at night."

"Kidnapped by Dahlia. She brought you to Ethiopia?" asked Reece.

"I think so. I woke up in a cave. There was a man with a yellow hat inside. He's digging into the rock. That was yesterday."

Reece sat on the ground, trying to sit cross-legged, but he couldn't do it and leaned back on his elbow. "I'm from Alabama, but I flew here on a plane. I can't believe that you just showed up in a cave. That's crazy."

Mia's eyes misted, and she looked down. "I'm sorry. I just don't know what to say." She bubbled over into a sobbing cry and put her head between her knees.

"We'll take care of you. Don't cry." He reached out and touched her shoulder. She was real.

Mia cried for a moment, collecting herself. She could feel Reece's music and knew to trust him. "You've been kidnapped, too."

Reece gripped his knees, trying not to fall over backward. "How do you know that?"

"Your music. You're from another place, too," said Mia.

The music. She was right. Kentucky. An old man with knobs of white hair flashed through his head. He focused on her music. It registered in his head as an equation. He felt that anything was possible. He smelled smoke, and Afewerki was standing behind him. "Maybe so," said Reece.

"Someone will come to take her away. It has happened before," said Afewerki. He squatted, his butt hitting the ground.

"Dang, how do you do that?" asked Reece. He stood.

Afewerki just laughed. "It is the way of the peasant."

"Is someone coming to get you?" asked Reece.

Mia was sitting cross-legged. "I don't know. How will they know where I am?"

"Don't worry," said Reece. "We'll take care of you. We'll get you home somehow." But heck, she didn't have a passport, or did she? "Do you like bananas, oranges? I'll buy you some at the market. The enjera and wots are very spicy."

"The enjera is sour. I like dabo, the bread."

Reece had a sudden thought. "What have you been drinking?"

"Just water."

"From the clay pots?"

"I think so. Why?"

"It's best to drink filtered water. We need to take you to our compound."

Afewerki spoke. "The woman will charge some money to take her. This one is good luck."

"Okay, can you go and ask? How much?"

Afewerki frowned. "Okay." He stood.

"You're good for the economy," said Reece.

"I need some clothes," she said

"We can do that. What is the first thing you remembered when you arrived here?"

Mia hunkered down. She was silent. "I was being carried. I think. I went through the wall. It made me cry, but there was no sound. I was floating. There was a kind of darkness, a blank space, and I went into that. Then I was here." She shuddered.

"Wow," said Reece. He was thinking about the nighttime visits he had when he was a child. How he squeezed his eyes shut, hoping they wouldn't take him, pulling the sheet over his head. One of them had been a little girl. She'd done something to his head. There had been lights, sounds of moaning in the background, maybe a TV. *The Big Valley*, season one, episode 17. *Dahlia?*

EIGHTY-NINE

Had Mia not been there, Reece would have abandoned the schoolteacher's invite to dinner. Two hours had passed, and still no sign of food, just smoke.

Mia sat beside Reece. Afewerki went inside the hut to check on things. He emerged. "Just a few more minutes." He looked at his watch, which gave the correct time twice a day.

"Jesus, I hope so," said Reece.

"I'm hungry, but I want dabo, not the enjera," said Mia. She looked small and alone. She was seven years old and from Kentucky, where it was 2003. She was slender, with shoulder-length hair and bangs, and had bright green-brown eyes. Her mom's name was Jen. Her dad's name was Reece, too.

Reece tried to think of more questions to ask, but he felt like he was making Mia tired. How could it be true? But how else to explain her sudden appearance? "So, tell me more about Charlotte, the little girl."

Mia frowned. She didn't want to talk about it. "I want some fruit punch. I'm so thirsty." She waited a few seconds. "Charlotte had blonde hair and was always busy doing something. She came to our new house. She went to my new school. My dad didn't like her."

"Why didn't he like her?" asked Reece.

Afewerki cleaned his teeth with a chewing stick.

"He just didn't. Charlotte was bossy." She doodled in the dirt, flipping over small stones.

"What did your dad do for a job?" asked Reece.

"He was a teacher at college. I think that's why we moved to Kentucky. I wish we hadn't moved."

"You moved from Alabama? Birmingham?" asked Reece.

"Yes. I was born there."

Reece struggled to stand. "Need to stretch my legs. You say that there was another little girl that your dad didn't like...in Birmingham?"

"Oh brother, her name was Betsy. She really liked me. She lived with her grandparents, just like Charlotte. Dad said I couldn't play with her."

Abebe came from the hut, sweat streaming down her face. She wiped her hands on her dress and spoke to Afewerki. Dinner was ready.

"Hot dog," said Reece.

Mia laughed. "Hot dog!"

Abebe brought a colorful woven basket on top of which was a thin tin platter covered with enjera. She retreated and brought a large pot, which contained the wot with just boiled eggs, no hen. She poured the spicy wot, a mushy stew with chopped onions, into the center of the platter.

"Is very oily," said Afewerki.

"Shall we wash our hands?" asked Reece.

"Yes, it is for the best," said Afewerki. "But she has no soap."

"Oh, we need bread for Mia," said Reece.

Afewerki asked Abebe to bring a wheat roll from her neighbor's house. She bowed her head and hurried through the gate.

Reece took a bite of soggy enjera. He tasted oil, hot pepper, and a generous amount of salt. "Geez," he said. "How are we going to do this without water?"

Afewerki sampled the wot with enjera. "What a hell. So much salt."

"Salt wot, no?" asked Reece. He laughed.

"Ow, chow wot," said Afewerki, also laughing.

Abebe returned with a dark brown bun and handed it to the little girl, smiling nervously.

"Amenseganolo," said Mia.

"Yiqirta," said Abebe.

"Is Abebe eating with us?" asked Reece. He swallowed another bite, his head beginning to sweat and his mouth water.

"No, she is a single woman. It would not be right to eat with men," said Afewerki.

"Okay," said Reece. "Mia, we'll have lots of clean water for you back at our compound, okay? I can't believe how well you're doing."

"I miss my parents and my bed. I was cold last night. The lady didn't have any blankets. She was nice, though."

"Yes, you must be fright?" asked Afewerki. He was eating the enjera plain without the wot.

"I was at first, but no one has tried to hurt me." Mia nibbled her bread.

"What will the Snake think?" asked Reece.

"He is knowing," said Afewerki. "This is not the first time. He will not do anything."

Reece picked at the enjera. He was hungry, but the saltiness of the wot was overpowering. He broke open an egg and tried the hard yolk with some enjera. "That's not so bad. How do you say, 'salt wot?' Chow wot?"

Afewerki laughed and coughed. "Sshh, we must not.

We must eat more. She will be angry." He laughed.

Reece grinned. "Yuck. Need some katikala to wash it down."

Afewerki tried not to laugh but couldn't help himself. He drew his hand across his throat.

Reece tried very hard not to laugh. It was like trying not to laugh in church. He could feel the day cooling, a breeze washing over Gwar.

"What's so funny?" asked Mia. She was smiling. They were good guys. She could feel it.

"So, Mia." Reece changed the subject. "Tell us about Betsy, from Birmingham." His eyes were watering. He batted away a tenacious fly.

Mia seemed to be a wise old woman sitting there as if she understood the ages. "She came to the house every day. She wasn't in my classes at school, but she would always invite herself to dinner. Dad thinks she tried to kill my goldfish by putting something in the water. They got really sick and floated upside down. Funzo and Waterhead. We got them at the pet store."

"Pet store?" asked Afewerki.

"A store where you can buy pets like fish and dogs and cats."

Afewerki pondered that. Kind of like the donkey market.

"What did your dad do?"

"He found out where she lived and told her grandparents about it."

"Did she come back?" asked Reece.

"Not for a few days."

Abebe had been sitting on her bed, biting her nails.

She saw the little white girl as a bad omen. Did they like her wot? Would the ferenj talk about her badly? She took a deep breath and went outside to check on her guests.

Afewerki cleared his throat and spoke, telling Abebe that the meal was delicious. For good measure, he took an egg and ate half.

"Bataam taruno," said Reece. He took a big bite of enjera and the onions.

Mia laughed. She saw their game.

Abebe frowned at the little girl. Why would she not eat the meal? What to do? The three had not eaten very much. She went back inside to tend the fire, even though she would let it go out after they left.

"What does your father teach at the college?" asked Reece.

"I think it's philosophy. I'm not sure," said Mia.

"Interesting," said Reece. "That was my minor when I was at Auburn."

Mia nodded. "Daddy called them Dahlia. Betsy and Charlotte."

"Dahlia," said Reece. *Why?*

They finished the salty wot, and with much bowing and thanks, left the schoolteacher's compound with Mia. Abebe waved at them until they disappeared over the hill. She needed a husband, white or black didn't matter.

"Oh my god," said Reece. "That was terrible."

Afewerki laughed. "Yes, she is not a good cook."

Mia walked between them, thinking of her parents. She was still nibbling on her bread.

It was after dark when they arrived back at the compound. Everyone had eaten. Svana, Eydis, and Gudmunder were drinking tejj, brought to them by Gebremariam, and sitting beside a small fire. All three stood when Afewerki, Reece, and Mia entered through the fence. Who was the little girl?

Reece ushered Mia to the fire, standing there reflecting.

"Who is this?" asked Gudmunder.

"Yes, who?" asked Eydis.

"This is Mia," said Reece. "She has arrived, found by the Abba Paulos. She is from the future, 2003."

"The future?" asked Svana. She was squatting. "Hello, Mia. I am Svana." She stumbled and stood.

"Nice to meet you," said Mia.

Gudmunder and Eydis nodded, confused. The future?

"The future?" asked Mia.

"It's 1987 here," said Reece. "You're from 2003."

Mia walked to the fire and sat on the ground. She took a crooked stick and poked in the coals. Her parents had taken her camping several times, and fire was magical.

"It's what she says," said Reece. "I believe her."

"Where do you come from?" asked Gudmunder.

"I live in Kentucky," said Mia. "Dahlia sent me here. She's pretending to be me."

"In the US," said Reece. "Kentucky." *Dahlia.*

"Who is Dahlia?" asked Eydis. She settled beside Mia, sitting in the grass.

Mia thought. "She wants to learn from me. Something about my music."

"Oh," said Eydis.

Reece seemed to have some vague understanding. "Dahlia travels between universes." He wondered at the insanity of his own words.

"Yeah," said Mia. "Dahlia...Nice to meet all of you. Do you have any water?"

"Right," said Reece. He went to the supply house for a bottle of water.

Mia settled into a pose, legs crossed, her shoulders hunched.

No one spoke, waiting for Reece to return. Reece handed her the bottle of water.

"Thank you," said Mia. The bottle was heavy. She drank slowly. "Cold."

Reece felt a slight thrill of joy.

Gebremariam came to see if anyone needed anything.

"We are fine," said Gudmunder.

"Yiqirta," said Afewerki.

Gebremariam nodded. "Ishi," and he withdrew to the gap in the fence. The bats were out, seemingly chasing the swallows. The little white girl was a visitor. He touched his heart and prayed that his family would be blessed. He prayed for evil to leave Gwar.

Mia sat in the grass, thinking of her parents and grandparents. The smoke from the fire comforted her, one step closer to reality.